HIGHER AUTHORITY

Stephen White

SIGNET
Published by the Penguin Group
Penguin Books USA Inc., 375 Hudson Street,
New York, New York 10014, U.S.A.
Penguin Books Ltd, 27 Wrights Lane,
London W8 5TZ, England
Penguin Books Australia Ltd, Ringwood,
Victoria, Australia
Penguin Books Canada Ltd, 10 Alcorn Avenue,
Toronto, Ontario, Canada M4V 3B2
Penguin Books (N.Z.) Ltd, 182-190 Wairau Road,
Auckland 10, New Zealand

Penguin Books Ltd, Registered Offices:
Harmondsworth, Middlesex, England

Published by Signet, an imprint of Dutton Signet,
a division of Penguin Books USA Inc.
Previously appeared in a Viking edition.

First Signet Printing, February, 1996
10 9 8 7 6 5 4 3

Printed in the United States of America

PUBLISHER'S NOTE
This is a work of fiction. Names, characters, places, and incidents either are the product of the author's imagination or are used fictitiously, and any resemblance to actual persons, living or dead, events, or locales is entirely coincidental.

to Alexander

A NOTE TO THE READER

Higher Authority is a work of fiction. The characters and events described are entirely the product of the author's imagination.

Much of the story takes place in a uniquely American and uniquely western world, that created by the Mormon followers of Joseph Smith in a land Brigham Young called Deseret. We call it Utah.

The Church of Jesus Christ of Latter-day Saints, popularly known as the Mormon Church, is depicted in this story as an essential cultural and religious backdrop to fictional events and fictional characters. All locales described in the book are used fictitiously. No actual event or incident is intentionally portrayed; any resemblance is coincidental.

Although certain prominent Mormons, some alive and some deceased, are quoted in the book to provide contemporary context for the story, any resemblance between a character and an actual person, living or dead, is entirely coincidental, with the exception of Senator Orrin Hatch, who appears briefly as a character. In no way does the book attempt to portray Senator Hatch's actual conduct.

I left Great Salt Lake a good deal confused as to what state of things existed there—and sometimes even questioning in my own mind whether a state of things existed there at all or not.

MARK TWAIN,
ROUGHING IT

It is almost impossible to write fiction about the Mormons, for the reason that Mormon institutions and Mormon society are so peculiar that they call for constant explanation.

WALLACE STEGNER,
MORMON COUNTRY

PROLOGUE

Blythe Oaks ran almost every morning. Early. She liked to time her workouts so that she was heading east just as the sun cracked the horizon.

This late-summer Monday she was on the Mall in full stride, the Air and Space Museum on her right, the Capitol dome ahead of her. As she approached the border of the Reflecting Pool she stopped abruptly and pivoted to check the path behind her.

It was deserted. A few homeless people had begun to stir on the periphery of the Mall. But no other runner was within a hundred yards.

Blythe ran in place while she monitored the progress of a far-off jogger and watched a woman glide gracefully in the distance on in-line skates. Neither approached her. Neither even seemed to take notice of her. Despite the respite from her workout, Blythe's pulse didn't slow. She glanced at her watch and took off again, striving to cleanse her mind of fear by concentrating on achieving good hip extension and not landing too far back on her heels. In minutes, she covered the long stretch of ground that extended west toward the Potomac.

Blythe Oaks ran fast when she thought she was being followed.

As she approached the street where she lived alone in a second-floor apartment, she prayed that she wouldn't find a flower waiting outside the front door to the building. She mouthed the prayer, her mantra to God, "Please, no flower, please, no flower, please, no flower."

Please, stride, *no flower,* stride.

Blythe had already decided that her stalker bought a fresh bouquet only once a week, because every morning for seven days the single stem left by her door would be of the same variety. The flower was always wrapped in tissue paper color-coordinated with the hue of the bud. The flowers were freshest on Saturday. So, she had concluded, the stalker bought them on Friday. Maybe Friday night after work. But this past weekend, no flower. Before her run this morning, no flower.

A month before, a blue Toyota Camry with D.C. plates had prompted Blythe's paranoia. The first time she had spotted the car it was parked on the street outside her apartment building, directly across from her own beige Taurus. Blythe remembered noticing the car that first time mostly because the person behind the wheel had turned away abruptly when Blythe looked toward the car. In her mind she had a snapshot image of the driver, recalling long, dark brown hair, a suede jacket, and a baseball cap—the Orioles?—with a plastic adjustable strap in back. Later that day, she thought she spotted the same Camry outside the Supreme Court Building, where she worked. The next day she saw it again, back on the street in front of her apartment. Sometimes she was certain she saw the car drive past her when she jogged. Once, the blue Camry had parked right next to her Taurus at the supermarket.

Blue Camry.

After six strong miles Blythe turned the final corner toward her building and decided she liked her new Nikes. A clerk who had assisted her on Saturday had suggested this shoe. The woman apparently knew what she was doing. Blythe fantasized briefly about returning to the store and asking the clerk if she wanted to go for a run sometime. She shook off the impulse. She knew she wouldn't ask. One reckless mistake was enough. More than enough.

A reflexive vigilance intruded as she neared her building. Blythe was becoming a car expert. Between breaths she quietly called out the makes as she passed them in their slots along the curb: "Camaro, Buick, Honda, pickup, minivan, Saab."

Stride, stride. *No Camry, no flower.*

One step up to the walk. Five more to the door.

With what felt like monumental effort, Blythe forced herself to look up. Immediately she started to cry. Such pretty blue buds. A note card of heavy gray paper. The beautiful cursive hand.

"Nice shoes!! Soon everyone will know about us!" the note read.

Standing by the door, the card between her fingers, the flower at her feet, Blythe smiled awkwardly through her tears to greet a neighbor who was heading out the door to go to work. Inside, she took the stairs two at a time to the second floor, now crying in a desperately muted voice, "Please don't call, please don't call, please don't call."

She knew she was talking to the stalker now, no longer to God.

She unclipped the safety pin that secured her key to the waistband of her sweatpants, unlocked the door, and walked into her quiet apartment. Long, lean shafts of sunlight cut a diagonal swath across the living room. Breathing deeply twice, she tried to stem her tears. Involuntarily she looked at the kitchen telephone, then quickly away. If she didn't look at it, she wanted to believe, maybe it wouldn't ring.

A minute passed. Her breathing slowed. Warily, Blythe moved into her bedroom to shower and get ready for work. She had almost finished stripping off her running clothes when the telephone came alive. With the back of one hand she covered her mouth and focused her eyes like lasers on the bright red phone by her unmade bed.

If she picked up the receiver, the stalker would say nothing. No breathing. No profanities. Nothing. As if the stalker's only wish was the vacant connection and the sound of Blythe's once confident, now hollow "Hello."

Soon everyone will know . . .

No! No one can know. For the first time that day, the hundredth time in a week, she reviewed her options. A meager, familiar list. Call the D.C. police. Or the Supreme Court police. Report the stalker.

"A woman? Why might a woman be following you, Mrs. Oaks?"

"Well, Officer, perhaps it's because I'm a closet lesbian."

She admonished herself for the fantasy. *Right, Blythe. Not a chance. Maybe I should just leave. Go back to Utah. Give up my job. Give up my dream.*

Steam drifted from the shower. Water pelted the tile. The phone rang and rang. Standing naked but for her sweaty socks, Blythe Oaks cried again, loudly this time. She didn't know what she was going to do.

PART ONE

EVIL SPEAKING

Those who would take prophets out of politics would take God out of government.

EZRA TAFT BENSON,
PROPHET, CHURCH OF JESUS CHRIST OF LATTER-DAY SAINTS

Criticism is particularly objectionable when it is directed toward church authorities, general or local. Evil speaking of the Lord's anointed is in a class by itself. It is one thing to depreciate a person who exercises corporate power or even government power. It is quite another thing to criticize or depreciate a person for the performance of an office to which he or she has been called of God.

It does not matter that the criticism is true.

[*Emphasis added.*]

DALLIN H. OAKS,
FORMER JUSTICE, UTAH SUPREME COURT;
APOSTLE, CHURCH OF JESUS CHRIST OF LATTER-DAY SAINTS

Robin Torr tapped the eraser end of a pencil against the cleft in her chin and said, "The truth, Lauren. Why did you come all the way to Salt Lake City?"

Lauren Crowder crossed her legs and tried to shake off the mental malaise of her cross-country flight from New York. "Because," she said, lifting one eyebrow, "I thought it would be harder for you to turn my sister down if I was sitting in the same room with the two of you."

Robin laughed. "That's just what I figured. But it's been a lot of years since law school, Lauren. And I've gotten tough." She raised her right arm and flexed her biceps. "I'm not the same little flit you remember from Berkeley."

"Given your record lately, I suspected that," Lauren said. "And that, of course, is really why we're here."

Robin Torr smiled again. Lauren knew her old friend would be pleased that her blossoming reputation as a civil rights litigator had hopped the state line from Utah to Lauren's home in neighboring Colorado.

Robin hooked her thin hair behind her ears and adjusted the frame of her eyeglasses before speaking again. "You should know from the outset that I go into this willing to disappoint you. Both of you." Lauren's expression conveyed her skepticism. Robin persisted. "If your sister's story has merit, Lauren, I'll listen. If it doesn't, I'll pass. I step on toes all the time now. It doesn't bother me anymore, not like before." She caught herself, realizing she was treading the thin line between confidence and bluster.

Now it was Lauren's turn to smile. "Have you stepped on the toes of any United States Supreme Court justices lately, Robin?"

"What?"

"Why don't you hear Teresa out? Okay?"

Teresa Crowder tugged at her skirt before she spoke. Her smile was magnetic. Although she was able to adopt a posture of composure and confidence, at twenty-five an aura of postadolescence still hung over her. People would describe her as a young woman. A beautiful young woman.

She opened with a question. "Do you remember when Orrin Hatch died? In the men's room in that hotel in Los Angeles? That's actually when it all began, I think. Should I start there?" Teresa turned toward her sister for a signal.

Lauren gave a permissive smile, trying hard not to influence the meeting any more than she already had. She wanted to see how her little sister and her old friend would negotiate this territory without her interference.

Robin looked at the slender young woman with the perfect posture and the long legs who was sitting across from her. It was like a time warp. Teresa *was* Lauren, the last time Robin had seen her in Berkeley—what, eight years ago, nine? But she wondered if Teresa possessed her sister's fire. Lauren's intensity had been almost a legend in law school.

Without any effort Robin recalled the news stories about Senator Hatch's sudden death in a deserted men's bathroom on the meeting-room level of the Bonaventure hotel in L.A. She thought, *What does that have to do with anything?* With barely suppressed irritation she said, "*This* has to do with Orrin Hatch? Senator Orrin Hatch? I don't get it; the man's been dead at least a year. I thought you said on the phone this was about sexual harassment?"

"It is." Teresa flicked another tense glance at her sister.

Lauren smiled her encouragement. "Go on, Teresa," she said.

Robin Torr stifled a tired sigh. "Yes, please. Start wherever it makes sense. But it's getting late, so let's start somewhere."

"Well . . . after Orrin Hatch died, and Lester Horner was appointed to fill his Senate seat, he—"

"Wait. This is about Justice Horner? You *know* Justice Horner?"

"I didn't. I met him on an airplane. And he offered me a job and I took it. I worked for him—well, indirectly worked for him—for a short time when he was in the Senate."

Robin's stomach flipped. The contentious confirmation hearings that had ultimately vaulted Lester Horner from the U.S. Senate onto the U.S. Supreme Court had been nasty and divisive. He had been confirmed by a single vote. She said, "Hold it. This harassment complaint we're discussing isn't about United States Supreme Court Justice Lester Horner, is it?"

"Well, sort of indirectly it is, I guess. But no, not really."

Robin forgot all about trying to grab dinner somewhere before the Jazz game started. She reminded herself that it was only the preseason. She'd just have to eat concession food at the Delta Center.

"And the job was in his Senate office here in Utah?"

"No, no. It was with the Utah Women's Symposium. I think I was their token gentile."

Robin Torr was familiar with the symposium, a nonprofit organization that ran a huge annual meeting that paid lip service to women's issues in Utah.

"And the job was . . . ?"

"Assistant to the coordinator."

"And you took it?"

"Yes, sure. I was getting tired of what I was doing at the time. The job he was offering me sounded great."

"And the coordinator of the symposium? She was your boss?"

The young woman nodded.

"And she's the one who harassed you?"

"Yes."

Finally, we're getting somewhere, thought Robin. "Go on, then. Tell me exactly what happened. Please don't leave anything out. "

For the next fifteen minutes Robin listened without interruption to the obviously rehearsed presentation. During the entire discourse the Salt Lake City attorney was fighting an impulse to shake her head in disbelief at the story she was hearing. She desperately wanted to cut this interview short, to smile and say, "Toto, I've a feeling we're not in Kansas anymore," but she feared the young woman wouldn't get the allusion.

Lauren watched as Robin sneaked another glance at her watch.

In her mind, Robin computed that she had ten minutes to wrap this up and still have a chance to eat something other than dubious pizza at the basketball game.

Robin Torr was the youngest and only female partner with the Salt Lake City law firm of Lewis, Frank and Zelem. In her relatively brief trial career she had forged a solid reputation in labor and civil rights cases and had recently made a couple of big splashes in the Tenth Circuit on Title VII appeals. That reputation now attracted to her door a steady Great Basin parade of discrimination victims and discrimination-victim wannabes. Torr prided herself on her ability to differentiate between the two groups with accuracy and dispatch.

Teresa Crowder paused at the conclusion of her presentation. Although the young woman's wide smile was as pleasant as spring, Robin detected heat in her tight eyes. In an effort to fight a reflexive temptation to smile back, she slid her long fingers beneath her round eyeglasses and squeezed the bridge of her nose.

Lauren's eyes were intent on her old friend. A prosecutor in Boulder, Colorado, Lauren found herself fascinated not only by the novelty of Robin's edgy demeanor but by her little sister's unusual resolve.

Robin couldn't resist tipping her incredulity at what she had heard. Her voice was hoarse from the residue of a cold. She hoped, instead, it sounded husky.

"You haven't lived here long, have you?" she said.

Teresa Crowder shook her head. "Not quite a year."

Robin cleared her throat and focused on her prospective client. She tried to convince herself that her old friend from law school was temporarily out of this equation.

"And I take it you're not a member of the Church, are you?" Anyone living in Utah for more than a week would have immediately gauged the question for sarcasm. In Utah, the question of *what* church did not require clarification. And in this case the answer, Torr knew, was preordained.

The young woman shook her head again. "I thought about it for a while. Senator Horner—Justice Horner—certainly encouraged me to convert. But if you want a career, becoming a Mormon woman doesn't seem to have much upside. And the option of becoming a Mormon man wasn't ever discussed."

Lauren laughed out loud at her sister's joke. Robin didn't join in. She couldn't decipher how much of Teresa's response was editorial and how much was an attempt at humor. Either inclination in a prospective client concerned her.

"Do you have any idea how influential Lester Horner is around here?"

"Of course," said Teresa.

"He was a general authority of the Church. You must know that."

"Yes, I know. And now he's the newest justice of the U.S. Supreme Court," Teresa said. "I guess he got himself a promotion."

The attorney sighed. That morning she had lost two motions in what should have been a slam-dunk hearing. She damn well knew she shouldn't have lost either of them. The failure had soured a mood already foul from another night of too little sleep. Now she had to struggle with an old friend asking her to help a relative with a case that, despite its merits, was frosted with political land mines.

"What's a general authority?" asked Lauren.

Robin responded. "A Mormon leader. There's a group of men in Utah who run the business and spiritual end of the Church. They're called general authorities.

There are a dozen senior general authorities in a group called the Quorum of the Twelve Apostles. The president of the Church—the prophet, seer, and revelator of all Mormondom—has two advisers, like a cabinet, in something called the First Presidency. Below them is a group called the First Quorum of the Seventy. Lester Horner was a new member of the Seventy when he accepted the Senate appointment. That put him on a list to someday, maybe, become the prophet, to run the whole Church."

Robin turned back to Teresa. "Just for the sake of argument—or at least for your sister's benefit—let's pretend you don't understand how these things work in Utah.

"For Justice Horner, filling the remainder of Orrin Hatch's term in the U.S. Senate, and then moving on to the Supreme Court, can be considered a personal sacrifice, not a promotion. If you had a choice between becoming a Supreme Court justice and being on a shortlist to become God's next prophet on earth, which would you prefer?"

Deadpan, Teresa replied, "Well, at least they're both lifetime appointments."

Robin Torr cracked a smile.

Teresa's confidence ballooned. She said, "Ms. Torr, I'm not accusing Justice Horner of anything. He has been incredibly kind and generous to me from the first day we met. He has always treated me with, well, with dignity and respect. This isn't about him."

Robin cleared her throat again. Her voice sounded normal to her, finally. She flashed a sympathetic smile. "Teresa—may I call you Teresa? It doesn't make any difference that you're not accusing Justice Horner of anything improper. I wish it did, but for the purposes for which you are seeking my representation, it just doesn't make any difference. If you accuse his lifelong friend and chief clerk of harassment and discrimination, you might as well be accusing him."

In as even a tone as she could muster, Teresa said to the attorney, "I guess you're right, Ms. Torr. I guess I don't understand. I'm sorry. Why doesn't it make any difference that I'm not accusing Justice Horner of being involved in any of this?"

Robin removed her glasses and lay them on the desk beside her buff-colored legal pad. Turning back to Teresa, she arched her eyebrows, despite knowing what that little act did to highlight the spray of wrinkles at the corners of her eyes. She said, "It's 'Robin,' okay? And the answer is: Because, Teresa, we're in Utah."

Robin hoped that pointing out the simple geographic and cultural reality of the current circumstances would be sufficient argument to convince Teresa Crowder of the foolhardiness of pursuing any action against the senior clerk of the only Mormon ever to sit on the United States Supreme Court.

Teresa nodded. She said, "Yes, we are. I've noticed, believe me. It's *so* hard to get a good cup of coffee."

Lauren laughed again. Robin smiled reluctantly before she continued her argument. "Some recent history might be helpful in putting this in context. The LDS Church was ambushed by Horner's appointments to the Senate and then to the Supreme Court. If the Church leadership had anticipated either appointment, the prophet would never have called Horner to serve on the Seventy in the first place. The Church ended up enduring a very unpleasant inquisition and expending an incredible amount of political capital to get Horner confirmed to the Supreme Court. The person you're accusing of harassment is just too close to him for him to escape your allegations untainted. Hell, Justice Horner handpicked her.

"And speaking of 'her,' I doubt that I need to point out that the accusation you're making is of *female-female* harassment. Do you have any idea what an abomination homosexuality is to the Mormons?"

Teresa knew. She was unswayed. She looked toward her sister. Past her.

"And I guarantee you that there are a lot of influential people in Utah—in the LDS Church in Utah—who will not want you to prevail. And where there is an abundance of Church influence in Utah, there is also an abundance of Church money. And what you want me to help you with will be terribly expensive."

What Robin was implying, but didn't say, was that the other partners in Lewis, Frank and Zelem were about as likely to agree to take this case on contingency as Utah was of reviving the ERA.

Teresa glanced down at her hands, folded in her lap, offered a rueful version of her wonderful smile, and looked back up at the woman who she was hoping would agree to represent her in a complaint alleging sexual harassment and job discrimination that she wished to file against her former superior on the Utah Women's Symposium. As sincerely as she could, she said, "I know we're not in Kansas anymore."

Robin finally laughed out loud. Then she caught Teresa's gaze and held it. As compassionately as she could, she asked, "Why do you want to do this? Other than because you feel you've been screwed, why do you want to do this?"

Lauren waited with Robin for her sister to respond to the blunt confrontation.

Teresa handled the challenge deftly. "I look at the question differently, Ms. Torr—Robin. I see every reason *to* do it. She harassed me. She punished me for refusing to have sex with her. She expected me to take the punishment quietly and not be a problem to her. The only reason not to do it, not to sue them, is because these people are more powerful than I am. It's taken me a while, but I've decided that that's a rotten reason."

Lauren was surprised at the cogency of her sister's reply.

Robin said, "What about the cost? This sort of thing isn't cheap."

Lauren jumped in. "Money's not an issue for now, Robin. I've got money from my divorce, and I'm going to pay for this for a while. At least until we see what we have. How strong a case we can put together."

Shit, thought Robin. She had been hoping for an easy way out. She said, "It's not just the money, Lauren. This is political dynamite. And you both know it."

Lauren remembered her friend as an old-time rabble-rouser. With a hint of a smile, she asked, "Is that good or bad, Robin?"

Robin was all business. "You know me. I don't mind

causes. I don't even mind high-profile causes. But I'm not particularly fond of stupid."

"And what do you think this is? Is this stupid?"

After going to exaggerated lengths to be certain the bottom edge of her legal pad was perfectly aligned with the bottom edge of the desk in front of her, Robin Torr decided to ignore the question. Instead she said, "Let's make sure we all understand what we're discussing here today. I want to say this once, out loud. For all of our benefit.

"Your boss, ex-boss—the one you refused to have sexual relations with, and the one who, you maintain, shortly thereafter sabotaged your continued employment by the Women's Symposium—is a woman? Right?"

Teresa shrugged her acknowledgment.

"And this woman is, at *this* very moment, the chief clerk of the first and only Mormon ever to sit on the United States Supreme Court?"

"Yes."

"So, in a nutshell, this is what we've got: You, a very attractive young *gentile* woman, are retaining me to file a sexual harassment suit against a respected, married *Mormon* woman who is a lifelong friend of one of the most influential men in the Church of Jesus Christ of Latter-day Saints. And who now happens to be his chief clerk on the United States Supreme Court?"

Another nod from Teresa. "Yes, that's right, Ms. Torr."

"And you want to do this little trick in Utah?"

"Again, yes, Ms. Torr."

"This," said Robin, "is nuts."

"Probably, Ms. Torr. Probably." Teresa looked at her lap. "There's one other thing I should tell you."

"Yes?"

"My new career? Since I got canned by the symposium? I'm trying to get established as a stand-up comedian. I wait tables sometimes, too." She forced a self-conscious smile. "I thought you should know."

Robin Torr broke out laughing. She was beginning to find something about this woman irresistible. Shaking her head, which released her fine, straight hair from behind her ears, she said, "What about before that? What were you doing when Horner recruited you for the symposium?"

"I was skating with Disney's World on Ice. For the last six months before I retired I was the Little Mermaid."

Robin held out her hands as if to say, I give up. She couldn't help beginning to compose tabloid headlines in her head. "Little Mermaid Hooks Horner" came immediately to mind. She turned to Lauren. "I have a feeling I'm going to regret this, but I'll seriously consider taking the case on one condition. Lauren, how long can you stay in Utah? If I'm going to get into this mess, you're not going to get off just writing me a check. I want to put you to work for a while."

Robin's unexpected plea caused Lauren Crowder to sit up straight. She said, "I don't know, Robin. I was only planning on visiting with Teresa for a few days. I've already been away from Boulder for a long time. Alan, the guy I'm seeing, might kill me if I don't come home by the end of the week."

"Well, think again. If I'm going to agree to look into this, you have to stay long enough to help me see what we've got. If we find we have something strong enough to run with, I'll commit, okay? And then you can go home."

"I'm not actually due back at work until the end of October. I guess I could stay," Lauren said. "But, Robin—"

"That's a great idea! Lauren, please?" said Teresa.

"What?" asked Robin.

"I don't think I'm quite the same person you might remember from law school."

Teresa smiled at her sister and said, "Lauren, don't be silly. I think it's a wonderful idea."

Robin wondered what Lauren meant by her last comment. "Good, then. We're set. And one more time, just for the record," she said, touching her pencil to her legal pad, "what's the name of this woman we're about to make world-famous?"

"Her name," replied Teresa Crowder, "is Blythe Oaks."

Where the state of Utah isn't mountain it is high desert.

In 1847, when a revelation from God directed Brigham Young to lead his saints in search of Zion, the Kingdom of God on earth, he guided the first of his flock of fourteen thousand Mormon followers from their beseiged home in Nauvoo, Illinois, across the Great Plains through the Wasatch Mountains to the Great Basin and the banks of the Great Salt Lake.

The emigrating saints arrived to find a high-desert paradise sparsely populated by Indians, mostly Utes, ringed by mountains, and bordered by the southeastern shore of one of the largest dead seas in the world. For the Mormon pioneers the most important features of the topography were the natural barriers that Brigham Young felt would protect their nascent state of Deseret from the influence of belligerent, unholy gentiles. Standing guard to the east were the Wasatch Range and the majestic Rocky Mountains. To the west were the huge lake, vast deserts, and the imposing Sierra Nevada.

Almost one hundred and fifty years later, Lauren Crowder had arrived in Utah's capital city to find a sprawling metropolis with a small, modern downtown that had a familiar, conventional, western appearance that belied its underlying character. In truth, Salt Lake City is no more a typical western American city than Mormonism is a typical Christian religion.

Salt Lake City is probably the only major western American city where ice cream parlors outnumber bars, and where streets are assigned names based on their geographical relationship to a temple.

And the Church of Jesus Christ of Latter-day Saints is surely the only Christian faith whose Word of Wisdom includes rigid codes regarding the underwear to be worn by believers, and whose beliefs include the surety that the biblical Garden of Eden is really in Jackson County, Missouri.

On a roundabout drive from Robin Torr's office to her small rented brick bungalow just off Fifth South, below the University of Utah, Teresa pointed out the sights to her sister.

Despite the fact that Salt Lake City was, at only fifty percent LDS, the least Mormon city in Utah, the sights in Salt Lake City were almost all Mormon attractions.

In Teresa's old Volkswagen Rabbit, afflicted with a bad muffler and a worse clutch, they drove downtown to Temple Square, parked close by, and walked to the walled site of the Mormon Tabernacle and the Mormon Temple.

Teresa was determined to inject her sister full of Mormon significance and Mormon culture. "This place isn't what it seems to be," she said. "Utah. It isn't like any place else in the country. If you're going to be helping me with this, everything depends on your understanding that." Acting as an unofficial guide to the attractions of Temple Square, she spent a few futile minutes trying to explain to her sister the significance of the bronze handcart and the Sea Gull Monument.

When Lauren interrupted her and asked, "A miracle? Really? Just because some birds ate some grasshoppers?" Teresa finally gave up in frustration and led her sister to the center of the square to wait for a guided tour.

As they lingered in the beautifully manicured courtyard awaiting a sufficient number of tourists to assemble to justify a tour, Lauren turned to her sister and said, "I didn't know some of the details you told Robin today."

Teresa said, "It's not a nice story, Lauren. I don't like to think about the details." She looked away.

"No, it's certainly not a pretty story." But Lauren wanted to go over it again. "She called you a slut? I didn't know that part."

"After dinner, in the bathroom at the restaurant, when I threatened to scream, yes, she did. She called me a few names. That was one of them."

"And she actually touched your breast? I thought—I guess I assumed—she'd just, like, fondled you through your clothes."

"No. By then she had me backed up against a toilet. I was using both my hands to prop myself up on the wall to keep from falling over backwards. She touched me on my throat, very gently"—Teresa's hand rose to her neck, to a spot just above the hollow—"then she slid her fingers inside my suit jacket and . . . and she touched my breast."

"You weren't even wearing a bra?"

Teresa laughed at the question. "Lauren, with my boobs? Are you kidding? When have you ever known me to wear a bra?"

"And that thing that happened in the shower. That was before dinner?"

"Yes, that was earlier." Teresa looked up to be certain that her sister wanted her to continue. Lauren's face was all curiosity and compassion. Teresa said, "We had adjoining rooms in the hotel. When we came back to the hotel from our last meeting on Capitol Hill, she came into my room with me. We were talking about something, visiting the Holocaust Museum the next day, I don't know, something. She stayed for a couple of minutes. Then, when she went next door to her room she used the connecting door. I guess I never closed the door on my side all the way after that. Five minutes later I saw her reflection in the mirror. She was standing in the doorway to my bathroom. She said she'd come over to find out whether I wanted to stay in the hotel for dinner or go out."

"But you were naked?"

"I had a washcloth. Does that count?"

Lauren smiled at the joke. Her sister could find humor anywhere. "And she didn't leave right away?"

"No, she stood there asking me questions."

"What, like 'Pizza or Chinese?' "

"Basically, yes. I remember she asked me if I liked sushi."

"Was she dressed?"

"She had a bathrobe on."

"Was she modest?"

"Yeah, she must have been. I think I'd remember being flashed."

"Was she, like, looking? You know what I mean. At your body?"

"In retrospect, I guess, yes, she was. But she wasn't staring. I didn't feel ogled."

"Did you tell her to leave?"

"Not right away. I tried to act cool. Lauren, for the last three years I've been in a hundred locker-room situations with dozens of different women, including some who were my bosses. Being naked in front of another woman like that just wasn't that strange for me after all the time I spent on the road with World on Ice. I mean, it eventually got weird when she just stayed and stayed and stayed. But showering in front of a female coworker just wasn't that awkward for me. Finally, when it seemed like she was never going to leave, I said something like 'I'll be done in here in a few minutes, okay?' And she left."

"But you were pleasant about it?"

"Yes. Of course I was pleasant."

"And the whole time you didn't do anything to cover yourself?"

"No, I didn't. Again, if you don't count the washcloth."

"You didn't think her behavior might be inappropriate?"

"Then? If I had thought about it I might have considered it, I don't know, odd, maybe. But inappropriate, no. Not until later."

Lauren tried to picture the situation and wondered what she would have done. "Whose idea was it to stay at the hotel for dinner?"

"It was mine. I was tired. I wanted to go to bed early."

Teresa looked up high in the sky at the statue of the angel Moroni on top of the temple. "You know, I don't like the way this conversation is going. I know what you're thinking."

"What am I thinking?"

"You're thinking that this isn't going to sound too good in court."

"You're right. That's what I'm thinking." Lauren decided not to push her sister any further. That was a task, thankfully, she could leave for Teresa's new attorney.

Teresa apparently wanted to change the subject, too. She asked how well Lauren knew Robin Torr.

"We were good friends for a while at Berkeley. Pretty good friends. For law school, anyway. But she was a year ahead of me. Then she got involved with somebody, and I met Jake, and, I don't know."

"You drifted apart?"

"We were never that close. The friendship was really just starting. Jacob didn't like the guy Robin was seeing. And vice versa. Just one of those things. She's different now."

"How?"

"I don't know. Robin was always kind of meek in school. She was a pleaser. Bright and energetic, but a behind-the-scenes person. Now she's got herself quite a reputation as a scholar, and she's become a scrappy litigator, too."

"You somehow don't sound too pleased with the change."

"I've been struggling with it since we left her office. She's—I don't know, brittle now. She has an edge to her I don't remember. Maybe she's too determined to appear like a hardass. She reminds me of somebody I don't like to remember."

"Jacob?" asked Teresa. Jacob was Lauren's ex-husband.

Lauren took two steps before she replied. "No, T. She reminds me of me. Not too long ago."

Soon, a call to assembly intruded.

For the next hour they heard Sister Cella, from Tucson, Arizona, tell the parts of the story of the LDS Church that the Mormon leadership deemed appropriate for public consumption. Although the tour group never got closer than ten yards away from any door to the imposing granite temple, they visited the famed Mormon Tabernacle and for most of an hour digested a version of Mormondom so sanitized that the Church could have been mistaken for a mainstream Protestant sect.

The terminology spoken and the icons visible during the tour were traditional Christian ones. The themes presented were fundamental and conservative; the tone was subtly, but richly, patriotic. Overall, the impression made was as perfect as if it had been produced by Universal Studios Tours. Just as the benches in the cavernous tabernacle were made of western pine but had been meticulously hand-finished by Zion pioneers to make them appear to be of oak, the Mormon religion was packaged for the general public to appear as something other than it was.

That effect was exactly what Church leaders intended.

When the sisters returned to the car, Teresa drove east into the steep foothills of the Wasatch Front, past the University of Utah, and up Emigration Canyon to the base of the monument honoring the leaders of the Mormon pioneers.

She parked the car. She was frustrated. Her sister, she was afraid, wasn't getting it.

"You can't help me much, Lauren, unless you know this place. Utah. The version you just heard was pure vanilla. But it's not the way it is here. It's not what Mormondom is all about. At least it's not what Utah Mormondom is all about. Salt Lake City isn't just a funny western town that used to be full of polygamists and now has a great choir and wants to host the Winter Olympics. This"—she spread her left arm toward the sprawl of the Utah Valley as the light waned in the desert—"is the center of one of the fastest-growing and wealthiest Christian churches in the world. Salt Lake City is a true religious capital—a major one, like Rome, or Jerusalem, or Tehran. You can't forget that, ever, if you're going to be of much help to me."

Lauren was about to offer some reassurance, but Teresa bulled on, her voice swollen with passion. "Considering a lawsuit here isn't the same as doing it in Denver or Seattle. Robin Torr is absolutely right. How can I make you understand this place?

"Can you imagine going to Rome and not being able to visit a church? Or going to Israel and being excluded from a synagogue? Well, the holiest place in the LDS Church was in that square we just left, and no one is ever, ever allowed in it who isn't a Mormon in good standing. And part of being in good standing is promising—pledging your life *and* your afterlife—never to reveal the secrets of what happens in that temple. Because in that temple there are secret ordinances with secret handshakes and theatrical baptisms of dead relatives and dramatic re-creations of your entrance into heaven.

"Don't be fooled. This is not a conventional Christian denomination. They don't tell you that on the tour we were just on. They don't tell you that in heaven, the holiest of Mormons—but only men—will progress to become gods themselves, that Jesus is but one god among many. They don't tell you that the spirit of every living soul, born and unborn, is as old as God. They don't tell you that every twelve-year-old Mormon male begins to accumulate priestly powers that allow him to communicate directly with God and to heal in His name. They don't tell you that they take the Book of Revelation literally and that the year 2000 marks the beginning of the millennium and that the work of the LDS Church is going to change earth into its version of a moral, just, and saintly place to prepare for the gathering of the faithful in the Wasatch Valley. Then, Jesus Christ, in His next coming, will lead the faithful back to Eden, which is someplace near Kansas City, Missouri, for heaven's sake."

Teresa's eyes were dappled with greens and grays. The sky to the west was awash with the colors of fruit ice. Despite the beauty of the setting, Lauren was transfixed by her sister's unusual intensity. She saw some of her old self reflected in the passion. Whatever was fueling the change in demeanor on her sister's part, it was working. Teresa had captured Lauren's attention.

"It's hard to explain the culture here, and I don't

know if I'm doing a good job. I'm afraid you actually have to live here to understand it," Teresa said a few minutes later, almost apologetically, as she stood with her sister beneath the imposing statue of Brigham Young, Heber Kimball, and Wilford Woodruff in Emigration Canyon.

"Some of the time living here feels normal. It's a beautiful, peaceful place—clean, not too much crime, wonderful mountains, great climate. Then one day I realized that it's the most segregated place I've ever lived. There are two absolutely parallel communities here: one LDS, one gentile.

"Mormons make up about half of Salt Lake City, closer to eighty percent of the rest of the state. But even after being here over a year, I have no close friends who are LDS—none. And none of my friends have friends who are LDS. Acquaintances, sure. Neighbors, yes. Coworkers, yes. But except for the brief time when I was working for the Women's Symposium, I don't even speak with any Mormons on a meaningful basis.

"I don't want this to sound anti-Mormon. It's easy to make fun of the Mormons. People have been doing it, apparently, from the start. See, with one another, these saints can be remarkable people. They help one another as unselfishly as you could imagine. Some of them actually do seem filled with grace at times. Justice Horner's a good example. As a group of people they are absolutely consumed with the welfare of their own community. But the rest of us, the nonmembers—the gentiles—once we're identified as not being interested in conversion, it's like we disappear.

"And every day there's something here that makes you remember how powerful the Mormons are in Utah—economically, politically, culturally."

Lauren couldn't tell if her sister's version of the Utah LDS Church was just bitterness talking. Or maybe fear. For the first time she wondered whether there was some political motivation behind her sister's allegations. Teresa's slant could not have been more different from the presentation they had just endured in Temple Square.

The Crowder kids had been raised Episcopalians. Over the years Teresa had toyed with fringe spiritual groups Lauren considered much stranger than the Mormon Church. "Were you ever tempted to convert? You've always been the family seeker, T."

Teresa examined her sister's face for signs of criticism. "I thought about it. Sure. At first, every Mormon you meet checks you out as a potential convert and begins to indoctrinate you. What they do is they entice you with the sense of community. It can be subtle, and it's seductive, believe me. Especially for a newcomer. The fibers of the Church community are everywhere in Utah. Births, deaths, community projects, welfare projects, constant meetings at the ward house or the stake, classes for the kids, or visits to the temple to perform ordinances. Girl Scouts, soccer and basketball leagues—it's all run by the Church in Utah. And when Mormons aren't going out to participate in Church activities, home visits, firesides, and home teaching come to them, with elders constantly checking their allegiance to the lines of authority. It's constant. Constant. An active Mormon will be involved with the Church twenty hours or more a week. If you don't happen to have one of your own, it's an entire life. But it was months before I really learned any doctrine, and even that I had to do on my own.

"Senator Horner was always pushing gently on me to join. He invited me to services with his family when they were in town. He was constantly alluding to how wonderful and comforting being a Church member could be. He would quote little tracts from the Book of Mormon or remind me, as I sipped a Coke, how right Joseph Smith had been a hundred and fifty years ago about the Word of Wisdom. But nobody, not him, not anybody else, would really talk to me about doctrine. And *nobody* wanted to talk about the structure and inviolability of the Church's authority.

"It feels like a secret club. Once you join you get to find out the rules. And the first rule you learn after you join is, Do not *ever* question what it is you've joined."

"And the doctrine? What's so strange?"

"It's funny. The Church leaders encourage saints—they call themselves saints—not to focus on the doctrine. The party line from the top is that intellectual inquiry into doctrine and Church history is misleading and can only serve to undermine spirituality and obedience. The LDS Church has this amazing concept: activities, behaviors, and even thoughts are defined as either 'faithpromoting' or 'not faith-promoting.' And the Church leadership, these men called the general authorities, get to decide which is which. They decide what you should think. What you should read. What you should do. How you should act. With whom you should associate."

"Horner is one of these general authorities?"

"Yes. Was briefly, anyway, before he went to the Senate. He's young and he's pretty influential in the Church. He's only fifty-four or something like that. What makes Lester Horner unusual is his age. Most of the top guys are antiques. I mean ancient. A prophet younger than eighty would be considered youthful, maybe even unseasoned."

Lauren wanted to lighten things up. "So, if I understand you right, what you're doing with this lawsuit is the rough equivalent of accusing one of the pope's lieutenants of messing around with an altar boy?"

"The Mormons wouldn't have much patience with the Catholic analogy, but yeah. Even though I haven't accused Lester Horner of a thing, to accuse a Mormon as prominent as Blythe Oaks of homosexual behavior is about as irreverent as you can get. The only thing I can think of that would be worse would be to accuse her of being an abortionist. To the Mormons, you could say I fall into the category of not being particularly faith-promoting."

Lauren Crowder took a step over to her younger sister and hugged her. She said, "I'm with you on this, Teresa. I don't know how I feel about anything you've just told me. But I can promise you that you're not alone. I'm here because I love you." Teresa, awkward with the show of affection, was slow to return her sister's embrace.

"Lauren? There's something else. I'm glad Robin asked you to stay, and I'm glad you'll be here for a while. But, um, I don't know how to say this exactly. I don't have as much faith in my ability to stick with this as I wish I did. What I need most from you, I think, is for you to believe in me and to help me keep from quitting, no matter how nasty it gets. Okay? It's gonna get nasty, right?"

Lauren said, "Yes, probably."

"Well, I don't want to run. Help me not to run this time. Even if they get mean. You know what I'm talking about, don't you?"

Lauren kissed her sister on the nose. Certain things about their childhood were only ever discussed in vague references. "Yes, I know what you're talking about. I'll be there. I'll give you a shove when you need it, Teresa." She caught her sister's gaze and held it. "It *is* a worthwhile fight. We'll take it to the end, together. Okay?"

"Thanks."

"But as fascinating as I find this tour of the promised land, it's time to go to your house. I'm exhausted. I need to rest. My indentured servitude with this case of yours starts tomorrow morning. I'd like to be awake for it."

Teresa put an arm around her sister's waist. "Lauren?"

"Mmm."

"No running? Even when it gets mean."

"No running."

Lauren wasn't certain how to tell Alan she wasn't coming right home to Colorado.

As she lifted the receiver to place the call, she imagined him in his living room, reading. In jeans and a sweatshirt, on his green leather chair. She wondered how long he had let his hair grow. Whether this was a bearded phase or a clean-shaven one. Whether the leaves were changing below him in the Boulder Valley. Whether he would be longingly disappointed or just plain angry.

What she said after she said "Hi, sweetheart" was simply "It looks like I'm going to have to stay in Utah for a while, Alan."

A few heartbeats of silence followed. Then Alan asked, "Why?" Although his voice stayed as soft as ever, his tone was challenging and not particularly curious.

Lauren said, "You're disappointed, aren't you? I am, too." She'd been away from Boulder and from Alan Gregory for a long time already. Her stop in Utah on her way home to Colorado was supposed to have lasted three days, just enough time for her to give her sister some support while she shopped for an attorney.

"Of course I'm disappointed, Lauren. I really miss you. What's a while?"

"Couple weeks. Maybe three. Depends. Teresa's attorney, my old friend from law school, wants me to help her out here while she investigates the complaint. Teresa wants me here, too. It's not a bad idea. It could save me a lot of money in legal fees." The last part was a rationalization.

"Oh," he said.

"You can come to Utah and see me. It's a lot closer than New York, and I won't be here that long." She realized he wasn't inclined to make this any easier for her. "Look, I'm sorry," she said. "I want to come home and be with you, too. But this is important for Teresa." When he didn't respond immediately, she added, "I don't ask for much, Alan."

"No, Lauren, you don't. But when you do, it usually has to do with me tolerating not seeing you for one reason or another. It's hard for me. And I don't think I can come to Utah. I've already got that bike trip planned with Sam Purdy in Crested Butte in a couple of weeks. I can't leave work any more than that." Alan Gregory was a clinical psychologist trying to rebuild a practice that had been decimated by misconduct charges.

"Maybe I can get away and meet you in Crested Butte for a few days."

"With Sam there?"

She laughed. He joined in. The tension began to ease.

She said, "That would be an unusual weekend, wouldn't it?"

"To say the least."

Ten minutes later, after they had hung up, Lauren took off the clothes she had been wearing all day and pulled on a robe. She had expected Alan to be upset about her decision to stay in Utah. She had also expected that they would work it out.

The exact same set of circumstances would have led to a tantrum from her ex-husband.

She curled up on her side on the bed in her sister's spare bedroom. The room oozed nostalgia. The furniture was from Lauren's childhood bedroom. It had been handed down to Teresa. Lauren closed her eyes. Something, she knew, wasn't right. The doubts that stirred her discontent felt as juvenile to her as the surroundings.

Alan's disappointment tugged on Lauren like gravity. She *had* been looking forward to seeing him. But she also knew that her own letdown at not being able to go straight home to Colorado didn't approach the intensity of his chagrin.

That worried her. She was planning to marry the man. She should yearn for him, shouldn't she?

Pratt Toomey was ten minutes early for his three-o'clock meeting with Robin Torr the next day. Elsic Smith, Torr's secretary, had been anticipating Toomey's arrival and had a cold can of 7 Up waiting for him on the corner of her desk. Elsie's grief over her thirty-eight-year-old husband's death from cancer was waning after a year, and she had her eye on Pratt Toomey, whose own wife had surreptitiously left Pratt, the Church, and Utah with the five Toomey children while Pratt was volunteering during the previous July's Pioneer Day celebration.

Elsie had decided, for both herself and Toomey, that enough grief was enough grief.

Pratt gently lowered his tall frame onto the chair next to Elsie's desk. "Your boss hasn't been requiring my services enough lately, Elsie. I'm finding myself having to manufacture excuses just to spend a few extra minutes in your company."

"That's so sweet of you, Pratt. But you don't need an excuse as far as I'm concerned. As a matter of fact, I was sitting here wondering if—"

The static of the intercom interrupted Elsie before she had a chance to suggest that Pratt join her and her kids for a picnic that evening. Robin Torr's voice. "Elsie, is Pratt there yet? You know he's always early. Anyway, if he's there, send him in, please."

"Duty calls?" asked Pratt, just a tad too much disappointment in his voice. He stood, the soft drink in his hand, and let himself into Robin Torr's office.

Pratt didn't recognize the woman sitting on the small sofa across the room. Robin was behind her desk, her hair held back from her face by a pencil over each ear, her glasses on top of her head. In a conspiratorial whisper, without looking up, she started teasing Pratt about Elsie. "Pratt, someday, I swear, Elsie is going to thank me for protecting her from a fate worse than a month of nonstop temple tours. Whether you know it or not, Elsie has decided you are The One. A few more visits out there and she'll be sizing you up for her dead husband's old clothes and start asking you for help tuning up her lawnmower. And, Pratt—all revelations aside—she's much too sweet for you. By the way," she continued, raising her voice to a conversational level, and looking up and gesturing across the room, "that's Lauren Crowder. She's an old college friend of mine and an attorney from out of state who's going to be assisting on the case we'll be talking about today."

Lauren nodded an acknowledgment.

"Lauren, this is Pratt Toomey, one of the investigators we use. He's a good investigator and a great flirt. Actually, I'm giving him a little too much credit. Pratt's a fair investigator and a slightly better-than-average flirt."

Pratt mentally checked his posture and smiled. "As I've told you before, I can manage Mrs. Smith's affections just fine, Robin. And it's very nice to meet you, Miss Crowder. Delighted to have you in Utah, and I do look forward to working with you."

Robin continued to tease. "Pratt, you can cut the charm. One, she's engaged. Two, she's not LDS. And three, she's more than smart enough to see through your crap."

"Robin, I'm offended."

"Yeah, right, Pratt."

Lauren waved across the room at Pratt Toomey. "Hello, Mr. Toomey."

As Robin searched around on her desk for her glasses, one pencil fell out from behind her ear and her thin hair shadowed her face. She said, "Enough pleasantries. Let's get to work, folks. We've got some chores to divide up."

"What's the case?" asked Toomey.

"The stuff of your nightmares, Pratt."

"Truly?" Pratt smiled like a man whose nights held no terror. "And what might that be, Robin?"

"Well, one that involves the hierarchy of the LDS Church, lesbianism, and sexual harassment. What did Boyd Packer say were the three big dangers facing the Church in the nineties, Pratt? I think they were feminists, gays, and so-called scholars. Well, this case looks like it should be all-inclusive." Elder Boyd Packer was a senior member of the Quorum of the Twelve Apostles.

Pratt thought she was joking.

"Do you have a problem with it, Pratt? I'm serious, now. This case will probably involve some serious Church intrigue. Tell me now."

Pratt Toomey paused until he was sure he had the floor. He wanted to ask some questions, see what he was agreeing to. But he hated appearing indecisive, especially around attractive women.

"Robin, the Church and I have an understanding. I've got to make a living if I'm going to tithe. And the Church certainly does like for me to tithe. And the immutable truth, in case you haven't noticed, is that the woods in these parts are full of LDS. So if you're going to hike in these woods—as I've been known to occasionally—you're occasionally going to step in the droppings of a member. But where providing for one's family is concerned, both God and the Church believe that a man's got to do what a man's got to do."

Robin didn't look up. "Nice speech, Pratt, but get real. Around here a man's got to do what his bishop tells him he's got to do. I don't want platitudes. I want you to consider whether you can offer unbiased help on this case. We're talking about the possible involvement of general authorities. Who knows, maybe even apostles."

Darn, thought Pratt. *I wish I didn't need the work.*

"Big bears, little bears, all God's creatures defecate, Robin. And it's all the same when you step in it."

At the conclusion of his metaphor about bears in the woods, Pratt took three steps toward the sofa and lowered himself onto a chair across from Lauren Crowder. He was prepared to gaze warmly into her eyes, but she didn't bother to look up.

Torr stood at her desk and made her way over to the

sofa. She said, "By the way, Pratt, I may have forgotten to mention it, but Lauren here is the plaintiff's sister. The plaintiff's name is Teresa Crowder." She sat down.

"Here's the story. My client was offered a job working in the Utah Women's Symposium by Lester Horner when he was a new U.S. senator. You heard of the symposium, Pratt? You know, the Mormon version of feminism in the nineties. Now there's an oxymoron if I've ever heard one. Anyway, it's right up your alley."

He nodded. He didn't know what else to do.

"Teresa's immediate superior was Blythe Oaks, whose husband, by the way, is assistant director of the Missionary Training Center in Provo. Another Church hotshot. Rumor is that when Blythe comes to her senses and resumes her rightful place beside him in the home, he'll be on a bullet train to the Seventy. Anyway, Teresa traveled with the female Oaks to Washington, D.C., on a business trip to meet with staff members of the Utah congressional delegation. Okay so far?"

Pratt said, "Sure."

"On the last night of the trip, Oaks unexpectedly drops some of her Mormon decorum. At dinner, she drinks a significant quantity of pretty good white Burgundy and begins to seduce our client. Our client is no virgin. She knows when she's being seduced.

"Our client is uncomfortable with her boss's advances, to say the least, and excuses herself from the table to go to the ladies' room to ponder how to make a graceful exit.

"Oaks follows her. Ends up pushing her into a stall and kissing and then intimately touching our client while she is straddling a toilet trying to get away.

"Shortly thereafter, Lester Horner is appointed to the Supreme Court. Our client, who has been led to believe she is doing great work, is told her services are no longer needed by the symposium. In no time, Blythe Oaks is heading off to D.C. to clerk for Horner."

Pratt had heard enough. He felt like bolting. Instead, he swallowed and asked Torr where she wanted him to start work.

"Our first problem, Pratt, is finding some evidence to support our allegation that Blythe Oaks has a harassment history, primarily with other women. If we can't find evidence of that, then we'll probably have a pretty difficult time convincing a Utah jury that the harassment occurred."

She turned to Lauren. "And except for her harassment of your sister, Lauren, we have no indication that Oaks has been anything other than an exemplary Mormon wife. I made a couple of phone calls, and the picture I get of Oaks is that if you forget her legal career, she looks like a textbook Mormon wife and mother; temple recommend, just enough kids, Relief Society, welfare farms, basement full of old food, the whole nine yards. Only blemish is her employment history."

"You mean the type of work she did?" asked Lauren, puzzled.

Robin smiled. Time for a Utah lesson. "No, I mean the fact that she worked at all when she didn't have to. Although many do, it's not considered desirable for Mormon women to work."

Lauren made a mental note to ask someone to translate into English for her the other characteristics Robin had listed that make up "an exemplary Mormon wife."

Lauren said, "Don't forget about Washington, Robin."

Robin turned back to Pratt Toomey. "Right. Our client thinks that some people, specifically the restaurant staff at the hotel in Washington, D.C., may be helpful to us. We'll probably need to interview them at some point. But Lauren has already made some calls today and will do the initial phone contacts there."

"So where do we look around here for evidence of harassment?" Lauren asked, her gaze going to Robin Torr before settling on Pratt Toomey. "I take it the Mormons don't keep a register of lesbian members that we can refer to."

Robin waited for Pratt to answer. When he didn't, she said, "The LDS Church is actually quite fond of lists. Almost as fond as it is of secrets. So the odds are that they do keep a register of suspected lesbian members, but it's not terribly likely they'd let us see it. That would definitely not be a faith-promoting piece of paper. So I think we're left to start looking in all the places where Oaks worked.

"Teresa's harassment happened on the job. We begin there, and see if we can find any evidence that Oaks has done this before. It turns out she's worked for Horner for years. First at BYU—Brigham Young University—that's in Provo, Lauren, about an hour south of here. Then she clerked for him during the brief time he was on the Court of Appeals. Then she ran the Utah Women's Symposium when Horner was in the Senate. It's a privately funded nonprofit thing that was loosely tied to the senator's office. That office is downtown, a couple of blocks from here. That's where Teresa worked. All in all, we probably have a lot of people to talk to. We just need to pray that Oaks hasn't been too discreet. Or, at the very least, that she's angered somebody enough that they'll talk to us. Pratt, any thoughts?"

Pratt Toomey would rather have talked about anything other than gays and lesbians. As far as he was concerned, the Church had no homosexuals.

He waited until neither woman was talking before he spoke. "You may find that somebody's willing to say a few discouraging words about Sister Oaks, Robin. That's possible. There are going to be folks around here who think she had no business going to Washington to work for Justice Horner at all. Leaving her husband and kids here, like she did. I know the kids are grown. Still, some—more than a few—will say it wasn't a woman's place. But the homosexual thing, I think it's a dry hole," he said.

"Why?" snapped Lauren. She immediately scolded herself for not being more level.

Pratt responded evenly. "You're talking good, moral, conservative, God-loving people. God-fearing people. Not homosexuals. We're talking Brigham Young University in Utah County, Utah. A great university. We're talking a Women's Symposium that was started by a fine, fine man, Orrin Hatch. We're talking the United States Senate office of onetime general authority Lester Horner. We're talking the Supreme Court of the United States of America. What Mormon women you're going to find in these places are going to be family-oriented, God-serving women; you're not going to find any homosexuals. You might as well be looking for turds in an operating room."

When Pratt Toomey said "homosexuals" the word came out as "hummasexuals."

Lauren considered Toomey's preoccupation with excrement and his apparent homophobia while she was trying to decipher the expression on Robin Torr's face. Lauren was surprised that Robin didn't appear more troubled at the bias and skepticism they were hearing in her investigator's appraisal of the task in front of them.

Lauren turned back to face Pratt. She tried to make her voice sound merely curious, not disbelieving. "Pratt, are you maintaining that Blythe Oaks is a fine Mormon woman?"

"Some, as I said, may disagree. Some will say she shouldn't even have gone to law school. Some would say she should have just stayed at home with her kids and continued to volunteer with the Relief Society. Apparently, she's worked out of the home many years when she didn't have to. There are elders who frown on that. But what I'm saying is that she's going to look like a good Mormon woman on paper. And she's going to look like it to her co-workers. And she's certainly going to look like it to the Church, given the current circumstances. Many will stand up for her just to stifle the inevitable Utah-bashing."

Lauren's reaction was a few degrees shy of fiery. She swallowed twice trying to temper it. "What is it really, Pratt? You think my sister's making this up? Or do you think she somehow seduced Ms. Oaks into assaulting her in a hotel bathroom?"

The growing confrontation between her team members finally grabbed Robin Torr's attention. She sat up straight and rehooked her hair behind her ears, looking back and forth between Crowder and Toomey. She made a quick decision not to intervene. Yet.

"I don't know what happened that evening in Washington, Miss Crowder. I'm just sharing my impression about how fruitful I think it's going to be to interview a hundred of Blythe Oaks's co-workers, when ninety-eight of them are going to be LDS and when the Church is already going to have suggested to its members that speaking with us may not be in accord with promotion of the faith. You may consider what I'm saying to be nothing more than a professional opinion relating to strategy as it relates to the Church of Jesus Christ of Latter-day Saints—of which I am a proud, proud member."

Lauren's eyes flashed. Her voice stayed level. "If you think my sister's lying, Mr. Toomey, just say so. I'm sure we can find another investigator."

Pratt Toomey enjoyed a long pull from his 7Up and then placed both palms flat on his thighs before looking up. He made eye contact first with Robin Torr, then with Lauren Crowder.

"No. I don't think she's lying. To be frank, I think the three of you are nuts for thinking of pursuing something like this at all. But to consider the possibility that you would do any of this in Utah if you believed it weren't true, I'd have to admit to myself that I'm probably working with certifiable psychotics."

The room was ripe with silent tension until Robin Torr cleared her throat and said, "That's quite a vote of confidence coming from you, Pratt. It's nice to know we can count on your unbending loyalty up to and until the time that we begin drooling." The other pencil slid from its perch behind her ear.

"Lauren, anything else for Pratt?"

"No, Robin. Nothing else for Pratt right now."

"Well, then. Let's find a way to divide up this work. Because it seems we have the unenviable task of inviting a few dozen faithful saints to assist a gentile in indicting one of their own as a lesbian sexual harasser."

She looked first at Pratt Toomey, who was stone-faced, then at Lauren Crowder, whose face remained flushed with anger.

"Now tell me, isn't the law great?"

One Hand Laughing is on the garden level of an old stone building on State Street in Salt Lake City. When headliners who have cut their teeth on *The Tonight Show* or Letterman come to town for weekend engagements, the spartan room that holds the comedy club rocks with laughter. On Thursday nights, things tend to be more sedate. The acts aren't exactly open-mike, amateur-night stuff, but the comedians who hone their sets to sparse houses on slow weeknights in Salt Lake City, Utah, are generally no closer to an HBO special than Madonna is to an audience with the pope.

But on the Thursday night when Teresa Crowder took the One Hand Laughing stage, only three days after her initial meeting with Robin Torr, the comedy club had a few dozen more patrons than usual. Some of the extra chairs were filled with people made curious by rumors that had begun to spread around Salt Lake that aspiring comic Teresa Crowder was considering filing a lawsuit alleging that the Mormon female clerk of the newest justice of the U.S. Supreme Court was guilty of sexual harassment.

A smattering of applause rose, then quieted as the comedy club darkened. Teresa was dressed all in black—leggings and a long sweater. She walked confidently onstage and stood silent, staring up at the microphone. It jutted into the air about a foot above her mouth.

The owner of One Hand Laughing was a six-foot-seven in-betweener named Harold O'Shay who had played a couple of seasons for the Utah Jazz before the coach resolved the question of whether O'Shay was a big guard or a small forward by deciding he was neither, and cut him. O'Shay cleared waivers, stayed in Salt Lake, and invested a chunk of his signing bonus into launching One Hand Laughing. While introducing comedians he always raised the microphone stand to accommodate his atypical height, and he always left it way up there after his introduction. Touring acts were judged by the local audience on the elan with which they handled the elevated mike.

This was her home turf. Teresa Crowder was prepared.

She wore a stage face—blush high on her cheekbones, bright red lipstick, highlighted eyes. The makeup made her look more adult. She scratched her head and stepped away from the chrome stand until she was just out of the harsh ring of the spotlight. Gazing back up at the microphone, then behind her at the circle of light on the wall at the rear of the tiny stage, she said, "You know, never before have I noticed the *shape* of the shadow that thing leaves." Titters now from the audience, not laughter.

She hesitated, then she grabbed the pole and pulled it toward her, twisting the chrome ring that separated the two halves of the staff this way and that, futilely trying to release the extended mast. "The problem I'm having here is that it's not logical," she called up into the mike. "To get things shaped like this to come down, they usually don't need to be *un*screwed."

Lauren Crowder was sitting in the back row, left rear corner, watching her little sister's act for the first time. She was with Robin Torr and Robin's husband, Wiley. Wiley Torr's face was covered by a wide, cheek-puffing smirk. Without looking either at his wife or at Lauren, he said loudly, "Well, Robin, although it may be true that this new case of yours is stirring up just a smidgen of controversy, at least your client seems to blend right into the neighborhood."

Lauren reached over and touched Robin Torr's hand in a gesture of reassurance. Robin dropped her forehead onto her arms, already folded on the table in front of her, and thought seriously about taking a nap.

Before Teresa had gone onstage that night, Robin Torr had demanded and received assurances from her client that she wouldn't discuss her allegations during her set and that she wouldn't say anything inflammatory about the Mormons.

Teresa was true to her word.

Robin found herself laughing during much of the remainder of her client's routine, which centered mostly on making fun of fly-fishermen. She also found that she had arrived at a conclusion about how well Teresa's comedy would be received by the dominant culture in Salt Lake City: not well. Robin quickly decided that she would stop pressing her argument that her client shelve her touring aspirations and stay in town to be available to help with the case.

This was one act that would definitely play better in Peoria.

The Side Pocket sat on a dusty corner just a few blocks west of where North Temple Street shot straight as a laser from downtown Salt Lake City to the airport. From outside, the pool hall and tavern looked as if it had originally been designed as a small-town jail—salt-and-pepper brick walls, eight-foot-high security bars on the darkened windows, a shingle roof the color of weak tea. Half whiskey barrels with unhappy junipers planted in them were the management's only attempt at providing an enticement for strangers to enter. The occasional stranger who did enter the Side Pocket was either desperate for a place to shoot some pool or ignorant about the west side of Salt Lake City or, more likely, both.

On Friday, after a long two days helping Robin manage the media fallout from the rumors spreading around the city, Lauren had stopped back at Teresa's house just long enough to hang her suit, tug on a pair of old jeans, and get directions to the only place her sister knew in Salt Lake City where Lauren could find a pool table. Lauren parked Teresa's recalcitrant Rabbit on the viaduct side of the tavern and walked self-consciously into a smoke-filled room scattered with a half-dozen people who probably wouldn't have been welcomed with open arms in nearby Temple Square.

She carried her cue stick in its narrow case in her left hand as she approached an unremarkable laminate-capped bar on the far side of the room. The bartender stacking glasses behind the scratched counter sucked hard on the butt of a Marlboro and took her sweet time turning her head to talk to Lauren, who immediately surmised that the blouse she was wearing was the only silk the Side Pocket had seen in a long, long time.

"Yeah?"

Lauren smiled. "I understand you have pool tables?"

The woman sucked the filter on the cigarette so hard her gaunt cheeks collapsed in on her pitiful teeth. "In back," she said, raising her right cheekbone to indicate the appropriate direction. "You wanna drink?"

"Sure. Please. A beer."

"You gotta be a member."

"Of, of what?" Lauren asked, momentarily fearing that this odd establishment, too, required some unusual LDS initiation.

The woman smiled, exposing gums eroding and black. "This is Utah. This is a private club. You need to join. To play nine ball. To have a beer. You gotta join. Just fill this card out, we'll make you a member right quick."

Lauren dug her driver's license from her wallet and filled out the little application card, and in short order she received her membership card to the Side Pocket.

"Kind of beer you want?"

"Anything but Coors."

The woman nodded once, affirmatively, and said, "All *right.* I'm from Philadelphia, myself," and gave Lauren a Rolling Rock in a long-necked bottle. "Glass?"

"No thanks."

"Jerry'll set you up in back. It's not busy yet." The bartender nodded at Lauren's cue case and said, "You look serious about this, hon. Tables four and six have new felt and decent cushions. Tell Jerry I said to give you one of those. I'm Odelle."

Lauren's tension eased. She said, "Thanks," and walked down the narrow hallway toward the pool room. She tripped over a piece of loose carpet strip and had to shake a little tack from the sole of her shoe before she continued. Jerry was easy to find. She gave him the message from Odelle, and he set her up on table six. Two other tables, neither nearby, had players.

As promised, the felt on table six was new. A quick examination showed the cushions to be serviceable, and the pocket level she kept in her case revealed the slate to be true. Lauren was impressed with the quality of the table, despite the fact that the back room of the Side Pocket was absolutely the grubbiest place in which she had ever unpacked her cue.

She racked up the balls and broke hard and started to limber up. Four in the corner. *Thwack.* Six-eleven combination. *Tap.* One ball off the cushion. *Crack, thwop.*

Halfway through the first rack she failed to sink the seven on a tough but playable angle across the table. Her concentration wavered for just a moment while she reflected with some regret about how things were going with Pratt Toomey. She cursed his condescending manner and her own impatience and then deftly sank the seven with her next shot.

Pratt, she surmised, wouldn't be so easy to pocket.

She was rusty. Over the next two racks she missed at least four shots she should have made. After one cross-table touch-shot missed by a hair she checked the slate again with her level and again, to her disappointment, found it to be true.

Two large, loud, Budweiser-fortified men began playing on table five, next to her. Lauren spied them for a spare second before her concentration returned, and she played on. An hour stretched into two, and the big room filled with players and sharks, and the sharp sounds of colliding billiard balls swelled the air along with the aroma of smoke, stale beer, and male sweat. Everyone who entered the back of the Side Pocket noticed the black-haired stranger in the silk blouse with the hot hand. Twice she was approached and offered a game. Twice she politely declined.

A man wearing worn corduroys and an orange polo shirt came over and straddled a beat-up metal folding chair near the wall across from table six to watch Lauren Crowder's impressive style. After five minutes or so he got up and retrieved a fresh Rolling Rock from Odelle.

He placed the bottle next to Lauren's half-finished one and said, "Only drunks and Englishmen drink them warm, you know. Here's a fresh one for you."

Lauren was racking the balls. "Thank you," she said,

her voice pleasant but not inviting, "but I can get my own."

"I'm quite sure you can. I am quite sure you can. Mind if I watch?"

"You've already watched. I'm not interested in a game, if that's what you're wondering."

He laughed. "With you? Me playing pool with you would be like me arm-wrestling one of those boys from Tonga over there. My watching you is from pure admiration. I am a man who admires quality wherever I find it, but I am both blessed and cursed with absolutely no competitive zeal. If you want, I'll play a game of darts with you. I'm passable at darts. But pool? There's only two players I know who could take you on, and that's only because in addition to being good, they're both stupid. You would destroy either of them. My name is Harley, by the way." He smiled mischievously. "I can tell you've been dying to know that."

Harley drank from a can of Diet Pepsi.

Lauren smashed the racked balls. Although she found his manner charming, she didn't return his smile.

Harley persisted between shots. "I'm not trying to annoy you. Although on more than one occasion I've been told I can be annoying, even at those times when I'm not particularly trying. I am trying to be friendly, however. And you are not making it easy thus far. But, among other things, I am known as a patient man."

Lauren rested her cue butt-end on the linoleum floor. "Harley?"

"Actually, my name is John Harley. But everyone calls me Harley."

"Harley. You seem nice. But I'm not here for company. I'm just here to shoot some pool. It relaxes me. I've had a hard week and I need to shoot some pool. Please. I don't mean to be rude."

Harley scratched his neck. "What kind of hard week?"

"I'm not sure that's any of your business." She didn't look up.

Harley guarded his smile, his gaze directed at the floor.

"Please, I don't disagree with you," he said. "I'm

quite sure it's none of my business. See, where I come from, which a long time ago was Charleston, South Carolina, this banter I keep starting with you is called conversation. You tell me you had a hard week. I say, 'Oh, really, tell me about it.' You say this and that, and I commiserate. Then you notice that I'm drinking diet pop instead of cold beer and you ask me about it and I tell you I'm a recovering drunk. Then I ask you if you're married, and you say no, and then, in obvious non sequitur, you say you're here on business, and immediately regret the disclosure. And then you don't ask me if I'm married, because you really could care less, but I tell you anyway that yes, I am, and I've got two girls, seven and nine. And then I surprise you by telling you I love my wife but she wants nothing to do with me right now cause I smoke and drink and hang out with gentiles in pool halls."

Lauren opened her eyes wide. "Really. That's how it would go were we to have a conversation?"

Harley nodded. "Just like that. I've done it a thousand times. Well, maybe five hundred."

"Well, if all you say is true, why does it seem like you're trying to hit on me?"

"Hit on you?" Harley pulled his patrician hands to his chest and put on his most innocent face. "Please don't misread my intentions. I'm here solely because of what we have in common."

Lauren had returned her attention to lining up a shot. Harley's last words interfered. She looked up from the table and said, "You and I? We have something in common? What on earth is that?"

"We're both polite renegades. At this minute, you are the only female hustler in the pool-hall end of the Side Pocket. And I am the only Mormon, recovering alcoholic, associate professor of sociology in the pool-hall end of the Side Pocket. You and I are renegades. But we've got a certain class. Don't you think?"

Lauren said, "I am *not* a hustler."

Although Blythe Oaks knew her stalker's gentle handwriting almost as well as she knew her own, she had never heard the woman's voice. Blythe had studied the curves and loops on the note cards that always accompanied the flowers and had matched them to examples in a book she had purchased on handwriting analysis, all in an attempt to begin to know something about this woman who was stalking her. But the soft handwriting was all Oaks had; her stalker's voice was only a whisper in Blythe's nightmares.

Owing to her ignorance of her stalker's voice, and a lifelong propensity toward denial, Blythe wasn't at all alarmed by the pleasant young female who greeted her on the phone at work. The voice, breathy and unaccented, anxious only to an attuned ear, said, "Blythe Oaks, please."

"Speaking," she said.

The young woman who had placed the call swallowed once and stared at the crib sheet in her hand. She had rehearsed possible variations on this conversation at least a dozen times. Still, as her hair blew into her face and her wet palms clung to the black handset of the pay phone—foul and sticky from a thousand grimy hands before her—she felt as though she couldn't even remember her middle name, let alone the direction this conversation was supposed to take. For a moment she was distracted by thoughts of what might have fouled the disgusting receiver she gripped much too hard in her hand.

"It's me," she said finally, awkwardly.

Blythe's denial about her vulnerability included an assumption that she was unassailable at the Court, that no one—*absolutely no one*—would be foolish enough to mess with her while she was in Lester Horner's chambers at the United States Supreme Court.

"I'm sorry. Who is this, please?" Blythe was reviewing a draft opinion written by one of Justice Horner's other clerks on a case involving the Shoshone tribe and high-stakes gambling.

The young woman looked at her notes before she responded. She read aloud, "You know. Your friend with the flowers."

Blythe's glands pumped adrenaline.

"What? Oh God! Oh God!" Her voice rose in exclamation, then crashed into a whisper. She wheeled around in her chair to see if anyone was within listening distance.

This person talks. She talks. I don't want her to talk. Please, please no.

"Why are you calling me here?" Oaks demanded, as though the caller's sin involved this new intrusion into the sacred halls of the Court and not her persistent violations of Blythe's life and privacy.

The young woman practiced her next line silently once, then said aloud, "I want to meet you. I want you to meet me, really. I already know that I like you. I want you to see how much you can like me."

Blythe's voice rose involuntarily, and the next words tumbled out rapidly, the softer sounds masked by the shear volume of air escaping her lungs. "Why are you following me? Who are you? You sound so young. What do you want with me? Please leave me alone. Please."

The young woman recoiled at the alarm in Oaks's voice. Of course she'll sound scared, she reminded herself. That's the point.

She forced her attention back onto the sheet of paper in her hands, grateful that she had brought the script to keep her focused. She had tucked the phone down between her shoulder and her head. The plastic seemed to stick to her ear. Her skin crawled. She yearned to rush home and bathe in the hottest water she could tolerate.

"I can't leave you alone," she read. "You must know that by now. I need for you to meet me. To know me. To give me a chance."

"No. No. That's crazy. I can't meet with you. I can't. Please leave me alone. *Please.* Just leave me alone. I'll call the police."

She had assumed they would end up here. Still, she dreaded it. *Just stick to the script.* Every whisper of threat absent from her voice, as she'd rehearsed, she read, "And what will you tell them? Will you tell them about visiting the Laredo? Or maybe another lesbian bar. Or about what really happened at the Mayflower Hotel? Will you tell them why a woman is following you and why she wants to meet you? Of course you won't. If you just meet me and give me an hour and you don't want to see me ever again, then I'll leave you alone. I think you'll like me. I'm a nice person. You'll see."

Blythe was stunned by the new implication of threat. This woman knew *everything.* Despite the blackmail implicit in the young woman's words, Blythe desperately wanted to believe the innocence of the offer. An hour with this woman—heck, girl—and then freedom. Despite an attempt to stay even-tempered, a scolding anger leapt into her tone. "You're a *woman.* Don't you know how terrifying it is to be followed? How can you do this to me?"

"I want you to meet with me. I need you to. I don't want to hurt you."

"What kind of car do you have?" Blythe demanded, seeking credentials. The shock and anger in her voice were being replaced by desperation.

"A Toyota," the young woman said.

No Camry. No flowers.

Oh God, please no. "What *kind* of Toyota?"

This wasn't in the script. But she figured she had better answer. "It's a Camry," she said, then panicked and thought, *Please don't ask me what year. I don't know what year the stupid car is.*

"What color is it?" demanded Oaks.

"It's blue."

Blue Camry. Blue Camry.

Blythe Oaks promised herself she would consider her options carefully before following through with the rendezvous, but right now, she decided, the best course of action was to be agreeable and meet with this young woman. Maybe then at least the flowers and the phone calls would stop.

The young woman insisted that the meeting be late the next afternoon. A picnic in Virginia, along the Potomac. She gave directions. "I'll bring everything. You don't have to do a thing. We'll have a great time."

After a day of second thoughts, and three conversations with her friend Audrey Payne in Utah, Blythe parked her Taurus in the agreed-upon location an hour before the four-o'clock rendezvous and hid in a carefully selected spot in some woods above the picnic area. Oaks wanted to watch the blue Camry arrive; she wanted to control this encounter as much as possible. Ultimately, she planned to be the one who decided whether to go through with the meeting.

Her friend Audrey had advised her to forget the meeting, to just pack her bags and get out of Washington. But Blythe had convinced herself that too much was at stake. And maybe this demon in her life was nothing but a confused, harmless kid.

Though she needed to be sure.

Blythe Oaks was so intent on watching for the arrival of the blue Camry and on making an early assessment of her stalker that she paid almost no attention to a person who was walking a dog through the woods where she was hiding.

She was sitting cross-legged between a hollow log and a hefty maple tree. At first, Blythe thought that the man behind her was ambling the forest aimlessly. But when he began throwing sticks for his dog to retrieve, he seemed gradually, almost purposefully, to be approaching Blythe from the rear. With each call to his dog, with each footfall of the man, Blythe felt the distance close between them. She found his presence distracting.

Finally, to her dismay, she heard him arrive right behind her, his feet crackling loudly on the kindling and twigs. He was preceded by his dog. Reflexively, Blythe reached out and petted the friendly dog that snuggled up to her. *Please go away,* she implored the man silently. *I don't want to talk.*

The wide brim of the felt hat she was wearing kept her from seeing above his waist without turning or twisting her head. Irritated at the intrusion and at the familiarity with which the man had approached her, she rested her weight behind her on her palms and tilted her head back to look up at him. She hadn't quite decided what to say when he reached down and slit her throat with a single rapid motion of a three-inch pocket knife.

Blythe Oaks's blood spurted from her neck for twenty diminishing beats of her dying heart, then drained slowly from her severed artery, down through the mulch and leaves, until it saturated the earth at the man's feet.

The man watched, grateful that her felt hat had fallen forward to cover most of her face and that he couldn't see her eyes. He tightened his grip on his curious dog's lead to keep her from the warm, aromatic blood.

Finally he nodded in somber satisfaction. In as soft a voice as he could manage, he said, "Heel," and returned up the hill in the direction from where he had come.

He had expected that his pulse would be racing. It wasn't. He had thought he might vomit. He hadn't.

And his judgment had been correct all along. The dog's presence *had* made his approach less threatening. As they crossed a narrow swale, he reached down and scratched her neck.

He said, "Good girl."

A couple of harmless hours with John Harley, Lauren rationalized, would at least provide an opportunity to get some of her Mormon questions answered. Although she was reluctant to admit it, even to herself, she was also a bit intrigued by Harley, a Mormon so different from Pratt Toomey that the two might have been separate species. She agreed to accompany him someplace for what he called breakfast. Harley explained that there were only a few places open all night in Salt Lake City, which severely limited the collection points for the drunks who spilled from the clubs when the bars closed. Bill & Nada's was Harley's personal favorite.

Although Lauren accepted Harley's offer of midnight breakfast, she declined his offer of a ride. She climbed into her sister's cranky Rabbit and followed Harley's Ford Escort, which was belching blue smoke, to Bill & Nada's. Her shoulders ached and she quickly decided she would gladly trade her sister's car for a good massage.

Bill & Nada's was an aging shack with ample parking out front and friendly, nonjudgmental people inside. The coffee was hot, the food either white-bread plain and reliable or downright eccentric, like brains and eggs, veal heart, and pig's tongue. The decor was an eclectic mix of western kitsch and the owners' collections of ethnic oddities from around the world. In the high desert of Utah, Bill & Nada's was an oasis for the underdog.

The waitress delivered coffee and toast to Lauren and

decaf and pecan pie to Harley. Lauren sipped once from her coffee and directed a question to John Harley. "What sort of characteristics would make up an exemplary Mormon wife?"

Puzzled, he replied, "Let me get this straight. You want to know what constitutes an exemplary Mormon wife?"

"Please, Harley, it's important."

"You're sure this isn't a tourist question, like going to Orlando and asking what's the best ride at Disney World?"

Lauren assured him that her question was sincere.

"Okay, then, I'll tell you about my wife. She's a good Mormon woman. There'll be some caveats here, but by and large, Jules is a fine example of a Mormon wife.

"Caveat one: She can't have any more kids. Two kids in an LDS family is seriously below average. Let me play sociologist here for a minute. Did I tell you I'm a sociologist? I did, didn't I? The birth rate in parts of Utah—like Utah County, for instance, that's where BYU is, in Provo—exceeds the birth rate in some third-world countries—heck, probably most third-world countries. LDS believe that the spirits of all human beings already exist and that those spirits can only be rescued and endowed with an afterlife through birth and then through sacred temple endowments and ordinances. So each birth is the essential step in the beginning of the rescue of a soul. A spirit-baby. It's why Mormons are so ardently pro-life. To make a soul eligible for an afterlife, it first must be born. Large families rescue more spirit-babies, just by definition."

Lauren's mind was generating questions faster than a curious four-year-old's. But she let Harley continue talking unimpeded.

"So Jules, through no fault of her own, hasn't rescued a large enough quota of unborn souls through childbirth. She tries to make up some of the deficit through genealogy. The other way saints can rescue souls is by doing proxy baptisms for relatives who have died without the good fortune of a temple baptism. Since the angel Moroni led Joseph Smith to the gold plates only around one hundred and seventy years ago, countless generations of ancestors had already died ignorant of the teachings of the Book of Mormon. They all lie waiting in their graves for proxy baptisms so that they may enter the celestial kingdom. Identifying those relatives is the province of genealogy. My Jules has a true gift at mining obscure sources for ancestors whose souls are hanging around in need of redemption. She has already greatly exceeded the four generations that are expected of her.

"Caveat two for Jules is me. She, it could be argued, made a mistake of spiritual judgment by marrying a recently converted man, yours truly, who had a relatively short and questionable track record with the Word of Wisdom. You know the Word of Wisdom?"

Lauren looked at Harley wide-eyed and shook her head.

"It's a book of pronouncements by Mormon prophets, starting with Joseph Smith, about what we saints should and shouldn't do in order to live faithful, obedient lives. I'm sure you've heard about the famous ones: no caffeine, no alcohol, no tobacco."

Harley sipped at his coffee. "Well, as I've said already, I'm a drunk. Currently a sober one, for about nine weeks now." He knocked on the scratched laminated tabletop. "And although I don't smoke when I'm drinking, I smoke a hell of a lot when I'm quitting drinking. And caffeine is something I've never been able to get too worked up about, spiritually speaking. I'm pretty sure I can dump caffeine if I ever succeed in stopping drinking and smoking simultaneously for any reasonable period of time.

"So I, John Harley, am another black mark on Jules' record. Good Mormon women have husbands who are a bit more spiritually exemplary than yours truly.

"What else? Jules and I tithe based on my salary. A straight ten percent to the Church, off the top. That's just good Mormonism. Good LDS women don't work. Their primary responsibility is taking care of their husbands and their families. So Jules doesn't work outside the home. The president—of the Church, not the country—has said that a married woman should not compete with men in employment, that her place is in the home, not the marketplace. Jules listens to the elders. Good Mormon women do that.

"Jules and I attend our ward-house services and we do temple ordinances whenever I'm being righteous and have earned entrance into the temple. We raise our children according to Church guidelines. We do family home evenings. Our basement is full of preparations for Armageddon. She's constantly replenishing our seventy-two-hour kit to take us through any emerging catastrophe, and she has a two-years'-plus supply of food in the basement to provide security for the family during the end-times. She's an active volunteer in the Relief Society—that's the Church's welfare organization.

"She respects the priesthood in the home. That means she recognizes that I am the authority on matters of faith and reason within our home." He teased her with his eyes. "That's a scary thought, isn't it?"

Harley grew somber as he reflected further on his wife's qualities.

"She's a good woman, Lauren. Jules is an honest, funny, reliable, good woman. She's a great mom to the girls. She's been beyond patient with me. If I'm sober through the end of the semester and stop smoking and I clear things with my bishop, I'll be able to move back home."

Lauren thought she saw something poignant slide across John Harley's face. She remained quiet.

"But, you know, the things that make her a good LDS woman aren't the things that make Jules shine in my eyes. Maybe that's a failure of the spirit on my part. Maybe I should appreciate more the things she does for her faith. She would say that being a good Mormon woman is as important or more important than being a good woman, or maybe she would say it's all the same thing. The fact that I don't agree, she might say, is an argument for the weakness of *my* faith."

Harley accepted a refill on his coffee and scooped up the remains of his pie. "Another thing Jules is, Lauren, is that Jules is nothing at all like you."

As Lauren pondered how to respond to Harley, Pratt Toomey marched up to the booth where they sat and said, "Miss Crowder, good evening. Please excuse my interruption."

Lauren flushed at the sight of him but recovered to make an awkward introduction. "Pratt Toomey, this is John Harley."

"Hello, Harley. Nice to see you again."

"How you doing, Pratt?"

"Just fine, Harley. Jules and the girls are doing well?"

"Great, Pratt. Great indeed. Thank you for asking."

Lauren watched, intrigued, as the two men resumed some strained acquaintance. She was momentarily distracted from her initial surprise at seeing Pratt Toomey in Bill & Nada's after midnight.

Pratt turned to Lauren, and with exaggerated politeness said, "Miss Crowder, may I speak with you a minute? Privately?"

"Please, Pratt, call me Lauren. Can this wait?"

"Mrs. Torr doesn't think it should wait. She asked me to find you."

"What is it then, Pratt, that can't wait?"

"May we speak somewhere more private, please?"

"This is fine with me. Go on."

Toomey scratched his forehead. He was perplexed at the very fact that his suggestion had been rejected. He said, "Mrs. Torr asked me to tell you that Blythe Oaks is dead. She was murdered this evening in Washington, D.C."

"Murdered?" Lauren said the word as though its meaning weren't clear. Her silver eyes instantly darkened to gray and seemed to lose their sparkle.

"Yes, ma'am. And Mrs. Torr is concerned because we've not been able to locate your sister. She thought you may be able to help us find her."

Her breathing quickened. "She's not at her house?"

"No, ma'am."

"Oh, shit."

"Yes, ma'am. Although I'm not particularly fond of profanity, that does about cover it."

News of the brutal murder of the chief clerk of the junior justice of the United States Supreme Court was splashed on page one of virtually all the major metropolitan dailies. The story value was significantly enhanced by the fact that the victim had been the object of recent allegations of sexual harassment made by an obscure stand-up comedian from Utah named Teresa Crowder.

Law-enforcement authorities scoured the woods along the Virginia banks of the Potomac for clues about Blythe Oaks's murder. Local homicide detectives and U.S. Supreme Court police were left wondering about a motive for the attack, and the tight-knit LDS community in Provo was preparing to bury Sister Oaks's body.

And Robin Torr was contemplating how, and whether, to proceed with Teresa Crowder's case, given the tragic death of the defendant.

All things considered, Torr's impulse was to retreat.

During warm-ups before the Jazz's preseason game against Indiana that afternoon, Lauren told Robin she still hadn't heard from Teresa and was a little worried. Robin responded that she wasn't sure how much it mattered anymore. She wanted to recommend that Teresa drop the complaint, anyway.

Lauren was surprised and said so.

Robin had anticipated a protest and had prepared herself to counter any arguments. "Let me state my case, okay? I'll grant that there are ways to proceed despite the murder. First, we can go ahead and press a suit against Oaks's estate instead of suing her as an individual. That's simple. Second, her death doesn't really affect any action we might take against the Women's Symposium. So, yes, legally there are ways to proceed. We both know that.

"But now, with Blythe dead, we'll also have to contend with the complications posed by Utah's Dead Man's Statute, which could conceivably compromise the testimony we thought we could use from those restaurant staffers in D.C. about what they overheard Oaks say to your sister. In Utah, the Dead Man's Statute provides limitations on testimony in civil cases about what a dead person said. If we're facing a competent defense attorney and a solicitous judge—and I can pretty much guarantee you that if we file suit against Blythe Oaks in Salt Lake City, we'll be facing both—the odds are at least even that the defense attorney will make a motion to suppress the testimony and that the judge will grant it.

"But even if we ignore for now the complications posed by the Dead Man's Statute, we still have new problems with how Teresa's going to be perceived. With Oaks dead, especially given the way she died, she's become an even more sympathetic figure than she was already, which was a significant hurdle in a battle like this from the start, and—"

Lauren grabbed Robin's shoulder as the Jazz players strode casually onto the floor of the Delta Center. "These guys are *huge,* Robin!"

"The Jazz aren't actually that big a team, but—"

"Why do they call them the Jazz? Is that a Mormon thing, too?"

Robin laughed. "No. The team used to be in New Orleans. Utah kind of hijacked them. Salt Lake's a pretty small market for an NBA team."

Their fifteenth-row seats were about even with the foul line behind the Jazz bench. The arena was filling slowly.

"Are they any good?"

"The Jazz? Yeah, we're good. We used to be on the verge of great. But we're getting old."

Lauren thought it was an apt metaphor for her entire generation.

"Can I get a beer here? Or do I need to become a fan-club member or something?"

Robin smiled. "You can buy three-two beer without joining anything. And that's all they sell at games, anyway."

Robin pressed her argument for quitting the case. "You know, with the exception of those witnesses in D.C.—who may be of limited use to us now—you and Pratt and I haven't exactly been discovering a treasure trove of new information to help our case. All we have so far, really, is Teresa, and that's it. There's got to—" Robin interrupted herself, grabbed Lauren's wrist, and began whispering in her ear. "There, standing in the aisle. Here's what you were asking about. See that couple? The lady with the red hair? They're LDS. You can see the lines of her garments through her clothing. See? That underwear she's wearing, those are temple garments. Half the people here, more or less, are wearing them."

Lauren tried to imagine what kind of undergarment would leave lines like the ones she was seeing etched beneath the woman's tight clothing—a scoop just below the neck, lines a couple of inches above the knees.

"Is it one piece?"

"Yes, I think so. I've never actually seen one."

"I want some, Robin. As a souvenir of Utah."

Robin shook her head in amusement. "You just don't get this place, Lauren. Those garments aren't quaint, they're sacred. The local stores won't sell them to you without a temple recommend."

Lauren looked over at her friend. "Let me get this straight. I have to join a club to buy real beer and I need ID to buy underwear? Utah," she said, "is a very interesting state."

As the moment of the introductions of the players neared, the mood in the Delta Center became electric.

"How do you have time for this, Lauren? To give your sister all this time? When I asked you to help, I actually expected you to say no, which I thought would have let me bow out of this mess gracefully. What about your life? Your cases in Boulder?"

Lauren had been anticipating this conversation. She said, "I'm on leave from work," suspecting the inquiry wouldn't end there.

"Like a sabbatical?"

Lauren and Robin had to stand to permit a family of eight to move past them to their seats.

"No, I'm on medical leave. I've been off work for over six months. I'm due back soon."

Robin turned and examined Lauren's body as though she expected to find evidence of a tumor she had previously overlooked. "You look fine to me, sweetheart. I'd die for your hair."

Lauren sighed, looked away, then back. "I have multiple sclerosis, Robin. The reason I was in New York City before I came here to help Teresa was to receive some experimental treatment with a new drug. But I am fine."

The lights in the Delta Center dimmed. The national anthem started. Robin whispered, "Gosh, I'm so sorry."

"Don't be, it's—"

"My mom's sister has MS. She's my favorite aunt. She's in a, um, wheelchair."

The crowd sang robustly. Lauren was grateful for the interlude. She moved the conversation back to the consequences of Blythe Oaks's death. "Well, I want to go on record with an opinion. I would very much like to continue to investigate as though we were going to file suit. At least until we know what supportive evidence we can put together."

"Lauren, you know it's not up to you or me; it's up to your sister. I'd rather see what she'd like to do. Her vote is the one that counts most here."

"So if she wants to go on, you'll continue?"

"Yes. At least until we see what we dig up in the next couple of weeks. No promises after that."

"Well, then I guess all I have to do is track her down."

"Finding my elusive client would be of significant help. There's no doubt about that."

Teresa still hadn't surfaced. She hadn't left Lauren any indication of where she was going, only a cryptic note that she would be away for "a few days." Lauren tried to explain that she considered it progress that Teresa had left a note at all. Robin professed skepticism and small faith in that progress.

"Is it really that much of a problem that she isn't in town, Robin? I mean, do you really want her going onstage in Salt Lake City two or three times a week? You saw her act. It's not likely to create a lot of sympathy around here."

"You won't get an argument from me about that. Maybe it's not so important that she be here. I guess what I need is, I need to know her heart's in it. All the way in it."

"I've never seen her this intense about anything but ice-skating. She's in it. Trust me."

"I also need a way to reach her. I'll insist on that."

Lauren said, "That's reasonable."

Robin told Lauren that she hoped Teresa hadn't used her brief holiday to visit Blythe Oaks. She didn't think the case could endure any evidence linking Teresa and Washington, D.C., during the time of the murder.

Lauren brushed off the concern. "I'm not worried about it. That's not her style, Robin. When Teresa goes off, she goes off alone. She gets as far away from stress and pressure as she can. As a kid she would go off into the woods or to a friend's house. Now that she's older she tends to take vacations she can't afford. Once, after she broke up with some guy and he refused to accept that it was over, she went off to Hawaii for a weekend and charged the whole thing. Another time, believe it or not, I had to wire her money in Quito, Ecuador. I've told you before that my dad drank, haven't I?"

Torr nodded, puzzled at the apparent non sequitur. John Stockton controlled the opening tip, immediately drove the lane, and dished off to Karl Malone underneath. Robin tried to follow the action and listen to Lauren at the same time.

Lauren said, "He went on benders, my dad. That was

the extent of his drinking. Every so often—sometimes it'd be six weeks, sometimes six months—he'd get in the Ford and go to town, always by himself. Him being by himself was the tip-off, because other times when he went to town he would rustle up one or two of us kids to ride along with him. Buy us some candy or a pop. Brag about something we had done. Tell people how proud he was of us. But on those trips to get beer he always went alone. Probably went to the next town, or even the next county, so nobody would know.

"As the pickup would head off down the lane kicking up dust, my brother would say, 'Everybody get ready, I think the Schlitz is about to hit the fan.'

"We'd all just wait to see if we were going to get targeted, every one of us feeling absolutely out of control.

"Except for Teresa. Teresa would split. She would hide someplace where she could watch the pickup come back down the lane, and she would count the cases and then she'd be gone. And then we'd count the cases and we would know how long Teresa would be gone. One case, one day. Two cases, two days. Holiday weekends, three cases, three days. The first time it happened . . ."

Robin touched her friend's face. From the baseline, Stockton sank a three. The crowd roared. Robin didn't even look at the court. She said, "I know this is important, and I want to hear every word. But will you tell me about it during halftime? I want to see if this first-round pick we drafted out of North Carolina is truly the next David Thompson."

The first time Teresa ran, Jersey Crowder was six hours—ten beers, maybe fifteen—into a two-case bender.

When Jersey exploded—and everyone in the family had known he would explode sometime on that July third Saturday—Teresa, eight years and two days old, was arguing with her mother about how she was going to dress for church the next morning, insisting that her friends would not be wearing dresses, and neither would she. Jersey Crowder—a big man, six-one, two hundred and ten pounds—came up behind the argumentative Teresa and hefted his fifty-pound daughter under her arms, spun her around in the air, raised her face to within an inch of his own, and shook her.

Of what happened next, Teresa remembered only the roar and the smell and the fear.

The terror chilled her like a blast of freezing rain, and she trembled. She looked to her mother, who stood across the room impassive and tearful.

No more than ten minutes later, Teresa ran.

That first time she ran she just hid in the orchard. Twice that day she eluded family members and neighbor kids whom Lauren had rounded up to go searching for her. Teresa didn't eat; she didn't want to. Late at night, she crept into the garage, into the back seat of her mother's LeSabre, and slept there until she retreated back to the orchard just after dawn. The Crowders didn't see their younger daughter again until the annual fireworks show down by the river on Sunday night.

At dusk, Teresa weaved unselfconsciously through the crowd waiting impatiently in the riverside park for the start of the fireworks, walked up to the blankets where the family picnic was spread, sat down next to her sister, Lauren, and said, "Is he asleep?"

Lauren nodded solemnly.

Teresa said, "Good," fetched herself a piece of cold fried chicken from a covered dish, smiled at her mother, and acted as if nothing at all were wrong.

Her mother offered a silent prayer to heaven and asked Teresa whether she would like some potato salad.

Before they fell asleep that night, Teresa told Lauren all about it.

"So she could be anywhere?" said Robin Torr, trying to process the story Lauren had told her during halftime.

Lauren was distracted, gazing up at the distant rafters of the Delta Center. "You know, I can't believe how many people are here. But, yeah, Teresa could be anywhere you can imagine. Even some places you wouldn't imagine."

"How long will she be gone?"

"We'll hear from her soon, would be my guess. She'll be back. Just show up, no apologies. Or else she'll call me from someplace to send her some money."

"I'm beginning to fear that judgment is not one of your sister's long suits."

Lauren was tempted to argue. She tried hard to stay even-tempered.

"It's not her judgment I question, Robin, although when she's under stress she can be pretty impetuous. Teresa doesn't pick fights; you have to keep that in mind. She runs from fights, from conflict. That's what's so important about this stand she's taking now. It's different. She's telling us she's being pushed around, and she wants to fight."

"Lauren, I'd like to believe you. I like your sister. And I'm trying to help her. My increasing concern here, however, is that Teresa is having second thoughts about this particular battle and she's decided that it is you and I who she wants to do the fighting on her behalf. I won't stay in this crusade unless I know real soon that she's in it to the end. There's too much at stake here. You wanting her to stay in it till the end isn't enough for me."

"Crusade?"

"Yeah, it's a crusade. Who are we kidding? Teresa is fighting for the same damn territory that Anita Hill failed to capture. Hill had impeccable credentials, credibility, and nothing to gain. The fight was good media—black-on-black, national TV, gloves off. And I want to remind you that for all the territory she might have captured during the battle, in the end, Anita Hill lost.

"Teresa, on the other hand, is young; her credentials are in a rather odd corner of show business, not on a law school faculty; and regardless of her principles, she'll end up suing for monetary damages. The publicity will help her career, so she's not going to appear pure no matter how we wrap her. And this is in no way a clean fight that I've been enlisted to coach. By taking on Oaks, she's taking on Lester Horner, and by taking on Lester Horner, she's taking on the hierarchy of the LDS

Church, whether she likes it or not. And the LDS Church is absolutely not going to permit Lester Horner to be soiled by this, even indirectly."

Robin looked hard at Lauren. "Do you understand why this is so important to the Mormons? I mean, do you *really* understand?"

Lauren said, "I don't know. I keep thinking I do. But maybe I don't."

"As a general rule, the LDS Church shuns secular attention. The only reason the Church risked the shellacking it endured during Horner's confirmation hearings is that the Mormons consider the U.S. Constitution a divinely inspired document. I mean that literally. The Church leadership feels that the forces of Satan have eroded God's constitutional intent over the years. Abortion rights, strict separation of church and state, soft treatment of criminals and drug dealers, erosion of family values, permissive homosexual rights—you name it, Satan has poisoned it.

"Lester Horner is the first advocate of the Church's interests on the high court, ever. And with the ridicule they've had to endure to get him there, they feel they've earned that seat. They have been waiting, planning, and plotting to land this level of judicial influence for over a hundred years. Now that they have it, Horner will absolutely be protected from the slightest blemish. The leadership of the Church has wanted to get a saint on the U.S. Supreme Court for over a century, and now that they have one, they are not going to let a twenty-five-year-old female, gentile, stand-up comic blow it for them. If it is in their power to stop her, they'll stop her."

"Are you implying something about Blythe Oaks's murder, Robin? You're not suggesting the Church might have had something to do with that, are you?"

"No, of course not. Well, no, not really. No. But now that Blythe Oaks is dead, the Church will expect your sister to put her tail between her legs and go away. You can bet on it. They will not expect us to continue to investigate this."

"Why not? They must know we're not Mormon."

Torr laughed. "By now, Lauren, you can assume the Church knows what brand of tampons we use. My point is that they will expect us to fold, because with Oaks gone, the path of this arrow we're shooting goes directly to Lester Horner—his judgment, his credibility, his reputation—and they'll think we're too smart to take him on."

"Are we too smart?"

Robin paused and picked at a pebble of yarn on her sweater, reflecting on the good will this case was going to cost her with her partners. She said, "Apparently, I'm not. I don't know about your sister or you, but I'm suspecting that this particular dementia is rather contagious."

The lights changed inside the Delta Center to highlight the court for the start of the second half. As the players strolled back onto the court, a high-pitched chirping caught Robin's attention, and she dug around in her purse and pulled out a portable phone. Distractedly, she extended the small antenna, flipped open the mouthpiece, and said hello, expecting some mindless reminder from her husband, Wiley. The phone was his; she didn't usually carry it. Lauren found what Robin was doing much more engrossing than the basketball game.

Robin's end of the two-minute conversation consisted of "Yes," "Yes," "You're sure he said that?" and "Of course, I'll do my best. Bye."

She closed the phone and turned to Lauren. "That sound you just heard was the other shoe dropping. That was Val Zelem, our senior partner. The FBI is looking for Teresa. They want to question her about Blythe Oaks's murder." She watched Lauren swallow. "I think we'd better find her before they do."

Wiley Torr didn't look at his wife as he spoke. But these days, he rarely did. Sunday-night dinners together as a couple had become a tradition with them since they moved to Utah. Between the demands of working late during the week and the pressures of socializing with friends and colleagues on Friday and Saturday nights, Sunday had become the only night they could count on being alone together.

". . . because your defendant's dead, Rob. And because the facts as you present them don't exactly seem to support an EEOC filing, anyway. The statute says a hundred and eighty days, and you're way past it. It's that simple." Wiley Torr grabbed a chunk of bread and scanned the small dining table. "Can't you ever remember to put butter out? Just because you don't eat it, it doesn't mean that nobody does." Wiley walked over to the refrigerator and retrieved a blue tub of margarine. The tub was decorated with little flowers.

Robin Torr momentarily addressed herself to her husband's empty chair. Since when did he read Equal Employment Opportunity regulations? "I didn't know that you wanted any. And I know the EEOC criteria, Wiley. And if it turns out that I can't pursue a Tide VII filing, then I'll just go with a tort, since Utah's FEP is such a joke. I've done it before. Going straight for the tort has its advantages. It may even be the strategy of choice."

Wiley sat back down. "Political advantages, sure, Rob. I think you're managing to be naive and political at the same time. It's your Donna Quixote complex again. Now that Oaks is dead, you think Lester Horner's going to try to coax a settlement just to avoid some publicity? Wrong. Heck, he's just going to sit back and hide behind the biggest darn bench in the country while you spin your wheels. His supporters here will file a zillion motions and delays and bleed your client absolutely dry, until you're backed into a corner that even *you* can't squirm out of. And don't count on the press. They'll lose interest in Utah. They always do. This case is going to bury you in paperwork, and your partners are gonna scream about the costs. Anyway, a tort based on what?" Wiley looked around for his napkin, which had slid off his lap onto the floor.

"Assault and battery, for openers."

"For propositioning her? This whole thing is preposterous, anyway. Blythe Oaks? Come on. Them words in that fancy toilet in Washington must have been fighting words."

"There's more to it than that, and you know it, Wiley." Robin wondered why her husband was being so combative and tried to consider why she was being so argumentative. Maybe this was just another edition of their already copyrighted Mormon argument. Wiley had grown up viewing the LDS Church as a largely positive influence in Utah. Robin viewed the monolith in her adopted state a little less benignly.

"I don't know anything. You won't talk to me about the details. Please pass the salt. And what about damages? You can't prove that's why she lost her job. It's almost impossible to prove." Wiley Torr was a hectic eater. His inborn agitation always seemed to be least bridled while at the table.

"Well, like emotional distress."

"What? The poor girl's in therapy? Like half the goshdarn world's in therapy. So what? Ever wonder why there are so few Mormons in therapy? Huh? Ever wonder that?"

"Because their bishops tell them not to. Because the housewives eat Valium and Xanax like M&M's. That's why. And my client's a woman, not a girl, Wiley. And I know what the hell I'm doing. I know this law better than you do, and I'm not at all certain I can't use loss of employment and failure to promote. There's more to this case that we haven't talked about. Okay? Trust me."

Robin's appetite had evaporated. She set her fork down, put her forearms beside her plate, and tried to capture her husband's elusive gaze.

"And what do you mean by Horner's supporters, Wiley? This isn't about the impregnability of the United States Supreme Court. Your interest in this case is because of the Church. Did your partners ask you to shut me up? The mighty Seventy doesn't want the bad press, huh? Sexual harassment by a *Mormon woman,* Wiley! By the *Mormon* clerk of the first *Mormon* Supreme Court justice!

"The apostles don't want the press. And the prophet certainly doesn't want the press—if he's not already too senile to read it. This is juicy; Wiley. *New York Times, Newsweek, USA Today* stuff."

He didn't even look up from his spinach lasagna.

"So what are they going to do to stop this woman, Wiley? I mean, let's face it, with the right slant this particular little tumor has the potential to make the Salamander thing look like a goddamn zit by comparison. So what's it going to be? You should know. Your firm does plenty of Church work. Will it be the pimple-faced boys in suits, two by two, proselytizing at her door day and night, quoting the Book of Mormon until she either tithes or goes crazy? Or are they going to play hardball? Bring out the fabled Danites? *Ooooooooh.* Or maybe sic the FBI retreads in Church security on her? Or maybe this will be treated as a bloodless indiscretion and she'll get to get rich like Mark Hofmann and I'll end up having a discreet meeting in the foundations department at ZCMI with a representative of some apostle who will offer my client a sizable sum to confess the error of her ways and drop her action."

Wiley looked up from his plate. He was pleased that he had finally goaded her into sounding shrill. "Please don't curse. And you know I don't like it when you ridicule the Church. I think you're overreacting, anyway. Which is my point. You know the local terrain as well as I do. You know the rules. This lasagna's great, by the way."

Robin Torr clenched her already taut jaw and sighed. She knew the law. Maybe she didn't know the rules. She only knew one rule. The Utah rule. *Don't piss off the Church.* And with this lawsuit, there was little doubt, she was breaking that rule. Wiley, in his uniquely condescending manner, had just reminded her of that. She sipped at her iced tea and manufactured an artificial smile.

"Thanks. But don't you think that's enough salt, Wiley? Gosh. You know you use too much."

Later; she sat across from him and watched him sleep.

His blond hair was as bright as it had been when they had met, but his once-firm body had begun to soften. She reflected that she had probably changed much more than he over the years. He had been in the top ten percent of their law school class. She had been solidly in the obscure middle. She had always felt that he was more attractive and competent than she. Lately, with her promotion to full partner, things had begun to change. Maybe she couldn't outlawyer him, but she could outwork him. Could begin to level out some of the power.

He had been the man she couldn't get—handsomer than she deserved, more successful. Her mother had warned her. "You're marrying up, dear. Just like I did. It's a dangerous direction to have your nose."

Now she had changed. She could easily be moved to guilt about that, as though it were her job to be static and not challenge him with change, with confidence. But why did it always have to come out sounding so hostile?

Wiley was unmoving in sleep, soundless. "I swear you could sleep in an envelope, Wiley," she had joked early on in their relationship, astonished at how still he slept, how unmussed he left the covers. "I could just slide you in and lick the flap and you wouldn't even wrinkle the paper by morning." At the time, he had responded that she could "lick his flap anytime she wanted." Now, ten years later, she had difficulty recalling the last time either of them had had their flaps licked.

After cleaning up the dishes from their late dinner,

Robin Torr recognized an urge to have sex. She considered making the first move. She didn't. She pondered whether she would like it if Wiley made the first move. She wouldn't. For Robin Torr; the desire to make love no longer had anything to do with Wiley Torr.

Robin debated making some zucchini bread, didn't, and scanned the *Tribune* mindlessly instead. Later, she moved from the living room to the cozy window seat in the bay in their bedroom and read a novel. A three-quarter moon filled the valley with light and twinkled off the forbidding granite faces of the Wasatch Front. She tried not to look at the flash of blue light made by the illuminated clock on the table by the bed and tried not to consider the now familiar dilemma presented by her desire when her only prospective partner didn't interest her.

Always careful with words, Robin played with "repulsed" before settling on "didn't interest."

Why did I take that damn case? And why can't I shake this need to shove it back in their faces? Where the hell is my client?

Why did I say "I do"?

She masturbated and faced the dawn without a memory of sleep.

Pratt Toomey's contacts in Salt Lake City significantly outnumbered his contacts in Provo, so Robin Torr decided that it made sense for him to continue to stay in the metro area to learn what he could about any evidence of previous harassment by Blythe Oaks. Although Lauren remained suspicious that Toomey's enthusiasm for the task was less than sincere, she judged that her latitude for arguing with Robin had ebbed dangerously low, and she decided to let it alone.

She took some solace in the fact that Pratt's assignment in Salt Lake left her to fend temporarily for herself, and she had no trouble talking Robin into permitting her to sniff around Provo, Blythe Oaks's hometown, and the site of one of the most homogeneous LDS populations in Utah, and therefore the world.

The Monday morning after Blythe Oaks's murder, Lauren, with nothing but distrust for her sister's Rabbit, rented a car and drove south out of Salt Lake City shortly after rush hour, with morning shadows still darkening the Wasatch Front to the east. The mountains on the western edge of the narrow valley south of the Great Salt Lake were already washed with daylight. Lauren left metropolitan Salt Lake City behind sooner than she would have guessed, and in less than an hour she was skirting the high bluffs above Utah Lake, where the city of Provo sits wedged against the towering faces of the Uinta National Forest.

The little college town was still shaded by the cliffs looming to the east. A surprising chill laced the air.

Lauren's home of Boulder, Colorado, had a geography similar to that of Provo, but she had to admit to herself that morning that in the category of breathtaking beauty, the compact city of Provo held a significant aesthetic advantage over Boulder's relative sprawl.

The highway into town took Lauren directly to the campus of Brigham Young University. She stopped her car and received directions to the law school from a young man dressed in dark gray slacks, a white shirt, and a tie. The student had been walking with two other young men who were dressed virtually identically, and with two young women dressed in chaste blouses and skirts that hung nearly to their ankles. All carried day-packs or oversized purses crammed with books.

Lauren mused to herself that despite the geographical similarities between Provo and her hometown, there were certainly some differences. The only time she ever noticed University of Colorado students dressed as formally as these BYU students was during rush week for the sororities and fraternities. Even then, she reminded herself, their styles were a little more adventurous than these. No, make that a lot more adventurous. In Boulder, the dressy fabric would be stretched tight over young male buttocks, high up young female thighs.

These BYU kids certainly were polite; she had to give them that.

A minute later, lost already, she stopped another student in a white shirt and a tie, who directed her to a visitors' parking lot not far from the J. Reuben Clark Law School. Lauren Crowder was dressed modestly, she thought—a loose cotton crewneck sweater and a rayon skirt that reached to the top of her knees—but as she walked the short distance from the car to the law school, she felt almost naked. Male students looked at her, then quickly away. Two female students actually seemed to stare, their stares confirming their initial impression: this lady was no saint.

Lauren started her quest at the office of the dean of the law school. Without an appointment, with the last name of Crowder, and with the hem of her bright skirt above her knees, Lauren found that her inquiries about

Blythe Oaks were received less than enthusiastically. The receptionist in the dean's office politely but firmly dispelled any illusions Lauren might have had about seeing anyone that day and left her with the impression that other days were no more likely. And, no, the receptionist could not think of anyone else at the law school who might be of any help.

Lauren walked across the campus to the Registrar's Office and learned that Blythe Oaks, born Blythe Truste, had received her A.B. from BYU in 1963 but hadn't earned her law degree until 1989, when she had graduated in the top five in her class. Lauren already knew that quite a few of the intervening years had been spent on the law school staff as Lester Horner's secretary. A brief visit to the Alumni Association and a perusal of their database provided information on Oaks's activities since leaving law school. Blythe Oaks had spent one year clerking for a judge on the Utah Supreme Court, one year clerking for Lester Horner on the U.S. Circuit Court of Appeals, a brief period coordinating the Utah Women's Symposium, and part of the last year of her life as the chief clerk of the newest justice of the United States Supreme Court.

Crowder walked back across campus to the law school library and used a computer search to look for evidence of Oaks's scholarship. She found two law review articles and two co-authored pieces in major journals. A brief examination revealed the work to be thoughtful and cogent. Not brilliant, but damn good.

As Lauren tried to remember what her rental car looked like and where in the spacious lot she might have parked it, she reflected that Blythe's curriculum vitae was as impressive as anyone could hope to assemble four years out of law school.

Now all Lauren had to figure out was what forces conspired to cause her sister and Blythe Oaks to collide in the ladies' room of the Mayflower Hotel in Washington, D.C., and whether Blythe's murder might have anything to do with what transpired that night.

Lauren found a small restaurant a couple of blocks from campus, and after finishing a quick lunch, innocently ordered a cup of coffee. The waitress looked at her in a slightly embarrassed manner before pronouncing, "I'm sorry, we don't serve coffee, ma'am."

Lauren said, "Of course, I'm sorry," and immediately scolded herself for apologizing for wanting some caffeine. MS-driven fatigue tended to grip her sometime between late morning and mid-afternoon each day, and she despaired at the thought of making it back to Salt Lake without a caffeine boost.

She plotted strategy for the rest of the afternoon, jotted some notes in her appointment calendar, and paid her bill. Outside the restaurant, she received directions to the main BYU library from yet another gray-slacks-white-shirt-and-tie twenty-one-year-old.

At the main information desk, Lauren asked where she could find old BYU yearbooks and was directed to the Special Collections department on the fourth floor. The librarian who led her to the stacks examined Lauren's outfit as though Lauren were the only female in Tehran without a veil. The collection of BYU yearbooks dated back to 1909. Lauren pulled the 1960 through 1963 editions from the shelf and retreated to the anonymity of a carrel.

As Lauren flipped through the pages of pictures of the freshmen entering in 1959, her eyes were drawn to the photograph of Blythe Truste well before she spotted her name. At the age of eighteen, Blythe Truste had eyes so bright and lively that they twinkled even in black and white. The only other yearbook references to the young Blythe Oaks related to membership in two campus religious organizations.

Lauren searched a little more but discovered nothing further of interest other than the unsurprising news that both Paul Oaks and Lester Horner were also members of the Class of '63. She asked where she could find a copying machine and then spent a few dollars making copies of the class pictures from all four years before going back downstairs.

She found a bank of public telephones and the Provo directory. In a minute she had located a long column of listings for the wards and stakes of the Church of Jesus Christ of Latter-day Saints. Teresa had explained the congregational structure of the LDS Church. The basic unit was the ward. A stake comprised four to eight wards, and from a thousand to four thousand members. There were too many wards from which to choose, so Lauren punched in the number of a stake.

To her surprise, the voice that answered said simply, "Stake president."

"Hello, is this the president himself?"

"Yes, this is the stake president—in the flesh. How may I help you?" Lauren thought she detected the residue of an ancient Texas drawl.

"Well, I'm trying to find the location and time of Blythe Oaks's funeral. I was hoping you could help."

"I think I might just be able to. Sister Oaks will be buried this afternoon after a service here in the chapel at the stake center. Bishop Charnes, from her ward, will conduct the service. The service will begin right at three-thirty. And I suggest you arrive early. We expect quite a crowd. Sister Oaks was a beloved lady."

"Thank you. I think I will try to arrive early. Could you please give me directions to the stake center? I'm not familiar with Provo."

Lauren jotted down the directions offered by the kind voice on the telephone while she checked her watch and made a quick computation of how long it would take her to get to the mall she had passed on the way into town to find an outfit suitable for a Mormon funeral.

She decided she could make it if she hurried.

The service in the stake chapel surprised Lauren with its air of celebration. She had heard so much innuendo from her sister and Robin Torr about bizarre secret Mormon ritual that she was confused by how conventional and traditional and uplifting the funeral service was.

The chapel was jammed with mourners, who raised their voices proudly with the opening hymn. A prayer from Bishop Charnes followed, and then two old friends of Blythe Oaks, one man and one woman, spoke at some length about her life. The anecdotes they related bore evidence of Oaks's good humor; her athleticism, and her accomplishments, first as a mother and wife, and later as a legal mind of whom the entire community could be proud. Her generosity to the community was applauded, her faith revealed and polished. Then, one after another, a long succession of friends and colleagues stood and shared warm memories of Blythe.

Supreme Court Justice Lester Horner spoke last. He addressed a hushed room. His presence and his accomplishments, both within the Church and in the government, quieted the congregation as though he had raised a finger to his lips.

Horner described Blythe Oaks as one of his oldest, dearest friends. He told tales of their college days and of their many years working together. He thanked Paul Oaks and the Oaks children for sharing their wife and mother with the Church and with the Lord and with the community and with him, and asked them to take great pride in all that she had offered and accomplished. He asked forgiveness for taking her to Washington and ultimately to her death. And he asked everyone to celebrate her journey into eternity and the steps she had taken to be closer and closer to the Lord.

Another prayer, another hymn, more tears and more smiles, and the service ended. Lauren stuffed the photocopied description of the service she had been handed at the door into her purse and joined the congregation as it departed the chapel.

She left certain of one thing and nursing doubts about another. The certainty was that Blythe Oaks had been loved and respected by a lot of people. The doubts were about all the negative things she had been hearing from her sister and from Robin about the Mormon Church. What, she wondered, is so odd about this religion? The memorial service she had just attended had seemed absolutely normal, uplifting even. *What am I missing?*

Exhausted, Lauren found a motel and slept until the Utah Valley was almost dark. She woke slowly, showered, and, after watching the little bar of soap slither around the shower for the third time, noticed with some curiosity how difficult it seemed to be for her to grip the little thing. Although the depth of her fatigue tempted her to spend the night in Provo, she was eager for news of Teresa's return. She checked out of the motel, stopped for some fast food on her way out of town, and drove north toward the Great Salt Lake. Her curiosity about the lack of coordination in her hand developed into moderate concern as she realized she was having trouble gripping the steering wheel of the small car with her right hand.

By the time she reached her sister's house, Lauren Crowder was incensed that her arm no longer seemed to be taking specific instructions from her brain. For Lauren, when it came to her multiple sclerosis, anger always came first. Fear was just an echo.

She searched the house for evidence of Teresa's return, found none, tried Robin Torr at home and got her machine, and finally, furious at her failing arm, called Alan in Boulder. His soft voice brought her to tears. He had gotten over his disappointment about her extended stay in Utah.

She told him everything that had been going on with the case. About her frustration at not being able to find her sister. "I've called everybody in the family," she said, "all her friends, everyone I could think of."

"It sounds like you haven't ruled out the possibility that the murder is somehow related to your sister's lawsuit."

"I haven't. Obviously, the cops haven't, either. What do you think?"

Alan exhaled. "I don't know much about the murder, sweets. Just what I've read and seen on the news. The woman had her throat slit in some park. Wasn't raped. Wasn't robbed. No suspects."

"That's all we know, too, basically," Lauren said. "Except for the suspects part. I keep wondering about the Church or Horner, but I guess it doesn't make sense.

Murdering her would be such an inelegant way to stop us. They could just settle the case and gag us that way."

Alan perceived a hole in her reasoning. "Settling might stop *you*. It wouldn't stop her—the defendant. Not if whoever killed her saw her as a loose cannon. You know, somebody who was likely to do something like she did to your sister again. Someone who would keep bringing dishonor on the Supreme Court and all that."

"That's something I hadn't considered. Still, it's probably a coincidence. The murder."

"You don't sound convinced, Lauren."

"I guess I'm not. Apparently, neither is the FBI." With some difficulty she told him about her arm. They talked for most of an hour before hanging up.

During his days investigating in Salt Lake City, Pratt Toomey learned little about Blythe Oaks's character that he couldn't have learned simply by attending her funeral. After a futile flurry of phone calls he succeeded in coercing two of Blythe's former co-workers in Salt Lake City to speak with him. Actually, what it turned out they had agreed to do was to lecture him. They praised Oaks and defended her, and chastised Toomey for working for gentiles and against the faith.

"What's going on here is Utah-bashing, Pratt. Pure and simple. You're just a tool."

One of the two people who spoke with Toomey pointed out that Blythe and her classmates from the BYU class of 1963 might actually be the single most distinguished and successful group of saints in the twentieth century.

The alumni group included two general authorities—three if you counted Lester Horner. Paul Oaks was the assistant director of the Missionary Training Center in Provo. The class also boasted an internationally famous cardiac surgeon, a member of the BYU board of trustees, an assistant director of the FBI, and a former secretary of transportation. Blythe Oaks herself was the chief clerk of a justice of the United States Supreme Court. And, of course, there was the brightest star of all, Lester

Horner, once a general authority and now the first LDS member of the United States Supreme Court.

"And that," said Blythe Oaks's friend as she spoke to Pratt Toomey in the dead-end corner of the corridor outside her office, "is mostly just Blythe's group of personal friends from college. Who knows what the rest of the class has done." She listed a few other names from memory. "You, Pratt Toomey, should be ashamed of yourself. If I were you, I would certainly consult with my bishop before proceeding any further on any of this."

First thing Tuesday morning, Supreme Court Justice Lester Horner dropped off his rental car at the Salt Lake City airport and climbed into the narrow cabin of a commuter plane for the short ride south to Farmington, New Mexico. The seat he filled was next to that of his old friend Will Price.

Horner's impression of Blythe Oaks's funeral service was that it had been marked as much by shock at the circumstances of her death as by either grief or rejoicing at her welcome into heaven. A mind-numbing reception had followed the brief graveside service. A thousand condolences still echoed in Lester Horner's ears and left him feeling as hollow as a dry kettle.

Blythe's husband, Paul, had whispered something to Horner about shared pain, which he had struggled to recall for a while after the service. He never was able to remember precisely what Paul had said.

Justice Horner had considered trying to escape his remorse and his pain either by visiting with old friends in Salt Lake and Provo for a few days or by returning immediately to Washington and immersing himself in the intensity of the Court's new term. Ultimately, though, he accepted Will Price's invitation to go south and spend a couple of days on their hands and knees digging in the kiva they had been working on the tribal lands of the Ute Mountain Utes, in southwest Colorado. Horner made plans to catch a late commuter flight into Denver the next evening and connect with the red-eye back to D.C. He would be in his Supreme Court chambers by early Thursday morning.

This trip to the southwest with Will Price, Horner's ninth or tenth to the Ute Mountain reservation, was not only religious service but also personal therapy for the justice. He hadn't planned on being able to get a chance to work the dig again until the following spring. But the murder of his longtime friend left him in need of solitude and direct access to God. His most significant personal revelations from the Lord had occurred on Lamanite land.

He sat quietly in the passenger seat of the car Price had rented in Farmington, the morning sky a sharp blue sheet seemingly held aloft by buoyant white clouds. He thought of Blythe. Things decomposed slowly in the high desert in fall and winter. Leaves. Animals. Dear friends.

Horner could taste the slow, dry decay. With every breath, he could taste the decay. He wondered if his own ambition had killed his lifelong friend. Not a man prone to guilt, he wondered if that is what he was feeling.

He felt alone and blessed with the solitude. Farmington's dust and sand provided a degree of anonymity that Horner had begun to cherish since his elevation to the High Court bench. No one in the airport had even looked at him twice. No one knew he sat on the Supreme Court of the United States of America. It was arguable whether anyone would have cared.

One of Lester Horner's revelations from the Lord had revealed that the land of the Ute Mountain Utes would be the site where the first hard evidence would be discovered to support the Mormon belief in the emigration of the Lamanites and the Nephites from Egypt to the New World. Somewhere, Horner believed, in the enchanting canyons that branched out from the Mancos River, he would find evidence of the subsequent migration of the Lamanites to the Land Northward. He intended to still the doubters.

Now, he promised himself, he would dedicate the discovery to Blythe's memory.

Horner's friend Will Price was a big man with big features and a big voice. His head was no larger than average, maybe even a little smaller, but its parts—his eyebrows, his nose, his ears, his mouth—all seemed to have been taken from a much larger model.

Price's everyday voice boomed with such crispness and clarity that it cut through the surrounding clutter like a chain saw through pine. In an airplane, in a theatre, in a restaurant, if Will Price spoke in a normal tone, you heard his voice more clearly, and attended to it more readily, than you did to the voice of the person sitting right next to you.

Price's hands were meaty, each finger thick as a sausage, his arms heavy, like hardwood timber. His deep brown eyes were kind and warm. They invited. As always, Lester Horner accepted.

"You were right about Blythe, Will. You said I shouldn't ask her to be my clerk."

"Sometimes we know things, Lester. When I'm righteous, the Lord lets me know things. I'm grateful for that." Price's advancement in the Church had been much more pedestrian than Horner's. At various times he had been chosen to serve as bishop and as stake president. He had only recently finished service as president of the Church's mission in Baltimore. His current Church service was as a home teacher.

"I should have listened to you, Will."

Price said, "Tell me about Blythe going to heaven. It's a good story to tell. A cleansing story."

Though Will already knew most of the story, Lester Horner obliged. He told the whole saga of their friendship. He started with the day he met Blythe at BYU. Then the day he met Will. He wasn't quite done with his story when the two men pulled up to the Ute Mountain Ute Cultural Research and Education Center in Towaoc, on the eastern face of Sleeping Ute Mountain. The men checked in with their old acquaintances and exchanged pleasantries before getting back into the car, crossing the highway, and entering the tribal park. Will Price waited patiently until Lester resumed his tale, which he finished just as the men arrived at Lion Canyon.

Lester finished his story with the day Blythe died in a riverside park in Virginia.

Will hooked a hand around his friend in the front seat of the car and squeezed the taut muscles of his neck. Then he got out of the car and began to unload their supplies in the usual place.

Lester Horner hadn't moved to help. He sat in the passenger seat, immobilized. Will Price tapped on the glass until Horner opened the window.

Will said, "It's as it should be, Lester. As it was written. Now she's a step closer to God, just waiting for Paul to join her. But we have work to do. God's work. It's time for you to get unstuck."

Lester gazed vacantly at his friend. The red tints in Will's huge eyebrows were of the same hue as the exposed stones in the striated canyon. Lester smelled the slow decay. He smelled the rebirth.

He got out of the car and looked around for his hatchet.

Will Price slapped him on the back and drove down to the edge of the canyon to unload the supplies he would be carrying up the ladder to the kiva.

In prayer he said, "He's not strong enough for all this. If there's more that I can do, please show me how to help."

The morning after Blythe Oaks's funeral, Lauren met with Pratt Toomey in Robin Torr's conference room in Salt Lake City. They sat across from one another, each attempting to present a demeanor as flat as the big cherry table between them. Toomey viewed the meeting as an accommodation to good will and team spirit. He figured that the likelihood of his learning anything from Lauren's one-day visit to Provo was somewhere in the neighborhood of Salt Lake's likelihood of being flattened by a hurricane.

He listened to her recitation while feigning attention, but in reality he was absolutely unimpressed by what Lauren had discovered at BYU. Twenty minutes on the phone would have earned him more information than she'd gotten in a day.

He hoped at least she had enjoyed the scenery.

Lauren showed him the copies she had made from the BYU yearbooks and the photocopied program sheet from Blythe's memorial service in Provo. By cross-checking she had discovered that the first two people to speak at Oaks's funeral were classmates of Horner and Oaks at Brigham Young. "I've circled their pictures. Lester Horner's, too. Oaks was Blythe Truste back then. And I've circled her husband, Paul's, picture. He was part of the class as well. This group of people go way back—all the way to their freshman year. Do you know anything about any of them?"

Toomey was wondering if he had dressed too warmly. That morning he had pondered whether to wear worsted wool or cotton and had opted for the wool, mostly because his one clean shirt went better with the gray slacks. But now his crotch felt sticky, and it wasn't even midmorning.

"Excuse me?"

Lauren sighed. "I asked if you knew anything about any of this group from BYU. Oaks's old friends?"

"Let me see." He flipped through the photocopied pages and looked at the circled pictures. He recognized names, not faces. With a mechanical pencil he lightly circled a few more pictures. As he circled he said, "These names came up in some of the interviews I did here in Salt Lake yesterday. This one"—he stabbed at one of them with the tip of his pencil—"this one came up almost every time somebody actually agreed to speak with me, which wasn't that often. They were roommates at BYU and apparently remained good friends."

Lauren leaned over and read the name below that picture. Audrey Hayes.

Pratt continued, "Don't bother with her. I called her already and got nowhere. She just kept crying, saying she had told Blythe she shouldn't go to Washington. And a couple of these other people are prominent Church leaders."

When Toomey was twenty, just after his two years of missionary service, which he had spent in Australia, he had applied to BYU but hadn't been accepted. Instead, he'd gone to Utah State. The resentment from his failure to get into BYU hadn't faded over the years and still caused him discomfort when he was forced to deal with the school or its alumni.

Pratt looked uncomfortable to Lauren, who wasn't aware of the problems posed by his trousers or his history with BYU. She stood, frustrated that Toomey was not more forthcoming. She forced herself to be civil. "Can I get you something to drink, Pratt? I'm going to find myself something."

Pratt was taken aback by the unexpected offer. "Well, thank you for asking. Please ask Elsie to find me something cold. She knows what I like."

As Pratt began to jot down the names that accompanied the circled pictures onto the page in his notebook where he'd begun to compile a list of follow-ups he needed to make, Lauren left to get the drinks.

The list was developing uncomfortable dimensions. In Pratt's dozen years as an investigator, he had never, not once, had compelling reason to interview a general authority of the LDS Church. His roster of follow-ups now included at least three, and he had a suspicion the number was going to grow.

Pratt had seriously considered giving the case back to Robin Torr. She would have no choice but to accept his resignation, and he knew that if he caught her in the right mood she would be gracious about it. But he also knew that if he dropped the ball on this one, he would never see another controversial investigation involving the Church from this law firm. And word would certainly spread to other firms. The fallout could be devastating to his business.

Although Toomey was an inveterate flirt and affected a constant swagger, he wasn't naive about his business. He had argued to himself that the Church—his church, the Lord's church—would be best served by having a saint involved in the investigation into the allegations against Blythe Oaks. Who else but a member was going to be able to keep this stupid creature from feeding on slime and becoming a monster?

The Crowder sisters certainly wouldn't know when to stop. Robin Torr was as tenacious an attorney as he knew, but at least, he reassured himself, she could be trusted to follow a trail judiciously. She wasn't reckless and until now had never shown an inclination to forget that she was in Utah.

Toomey's bishop was as ambivalent about Toomey's role as he himself was. Toomey had explained to Bishop Fortin that if he quit, Robin Torr would get a gentile to replace him, probably someone like Gil Holmes, whom Toomey considered a closet Mormon-basher. Holmes would relish this case. He would leak to the media after it was over—maybe even before it was over.

Bishop Fortin said he wanted to speak with some other leaders about it, but in the meantime, he suggested praying to the Lord for guidance. Without any sense of peace, Pratt prayed about his choices and decided to stay with the case. As he had discussed with his bishop, he planned to make some discreet inquiries from his ever-growing list of follow-ups. And maybe he would learn just enough from one of these people to convince Robin Torr to put this baby to rest.

Pratt consoled himself that at least he wasn't learning anything that was giving the case new life. At least there was that.

Lauren relayed Toomey's message to Robin's secretary, and Elsie Smith hustled off to fetch him a cold drink.

The strength and coordination in Lauren's right arm and hand had returned after a night's sleep, but the muscles in her shoulder ached, as if she'd spent the previous day digging a ditch. On the short walk from the conference room to Elsie's desk, Lauren had noted an unfamiliar tingling in her right leg. Her MS hadn't flared up with a new symptom since she'd left Boulder for New York to begin the experimental drug treatment.

Now her remission seemed to be ending.

Elsie chugged back by Lauren with a can of Sprite in one hand and a cup of ice in the other, making a beeline toward the conference room and Pratt Toomey and, if Robin Torr's suppositions about Elsie's intentions were correct, dreams of a temple marriage.

Robin Torr's office door was open. She was on the phone but waved Lauren in with her free hand. A yellow number-two pencil held her hair back over her ear. To Lauren, Torr's call sounded contentious and unprofitable. Lauren assumed, based on personal experience, that Robin was talking with another attorney about a case.

Robin hung up and looked out the window at the rooftops of Salt Lake City and the blunt face of the Wasatch Front. The angle from her window prevented her from seeing Temple Square. Sometimes she was grateful for that.

She said, "That was Wiley. My husband. Sorry I had to make you sit through all that mushy, romantic stuff. He called to tell me that Oaks's estate has retained one of the partners of his firm, James and Bartell, to represent them against our planned action."

"I take it things aren't going well at home."

Robin stuffed a pencil over her other ear. "You could say that." She scratched her upper lip with her teeth before continuing. "Wiley and I haven't been doing well for a while. This case hasn't helped. James and Bartell is one of the bigger local firms. They're old and established and mostly LDS. They do a lot of Church business with a lot of Church businesses, and a lot of personal stuff for the authorities. Now it turns out that one of the partners will be defending the symposium and Blythe Oaks if and when we file a lawsuit. Wiley is one of the firm's token gentiles. It's been a good marriage for both of them."

"Why? What makes it work?" Lauren asked.

"Wiley's family is old-line Utah Irish-Catholic. They made lots of money from mining and banking at the turn of the century. The old-guard Utah Catholics and the Mormons came to a profitable accommodation a long, long time ago. So Wiley's family has been working hand in hand with the saints for generations. It's in his blood now. He knows which side his bread is buttered on and is almost as conservative politically as the senior partners of James and Bartell. He fits in okay. Better than okay. And to top it all off, he's a pretty damn good attorney."

She yawned, suddenly extremely tired. "My suspicion had been that this new tension between him and me is because his superiors have asked him to keep an eye on me and on your sister's case. And that was even before they were retained as counsel. I've asked him about it. He denies it. But the more he pushes, the more I get an idea of how worried the Church is about this.

"I'm using it sort of like a divining rod. When he increases the pressure on me, I figure I must be getting close to something. Now the pressure is going to be worse. What's so disconcerting is that I still don't know what we're close to. I'm really counting on you and Pratt being able to tell me something soon. We can't go with what we have. We'll look like opportunists."

Reflecting on what she had just said, Robin shook her

head. "God, this must sound terribly calculating to you. I haven't seen you for years. This man I'm accusing of spying on me is my husband."

Lauren didn't know what to say. Robin's story sounded too familiar. She remembered how estranged she'd been from her husband, Jacob, in the last year before their divorce.

Robin's long face broke into a smile. "And, oh shit, I almost forgot, there's good news. Before I got in this morning, we finally heard from your sister. I was in court so I didn't actually speak to her, but she told Elsie that she was in Reno and that she'd be back tomorrow. Elsie got a number where I can reach her later today. Does she have friends in Reno?" Robin paused a second at her own question, and a dart of dread struck at her bowels. "She doesn't gamble, does she?"

Reno? thought Lauren with relief. *At least, thank God, it's a long way from D.C.* "Gamble?" she replied. "No, no, not usually. Not Teresa."

Robin said, "Good. Finally, I can call the FBI and tell them we'll be happy to drop by for an interview."

Pratt Toomey's old Audi was pushing 130,000 miles, but he didn't question its reliability for even a minute. Barring a new motor for the cooling fan and a new compressor for the air conditioner, Toomey hadn't invested a cent in the car except for maintenance, tires, and brakes. Once he'd checked the oil and the tire pressure, Pratt would trust his little car on a midsummer trip across any of Utah's deserts or a midwinter trip over any of Utah's mountains. The current road trip would lead him across two high deserts and over two higher mountain passes. The Audi would do just fine.

The driver's side of the Yakima roof rack held a tray for his mountain bike, and the passenger side held a slot for his downhill skis. Although he had once made a concerted effort to do so, he couldn't remember a single journey of greater than a day's duration out of Salt Lake City when one side or the other of the rack hadn't been filled with his toys. He fondly recalled a couple of brief trips where both sides had been filled.

This trip was no exception. Pratt didn't need to consult a map to know that the route to his destination would have him shooting east down I-70 just thirty miles north of Moab's famed slickrock trails. Being that close to Moab and not riding was as unimaginable to Pratt Toomey as spending a winter day in Snowbird and not skiing.

Mountain biking was not typical recreation for a Mormon of Toomey's generation; it was both too solitary and too time-consuming. He rationalized his indulgence by the fact that his passion for fat-tire riding had been spawned by a series of Church youth-group trips he had chaperoned for his ward a few years back.

Twice Pratt checked the straps that secured his mountain bike to the rack, and twice he checked the tension on the clips that secured the rack to the car. Though he hadn't consulted a Kelly Blue Book lately, he knew there was a good possibility that his bicycle was worth considerably more than his car. He would hate to discover, upon glancing in his rear-view mirror, that his beautiful mountain bike was bouncing riderless down the highway.

Preparing for road trips was routine for Toomey. He threw a small single bag of clothes into the back seat and a larger duffel bag with his bicycling gear into the trunk, gently placed a cooler packed with sandwiches and lemonade on the floor of the front seat, stuffed a bag of pumpkin seeds into the glove compartment, and cruised south out of Salt Lake City. He would be in Moab by early evening.

Emmylou Harris and Tanya Tucker were his only companions.

Thursday evening, forty-eight hours later, two days of invigorating mountain biking under his belt, Pratt Toomey headed south out of Moab. He had an investigation to complete.

Early-autumn-evening traffic on Utah State Highway 191 on the high desert plains east of Canyonlands is typically as devoid of cars as the wondrous landscape that surrounds it is devoid of people. Pratt wasn't particularly familiar with the terrain in the southeast part of Utah, but from a quick glance at his road atlas he guessed he was approaching the tiny black dot his map labeled Hole in the Rock.

In his rear-view mirror, he watched with some interest as a distant pair of headlights rapidly covered the long stretch of highway behind him. A few seconds later a big green sedan blew past Toomey's Audi. The driver was wearing a cowboy hat, and Pratt guessed the guy was doing at least ninety.

Each night the setting sun created a magical quilt of shadows and stone in the high desert. Toomey was captivated by the panorama and paid no further attention to the sedan as it accelerated off into the encompassing dusk.

Fewer than ten minutes later, in the inky darkness of the La Sal Mountains, Toomey came across the green car. This time the sedan wasn't moving. Instead, it hung like an apparition hundreds of yards ahead of him.

The driver's door was open. The front of the car had come to a stop a few feet from the edge of the southbound lane, the headlights pointed back across the highway, obliquely toward Toomey's approaching Audi. A hundred and fifty feet of skid marks in the shape of a long comma marked off what seemed to Toomey to be a world-record fishtail.

Toomey slowed, mesmerized by the rush of light in front of him. At dusk's end, in this lonesome terrain, the big car with its door open looked as alien to Toomey as a spaceship that had alighted in the desert.

He brought the Audi to a gentle stop about fifty or sixty feet from the green car. He switched his headlights to bright, their brash glare effectively washing out the eeriness of the scene in front of him.

Toomey was alert and attentive. His typical vigilance was heightened by the apparent absence of the other driver from the scene. Pratt immediately considered and then rejected as inane the possibility that the driver had taken off down the highway toward La Sal Junction, the next town, on foot. What then? Maybe the driver had banged his head, was disoriented, and had wandered off into the wild night of these mountains. Pratt glared into the blackness off each side of the highway. He saw nothing but desert silhouettes.

He rummaged around his glove compartment for his flashlight, palmed it, then stretched his neck muscles by rotating his head from side to side. With the reluctance of a man facing a prostate exam, he pulled himself from the Audi and prodded his resistant feet to carry him the twenty yards to the green sedan.

Behind him, Emmylou Harris wailed mournfully from the open door of his car.

At a distance of ten feet or so, Toomey stopped and peered inside the car, an old Cadillac in great shape. He half expected to see the driver slumped on the floor. He didn't.

Pratt moved closer.

A folded copy of the *Deseret News* was visible on the floor of the passenger side of the spacious car. A copy of D & C—the Doctrines and Covenants of the LDS Church—had slid, spine up, to the crack between the front seats. Pratt relaxed a little. The D & C was almost as good a clue to Mormondom as was the wearing of garments. The driver of the Cadillac was most certainly LDS, and given that the person had been reading the *Deseret News,* the Mormon-owned newspaper from Salt Lake City, he was probably from Salt Lake as well.

Pratt searched the rest of the car carefully, looking for something with the driver's name on it, wondering if he might know the guy. Hadn't the man been wearing a cowboy hat? If he'd been hurt in this little incident, it's unlikely it would've stayed on his head. Where was the cowboy hat?

Where was the driver?

"Where's Pratt?" Lauren had asked Robin earlier that same day.

"Oh, I guess I forgot to tell you. He called Elsie and said he'd be gone a few days checking on some leads. Apparently he found some old friends of Blythe Oaks who he thinks may know something that can help us. Or, knowing Pratt, might know something that will convince us to desist."

Robin misread the consternation on Lauren's face. "Don't worry too much about the cost, Lauren. Pratt travels cheap, and he'll bill us on a per diem while he's gone, not hourly. Trust me on this. I've done a lot of cases with him. He's not wasteful, and he usually knows what he's doing."

"It's not the cost, Robin. I'm . . . he's not . . ." Lauren

Crowder pursed her lips to underscore her annoyance. "It's just that he should've filled me in before he left. We're supposed to be cooperating, aren't we? Now, what am I supposed to do while I wait? I mean, without knowing what he's learned or what he's looking for? What I'm likely to do is just spin my wheels. Look silly. That's probably exactly what he wants." She murmured a profanity. "He didn't tell Elsie anything else? Where he was going? Whom he was hoping to talk with?"

Robin Torr shook her head. "Sorry. You can ask Elsie yourself, but I don't think so. I didn't look at it from your perspective. But you've got a good point. What can I say? I should've insisted he fill you in."

Robin sighed a volume before she continued. "Pratt's LDS. He is not accustomed to answering to women. When I'm his paycheck, I get some courtesy. But on some level, I'm sure he's expecting you to act toward him like a Mormon woman would."

"Which is how?"

"Like he's a priest. Like he's a little god. But this is my fault, too. I'm not used to having so many investigators. Listen, why don't you lay off until he gets back from this trip and just help me figure out how to approach the people at the Women's Symposium? Then we can all regroup. When he checks in, which he's good about, I'll talk to him, tell him from now on he needs to keep both of us up-to-date. I promise."

"All right. What do you want me to do?"

"I'll need an hour or so to divide up the work and decide what order I want to do this. I'll let you know by ten. Is that okay?"

Lauren nodded.

"Good. By the way, have you heard from your sister? She's still due back today, isn't she? We're set for four this afternoon with the feds. I don't think I can put them off again."

"No, I haven't heard from her since yesterday, but I expect her around noon. I can't tell you how relieved I am that she's been working in Reno. You know, I hate to say this about my own sister, but things may turn out to be easier for us if Teresa is on the road a lot. At least I won't worry about her as much. She's too controversial here. She's bound to get in trouble if she stays in town doing comedy."

Robin Torr remembered her evening at One Hand Laughing and agreed absolutely. But she didn't say a word.

Teresa's plane arrived late, and her subsequent reunion with Lauren was abrupt and unsatisfying for both of them. Robin had set aside much of the afternoon for a meeting to prepare Teresa for the FBI interview. Given her prosecutorial experience, Lauren had argued that she should sit in and help. Robin had been adamant in refusing. She wanted Teresa to get accustomed to answering questions without her sister's support.

At the scheduled time, Robin Torr accompanied Teresa Crowder to her interview at the federal offices downtown. Together, they were prepared to provide Teresa with an unassailable alibi for the time that Blythe Oaks was murdered. Teresa carried a file with the receipt for her airline tickets to Reno, her boarding passes, and the housing and meal vouchers from the hotel where she had performed. She had the name and phone number of the club manager, who would verify her show times.

The special agent who conducted the interview didn't seem particularly interested in Teresa's paper trail. He acted as if he already knew everything about her being in Reno; in fact, he acted as if he might have known exactly where Teresa Crowder had been every minute since she had last sung "Under the Sea" for Disney's World on Ice.

But he did have a lot of questions about the allegations she was making about being sexually harassed by Blythe Oaks.

And he was particularly intent on assembling a complete set of Teresa's fingerprints and acquiring a sample of her handwriting.

He could produce a warrant for those, he said, if it was necessary.

Lauren waited in Robin's office for Teresa and Robin to return from their meeting with the FBI. Shortly after 5:30, Robin called her office and asked Lauren to join them at a nearby restaurant. Elsie Smith provided Lauren with directions to the Judge Cafe, a Salt Lake lawyers hangout, and she walked the few blocks across downtown to the restaurant.

From the narrow entryway Lauren spotted their table across the dining room, near the windows by the street. She thought Teresa looked as though she had just survived an interrogation by the KGB. Her face was pale, her eyes puffy and dull. She was sitting far back on her chair, almost reclining, both hands wrapped around a tall glass of water. In contrast to Teresa's catatonia, Robin seemed energized and animated. She sat leaning forward, her elbows on the table. As Lauren walked up she could hear Robin saying, "Think. Come on. There has to be something."

"Hi," Lauren said, sitting down. "Why do I have the feeling this was a rather grueling interview?"

Teresa tried to smile. She said, "It actually wasn't so bad. I think they believe I was in Reno." She paused. "I hope you don't mind coming down here. I needed to eat something."

"It's no problem," Lauren said, shifting her focus to Robin, whose face was stern. "Were you able to figure out why the FBI is involved in this? Did they tell you?"

"It's a 'police cooperation matter.' The FBI says its

involvement—'at this time'—is a courtesy to the Virginia police."

Lauren then asked the question that had been needling Robin and her for days. "Why have they been so patient in waiting for Teresa to show up for the interview?"

Robin glanced at Teresa before she responded. "Because I think they've known all along that Teresa wasn't in D.C. when Oaks was killed, and—"

"Then what was this all about? What did they want?"

"They wanted her fingerprints," Robin pronounced.

Lauren exhaled. *Routine,* she thought. "That's not surprising," she said. "They probably have some prints from the crime scene. They'll use them to rule out Teresa as a suspect."

"And," Robin said after a pregnant pause, "they wanted a sample of her handwriting."

Her handwriting? Shit, that is surprising. "Why?"

"The special agent wasn't saying."

"Did you provide it?"

"Yes, we volunteered the sample. They would have gotten it anyway." Robin looked over at Teresa, who opened her eyes wide with what seemed like monumental effort, and shook her head. "Teresa can't think of anything she has written that would be of any interest to the police."

"Nothing at all," confirmed Teresa, looking at her sister, appearing very young.

Lauren's mind jumped at possibilities. "No personal notes to Blythe? Nothing suggestive? God, nothing threatening, I hope?"

"I've already asked," said Robin, finally settling back on her chair.

The waitress delivered Teresa a plate with a grilled cheese sandwich and a small bowl of soup. She dug right into it. "I've got to eat," she said.

No matter how late in September the heat of summer lingers into the days in the high desert, the nights always bear the unmistakable chill of autumn. And higher still, in the narrow stone passes that snake into the La Sal Mountains above Utah's Canyonlands, the night air of September can be as cold as a flatland winter.

Pratt Toomey shivered from the chill. He returned to his car, climbed onto the driver's seat, and flicked off the tape deck. Emmylou Harris seemed to protest plaintively as she was silenced. Pratt grabbed the lined nylon shell he wore when he rode his bike on particularly cold days, pulled it on, and stuffed his hands into the pockets of his chinos. He trudged reluctantly back toward the Cadillac. His nose was running from the cold air. He sniffed hard.

Halfway to the green Cadillac he paused, hopeful that the sound he heard in the distance was the murmur of a car approaching, then decided the hum he detected was merely a trick of the supple wind. He continued toward the Cadillac.

He was getting annoyed at the puzzle of the empty car. At the darkness. And at his anxiety, which was itching at him like a lash in the corner of his eye.

He briefly considered the probability that if the driver of the Cadillac weren't LDS, he would simply crawl back behind the wheel of his Audi, crank up the heater, point due south, and try and make up the time he had already lost to this conundrum. He tried to tell himself that this situation, as unfortunate as it appeared to be, wasn't his problem. But this guy—by then he'd revisualized the image of the green sedan speeding past him and had decided that the silhouette of the driver had definitely been that of a man—was a fellow saint.

And Pratt Toomey felt an absolute, unquestionable obligation to assist a fellow saint.

Toomey clicked his attention to a new hypothesis. He examined the front of the Caddy for evidence that the driver might have hit a deer. But there was no damage. Frustrated, he shined the beam of his flashlight onto a long stretch of the asphalt along the path of the fishtail and found no dark puddled stains—no blood. He did identify some animal tracks that ran in the dirt behind the car. But he couldn't decipher what kind of animal had left the tracks, and he couldn't determine their age. He scratched beside his nose and sniffed hard again.

He called out, "Hello. Need any help?" and considered the possibility that the guy was merely relieving himself in the woods.

But no answer came. The only sound was the pulsating drone of the intermittent breeze cutting through the stone canyons. And, it felt to him, through his bones.

As much from cold as from curiosity, he climbed behind the wheel of the Cadillac and saw a fistful of keys hanging in the ignition. He cranked the starter. The engine popped immediately to life. The fuel gauge read more than half a tank. He backed the car up a few feet so that it was clear of the highway. He turned off the ignition and shoved in the button that turned off the headlights.

"Well, heck," he said out loud. "This makes no sense. No sense at all." He climbed out of the car.

Then Pratt heard a moan. Short. Desperate. To the west. In the darkness. He rotated his torch that way and slowly started walking. Maybe, he thought, the utterance was just another piece of magic from the wind.

"Hello. Anyone there?" Pratt called out. "Do you need some help?"

The answer came ten seconds later. Another moan. That's all. This one more drawn-out, lower in tone, but just as desperate. This one wasn't the wind.

"Shoot," Pratt hissed. "Where *are* you?" He stroked and prodded the night with the beam, methodically covering a one-hundred-and-eighty-degree arc in the direction of the mournful sound. Nothing. The light reflected off a wall fifty feet from the road, where ancient strata of rock rose up from the landscape ten or fifteen feet from grade. A shiver shot the length of Pratt's spine. He yanked the zipper of his shell up under his chin.

Why would somebody who is injured climb up there? Toomey wondered, gazing at the silhouette of the rock formation. He remembered his mother's brother, his Uncle Joseph, and the stroke that had paralyzed him. *Maybe the driver had had a stroke, gotten disoriented, couldn't talk. And there was Orrin Hatch. Senator Hatch had ended up in a deserted men's room after his stroke, hadn't he?*

With some alarm, Toomey considered the possibility that he might have stumbled upon a bishop or a stake president, maybe even an authority, one of the Seventy.

"I'm coming, brother. Where are you?" Toomey called into the night, duty, desperation, and fear mingled in his voice.

The moan again. And something else. Was that a gurgle? A whimper? What?

"Hang on. I'm coming," Toomey cried out as he searched the face of the rocks for a path up. He found a series of small horizontal shelves and began to climb. At the top he straightened himself, leaning into the wind, paused, and listened. The wind was blowing from the south, and he saw a distant beam of headlights before he heard the crooning of a downshifting engine. Toomey tracked the approaching car, which turned out to be a small pickup, until it arrived on the scene a minute or two later. He watched gratefully as it slowed next to his Audi. But it never fully stopped before zooming off, the echo of his, "Hey! Wait a minute, don't go" in its wake.

Toomey was momentarily distracted admiring the silhouette his mountain bike made perched on his Yakima rack, when he heard words spoken to him as intimately as a lover's.

"Just be still, brother, just be still."

The voice Pratt Toomey registered behind him seemed to rustle kindly, like the breeze, but the timbre was dense and rich. The words froze Pratt Toomey as solidly as the stone on which he stood.

"Yes, what you feel in your back is a gun. It's a big gun. It's loaded. And I'm prepared to use it. I'm sorry to make you climb all the way up here, but I didn't want us to be disturbed while we talked. Let's you and me just let that truck get a little farther out of here, and then we can have a chat about your salvation. I want you to consider this meeting to be as serious to your eternal life as you would a request from your bishop for an interview about the Lord."

Pratt looked down toward his feet and spotted the snout of a dog.

"How well do I know Pratt Toomey?" Harley laughed.

The chuckle sounded sardonic to Lauren Crowder.

"How well do I know him? Everybody in Salt Lake City knows somebody *like* Pratt. At least, everybody in the Church does. He's the Deseret equivalent of a good old boy. Pratt's everybody's friend. He's everybody's neighbor. As long as you're LDS, Pratt's your right hand. When the heavy spring runoff threatened the city a few years back and the authorities mobilized the stake presidents to mobilize the bishops to mobilize the brethren to protect our city from floodwaters, Pratt must have worked for seventy-two hours without sleep, organizing for the whole stake, planning for our ward, filling sandbags. When the New Year's blizzard buried Salt Lake in '93, Pratt was probably heading a brigade of snow throwers before the last flake fell. He does everything, anything. That's Pratt. He's the kind of saint who would have been fighting right next to Joseph Smith in Missouri. He is always striving for perfection in his faith. Pratt's dream in life would be to be a bishop. But he'll never be called."

"If he's so enthusiastic, so committed, why not?"

"Because urban Mormons are snobs. We promote success. Particularly righteous plumbers don't become stake presidents. Successful insurance brokers do."

"You're in the same ward, you and Toomey?"

"Yeah. Me and Pratt, we're brothers in God."

Lauren squelched a different question and asked, "Why the sarcasm?"

Harley smiled and looked down at his plate. His face was more somber and composed when he turned back to Lauren.

"Just the thought of Pratt and me being brothers. You know him, at least a little. Let's face it. If we're brothers, I'm the one who must be adopted." Harley eyed Lauren quizzically. "You know, this kind of hurts my feelings. I'm beginning to suspect you asked me to lunch just so you could quiz me about Pratt. My charm and wit are irrelevant."

"No, Harley. Yes. Well, no, not really."

"Good answer. I like that. I thrive on confusion, myself. It's territory I know so well, I could write a book about it. See, take a good look at me. John Jefferson Harley. I'm a thirty-six-year-old, maritally separated, drunken associate professor at a second-rate state university, hanging out with a slick Colorado lawyer—that's you, my dear—who some would argue is out to soil my sacred church. These facts don't exactly add up and make me what you would call the most trustworthy and faithful of Latter-day Saints, now do they?"

He didn't pause for an answer. "When I converted, I thought joining the LDS Church would bring me two things. I thought it would bring me Jules, and it did. She's a better wife than I deserve, I might add. My Jules is great. You want to see a picture?"

Before Lauren had stammered, "Sure," he had fished out his wallet and flipped it open to a picture of a tall, plain woman walking down a mountain trail hand in hand with two small girls.

"She's lovely, Harley. Very pretty. And your daughters are, too." He glanced at the picture a second time before snapping the wallet shut.

"And the second thing I thought the Church would bring me was salvation. Not necessarily salvation in a heavenly sense, although that would have been, and remains, absolutely fine with me. But I think what I was looking for was salvation from myself, from the devil within. The Church calls him Satan. I liked that he had a name.

"By then I was already a drunk. Jules, bless her, was so naive, she only saw my potential. She thought drunks were people who slept in doorways cradling Mad Dog. At the time, though I was far from admitting to myself that I was a drunk, I was smart enough to know I could use a serious dose of higher authority. And if LDS are big on anything, it's higher authority."

Harley read confusion on Lauren's face and was distracted by the shimmering in her sparkling hair. He conjured up an image of Jules and fought to keep his focus.

He said, "Don't worry, I'm not as lost with this story as I seem to be. Here comes the segue to Pratt. Pratt believes, soul and heart, in authority. He believes in Zion. In Utah. He believes in all that the Church is, and all that the Church teaches. When he gives his testimony to the truth of the Book of Mormon, he means it, literally. To him the book is true. He believes that his spirit is as old as God. He believes that Jackson County, Missouri, was actually the site of the biblical Garden of Eden, and that sometime in the seventh millennium all God's chosen people will return there for the final reign of the Lord Jesus Christ. He believes that God lives on a planet that circles a star called Kolob, and he believes that God is sexually active with the heavenly mother. He believes that the native American Indians are descendants of one of the lost tribes of Israel, called the Lamanites. He believes in these things because he has faith. He believes in the pre-eminence of the prophet, of the authorities, of his bishop. He believes in *his* authority in his own household, as man and as priest. He—"

"You don't believe those things? As a Mormon?"

John Harley held up a glass of water as though to offer a toast. "Boy. Believing is one thing, having faith is another. The reality is that I just don't care about the details. Being a drunk is humbling. Have you ever been loved by someone you don't deserve? Let me tell you, that's humbling, too. I don't feel particularly righteous very often. Mormon males need to be righteous to be priesthood holders. We need to strive for perfection. I wake up in the morning and look in the mirror, and most days, given what I see, the thought of me being the spiritual leader of anyone is ludicrous. The Church considers me a priest, solely because of my gender. Jules, bless her pure, righteous soul, is supposed to follow my lead as I converse with God. Is that ironic, or what?"

"So where's your faith, John?"

"I don't know. Maybe I don't have enough. I certainly don't have enough faith in Thomas Jefferson to make me believe that the U.S. Constitution is a document inspired by God. My bishop says I have a deficit of faith. And bishops, you know, are almost always right."

Lauren noted the return of Harley's sarcasm. She asked, "Mormons believe that stuff? About the Constitution? About Missouri? About the Indians?"

"Mormons like Pratt do. I don't know that he actually believes it as much as he's not troubled by it and doesn't question it. And if you want to hold on to your temple recommend, you do the same. It's part of the testimony."

"You sound cynical, Harley. I don't get it. Why are you a Mormon?"

He said, "You know, I don't even like to remember why I converted. Going back to then is like visiting a hole I've managed to crawl out of. But I guess it's important to go back sometimes. The truth of how I became a Mormon is actually quite trite. I was lost—in booze, in drugs, in women. I hadn't spoken to my family in years. I didn't know who the hell I was. Where I came from. Where I was going. The LDS Church had all the answers for me. They baked me this great three-layer cake. They told me where I came from. Told me who I was. And told me my future forever and ever.

"It's terribly ironic. The LDS Church in Utah may be as authoritarian an institution as exists anywhere in this country, but Mormon doctrine is sublimely egalitarian. If Joseph Smith wasn't really a prophet, he was most certainly a genius, because he invented one heck of an attractive religion."

He checked Lauren's face to see if she objected to his

preaching. Her eyes were soft and gray, like clouds after a summer rain. "Saints aren't just God's children, Lauren. We are *like* God. Mormons don't believe that God created man. We believe that our spirits are as old as His. Because of that, our doctrine is full of hope. There is no hell to fear. After our births, we can progress to become gods ourselves by improving and achieving in our lives. Think of that empowerment, Lauren. Not just going to heaven, but *becoming* God." His eyes were bright, his cheeks flush. "See," he said, "the promise can still move me."

Harley reached out and picked up the salt shaker, then returned it to its spot. "After the Church baked me that cake, they frosted it with Jules. I tasted it. For a while, I ate it up.

"Before I converted I was an outlaw. And the Mormon Church is, above all else, a great sheriff. We Mormons have rules for everything, from whether or not it's okay to play cards to what kinds of sex you can have with your wife. I was an out-of-control kid. Joining the LDS Church was like joining a spiritual version of military school. They straightened me out. Who knows, maybe they saved my life.

"If any of that makes any sense, then I guess that's why I'm a Mormon."

Harley's usually consuming gaze was suddenly elusive. Lauren tried to net it. Couldn't.

"And now—why the doubts?"

"Maybe my bishop's right. Maybe I lack faith. There are days that I envy Jules' faith, Pratt's faith." He shrugged his shoulders. "I haven't had one of those days for a while, though."

He finally looked up. "I thought we were talking about Pratt. He's not like me; he has no doubts. Pratt's a spirit-baby Mormon. He believes it all. Every drop of his blood is Mormon. His faith erases all doubt. He sees no questions. He looks at the Church and he just sees answers. His temple recommend will never be in jeopardy. Like I said, I envy it sometimes. The simplicity of it."

"And other times?"

He leaned forward until his face was a foot from hers.

"Other times, the blind obedience that's required to be a good Mormon scares the hell out of me."

Lauren made a mental note, for the tenth time, to find out what a "temple recommend" was. She prodded him. "I thought Pratt was supposed to be a philanderer."

"Pratt? What? Has he hit on you?"

"No, not really. But I thought it was only because I'm not LDS."

"Pratt's a flirt, Lauren. Not a philanderer."

"You seem pretty sure, Harley. How do you know?"

"Because I am a flirt *and* I've been a philanderer. That's how I know. I can assure you that I can recognize a member of my own species without having to sniff his crotch."

Harley's sudden candor stunned Lauren. She sat back on her chair, not quite sure what to say. "You're a philanderer? And I thought you told me that first night you weren't trying to hit on me." Lauren knew her words sounded coy. She didn't really care.

"I wasn't."

"Please."

"Seriously. I like bars. So these days I go into bars, shoot some pool, throw some darts, and I don't drink. I like women. I meet women. I talk, I flirt. I don't sleep with them. Now, anyway. I'm both proud and remorseful to say to you that I've been faithful a whole hell of a lot longer than I've been sober."

When he raised his gaze to meet hers, Lauren caught his eyes and said in a low voice, "Why, John Harley, were you just looking at my breasts?"

Harley blushed and affected a lyrical version of his ancestral southern drawl. "Indeed, miss, I think perhaps I was. But nothing shameful was intended. I merely wanted to be certain they were okay."

"And are they?"

"It seems that they are more than just fine."

Lauren struggled through a thick mist of fatigue that had begun to engulf her. His eyes gripped hers with an allure that she had always in the past identified as romantic and erotic. She felt herself being drawn in deeply. She didn't know what to make of it. But to have any hope of ordering her thoughts about Harley, first she needed to sleep.

"Am I boring you, Lauren?"

"Oh, Harley, no, I'm sorry. I didn't sleep well last night. I'm tired. That's all. I'm sorry." A hundred times she had scolded herself, told herself not to apologize for being ill. She winced at how easily she did it again.

"Do you need to rest? May I drive you home?"

"Gosh, Harley, I don't think that would be a very good idea."

Harley leaned across the table and, for the first time, touched her. His fingers on her cheeks felt like fire.

"Lauren, don't be misled by me. I am a man with much too much to lose. I have Jules. I have a couple of great girls. Right now, those three females are my bridge to God. Despite all my doubts about the Church, I'm safe on that bridge. When I'm with you I feel wonderfully alive, but I feel some danger. I feel my bridge sway. The danger, I think, comes from you. You either don't have very much to lose, or you're intent on losing what you have.

"I'm a good man. And I'm a drunk. My experience tells me that you know about drunks. And I think you know about good men, too. Don't you?"

She pulled her face away from his touch and looked at her lap. Despite a flicker of shame she couldn't resist the desire to sink into the crack in the earth where Harley lived.

In his years as a private investigator, Pratt Toomey had never carried a gun or been in a single fight. He had been threatened a few times, had been arrested once for trespassing, and had been chased by some dogs. But this was absolutely the first time he'd ever had a gun shoved in his back.

"Where are you going, Brother Toomey?"

How do you know me? Do I know you?

"Colorado. A little town called Ouray." Pratt's voice was as shallow as his breath. He clipped his words more than he intended.

"Ah. A pretty place, a very pretty place. And who are you going to see?"

The man's voice filled all the gaps between the puffs of wind.

"A woman named Rachel Misker. I'm a private investigator. I need to interview her for a case I'm working on."

"This wouldn't be about Blythe Oaks, would it, Brother Toomey?" The man's voice sounded sad.

How does he know that? "Yes. It is."

"Who else knows about your visit to Colorado?"

"No one else knows." Pratt guessed that his answer was the one the man desired.

"Not even your client knows?"

"No. I haven't reported to her yet. She only knows I'm following some leads. I'm hoping to find a reason to convince them to stop from pressing their complaint. You know about the complaint?"

The man ignored Pratt's question. "But you have been helping them? I'm afraid that's Satan's work, brother."

Pratt's voice cracked. "I've prayed about it. It's the Lord's wish that I keep an eye on them. That I protect the Church. Otherwise, a gentile would do it. I'm acting as the Church's eyes and ears. My bishop knows I'm here. He's counseling me."

The man seemed to huff at the rationalization. "Your bishop knows about Colorado. But he doesn't know about Rachel?"

"No. Nobody knows her name yet. Not Bishop Fortin, not my clients. Nobody."

"That's good. Because the truth is that the Lord doesn't wish them to." Discovering what he wanted to know had come much more quickly than the man had anticipated. He was grateful to Toomey for his forthrightness.

The echo of the explosion from the revolver filled the canyons and valleys of the La Sal Mountains and lingered there long enough for Pratt to think he was still hearing the reverberations when he died.

The impact of the slug caused Pratt Toomey to stumble forward before falling on his face.

The blood that drained from Pratt Toomey's ripped heart seeped slowly enough that he was able to reflect with some comfort on the joy of passing to the next level of salvation.

The man who had pulled the trigger of the .38 that was stuck in Pratt Toomey's back waited patiently for him to die. He waited patiently for the blood to pour from the exit wound in Pratt Toomey's chest and waited patiently for that blood to spill onto Utah's red earth.

But the blood didn't pour. Instead, the blood that oozed from the wound in Pratt Toomey's chest pooled thickly in the confines of his waterproof shell, soaking the fabric of his polo shirt and his sacred garments.

The man knelt next to the body and looked perplexedly at Pratt, as though he were a puzzle. He finally realized what was happening, why the blood wasn't flowing.

He gave a crisp command to his dog, who was lying on the ground ten feet behind him, her snout raised into the breeze to catch the scent of the blood. He repeated a command he had given her earlier. "Stay," he said.

The dog, again, obeyed.

The man knelt over Pratt Toomey, lifted his left shoulder, and rolled him onto his side. With a large pocket knife he cut a long slash in the purple ripstop over Pratt Toomey's heart, then rolled him back onto his abdomen. He waited, kneeling, until Toomey's rich, red blood seeped from beneath his body and then flowed properly onto the rocks. The man stood, stepped back, and followed the narrow red trail as it ran in a rivulet, finally draining off the edge of the rock and dripping down a hundred feet to mingle with the sand and clay of the already red-toned earth.

Part Two

Lying for the Lord

In the judgments of President Reagan and of President Bush, of the FBI and CIA (both replete with Mormons), of our armed forces (with many Mormon high officers), there are no more patriotic Americans than the people called Mormons. . . . Yet the Mormons, if they are at all faithful to the most crucial teachings of Joseph Smith and Brigham Young, no more believe in American democracy than they do in historical Christianity or in Western monogamy. Smith, Young, and their followers believed in theocracy, or the inspired rule of the Saints, and looked forward to each prophet in turn ruling over the Kingdom of God, as king, first here and then everywhere.

Harold Bloom,
The American Religion (1992)

Robin Torr had expected a progress report from the usually reliable Toomey on Thursday. It never came. Elsie insisted she hadn't heard from him since late Wednesday, when he had phoned with the news that he was in Moab. When no further word came from Pratt by lunchtime on Friday, Robin started making calls on her own.

The helicopter that eventually spotted Pratt's Audi later that evening wasn't part of an organized search. The chopper had been returning to its base after completing an aerial survey on a contract for the Bureau of Land Management. The wreckage of the Audi was such a blight on the Utah landscape that it couldn't be missed from the air.

Shortly after sunrise the next morning, Pratt's sun-bloated body was discovered close by. The body lay on top of the rock ridge where Toomey had been shot. It had been disturbed only by birds, small animals, and the cruel, fluctuating temperatures of the high desert.

A representative of the Utah Department of Public Safety phoned Robin Torr's home on Saturday morning with the news of Pratt Toomey's death. Wiley answered and called Robin to the phone. She took the call in the living room. Her conversation lasted just a few minutes.

She replaced the phone on the cradle, and softly, as though she were a balloon being slowly drained of helium, she dropped cross-legged to the floor next to the sofa. A sorrow as thick as lake fog covered her. In the same instant, she felt the tightening in her gut that she knew from experience was her body's first response to fear.

From across the room, Wiley stared at her, at a loss as to what was going on, or what he was supposed to do.

"Pratt's been murdered," she said, her voice hollow. Her anguish cried out for comfort. But her sudden fear, she realized as she watched Wiley come toward her with his arms extended, included a whisper of fear of her husband. She didn't know what that meant. Instantly, she found the energy to stand while she cried. While he held her. It felt safer that way.

The fear helped her to mobilize quickly. After a few minutes of tears, she relayed what she knew to Wiley, then called Teresa Crowder's home. Robin asked if she could come over.

Teresa was puzzled by the request for a Saturday visit. "Now?" she asked.

Robin replied, "Yes, right away." When her client followed with "What's up?" Robin replied simply, "It's important, Teresa. We'll go over it when I get there."

Robin's drive across town took fewer than ten minutes. The doorbell of her client's brick bungalow was covered with masking tape, so Torr knocked on the small glass panes high in the door and waited impatiently.

When Lauren answered, both concern and curiosity were clear in her eyes. Her dark hair was wet from the shower. It had the deep sheen of coal after a rain.

She said, "Hi, come on in, Robin."

"Hi, Lauren. Where's Teresa?" Robin stepped inside. Her demeanor was formal, difficult.

"She's on the phone trying to book some work. I'll tell her you're here." Lauren glanced over her shoulder as she stepped to the back of the house in search of her sister. Robin paced the front room while she waited. The red oak floors were scratched but clean, the furniture spartan but tasteful. A huge framed picture of the Crowder clan, probably taken around the time Lauren graduated from high school, was on the wall near the hallway to the bedroom.

A handsome group, thought Robin.

Though she was the visitor, when the sisters returned Robin asked them to sit.

Lauren finally recognized the awkward demeanor that Robin Torr was affecting. Lauren herself had worn it, or tried to wear it, each of the dozens of times she had been asked to tell the victim of an awful crime some terrible new information.

I'm afraid your daughter was raped before she was murdered.

Yes, the driver of the other car was drunk. Yes, he's been arrested for DUI at least three times before.

It appears your son is lying. His fingerprints are on the gun.

"Pratt Toomey is dead," Robin Torr said, sadness shaking her voice. She sat on the center cushion of a dirty gray sofa that was draped with a fake Navajo rug.

Teresa stilled the bentwood rocking chair on which she sat. As her lips silently formed the question "What?" she turned to her older sister for guidance.

Lauren was stone-faced. She had plastered on the nothing-will-surprise-me face she used to disarm detainees during interrogations. Instinctively, she knew that Pratt's death had implications she hadn't even considered. Without preamble, she asked, "Was Pratt murdered, Robin?"

Robin nodded, her eyes shining with tears, her hands in her lap. "I'm afraid so," she said. She twisted the wedding ring on her left hand. The wide expanses on the sofa, on each side of her, seemed as vast as prairies.

Teresa stared at her sister. Her tongue traced her upper lip. Her heart erupted a little bit with each beat. "Wait a second. What's going on? What do you mean he was murdered? Lauren, what's this about? Does this have to do with me?" With the last question, a frantic edge appeared in Teresa's voice.

Before either Lauren or Robin could respond, Teresa whispered, "This is because of me, isn't it? Oh, God." Lauren rushed to her sister. Teresa shook her off.

Robin began talking. Not to Teresa. Not to Lauren. She just needed to hear herself say some things out loud.

"I got a call a short while ago. Somebody in a helicopter spotted Pratt's car last evening on a state highway south of Moab. The car was wrecked. Apparently deliberately. Pratt's body was found a quarter of a mile away from the car. He'd been shot. In the back. They think he's been dead a while, at least a couple of days. They'll know more after the autopsy, of course."

"Does it have to do with the case?" The clarifying question came from Lauren.

"I think we have to consider that it does." Robin hadn't been aware of consciously reaching that conclusion.

Teresa turned to her sister. "It's time to stop all this, Lauren. Everything. They win. I've gotten someone killed now. I was wrong. This wasn't a good idea. It's time to stop."

Neither attorney tried to dissuade Teresa. Each knew that the decision to continue the fight or to desist wouldn't be made right then. Too much was unknown. But both understood Teresa's reaction. Both understood that with Pratt dead—murdered—the reasons to quit the investigation were stronger than ever.

Lauren remembered her commitment to her sister—not to let her run if things got tough.

Robin knew how pleased Wiley would be if they stopped.

But neither knew what to do next.

Teresa did.

Teresa split.

She had a reservation to fly to Las Vegas on Monday for an engagement that was due to start Tuesday night. Before she left, she asked Lauren whether, given Pratt's death, she thought she should cancel her gig and stay in Salt Lake City to be available to Robin.

Lauren couldn't think of a reason for Teresa to stick around, and told her that. If Teresa wanted to drop the investigation, she didn't need to be in Utah to do it. If she chose to press forward, being in Salt Lake City for a few extra days wouldn't change anything. To no one's surprise, Teresa was on her way out of town by dusk Saturday. She left the phone number of the hotel in Vegas where she would be working.

As Lauren dropped her off at the departure curb of Salt Lake City's airport, Teresa's parting words were "Sometimes it's hard to tell the difference between being prudent and being a wimp, isn't it?"

Lauren didn't have a response.

Her plans for Saturday night were simple. She wanted to do some laundry and get to bed early.

She phoned Robin and asked where she could find a decent laundromat. Robin suggested that Lauren come by her place to do her laundry. She'd fix them both some dinner. She said she needed to talk about Pratt's death with somebody besides her husband, who was up in Logan on business, anyway.

An hour later, Lauren was sorting dirty clothes in the small utility room off the hallway that led to the bedrooms of the Torrs' town house. Robin asked, "You mind talking about Pratt, Lauren?"

Lauren was momentarily distracted by the unfamiliar controls on the washing machine. When she turned back to Robin, she said, "Were you close, Robin? You and Pratt?"

Robin exhaled and tried to hook her hair behind her ears. The thin strands immediately escaped and shadowed her freckled cheeks. She hoisted herself up on the dryer.

"You know, I've been pretty surprised by my feelings about him since he turned up missing. The truth, I guess, is that I liked Pratt more than I ever acknowledged. Not that I'd thought about it much. He was just this guy who worked for me sometimes. I never socialized with him. But when I think about it now, I realize that as far as Mormons go, he wasn't, I don't know, exclusionary, like some of them are.

"I mean, in addition to doing his job competently, he would actually even give me the time of day. He didn't treat me as if I were unpure. Don't get me wrong—I'm sure Pratt thought I *was* unpure. But he wasn't condescending about it. Some LDS are. Spiritually speaking. As soon as some Mormons discover that you're not conversion material, you just disappear to them. Just"—she snapped her fingers—"gone. In Utah, especially outside Salt Lake, when I'm around LDS, I sometimes end up feeling like I'm spiritually homeless. But, looking back, I realize Pratt never left me feeling that way. He treated me like people."

Robin smiled privately, then laughed at her next thought. "Actually, Pratt didn't exactly treat me like people. He treated me like a woman. Which coming from a Mormon male in Utah isn't quite the same as being treated like people." She sipped from one of the two glasses of wine that she'd brought with her into the utility room, then stared hard at the pale liquid. "And, you know, he could be irritating as hell sometimes, too, Pratt could. His ego required that every women he met had to take note of him. I can tell you, that took some time for him and me to sort out. And if I were as pretty as you, Lauren, I guarantee you it would have taken even longer. That's for sure."

Lauren sorted more clothing, wondering where Robin was heading. Robin touched the glass to her lips and with the other hand pointed at some lingerie. She said, "I can't wear underwear like that. I wonder why? I guess it's because I don't feel attractive enough." She covered her mouth with her hand. "I can't believe I said that out loud." She turned her head and drank some more wine.

Lauren looked at her undergarments and felt self-conscious. Wondered how to respond. The washing machine cycled on noisily.

"You *are* attractive, Robin."

"Not like you. Or your sister. Look at me." She ran her fingers through her hair, then reached out and touched Lauren's. "I've never been the one guys want. I've always been the one they settle for. I've never felt desired. In my whole life. There are times in my life when I think I've actually hated women like you and Teresa. You're one of the women that Wiley interrupts a conversation with me to watch walk across a room. You don't know what that's like. To feel disposable."

Lauren felt like apologizing.

Robin didn't want a response.

"To answer your original question, no, Pratt and I weren't close. But, in a way, he was my only bridge into the biggest part of Utah—the part that's LDS. And I suspect I was one of his only bridges into the part of Salt Lake City that isn't. I'm going to miss him. That surprises me. But it's true."

Lauren got lost for an instant thinking about being pretty and wearing lingerie and about bridges and Mormons and about John Harley and what jerks men could be.

Robin wanted to go on. She sighed deeply, bracing herself with a mouthful of wine and a chestful of oxygen before continuing. "This has been real hard on my secretary, Elsie. I kidded around a lot about her predatory interest in Pratt. But she must have truly cared about him; she's devastated about his death." She stopped herself, yielding to a need to retreat from her feelings about Pratt. "We can look at the bright side of this, too, you know, Lauren."

"This has a bright side?"

"Sure it does. At least the FBI should be leaving Teresa alone now. I doubt that they're going to accuse her of killing her own investigator. Which reminds me—in regard to his murder, I've found out some things since this morning. From the police. As you've probably guessed, Pratt wasn't robbed. His wallet was in his pocket. And his gazillion-dollar mountain bike was still on top of his car when whoever shot him sent it over the cliff. Hell, if he hadn't died from being shot, that alone would have killed him.

"The Salt Lake police are assisting the local cops on this. They apparently have plenty of evidence from the scene: tire tracks, footprints, the slug that killed him. And they're going over Pratt's car looking for fingerprints and trace evidence. They've put out a public appeal for witnesses. They want to talk with anybody who might have passed by and seen Pratt's car. Or any other car around there. They want to know if anybody heard the shot.

"What they don't have, unfortunately, is a motive. Pratt's a guy who didn't make enemies. Well, certainly not LDS enemies. And like I said, he related as well to gentiles as just about any Mormon I know. So the cops have drawn a blank so far. At least that's what they're telling me." Robin paused and handed Lauren a bottle of fabric softener and showed her how the dispenser worked. She drained her glass of wine.

"Unless the lawsuit *is* the motive. Which I must admit is a thought that doesn't add up in Utah."

Lauren closed the lid of the washer. "You've said that before. But why? Why doesn't it make sense in Utah? I mean, to try to stop the lawsuit with violence. It's not a pretty thought, but it's not exactly unheard of, either."

"It's not modern Mormon style, Lauren. It's just not how things are done here. First, you have to understand that the Church's historical lust for power in Utah comes not just from some spiritual megalomania but mostly from the Mormons' sense of themselves, since their inception, as a threatened and persecuted people. And there's plenty of justification for that point of view. For the Church, having reliable political power and social clout is the Deseret version of the Israeli Air Force. It's the way they protect themselves. But as an institution, the Church prefers to appear tolerant, not monolithic—at least to outsiders.

"If you fight a public battle with the Mormon Church, they tend to win, mostly just by claiming that they are being persecuted for their beliefs, as they've been claiming for a hundred and fifty years. If you recall, that's the way they got Horner onto the Court, by claiming intolerance when he was criticized for his beliefs during his confirmation hearings.

"The Church leaders might want us to stop our investigation. Hell, I'm sure they want us to stop. But if they thought this lawsuit was going to really hurt Lester Horner, they'd call a private meeting with us and settle the damn thing. With money. Plenty of it. And we would all go home. If they wanted to pressure me to stop, they would do it through the law firm, through our big clients, or through Wiley. They wouldn't send somebody out to shoot Pratt. Maybe a hundred years ago. Not today; they don't need to. Their power in Utah is too entrenched."

Robin asked Lauren if she was ready to eat. They made their way to the small kitchen.

Robin removed a salad from the refrigerator, then refilled her wineglass and added half an inch to Lauren's. "And given the astonishing sympathy that's been created recently for the Oaks family, the police aren't especially eager to consider the possibility that anyone associated with her might have had a motive to deter Pratt from whatever it is he was up to in southeast Utah. And the fact that I'm not even able to tell the police what Pratt was up to down there doesn't add much to my credibility, either. I mean, the Oakses are such top-drawer LDS that Blythe really goes into this with the benefit of the doubt. The true and proper meaning of 'presumed innocent.' "

Robin dressed the salad, then shoveled some lettuce and vegetables onto a couple of plates and carried them to the small table in the dining room.

The two women sat silently for a few moments. Lauren ate, Robin drank. Lauren finally fractured the silence.

"And we still don't know what Pratt was up to on this last trip he took?"

"Not really, no. The police found his notebook in his car—you know, his address book–appointment book thing. It was a beat-up old leather book. I've seen it a dozen times. Anyway, I'm hoping there will be something in there that tells us where he was going, what he was looking for. I'm going to go down to the State Crime Lab and take a look at it tomorrow."

"I'd like to go with you."

"Sure, of course. I'd like that, too. It's funny, I've never tried a case before where I've actually needed a prosecutor on my side. This time, with the bodies that keep piling up, I think I do." She smiled warmly at Lauren. "And look who just happened to show up on my doorstep."

Lauren returned Robin's smile. "Well, this could be the prosecutor side of me speaking, Robin, but I think we need to consider the possibility that maybe Pratt had already been wherever he was going. Maybe he was on his way back from somewhere when he was killed. He may have learned something already, and scared somebody in the process." Lauren had finished her salad. It had barely dented her appetite. She eyed Robin's untouched plate longingly and prayed for prompt movement to the next course.

"You know, you're right, it's possible. But I'm not sure. There are a lot of somebodys and somewheres in there. The crime-scene people can probably determine which direction he was traveling by examining his tire tracks. I do know that Pratt was quite a mountain bike fanatic. Since we found out where his body was discovered, I've been guessing that he had spent some time, a day or two, mountain biking in Moab on the way to someplace else, someplace south of there, on or close to 191. You know about Moab?"

"Yeah. Alan—the guy I'm seeing in Boulder—he's a bicycle nut, too. He goes to Moab sometimes."

"But your question does raise an interesting possibility. I've been thinking since that call came this morning that Pratt was killed because somebody didn't want him helping us with Teresa's case in general. But maybe, just maybe, he was killed because he'd already stumbled onto something specific. Maybe he was on his way to see somebody who someone else just couldn't afford to allow him to see."

Lauren took a reading of her own fatigue level and considered the judiciousness of more wine. She reached for the bottle and poured, refilling Robin's glass, too.

"But who, Robin? Is Lester Horner going to go out and have somebody killed? Or is Paul Oaks? Given their reputations, they just don't strike me as the type."

"I agree with you. Absolutely. But who else is going to have a motive? I mean, if we sue, we'll be suing her estate, and that leaves Paul at some risk financially. And if we win, this whole affair is not going to look real good for Lester Horner. And there's the Women's Symposium. Lots of motive every place you look, but nothing compelling."

Lauren cupped her glass with both hands. The rim hung just below her chin. "Horner's exposure is small, Robin. He'll just hide behind the bench. The worst that happens to him is he'll be soiled a little bit by the association, but he'll survive it just fine. If anybody bothers to ask her, Teresa will tell them Horner was a perfect gentleman." She touched the glass to her lips but withdrew it before drinking. "From a purely legal point of view, Teresa's case isn't that great. We both know that. We've got a chance, but proving this particular charge against somebody this prominent is a true long shot. Still," she said, "somebody seems to be acting as though we're hot on the trail of something terribly important."

"I know. But if not Horner or Oaks, then who?"

"Despite your protests, I keep going back to my original thesis. I think the other suspect to consider is the Church."

Robin shivered once. She said, "No, you just don't get Utah. That's not how it would work here."

"It isn't even a consideration?"

Robin Torr placed her knife and fork over her salad in a gesture of culinary resignation. "Of course it's a consideration. Just not a realistic one. Listen. You haven't lived behind the Zion Curtain. You don't understand. In a way, you can't understand. If your home gets destroyed by an arsonist, you may end up wanting to inflict some kind of revenge on the creep. But if it gets blown to bits by a tornado, you just feel defeated; there's nothing you can do in the face of that immense power. That's what it's like here. In Utah, the Church is that big and that powerful. It's a true force of nature. If the leaders in the Church Administration Building wanted this case stopped, they wouldn't kill Pratt. They would simply pressure me or my firm, or, failing that, they would buy Teresa off."

"What if she wouldn't be bought off?"

"Lauren, if you and I manage to assemble an airtight Title VII case against Blythe Oaks—I mean, as tight as a beach ball—the judge we end up in front of is maybe going to treat us with some respect before he makes a series of rulings that make it impossible for us to prevail. He'll accept defense motions for delay. He'll restrict access to records or testimony of witnesses we don't think there is any reason to refuse to us. It'll be one thing after another. Why? Because there isn't a judge on the federal bench in Utah who wasn't hand-selected by Orrin Hatch, Jake Garn, or Lester Horner. Trust me, they will not let us win. We won't prevail in court. Period. If we get a decent settlement offer—shit, if we get any settlement offer—we'd be fools not to settle."

Lauren tried to understand what she was hearing. "Come on, Robin. Is the system really that insidious here? That's hard to believe."

Robin stared off across the dining room. Across the living room. Across Utah. "Yes and no. It doesn't feel insidious to me anymore. It just feels like our system. People in Chicago don't complain about Chicago politics as much as outsiders do. The problem in Utah is that with the Mormon Church, you just never really know what's going on. Most of what's controversial about Mormonism is hidden. From all gentiles. From most Mormons, too. Hidden in the temples or in the bombproof vaults in Little Cottonwood Canyon. It's all hidden by doctrine and history and threats of disfellowship and excommunication. In Utah, the Church controls history. They *own* the past. Literally. They have control over most of the original source material from the nineteenth century. If it's controversial, they don't let outsiders see it. Hell, they don't even let insiders see it.

"In the beginning, prior to statehood and just after, the Church used to have these enforcers—they were called Danites—who supposedly did the Lord's dirty work. Some say Brigham Young's own personal protector killed over a hundred people—you know, eliminated the Church's enemies. And the Church had plenty of enemies then. Actually, the Church *still* has plenty of enemies. I'm sure they consider me one now, too. Some people—gentiles, obviously—maintain that the Danites are still around doing the Church's murderous deeds. I don't think there's any evidence to support any of it except in some Mormon-basher's imagination. The Church scoffs at the idea; in fact, it uses the allegations as further evidence that the Mormons continue to be a persecuted people."

Lauren pressed. "What about you? What do you think?"

"Me?" asked Robin. "What do I think? Let's see. . . ." She tried to look wistful. "These days, *I think* that I want my husband to start treating me like I'm wonderful and witty and sexy and wise. I think I want to finally stop worrying about whether or not I'm attractive. I think I want my secretary to start treating me like my days in this universe aren't numbered. I think I want to find a diary written by Blythe Oaks admitting her sexual harassment of your sister. And I think I want the police to arrest a psychotic drifter, a Baptist or a Catholic or a Jew or a Muslim or even a goddamn agnostic, for the murder of Pratt Toomey. Yeah, I want the cops to tell me that his death was the random act of a deranged mind. That's what I think. Oh, and I want the Jazz to win the NBA championship once before I die. How's that?"

"Nice list. And nice diversion. But what about Blythe Oaks? Pratt's murder is the second one on our list. Was Blythe's death the result of the same deranged lightning striking twice? It makes no sense. First kill the defendant; then kill the plaintiff's investigator?"

Robin opened her eyes wide and stared. "Gosh, Lauren, you sure are a lot of fun tonight. I'm trying to digest one murder, and you're insisting that I swallow two and consider the possibility that my adversary is the most powerful institution in this state. Maybe I'll chew on that tomorrow. Or better yet, how about Monday? For tonight, can we talk about something I actually *want* to think about? Maybe for just a few minutes?"

Lauren smiled back at her friend and said, "Sure. Want to talk about your marriage? Or why you're always putting yourself down?"

Robin laughed, almost spitting out her wine. "I guess it's either that or the World Series. Though given the injury situation this year, it's never too early in Utah to start talking about the Jazz's prospects for the lottery." She made a devious face across the table. "Unless . . . we could always talk about this fiancé of yours in Colorado you hardly ever say word one about."

"Alan."

"That's a nice name. Yeah, Alan. While I get us the rest of our dinner—do you like spanakopita?—why don't you tell me about Alan, and why you aren't in Boulder, Colorado, picking out a silver pattern."

"Are you a vegetarian, Robin?"

"Kind of. I don't eat anything that has a mother."

By the time Lauren arrived home with her clean laundry after dinner she was determined to learn the purpose of Pratt Toomey's road trip. Pratt, she decided, had apparently been on the trail of something so important to Teresa's allegations that somebody figured it was worth murdering him over.

First, Lauren wanted to know if Robin and Elsie were right about Pratt making a stopover in Moab. And given the bicycle Pratt took with him, was the Moab stopover part of whatever lead he was pursuing on the investigation or merely part of some impromptu vacation? And she also wanted to know exactly where he was heading when he was ambushed and murdered on Utah State Highway 191 in the La Sal Mountains.

Lauren shared Robin's slim hope that the answers to all these questions would be spelled out in excruciatingly clear detail in the leather notebook that Pratt kept with him most of the time. But even the possibility that Pratt's itinerary was clearly etched in his log was discomfiting.

If the boundary line between church and state was as porous in Utah as it seemed to be, Lauren feared that whatever the authorities discovered in Pratt's notebook might soon make its way into the hands of whoever had killed him. That, in turn, would complicate not only the investigation of Pratt's murder but also, in all likelihood, the progression of Teresa's harassment action.

Lauren had already concluded that the fact that Pratt had been tracked so effectively on his trip meant that whoever had killed him might be close enough to Teresa's case to know the comings and goings of the principals. As far as Lauren was concerned, that supposition alone pretty much ruled out the option of Robin Torr hiring another investigator from Salt Lake City to try and ghost Toomey's trail. And, of course, it ruled out either Lauren or Robin trying to do the shadowing themselves. And using Teresa was out of the question.

Lauren spent a few moments sifting through the few options that presented themselves. Only one felt at all different from doing nothing. It was the one she chose.

What Lauren decided to do was to enlist some out-of-town talent. Although she didn't know Robin Torr well, she thought she knew her well enough to guess that her sister's attorney wouldn't endorse the new plan.

So she didn't ask.

She took two steps toward the telephone in the kitchen before she thought better of it and instead grabbed her coat and headed out the door.

Lauren's second phone call to Colorado late that Sunday evening was to Alan. After some brief small talk, mostly Boulder political gossip, and some prolonged sexual innuendo, mostly generated by Alan, she asked him if he and Sam Purdy would do her a little favor on their upcoming bike trip. Like, would they consider changing the destination from Crested Butte, Colorado, to Moab, Utah.

"You're going to be in Moab?" Alan asked with excitement in his voice. He was eager for an opportunity to do his usually self-reliant lover just about any favor.

"This is hard for me, sweetheart. You know I'm not particularly adept at asking for things. You've wanted me to lean on you a little more. Well, here it is. I need a favor from you. What I need from you is for you to check something out for me in Moab. Since you and Sam are going riding anyway, I thought you could just as well go to Moab as Crested Butte. There's something I absolutely can't do myself there right now or I wouldn't ask."

"Listen, it's no big deal, Lauren. I'm delighted to help. I can't speak for Sam, but Moab's great for me. Does this have something to do with Teresa's case?"

Quietly she said, "Mmm-hmmm. It does."

She stayed silent for a moment. He did, too. She was hoping he wasn't contemplating going into shrink mode on her.

She plowed on. "Okay. To be fair, Alan, what I'm asking might be a big deal. Let me tell you what's been happening here with the case. See . . . well, see . . . the investigator Teresa's attorney hired to help prepare the case was murdered last week, and—"

"Murdered? That makes two, doesn't it?" Alan's voice escalated with alarm.

"Yes." Lauren's voice, on the other hand, was as modulated as she could make it. "The investigator had been checking something out for us but had been out of touch for a couple of days. We finally got worried and started making some calls. The highway patrol found his body yesterday morning. He'd been dead a while, apparently. A couple of days."

The alarm he felt temporarily back under control, Alan adopted Lauren's terse tone. "Your investigator, he was killed because of the case?"

"Maybe. The cops aren't sure. But we think it's possible. Given the coincidence quotient, maybe even probable."

Alan knew that if she had been next to him, he probably would have spun on her and said something he would have instantly regretted. His impulse was to insist that she drop whatever she was doing and come home to Boulder. He rejected the impulse not because he rejected the thought but rather because Lauren Crowder as a general rule didn't listen to people, especially him, telling her what to do. He also didn't want to pass on the opportunity to do something important for her.

"What does Moab have to do with it? What is it you want me to do in Utah?"

"Pratt—the investigator—he was a mountain biker. Apparently, he was kind of a fanatic about it, like you. The police say he was in Moab riding just prior to being killed. But his body was found about twenty miles south of Moab on Highway 191. His car had a fancy mountain bike on it."

Alan had been to Moab twice before, both times to ride. But he'd always come in to Utah on I-70, through Grand Junction. He had never had a reason to go that far south of Moab on 191. Once, he had gone far enough to ride some of the wondrous trails in the La Sal Mountains, but he didn't have a clue as to what 191 did farther south than that. As he tried to puzzle out the geography in his head, though, he did manage to begin to read more clearly between the lines that Lauren was meticulously tracing in front of him.

"And what? You want me to go to Moab and snoop around for you about this murder? How would I learn anything the police haven't found out already?"

She did, indeed, want him to go snoop around.

"I don't know how, but yes, I'm hoping you can find out things that the police didn't discover when they were there. Or that they discovered and, for some reason or another, haven't told us. And anyway, they don't know you. They know me, and they know Teresa's attorney. No one will be watching for you."

Alan Gregory was sitting on his sofa in his living room in his little house on a gentle western slope a few miles from the eastern foothills of the Rockies. As Lauren said "they don't know you," he stood and began to pace his living room within the narrow range permitted by the confines of his twisted telephone cord.

He said, "Who are 'they,' Lauren?"

"See, we don't exactly know that yet. If we knew that, we would probably know what Pratt had been up to. Pratt had a lead he was checking out. But we don't know what it was. And we don't know whether he was killed before he checked it out or after."

"You don't know what your own investigator was doing? That's not like you."

Lauren resisted displaying some of the defensiveness that was mushrooming within her. "This isn't my case. You know that. And things had gotten kind of competitive between me and Pratt. We had both been talking to people, following leads, helping prepare Teresa's case. I think it—me helping—made him uncomfortable, especially since I'm a woman. I think he would have preferred to fly solo. Be the star. So he didn't keep Robin and me filled in on his next move."

"Robin is Teresa's lawyer?"

"Yeah. Robin Torr. She's good, Alan."

"She doesn't know what you're up to, does she?" Alan's tone said, "I know you."

Lauren paused. Exhaled. She gave up the effort necessary to resist sounding defensive. "No. Not exactly."

Alan sat back down and slung a leg over the arm of his big leather chair. The Front Range was silhouetted before him against a moonlit sky. Hundreds of miles across those mountains, the woman he loved was sitting awake late at night making what for her was a difficult request of him. During the year-and-a-half duration of their rather turbulent relationship, Alan could count the number of times that Lauren had leaned on him on the fingers of one hand. Her determined independence had been an irritating point of late-night discussion between them on more than one occasion.

He said, "Well, I've asked you to ask me for things. I'm getting exactly what I asked for, I guess."

"I try to oblige."

"So, if I come—I said, *if*—what's my reward? Do I get to see you when I'm done playing detective in Moab?"

"Not in Moab, I'm afraid. I think I'd better stay put in Salt Lake City. But you'll still get your long weekend with your bicycle between your legs. And from what everybody keeps telling me, riding in Moab can be even better than sex."

"Close, maybe, but not better." *And speaking of sex* . . . "I'll be lonely there without you."

"You'll have Sam."

"We haven't asked *him* about the itinerary change. And he's not exactly what I had in mind."

"Listen . . . I'm not naive about this favor I'm asking. This situation is obviously dangerous. So I've, um"—the next words spilled out at increased velocity—"already called Sam and asked him if he'd mind helping out."

"And he said?"

"Alan, this—what we're doing with Teresa's case—is apparently much more risky than any of us thought.

We're talking murder now, Alan. Pratt Toomey was shot in the back. At close range. By somebody who set a trap intended just for him. So even though I can't imagine anybody guessing that you're involved, I still want somebody around who can look after your cute little butt for me."

"And Sam said yes?"

"Sam likes me. And yes, he said yes."

"Why didn't you just ask Sam to do this by himself? He's a cop. He'd obviously be better at this sort of thing than I would."

"I don't know, your track record as a moonlighting detective is becoming the stuff of Front Range legend. But the truth is, I didn't want either of you doing it alone. I'd worry too much. I'll worry too much as it is."

The conversation moved gingerly to more stable terrain for the next few minutes. Alan withheld comment about Lauren's judgment and instead expressed his concern about her safety. She deflected his concern, insisting she was fine. He pressed. She maintained that she didn't feel that either she or her sister was in danger. Alan pointed out that that contention seemed ludicrous, given events.

A strange voice interrupted the conversation. On Alan's end the voice sounded muffled. Some banging followed immediately.

Lauren winced at the interruption, though she was able to muster some gratitude that the intrusion was interfering with Alan's prosecution of her judgment.

"Who's that? Teresa?" asked Alan.

"No, Teresa's in Vegas. I forgot to tell you. It's great! She got a big-time gig opening for a headliner at one of the casinos. She's real excited about it. You know, it's still so hard for me think of her actually on stage as a comedian. My little sister. But apparently this is all pretty real. I mean, Vegas, Alan, we're talking major league."

Joining Lauren in applauding her sister's success was an option—one that Alan had no difficulty ignoring. Instead, suspicious about why she might not be using her sister's phone at eleven o'clock on a Saturday night, he countered, "You're not at your sister's place, are you?"

An ancient reflex almost caused Lauren to say, "What business is it of yours?" But she didn't. She said simply, matter-of-factly, "No, I'm not."

Alan waited.

Lauren felt the density of the stillness on the line. In a reluctant voice, she admitted, "I'm at a pay phone."

While Alan was considering how serious the danger must be to motivate Lauren to truck somewhere late at night to find a pay phone to make the request she had just made of him, Lauren was reflecting on the relief she was feeling that she hadn't followed her initial impulse and gone over to John Harley's apartment to use his phone.

For Lauren, it was tough to acknowledge that she was using a public pay phone. She didn't want to have to admit to Alan that the case was so out of hand that she feared somebody might be monitoring her calls. Though, given Pratt's murder, at least such paranoia required no further explanation.

But being at Harley's apartment late on Saturday night, no matter how innocent her motive, would have been a miserable thing to have to acknowledge to Alan. And thus far, Lauren hadn't figured out how to explain John Harley, even to herself.

Despite repeated assurances to Robin, the Utah State Crime Lab didn't make Pratt Toomey's notebook available on Monday morning. When she and Lauren arrived for their appointment, they were told that they would have to wait until Wednesday to see the material. "Forensics take time," explained a tall, gruff functionary with a dense shadow of whiskers, who seemed to take significant pleasure in being uncooperative. Lauren knew the delay was strategic, not forensic, in nature. She said a silent prayer that the guy's superiors forced him to shave twice a day.

Robin telephoned on Tuesday afternoon and she was told by the same curt, condescending man that Friday was actually more likely than Wednesday.

Lauren was exasperated at all the time that was being wasted, frustrated by the lack of progress, and furious at the asshole running interference at the crime laboratory. The county sheriff from southeastern Utah, in whose jurisdiction Pratt had been murdered, had asked the Salt Lake City Police Department to assist on the case. Lauren urged Robin to phone the detective investigating the case for the Salt Lake police and imply that the press might be interested in knowing that it was taking the State Crime Lab five days to dust an appointment book for prints in a high-profile murder case.

Robin made the call. The detective offered to "clear a path through this bureaucratic jumble" for a meeting Wednesday morning at 8:30.

"Not much here, I'm afraid," explained the supervisor from the crime lab. He had greeted Lauren Crowder and Robin Torr pleasantly, shaking their hands firmly enough to cause Lauren to wince, and then apologized profusely for the runaround they had been getting. Crowder smiled her way through the whole routine. For five years she had watched Boulder cops stonewall defense attorneys, and this performance wasn't even close to award-winning.

The crime lab supervisor had one of those heads that looked incomplete without a hat. His collar was so tight that it pinched the skin on his neck in excruciating-looking little creases. As he completed his disingenuous apologies and prepared to actually discuss evidence, his voice grew hushed and serious. His collar seemed to grow tighter with the effort.

"Prints on the book are all the deceased's. Every last one. No appointments were written down in his log for the day of his murder or the couple of days before or after. There are a few phone numbers scrawled on the calendar for the previous week. One of them is your home number, Miss." He nodded at Robin Torr. "All of them check out but one. That one's a disconnected number. Phone company said it's been disconnected a while. I forget exactly—six weeks at least, anyway."

Robin listened intently to the man's recitation of the state's version of the contents of Pratt Toomey's appointment book. Lauren waited impatiently for him to finish his little speech so she could get her hands on the book. She fought to control her tongue while Robin asked a couple of probing questions. The forensic supervisor, his eyes as dismayed as a doe's in headlights, answered with seasoned ignorance.

Lauren's self-control waned and she finally interrupted the man's drill. She said, "Thanks so much for all your time. I think we'll go ahead and take a look at the book now."

Robin glanced over quickly, her face indicating that she thought Lauren's interruption had been ill-timed.

Lauren smiled at her friend. Her eyes said, *We're being treated as fools here.*

Robin glared back, made a quick judgment, turned back to the supervisor, and said, "Yes, thanks. We do appreciate all your help. May we see the book now?"

The man appeared uncomfortable, as though his bowels were full of gas. "Just a moment," he said, and stood and left the small room where they had all been seated.

As the door closed, both women started to speak simultaneously.

Lauren persisted over Robin. "He didn't even bring it in here with him. There's obviously something in there they don't want us to see."

"I know that. But you need to remember that we're not the prosecution, we're not in Colorado, and we're not LDS. Okay? We'll get the book. They don't want us to, but we will."

The man returned a few minutes later.

He carried a large manila envelope. "What is it exactly you ladies are looking for in here?"

Lauren opened her mouth to speak. Robin jumped in. "Work product," she said. "We can't be more specific. Mr. Toomey was doing work for me in the context of a legal case when he was murdered. We are looking for material related to that case." There was no smile on Robin Torr's face. She had leaned forward slightly before speaking. Her back was erect, her eyes unblinking.

"Miss, I—"

"It's 'Ms.,' and this isn't negotiable. If you would like to call Detective Jacobs for me, I'm sure we can work this out in no time."

"Ma'am, please. I'm just trying to be cooperative here. Save you from having to cover the same ground that the folks here at the lab have already covered. No need to reinvent the wheel, is there?"

The women stared at him, unconvinced.

He held up the big envelope with one hand and pointed at it with the other. "This is a difficult case for the department, this here is important evidence."

Torr spoke. "I'm sure it is. It's difficult for me as well. I lost a friend and a valued investigator last week. And one of my clients has lost valuable time, which I would like to begin to recoup. May I have the envelope?"

The man stood as still as a statue.

Torr said, "Please."

He said, "I'll need to stay here while you look at it, ma'am. The whole time. You may not remove anything. You may not make any marks in the book."

Before Robin could protest, Lauren interjected, "That's fine. Why don't you just have a seat over there?" She pointed to a chair by the door. "We'll work at this table. Robin, will you help me for a minute?"

At Lauren's direction, Robin helped her push the large conference table to one corner of the room and then set the blue plastic-and-chrome chairs so their backs faced the supervisor. The man didn't offer to help.

Robin walked back over to him, snatched the envelope from his hand, and then settled down at the table next to Lauren, edging her chair over so that their shoulders almost touched. As if on cue, each reached down and retrieved a legal pad from her briefcase. Robin fumbled around in the bottom of her case and found a couple of pencils. She stuffed one over each of her ears.

Lauren looked over her shoulder and offered the forensic supervisor an ironic smile. She held it until he appeared to be what she considered sufficiently uncomfortable, then she turned back to the table and poised herself to take notes.

The man didn't seem to be sure if he should sit where he'd been directed or go find someone higher up to whom to complain. Reluctantly, he sat and watched the two women go to work.

Not much here! scrawled Lauren on her legal pad after she and Robin had consumed about twenty minutes perusing the written record of the last ten days of Pratt Toomey's life. Lauren had methodically copied the details from each day onto a separate page of paper.

Toomey seemed to have used the calendar as a billing and expense record more than as an appointment book. Locations and durations of appointments were apparently filled in after the meetings occurred in order to provide documentation for billing. Expenses were logged meticulously.

The billing code Pratt used seemed straightforward. Meetings that were to be billed to Teresa Crowder's case had a circled *LFZ* next to them, in the margin right after the time and duration of the meeting. The initials stood for the firm name, Lewis, Frank and Zelem. Many of the recent appointments were going to be billed to Teresa. But Pratt apparently had at least one other large project going.

The initials next to the meetings for that client were intensely troubling to Robin Torr. *JB.*

JB. In law school, in Berkeley, it had been Wiley Torr's Scotch. Now *JB* was James and Bartell, Wiley's law firm. Robin hoped that Lauren wouldn't make the connection. Torr grew weary just thinking about discussing this conflict with Wiley.

Robin refocused and scribbled a note to Lauren. Her handwriting was small and precise. *He was always taking notes. Where's his note pad? He kept it in here! And these little pockets for credit cards? They're empty.*

Lauren remembered the note pad. She'd seen Pratt jot down reminders a number of times during meetings. She specifically remembered watching him write down some of the names she had culled from the BYU yearbooks in Provo.

She shrugged her shoulders at Robin and felt as though she were playing charades.

Robin picked up the leather notebook from the table and ran her thin fingers into the slim pockets inside the cover at the front and back. She found the perforated edge of a postage stamp. That was it. No credit cards. No business cards. No receipts. No note paper. No grocery lists.

Nothing but a piece of perforated scrap.

She whispered, "These were full of stuff. I'm sure of it."

Lauren nodded. The slender slots bulged as if they had once been stuffed full of something.

Torr turned to the man across the room and caught him in the middle of an anxious yawn. She gawked at his collar, thinking that the thread on that top button must be woven from titanium. She said, "Excuse me. Sir? Where are the papers from these pockets?" He looked confused. It was a studied look.

Crowder raised the book and opened it. "The pockets in the front and in the back of this book? Those papers."

He squirmed for a moment, rubbed his eyes, swallowed, and seemed to consider bolting out the door instead of answering. Finally, after staring at Lauren and chewing his bottom lip, he said, "We're not done with those items yet. And I'm not authorized to let you have them or even see them." Being defiant refueled him. "You can call Detective Jacobs if you want. But since my orders came directly from him, I'm sure he'll tell you the exact same thing. *Miss.*" Being defiant also made him petty.

Robin Torr snatched the pencil from behind her right ear and scribbled "SHIT" on her legal pad in precise small capital letters.

In the parking lot, the blustery, dry gusts that preceded an approaching cold front kicked up elm leaves and powdery sand. Lauren turned her back to the wind and grabbed her hair to keep it from blowing into her face. Robin held her red skirt in place with her free hand.

"What do you think it is that they're hiding?"

"I bet I know exactly what it is they're hiding. The last time I saw Pratt write something down in that book it was some of the names I had brought back from Provo with me. He was going to check them out, is what he said. I bet that list is at least part of what they're hiding."

"You know this area of the law a lot better than I do. Can we get what they have?"

Lauren didn't like the cards she and Robin were being dealt. She much preferred her usual hand—the prosecutor's cards. The liabilities of being a civil attorney were becoming increasingly clear to her. "No, not easily. Maybe not at all. If I were investigating or prosecuting this case, I wouldn't give us anything, either. Especially if it was politically sensitive. If we were defense attorneys and they had already charged our client, maybe we could force the issue in front of a judge. But in legal reality, we don't have any standing that would compel them to cooperate with us."

A bitter stab of wind sliced through Torr. She shivered. "I agree with you; I think it's political, too. The name of somebody important must be in Pratt's book." She tried to blink some blowing dust from her eyes. "Can we re-create that list? Cross-check? See who Pratt might have talked with?"

Lauren let go of her hair and nodded. She thought it wouldn't be that hard to do. Her black hair shrouded her face. She looked hard at her frozen friend. She realized that Robin had just tacitly signed on to continue pursuing Teresa's complaint.

"Robin. What are we investigating here? Teresa's lawsuit or Pratt's murder?"

Robin Torr hugged herself to ward off the invading cold. Her pleated skirt billowed like a bright red cloud. She ignored the immodesty. "Can you tell the difference anymore? I sure can't."

After leaving the State Crime Lab Lauren took a nap, grabbed a quick dinner, and drove to the Side Pocket to shoot some pool and see John Harley. Although he still refused to play a game with her, he had agreed to take an oft-postponed lesson.

She was on her second beer. He was still on his first Diet Pepsi. He was lining up a tough shot involving the six ball and an angle that looked impossible to him. She said it was makable.

"Go ahead with your list," he said.

Lauren had found the photocopies she had made from the BYU yearbooks and compiled a list of the names of the people whose pictures Pratt Toomey had circled with his mechanical pencil. She pulled the list from the hip pocket of her jeans and started to read. "Leroy Thomas."

"Really? Thomas? I've heard of him. Mmm-hmmm."

"Rachel Misker."

"Don't know her. Go on."

"Bruce Starkle."

"Good one, yeah." Harley slid the cue stick back between his fingers and tried to remember Lauren's instructions about precisely where to impact the ball. *Smack.*

"Too hard," Lauren said. Then, "But you got the angle, see."

Harley smiled at her as the six skidded off the corner of the pocket and rolled down the table.

"Any more?"

"Kevin Lee. That's it. What have I got?"

Harley planted his cue, bulb down, on the ancient linoleum floor and looked hard at Lauren. He quickly decided she was sincere. Naive, but sincere.

"You've got, I think, two relatively new general authorities. First Quorum of the Seventy. And one member of the Quorum of the Twelve, I think. I'm not exactly sure. And a woman I don't know. But mostly what you've got is a darn good set of reasons to pack up and go back to Colorado, where the bad guys don't write the rules."

"What do you mean?"

"These guys on your list aren't like you and me. These guys are *chosen*. They take their orders from God."

She was examining the table. She spotted a tough combination she was tempted to try.

"Seriously?" she said.

Harley picked up the chalk cube and caressed the end of his stick. "Yes, seriously, Lauren. LDS males—priests, bishops, yes, even me—receive direction from God. Not guidance, like through prayers. But direction, revelation. Conversation. What school their son should attend. Whether they should change jobs. Whether to let their daughter marry the kid next door. The operative word here is 'revelation.' The authorities and the apostles, the guys on your list, their revelations are not quite so mundane as mine and Pratt's. The authorities consult with God about what is best for the Church, for the faithful, for the dead, for the unborn."

Lauren was fascinated. "So if Pratt was going to interview one of these authorities about my sister, and somebody didn't want him to do that and killed him, and I follow that same trail, this game could turn out to be nasty for me, too."

"Nasty? Hardly. It appears that the game you so playfully refer to is already nasty. Two people are dead, if I'm not mistaken. What I'm talking about here is different. Have you ever read the Old Testament? Remember, we're talking plagues and pestilence and people turned to salt. God plays for keeps. The saints do, too. The means they use may be slightly more elegant than locusts and salt statues. But if they think that the Church is threatened in any way, I guarantee you they will be playing for keeps."

Lauren bent over to line up a shot for Harley and considered what she'd heard. Robin Torr kept telling her that the Mormon Church didn't settle scores that way. She grabbed her beer and drank deeply. "What do you mean, 'playing for keeps'?"

Harley pondered the question. "You ever heard of lying for the Lord?"

"No."

"It's sort of an unofficial doctrine used to excuse bending the rules. If what you're doing—even if it's wrong—is in promotion of the faith, well, there are Mormons who might not consider it a sin."

"Even murder? Would the Church murder people?"

Harley considered the question. He said, "Honestly? No, I don't think so. Despite all the terrible things some people like to think about Mormons. But something short of murder? Sure. The Church wouldn't think twice about pressuring your sister's attorney through her family or her partners. Or they might try to influence the judge if the thing ever went to trial. They would certainly discredit you or your sister without thinking twice. Failing all that, they would just get a well-heeled member to write out a check and settle the darn thing."

Lauren wasn't dividing her focus between Harley and the pool table any longer. Her attention was all on Harley. "Harley, why are you helping me? If what I'm doing is so potentially threatening to the faith?"

He didn't hesitate. It was a question he'd asked himself a dozen times since his separation from Jules, about various activities he knew wouldn't be considered faith-promoting by the Church hierarchy. "Don't misunderstand me," he said, "or Mormonism. It's easy to do. All Mormons aren't zealots. I'm not. Many have strayed even farther than I have. Some saints don't tithe anymore. They don't receive home teachers. They ignore the Word of Wisdom. Don't wear garments. They're on the fringe of the Church. The faithful say they're 'not active' and call them Jack Mormons. I can't speak for the origins of their doubts, but for me, my doubts, I think, are a question of imperfect faith. I still want to believe in the teachings; if you study them, you actually may find some of them somewhat compelling. But personally, I'm constantly having trouble with institutions and authority. It's my nature. And if the LDS Church is anything, it's certainly an institution and an authority.

"And I don't believe that justice is contrary to my faith or contrary to the Church's interests. I believe that saints sometimes sin, even high-ranking saints. To the academic in me, it's not different than what Ivan Boesky or Michael Milken thought they could get away with on Wall Street, or what Ronald Reagan and Oliver North did with the Contras. Sociologists call it 'elite deviance'—where people in power feel they should be immune from the rules. The Church would have trouble with what I'm saying. And they would have trouble with the fact that this whole affair you're investigating is already terribly public. But I don't feel like I'm betraying anything by speaking with you. Except maybe my sanity."

"What would your bishop say?"

"About my playing pool in a degenerate pool hall with a very pretty gentile while she plies me for information about the dark side of the Church?"

She nodded.

"I think he'd be pretty understanding."

She laughed.

"You don't?"

As she tilted her beer bottle back to drink, Lauren caught a man at the next table staring at her chest. Annoyed, she turned back to Harley. "You're as crazy as I am, Harley," she said.

He drained his pop and cracked a piece of ice between his teeth. "I don't think so," he said whimsically, " 'cause if I had that list"—he pointed at her pants pocket—"I'd crumple it up and throw it away and forget it ever existed. So what do you think, the thirteen in the corner?"

"No way," she said.

"Buy me a pop?"

"You're on."

In one smooth motion he lined it up and sank it.

Salt Lake's a small town, hon. Of course we used Pratt sometimes. Although we're a bigger firm, we probably work the same way you people do. We have a couple of regular guys who get most of our work. Pratt was one of two or three other investigators we use from time to time. You want some hot cider? I'm going to make some. Celebrate the first snow."

Wiley's failure to react with hostility to her question about Pratt Toomey's relationship to James and Bartell momentarily disarmed Robin.

"Yes, thanks. I'd love some," she said in a suspicious response to Wiley's offer to fix her something to drink, an event she couldn't remember occurring since the night George Bush was elected to the White House. She planned to dump some bourbon in her cider before she drank it. She didn't ask Wiley to spike it for her. He might comply, but he most certainly would disapprove.

She walked from the kitchen down the narrow hall to the bedroom. She reached under her red skirt and yanked down her pantyhose, then sat on the bed and pulled them off. She undid the top button of her blouse and then pressed firmly on her eyelids with her fingertips to ward off an impending headache. Wiley walked in with a mug of cider as she was massaging one of her feet.

Without looking at him, she said, "So it was nothing important? What Pratt was doing for you guys?"

He tensed. His breathing became shallow. After swallowing, he shook his head dismissively at his wife.

"Here's your cider," he said, and walked back out of the room.

Robin went into the walk-in closet and finished undressing. She wrapped herself in a heavy cotton robe before going into the adjoining bathroom. She began running a bath, lowered the lights, and retrieved her cider from the bedroom. She went to the kitchen and added a healthy dollop of Wild Turkey before using the cocktail to swallow a couple of Tylenol.

Wiley was on the phone in the den.

A minute later she dropped her robe, dumped a capful of bath oil in the tub, and lowered herself into the water. She sighed audibly. The hot water seared her skin. Within seconds the bath had melted the iciness from her bones and the whiskey had warmed her gut.

Robin held her eyes closed and cradled the mug on her navel. Bubbles and bath water lapped at the sides of the cup.

Wiley entered the room unannounced.

She jumped. "You scared me, Wiley."

"I didn't like your tone before. What you were implying."

He was huge above her, silhouetted against the dim light.

"What do you mean? The case? I didn't mean anything." She felt like cowering from his glare. There was nowhere to hide.

"You know what I'm talking about." His voice was sharp and bitter.

Robin tried vainly to lower herself beneath the water to hide her nakedness. Her pubic hair and the tips of her breasts were visible through the suds. She looked up and hated him.

"I'll be out in a minute. We can talk about it then. Okay?" She tried to force some pleasantness into a voice that was tinged with fear and loathing.

He towered above her. One of his hands held his mug of cider; the other was clenched in a fist at his side.

Please don't hurt me. "I'm sorry, Wiley. I didn't mean anything. I didn't." *You shit.*

"Like hell you didn't," he replied coldly. Wiley's language stunned her. Slowly, he poured the remainder of the cider from his mug onto her body. She curled away from it, fearing she would be burned.

"The *hell* you didn't."

"I'll be right out, Wiley. We can talk." Her voice cracked. She fought tears. She smelled cider and whiskey in the air.

He didn't move. *What is he going to do to me?*

She cried, "Please, Wiley, I'm scared."

"You should be," he said, and exited the bathroom, quietly closing the door behind him.

Without bothering to finish bathing, Robin jumped out of the tub. By the time she was out of her bathrobe and into jeans and a sweater she was fresh out of tears, her fright had abated, and she was stoked with undiluted rage. She whirled into the den, then the living room, and finally the kitchen in search of her husband.

He wasn't there. He'd left.

She slowly walked through every room of the town house. She fingered his things. Touched the waistband of his clean boxers. Ran her hands through his suits hanging in the closet. She smelled his pillow.

She was trying to discover how she had ever loved him.

"For a *bicycle*?"

Detective Sam Purdy's resonant voice filled every corner of the bicycle shop in downtown Boulder, Colorado. It was the third time he had said, "For a bicycle?" Each time his voice had grown louder. Each time his tone had become more incredulous.

Alan Gregory was taking some sadistic pleasure in watching the young salesclerk try to explain to Sam Purdy why a decent mountain bicycle was going to cost him at least five hundred dollars. Sam insisted on straddling each and every model she talked about as though he could decipher something important by having the thing stationary between his legs. With big pleading brown eyes, the salesclerk kept imploring Alan to help her out. He gazed back at her politely. Alan figured Sam would end up taking his advice and renting a bike, anyway.

Sam Purdy was big, maybe five-eleven, two fifteen. As he climbed on one bicycle after another, Alan Gregory was reminded of bears on unicycles. He smiled to himself. Sam Purdy would be his first endomorphic bicycle buddy.

The two men pulled south out of Boulder late on Wednesday afternoon, Alan's new Ritchey and Sam's rented Rock Hopper both securely mounted on the roof of Alan's Toyota Land Cruiser. Not far out of town the two men grew silent as they passed the entrance to Coal Creek Canyon, the ignominious sight of their last odd partnership. Neither especially wanted to talk about what had gone wrong and what had gone right that night eight months before. They had hashed that out already over far too many beers one night a few months back at the Walnut Brewery. Once was enough for both of them.

South of Golden, just before the entrance to the on-ramp to the freeway that would carry them west through the Rockies, Sam Purdy turned down the fan control on the heater and said, "I got the stuff Lauren faxed to us. It's pretty much as she said last weekend. Utah state cops are baffled. Guy's death looks like an execution. No motive. No witnesses."

"Any of it give you a better idea what we're supposed to be looking for?"

"Nah. I'm sure it's just some of the less sensitive stuff from the file. The cops in Utah wouldn't share much with a couple of attorneys working on a civil case. I imagine they gave them what little they did just to shut them up. No reason to poison the well. But the Utah cops definitely think our guy was in Moab. Lauren got us the name of the motel where he stayed. I changed our reservation; we're going to stay there, too. She wants us to find out whether this Toomey guy was in Moab just to bicycle or whether he was working on something while he was there. If he was working, she wants to know on what and with whom." Purdy lowered his voice from tenor to bass. "That is our mission, should we decide to accept it."

Alan had talked with Lauren almost daily during the week. What Sam was telling him so far wasn't news. He was hoping for something he didn't already know.

"Any clue in the police reports about what this guy might have been doing heading south out of Moab? Especially at night?"

"Nope."

"You familiar with that part of Utah?" asked Alan.

"Southeast?"

"Yeah."

"Sherry and I camped in Canyonlands a couple of times before Simon was born. The three of us did Lake

Powell last summer. God, was it hot. Ever been there? I swear, it was so hot the first couple of days that at first I thought Lake Powell was this beautiful spot where God let the privileged inhabitants of hell live on a lake. So anyway, yeah, I guess I know that area a little."

Alan Gregory was cold. He flicked the heater fan back up to high.

"Where do you think Lauren's investigator was heading?"

Sam was in the process of unfolding a road map. He prodded the ceiling of the car looking for a light switch. "Well, assuming he wasn't going to Canyonlands, which is a fair assumption since the reports indicate he didn't have camping stuff in his car, I think I can narrow down the possibilities to something manageable."

"Go on." Alan switched on a map light from his side of the car.

Sam stabbed at the map and said, "If Lauren is correct that he was traveling south on 191, I think he was either going to Navajo country, to northern Arizona, to southwest Colorado, to New Mexico—like to Sante Fe or Albuquerque—or to someplace absolutely obscure in Utah. Which, unfortunately, is most of it."

Alan smiled through a yawn in the dark car. He wished he had doubled up on caffeine before departing Boulder. "So that's just a few hundred thousand square miles for us to check, huh, Sam?"

Purdy fumbled for the fan control. Alan caught his hand in midstrike. "If you're so hot, why don't you just take off your sweatshirt?"

Sam sighed and yanked and tugged and finally peeled off his sweatshirt in the confines of the front seat. Underneath, he wore a long-sleeved T-shirt with a caricature of Ross Perot on it. He leaned forward and fumbled for the lever that would recline his seat into some configuration that he hoped would permit him a nap on their six-hour drive across the mountains. He pulled his Colorado Rockies baseball cap low over his eyes, unwrapped a Rolo and slid it into his mouth.

"To answer your sarcastic little query—give or take a million square miles, yeah. But we pros do it all the time, hotshot. Don't worry; most of it's fucking desert, easy to eliminate. Trust me."

Alan was quiet for a while. He popped a tape of *The Phantom of the Opera* into the deck and tried to settle into a highway rhythm. He couldn't.

"Sam," he said, somewhere just east of Idaho Springs, "why'd you agree to do this? Go to Moab and take a busman's holiday?"

At first Sam didn't stir; and Alan thought he had fallen asleep.

Sam said, "Remember a ways back—what was that, shit, one year, two?—we had that cult trouble up in Four Mile Canyon? It was right about the same time as that bullshit in Waco, Texas. You know; the Branch Davidians? I coordinated for the department with a couple of sociologists from CU when it looked like we might have us a confrontation with the Four Mile group. Anyway, Lauren remembered what I did then, and she called me a week or so ago and asked me would I check out some stuff she was hearing about the Mormons."

"As a *cult*?"

"Sure. It's not quite as far-fetched as you might think. The definition of a cult is pretty elastic. The difference between a cult and a church tends to be pretty much in the eye of the beholder."

Alan downshifted in search of some more power. "So, then, what's a cult?"

Sam sighed. "You want a lecture? Okay. The Mormons, like all of America's home-brewed religions—the Christian Scientists, the Seventh-day Adventists, the Scientologists—definitely started off as a cult. Basically, cults start off as small fringe groups united behind some obscure biblical truth. For the Mormons it was something called restoration. There's almost always a charismatic leader in these groups who separates his flock from the mainstream with a clear us-versus-them message. For the Mormons it was Joseph Smith. And there is usually a degree of control by the leader and obedience by the membership that most of us would find oppressive."

Alan didn't get the relevance. "But, Sam, Mormons

seem so mainstream. There are Mormons all over Boulder and Denver."

Sam said, "Do you know any? Like, socially?"

"No."

"Do you treat any in your practice?"

"No."

"Do you know anybody who hangs out with any Mormons?"

"No."

"So how mainstream are they?" Sam didn't wait for an answer. "See, the Mormons are unique among these religious movements in that they have succeeded at becoming integrated into society without ever becoming part of it. But like most of the splinter groups that everybody *would* call a cult, the Mormons practice isolation and exclusion socially, economically, and, of course, spiritually. The segregation is apparently much more pronounced in Utah than in other places.

"So what did I learn for Lauren? Nothing earthshaking. The Mormons don't like to publicize it, but they're the fastest-growing Christian church in the United States—six-percent growth a year, which is phenomenal. They are among the richest religions in the world, and they are among the largest private landholders in this great country of ours. The Mormon Church reportedly controls over a hundred major corporations, and the total income from all its sources—business income and member tithing—would place it solidly in the top quarter of the Fortune 500. Estimates of the Church's wealth go as high as eight billion dollars."

"That sounds pretty mainstream to me, Sam."

"I think that's the point. It's a huge, wealthy, influential church, yet one that manages to stay largely invisible outside of Utah and Idaho. The Mormon Church owns big-city newspapers and TV and radio stations all across the country—not Jerry Falwell cable crap, but network affiliates. Plus they make their own movies and TV shows and link Salt Lake with the world through an incredible private satellite network."

Alan remained skeptical. "So what? They're successful. But how does it add up? Are they dangerous?

Lauren is concerned the Church may be behind this guy's murder. Isn't that the question?"

"Dangerous? At face value, the Church is conservative in all senses of the word. Shit, it's the IBM of churches. To the public, the Mormons are pudgy men in gray business suits, women who are good housewives, and polite, well-behaved children. They keep their more colorful rituals secret in their temples. They keep their, shall we say, unusual doctrine to themselves. They live with a fraction of the vices of the rest of us. Unless we threaten them with drugs or abortion or pornography, they mind their own business and do more than pay lip service to family values.

"On the surface they seem to play by the rules. Politically, Utah is like a right-wing theme park. Mormons control ninety percent of the Utah legislature. The new governor just told the populace in his inaugural address that he will seek divine guidance on important issues. And I promise you he isn't talking about praying to some generic God. Legislative leaders routinely consult the Church hierarchy.

"You know how nuts everybody got because a hundred Branch Davidians were so ready to do whatever David Koresh told them to do in Waco? And how crazy everybody is in Montana because there are five thousand armed cultists living in bunkers? Well, there are almost a million and a half Mormons in Utah alone. And a healthy third of them are absolutely obedient to the Church's authority. If the Church leadership wants two hundred thousand Mormons in the streets of Utah with snow shovels, they apparently can mobilize them in thirty minutes in the middle of the night." He snapped his fingers. "Like that, I swear. They say so themselves. That's what kind of authority they maintain they have."

"Snow shovels are one thing, Sam, automatic rifles something else. To return to Lauren's question—is the Mormon Church dangerous?"

Sam seemed to be losing energy for continuing his lecture. "Who the hell knows? On the surface it sure as hell doesn't seem to be. The point, I think, is that a lot of Mormons are blindly obedient to their leader. And when that's the case, then all you need is one crazy leader to turn obedient into dangerous."

"You got something against the Mormons, Sam?"

"Personally? Nah. Well, maybe the Osmonds. I haven't actually forgiven them for that."

Alan laughed. "Be serious. You're asking me to believe that you agreed to contaminate our little biking vacation because you think Lauren is right to be worried about the Mormon Church murdering people?"

"No. I agreed because when I heard what she wanted, I knew you'd go along with it whether I did or not. And so far you've demonstrated an uncanny ability to get yourself into terribly deep shit, and you don't exactly have an illustrious record of getting yourself out of deep shit without significant assistance."

Alan chewed on that. "How'd you know I'd agree?"

"Because your girlfriend's a good lady. Because you love her. And because your sense of self-preservation is for shit. Gimme a break. This feels like teaching. I hate teaching. Good night, Doctor."

A while later, climbing the steep grade out of Georgetown toward the Eisenhower-Johnson Tunnel, Alan listened to the deep, regular breathing coming from the other side of the car and said quietly into the silence, "Thanks, Sam."

A moment later, Alan jumped when Sam said, "Don't mention it. But do you mind turning that crap down? I can't believe I'm going to have to listen to show tunes all the way to Utah. It's like going on a trip with my mother and her friggin' bridge friends."

Purdy hummed a few bars from *Oklahoma!,* pulled his Rockies cap farther down over his eyes, and was quiet.

Moabites have never owned Moab for long.

That night, even in the post-ten-o'clock-news darkness, when blue-collar towns like Moab should already be sound asleep, it was apparent to Sam and Alan that the moral title to Moab's stony splendor had officially been signed over to a new group of outsiders. And it didn't require an out-of-town detective to know that the latest owners were fat-tire freaks.

Like so many obscure Utah outposts, Moab was founded by Mormon pioneers in the first score of years after Brigham Young led the faithful from Nauvoo, Illinois, to the Great Basin. Young sent the new settlers out into the deserts and mountains of Ute country to set up missionary stakes that he felt would provide anchors for the long lines of the great spiritual tent of the Mormon state of Deseret.

A hundred years later, by the middle of the twentieth century, the forces of change that flooded the Mormon community of Moab were forces, appropriately enough, carved from Utah rock. In the 1950s, the nation's richest deposit of high-quality uranium was discovered outside of Moab. Almost instantly an army of pickup trucks pulling trailers invaded the pristine landscape, and uranium miners took over the little town and began to cut into the local terrain like crazed surgeons.

Thirty years later, in the early eighties, as the mining boom was suffering its final death throes, it just so happened that bicycle tires were growing fatter, bicyclists were leaving highways in search of off-road trails, and two-wheel enthusiasts were discovering the joys of another rock that Moab happened to have in abundance: red sandstone.

Not only because of Slickrock, a legendary route south of town, but also because of a thousand miles of more obscure sandstone trails nearby, Moab became known as the place that offered the best mountain-biking experience on the entire planet. Moab, Utah, a place where nobody wanted to be in 1980, became a place where over a million people would visit annually.

When the fat-tire craze began, almost a quarter of the homes in Moab were empty and a decent house could be had for under twenty thousand dollars. Now there were no vacancies in town, and when a house became available, most residents couldn't afford to buy. Moab, originally a Mormon enclave, once defiled by miners, boasted its own brewpub, and residents and tourists could pull their thousand-dollar bikes up to espresso stands all over town.

Joseph Smith's Word of Wisdom was, once again, certainly not the local gospel. Moab was a living, working monument to everything that Brigham Young preached would happen when the gentiles finally crossed over the Sierra Nevada and the Rockies and invaded their state.

Sam Purdy had been awake since Grand Junction, staring off into the brush and at the distant buttes, transfixed by the silhouetted mountains. He started shaking his head in dismay an hour later as Alan drove through the outskirts of Moab, the rusty detritus of booms past fouling the desert landscape.

The consequences of the current boom stared him smack in the face. A sign painted in huge letters on the asphalt highway implored visitors to use toilets. A block into town, Sam broke his silence.

"Bicyclists need to be reminded to use toilets?"

"Moab has been invaded lately, Sam. And, unfortunately, not only by considerate people."

"Using toilets isn't a question of considerate. Using

toilets is just, well, normal. I know lots of inconsiderate people who make it a habit to use toilets regularly."

Purdy looked out the window as Moab presented its face. The face was one of transiency, of catering to outsiders. "You know a town is lost when the folks who've lived there forever start calling themselves locals. I bet that's the case here. I bet the ones who are left call themselves locals."

Alan nodded in the dark. Examining the foot traffic on Moab's sidewalks, he was having trouble comprehending the reality that people would actually still be wearing Lycra at eleven o'clock at night.

"The cultural pollution is worse every time I come, Sam. I swear."

Bikes were chained to any horizontal or vertical fixture capable of securing them. Every other business seemed to be a bike shop. No single structure appeared to be more than a bad windstorm and a couple of coats of paint away from being classified as seedy.

"There's a reason why we're here, right? I mean, like a fun reason?"

"You gotta see it to believe it, Sam. The trails. Wait until tomorrow."

Purdy harrumphed.

Their motel loomed to the left. The new landscaping and the recently added shingled facade hadn't succeeded in hiding the lineage of the L-shaped building. This lodge had been built for the rough-and-tumble uranium boom, not the genteel fat-tire one.

Purdy stretched as he climbed out of the car. "I hope the beds in this place aren't as old I think they might be. I hate motel beds. Always feel like there's a crater in the center of 'em trying to suck you in. I have sinkhole dreams."

Alan returned after checking them into the motel and handed Purdy his key. "See you in the morning, Sam. Since I know how long it takes you to eat breakfast, why don't we plan on starting around eight?"

Purdy looked at his key. "We've got separate rooms?"

"Separate but equal. My idea. This way, I don't have to discover if you snore. It'll be better for our relationship to maintain a little mystery."

Purdy glared at him and then tripped over a bicycle clamped to a signpost that said "No Bikes in This Area." He cursed and said, "I'm going to bed."

"I'll lock the bikes inside the car. Then I think I'll take a walk. Good night, Sam."

"Good night, Doctor."

The first thing Sam Purdy said as he slid into the booth at Honest Ozzie's the next morning was "God, I'm glad I'm not a cop here. Nothing but entitled, rich tourists and poor, pissed-off locals."

"And good morning to you, Sam." Alan glanced at his watch. Eight-twenty. He smiled across the table. "Oversleep?"

Purdy glared at him through tired eyes. "I don't need you. I need some coffee."

The waitress came over. Purdy managed a smile for her. She was so thin her face seemed to have been carved on insufficient stock. Her approach to service was to appear distracted and annoyed, giving her a general air of reluctance that left the impression that she had been chosen for this job the way people are drafted for jury duty.

"What's good?" Purdy asked.

"My day off. The sunsets. That's about it."

Purdy extended his smile, showing some teeth. "Pretty stimulating job, huh?"

"You want coffee?" She elevated the pot she had in her right hand. Purdy and Gregory both nodded. She splashed some into both their cups, turning the saucers into little amber tide pools.

Purdy eagerly took a single long gulp and then poured the pond from his saucer into the cup. He checked out an argument the cashier was having with a customer across the room, then began talking. "He was here, all right. Our guy—Lauren's guy—Pratt Toomey. Stayed two nights. Room next door to mine, as a matter of fact. Acted like a biker. Rode during the day. Kept to himself. No sign of anybody else using his room. Maid said he was a neat freak. Asked for late checkout the day he left. Manager said no but agreed to keep his stuff in the office and let him use a shower so he could ride that day before he headed out. Couple of small bags, that's it. Left the motel just about dusk, maybe a little before."

"You've been busy."

"Well, a job's a job. I just showed his picture round. Everybody remembered him, knew he'd been murdered. Not too tough."

"Think he was just vacationing?"

"He was definitely here to ride. Don't know whether he was doing anything else, though. It's a small town. I'll find out." Purdy heard the awkward note of autonomy in his pronouncement. He said, " 'Scuse me, Watson. *We'll* find out."

They rode an easy trail that morning so Sam could take some lessons from Alan on the finer points of mountain biking. Alan was amazed at the ease with which Sam got the hang of shifting his ample weight fore and aft on the bicycle, and at the innate comfort he displayed at keeping his speed under control on the rougher and steeper terrain.

Purdy wore blue jeans, running shoes, and a neon-green helmet that left him looking like a tourist. Alan was in black-and-yellow Lycra and wore an expensive Gore-Tex jacket. His helmet sat on his head as naturally as a shell sits on a turtle. Sometimes other bicyclists stopped and watched them, apparently just for the entertainment value.

"This is great," said Purdy at the top of a particularly sharp stone incline that he'd scampered up as if he were riding a mountain goat.

In sincere admiration, Alan said, "You pick this up real quick, Sam."

Purdy examined Alan's face for evidence of sarcasm, didn't find any, and said, "I'm just a pretty athletic guy, I guess."

"Well, that may be true, but you don't see too many guys your size on mountain bikes. At least, not on trails like these."

"You mean fat guys?"

"No—well, yeah. I guess I mean big guys."

"Fat."

"Whatever, Sam. You're not fat."

Purdy patted his belly. "I like to think I'm shaped like Bill Clinton between diets." He looked at Alan. "You're more like Ross Perot after a month on the rack."

Alan laughed.

Sam said, "When we gonna eat?"

On the way back into town, the burden of Sam Purdy's extra pounds precipitated the failure of the quick-release that was supposed to secure the post of his bicycle seat to the frame. They stopped on the outskirts of town and Alan played with the faulty compression mechanism for about fifteen seconds. Diagnosis completed, he said, "Metal fatigue. We need to find a bike shop."

Sam gazed around at the town and then looked at Alan sardonically. "Gosh. That should be pretty hard around here. Like finding a drink in Vegas."

Alan made a face, straddled his bike, and pulled off ahead of Purdy, leading him to a shop called Rim Cyclery. They locked their bikes together, and Alan yanked Purdy's seat post from his bike frame and removed the quick-release.

"Sam, why don't you try to find some gloves while I'm taking care of this?" Alan suggested before weaving through the narrow aisles to the back of the store. The shop was crowded with bikes, mostly the mountain variety suitable to Moab's wonders. Alan's destination was the service department, to find a replacement for the stripped part.

Purdy, who after three exhilarating hours was getting into the sport of mountain biking with the fervor of a convert, waltzed over to check out a couple of bikes that were adorned with big red sale tags. Within seconds he had a salesperson on his tail.

The guy in the service department glanced over and saw the broken part in Alan's hands, made a quick calculation, and proceeded to ignore Alan while he continued to push a Campagnola crank on the other person at the counter. She was an attractive woman with ruby pinky rings on each hand and a gold Rolex on her wrist. As Alan eavesdropped on their conversation and watched what happened to the curves of the woman's chest as she propped her elbows on the counter, he thought he knew why Lycra had been invented. She tossed her long brown hair and mounted a wonderfully flirtatious smile while explaining to the service guy, "That's not what they told me in Santa Fe last week."

Five prurient minutes later, Alan tracked Purdy to a wall covered with at least a dozen different styles of bicycle gloves and was greeted with "Can you believe this? Forty-two bucks and these things don't even come with any fucking fingers?"

Alan raised a little plastic bag in his left hand and said, "I got the new quick-release. We're set." He looked at the two pairs of gloves in Purdy's hands. "Get the red ones, Sam. They go better with your hair."

Purdy poked the pair of blue gloves back on their spindle and called to Alan. "Hey, take a look at this bike over here. Whattya think, pretty good deal or what?"

Alan looked at the silver Cannondale, one of their lower-end models, and immediately recognized that the frame was at least five centimeters too small for Purdy. He tugged the big cop by his sweatshirt over toward the cash register and said he'd explain over lunch why it wasn't the right bike for him. The brunette with the pinky rings was in front of them, paying for her Italian crank.

One glance at her Lycra and Purdy forgot all about the Cannondale.

"Pratt was heading for Colorado when he left this yuppie amusement park." Purdy had a grin as wide as a mesa as he offered his pronouncement through a mouth full of bacon cheeseburger.

Alan pulled his sandwich away from his lips and gawked at his friend. "Now, how the hell do you know that?"

Purdy took another bite before he spoke. "I'm a cop. You're a shrink. I think that about covers it.

Alan muttered, "Jesus."

Purdy enjoyed a long drink from a bottle of three-two beer. "I showed his picture around the shop while you were playing bike mechanic. Everybody knew about him. He'd been in. He bought a new helmet. They had a sale that just ended. Gloves were on sale, too. I'm sorry I missed it. Could have saved ten bucks."

Alan figured he was supposed to wait patiently for Purdy to get to the good part. But Purdy was seriously involved with his lunch, and Alan couldn't generate sufficient restraint.

"And? What? People who buy new helmets in Moab are, as a general rule, heading for Colorado?"

Purdy laughed and said, "You know, I've forgotten how much fun it is to pimp you. What happened, ass-bite, was that Pratt asked the clerk who was helping him how the road south was at night. He was apparently trying to decide whether he should stop riding early enough to make the drive in the daytime or not. Clerk told him the road was fine, he should ride."

"And he was going where?"

"He said he was going to catch 46."

No map image that included a road numbered 46 filtered into Alan's consciousness. "Which goes where?"

"Eventually it goes up to Telluride."

"To Telluride? Really?"

Purdy nodded. "But the clerk's actually pretty sure he said 'near Telluride,' not 'to Telluride.' "

"Did Pratt happen to tell this guy why he was going to Colorado?"

Purdy shook his head. "Oh, my sexist friend," he said. Alan noted that Purdy's hair was still compressed from the pressure of his bicycle helmet. He had an image of Friar Tuck. "The clerk was not a guy, and no, she just remembered that he said 'near Telluride.' But she did say that there's some pretty good riding up there, too. Since I've come all the way to Moab, I want to do this Slickrock thing, and then I'm ready to go see for myself what Colorado's own San Juan Mountains have to offer. What about you?"

Alan took a moment to compose an answer. Finally, he said, "Sam, it's great what you've found out so far. Really, it is. I'm impressed. But to be honest, it leaves me feeling pretty useless. A bit like your personal trainer."

Purdy snickered. He was loving this vacation so far.

"There's more, too."

Alan slouched back onto his chair and waited.

"She said the cops never asked her any questions. And she didn't think what she knew was important. I'm the first snoop she's told."

Now, this was surprising. Lauren would be thrilled. "So they might not know about this?"

"Let me put it this way. You shouldn't underestimate cops. Criminals do it all the time. And it almost always costs them. But, then again, you shouldn't overestimate cops. The public does it all the time. And it almost always costs them."

"So we don't know what they know?"

"At this point, all we know is what we know. As far as what *they* know, we don't know. And please try to keep in mind that most of the time, I'm one of the 'they.' "

Lauren walked in the door to her sister's house, headed down the hallway, and noticed the message light blinking on the answering machine.

She had left John Harley at the Side Pocket. Leaving hadn't been easy. Harley had wanted to play a round of darts and then was planning to go to Bill & Nada's for something to eat before going back to his apartment. He had asked her to join him. She had declined, unsure whether the offer included only the meal or also the final destination.

One of the calls on the machine was from Teresa, who reported that Vegas was going great and wanted to know whether there was anything new on Pratt's murder. Lauren suspected that she really wanted a pep talk about continuing the lawsuit. At least, she told herself, Teresa is checking in. Another call was from Robin Torr, who sounded vacant and defeated and unsure as to why she had called. The first call on the tape had been from Alan Gregory in Moab, who said that he loved her and reported that he and Sam were on their way to Colorado to follow up on something.

Colorado?

Alan said he would call again the next day.

Sleep came easily until the phone started ringing. The metallic trill from her sister's bedroom seemed far away. Lauren awoke disoriented. Her heart rate accelerated in an instant. It took her three rings to identify the foreign sound as emanating from a telephone. Wearing only a long T-shirt, she ran to Teresa's bedroom and grabbed the phone. The house was cold, and her lean thighs were soon dotted with gooseflesh.

"Hello," she said, her voice full of sleep and barely caged alarm.

"I woke you. I'm sorry." Robin Torr's speech was clipped and pressured, but also hopeful, energized. The hopefulness calmed Lauren's galloping heart. "I need you to tell me I'm not crazy about something. Can you come downtown? To my office?"

Lauren gazed at the digital clock by her sister's bed. It read 12:42. "Now?"

"Yes."

Lauren ran a hand through her hair and said, "All right. Be there as soon as I can."

She rummaged for underwear, jeans, and a sweater. After running her tongue over her teeth, she decided to brush them, then she combed her hair. She grabbed Teresa's coat, which was heavier than her own, found a pair of gloves in the pockets, pulled them on, and plodded out the door.

Because Brigham Young had dictated that downtown Salt Lake City be laid out on a grid of streets that were wide enough for a wagon pulled by a team of horses to turn around, the feel of the city's downtown was spacious. But the width of the six-lane downtown streets also robbed Salt Lake of much of its intimacy and urbanity, leaving it feeling impersonal and vaguely suburban, even during the hectic rush of a business day. By one o'clock on a weekday morning the center of Salt Lake City was absolutely barren, the boulevard-wide roads like asphalt moats between the sidewalks.

Lauren spotted only one other car moving in the city's core as she made her way downtown past Brigham Young's house of many wives and past the renovated splendor of what was once the Hotel Utah. She parked Teresa's Rabbit by the curb in front of the new stone-and-glass tower where Lewis, Frank and Zelem had its offices. She was relieved and grateful to see Robin standing in the lighted lobby of the building. A security guard hovered in the background, just beyond the bank of elevators.

Robin pushed open the door. The gray granite entry seemed forbidding in the harshness of the security lights.

"Thanks for coming," Robin said, holding the door. She moved in to hug Lauren.

"Sure," Lauren said, perplexed by the physical intimacy and surprised by how much she welcomed the contact. The embrace temporarily stilled the fight that exhaustion and adrenaline were waging for control of her mood.

The guard held open the elevator door with a key and smiled pleasantly at the women as they entered. Lauren couldn't quite manage a smile in return but did say "Hi." Robin just nodded to him and punched the number eight on the brass panel of buttons. The elevator ascended smoothly. No one spoke until the doors glided open.

Robin had left the glass entrance door to the law firm unlocked. After she and Lauren entered, she carefully locked the doors behind them. Robin hurried down the hall to the largest of the conference rooms in the suite. Lauren followed on her heels, her friend's intensity contagious. The overhead lights in the room were blazing, and the one end of the big cherry table was carpeted with files, photocopies, and legal pads. An opened box of Vanilla Wafers and a can of root beer sat next to the chair where Robin had been sitting.

"Sit here." Robin pointed Lauren to the chair on the other side of the cookies. As Lauren sat, Robin reached over and stuck her hand deep into the box. "Want some?" she asked.

"No. Thanks."

Robin gestured toward a thin file in front of Lauren. With a Vanilla Wafer between her teeth, she said, "I think I've figured something out. Indulge me for a few minutes and follow my logic. But do it blind, okay? I don't want to contaminate your thinking with my theory yet. These are press reports and clippings that I've had Elsie collect from around the country on the murder of Blythe Oaks. Read. Please."

As she immersed herself in the impersonal words,

Lauren momentarily forgot that the victim of the brutal murder she was reading about was responsible for sexually harassing her sister. As long as she could forget that, she could read comfortably, like a prosecutor, the gruesome territory presented by these stories strangely familiar.

Blythe Oaks had been approached from behind while sitting cross-legged in a forested area along the banks of the Potomac in Virginia. She had a pair of binoculars around her neck. Her throat had been slit in a single motion by a right-handed person wielding a sharp knife. There were no signs of a struggle. No robbery. No sexual assault.

No witnesses.

Lauren turned the pages. She liked what she was feeling. She was feeling like a DA again.

When she indicated to Robin that she was done with the file of clippings, Robin shoved it aside and replaced it with a pile of reports about Pratt Toomey's death. "Now these. I know you've seen them once, but read them now in the context of what you've just read about Blythe's murder."

"You think you found something to tie them together?"

"I guess that's obvious. But why don't you read them first; then I'll tell you what I'm thinking."

Lauren shuffled one more time through the reports of Pratt's murder. She thought she saw the connection. She picked through the newspaper clippings from Virginia and D.C. and slid one across the table toward Robin. "The Virginia homicide people found a paw print in the blood by her body, right? That's what this one says."

Robin grinned. "You can't really tell much from the picture. But the caption below the photograph says that, yeah, it's a picture of somebody making castings of a shoe print and an animal print."

"So you're thinking maybe a dog?"

"Right. I called the detective on Pratt's murder at home about it tonight. It pissed him off. He said he knows about it. It was a dog print. The Virginia cops wrote if off as belonging to a stray. Or as a dog somebody was running in the woods."

"And the crime scene techs found paw prints all over the rock ridge where Pratt was shot?"

"It had rained the afternoon Pratt died. Some of the prints were well preserved in the mud, apparently. But the detective I talked to said the prints they lifted weren't of the same feet as the Virginia paw prints. Left front versus right rear, or something like that."

"You think this guy travels with his dog? And it was the same guy?"

"I know it doesn't *prove* it, exactly. But it is provocative, don't you think?"

"A wild dog could have come by after he died, Robin. Or maybe a coyote."

Robin leaned back and dropped her shoulders. "Could have been Rin Tin Tin, too." Her face reflected her frustration. "Why are you trying to blow me out of the water on this? I think I've got something here."

Lauren sighed. "Habit, I guess. I've spent too many hours in unpleasant meetings with cops who've brought me bags of evidence I can't use. Prosecutors get pretty cynical."

Robin smiled coyly and touched the top of Lauren's hand. "Was that an apology?" she asked.

"Sure," Lauren countered with a smile of her own, "if you'll apologize about waking me up in the middle of the night. So—to state the obvious—you think it might have been the same dog at both murders?"

"Who knows? It's something. At the very least, I think it's worth checking out."

"How? Has the FBI linked these crimes at all? The Utah cops must at least have considered the connection before they rejected it."

"I'm sure somebody considered it. Maybe they're still considering it. Maybe somebody's done it. But, in truth, why would anybody link the murders? Different states. Different MOs. Different weapons. Only thing that links them is Teresa. And, if I'm not crazy, maybe a dog. Oh, and the knife. Shit, I can't believe I almost forgot about the knife."

"What knife? Pratt was shot."

"Yeah, but somebody slashed him, apparently, either

before or after they shot him. Didn't cut him, but left a long gash in his jacket."

"Boy, if they could match the knives, that'd be a gold-plated link, wouldn't it?"

Robin shook her head. "I'm sure somebody thought of that. All you and I have is press clippings. They have better information than we do. *They* know why they wanted a sample of Teresa's handwriting. We haven't even figured out that little detail yet. And despite what they've got, it looks like they must have drawn a blank. There's just not enough. Nothing but the dog."

"Okay. What if I buy what you're selling? What if it was the same dog?"

"That's the question. If it was the same dog, then it was the same murderer. And if it was the same murderer, then maybe we have a conspiracy. And we have somebody who sincerely doesn't want us to look into this case any further."

"So how do we find out if it's the same dog?"

"You're the part of this team with criminal experience. Where do we find a dog-print expert? Can they match dog prints? I mean, like they do fingerprints? I'm a cat person; I couldn't even tell if it's the same stupid paw."

"Who the hell knows? There's got to be somebody who does." Lauren thought of Sam Purdy. "I have a friend in Boulder who will probably know someone we can talk to." Lauren endured a stab of guilt at not having told Robin about Purdy and Alan's trip to Moab. She quickly decided that now wasn't the time.

Robin reached into the cookie box and laid a Vanilla Wafer on her tongue as though it were a communion host.

Lauren examined her while considering the merits of the new theory. "We're all in more than a little danger here, you know. Teresa especially."

"Yes. I know."

"Should we stop? Maybe just go for a settlement?"

Robin scoffed. "Don't kid yourself. They're not going to settle this now. Our choices are to proceed at full steam or to give up."

"We must be on to something, Robin. You know that.

They have to fear we can prove these charges Teresa is making. Or why else would they kill Blythe? Why would they kill Pratt?"

Torr's hair was stringy, oily, tired. She tried to hang it behind her ears. "Who are we talking about here, Lauren? Who are 'they'?"

"Who has the most to lose?"

"The Women's Symposium. Lester Horner. Paul Oaks."

"The Church?"

Robin Torr exhaled through pursed lips. "I've told you before. This"—she waved her hand at the clippings spread on the table—"this isn't Church style. If the authorities wanted this lawsuit to stop, they would pressure us in other ways. If that failed, they would just get somebody to write Teresa a check."

Still, Lauren could feel fear emanating from Robin. Jokingly she said, "Maybe it's all coincidence."

When Robin raised her eyebrows and rolled her eyes, Lauren turned away, laughing. Finally she looked askance, back at Robin.

"Robin," she wondered, "what the hell are you doing here in the middle of the night?"

Robin wiped the silly look from her face.

"I'll tell you if you tell me where you were at ten forty-five when I called you the first time."

The thought that raced through Lauren's head in response to Robin's question startled her. Her heart downshifted and roared in her chest.

The words that never made it to her lips were *I was with my father.*

"He's somebody I met one night when I was playing pool. I do it to relax. Shoot pool."

"And? What? You're still seeing him, then."

"What do you mean, seeing him? We're not having an affair, if that's what you're wondering. He's married. Well, separated, and—"

"And you're planning to be married, I might add."

Robin jerked her head to one side. "Did you hear something in the hall?"

"Are you kidding?"

"No, I'm not kidding. Listen." The women sat as still as they could, slowing their breathing.

Nothing.

Lauren continued. "I know it sounds funny, but I'm kind of captivated by this guy. I don't exactly understand it myself."

I was with my father.

"And you know what else is odd? He's Mormon. He gives me Mormon lessons. Answers all my questions."

"Are you attracted to him?"

"I guess I am. But it's not really physical. He's okay-looking, but I don't think he's gorgeous or anything. It's more magnetic than that. I think I'm drawn to him. Alan, the guy in Colorado, is a pretty predictable man. He's very kind to me. But he's . . . he's not exciting. Though he is pretty cute."

Robin Torr considered her last image of her imposing husband, Wiley. "Exciting can be kind of overrated."

Lauren skated right over the poignancy in Robin's pronouncement. "Harley—that the guy's name, John Harley—I think he reminds me of my father."

There, I said it.

"Is that good? Or bad? Your sister doesn't sound too fond of your dad."

"I don't know. It's both good and bad, I suppose. My father, when he's not drinking, is a good man. The finest man I've ever known. I know that sounds very older-daughterish. But it's true." She paused, then grabbed the cookie box. "But when he drinks, God, life goes on edge. Then, every simple act of living is the equivalent of juggling a hand grenade with the pin pulled."

"So this Harley, he drinks, too?"

"He's sober now, for a few months."

Just like your dad.

Just like my dad.

"And you're intrigued enough to want to be around when he hits a steep bump and tumbles off the wagon?"

Lauren shivered and popped another round wafer into

her mouth. "I can't imagine that I want that. Why would I want that, Robin?"

Robin was surprised when her eyes filled with tears.

"Think I know?" She blinked twice to clear her vision. "Wiley, my husband, scared me to death earlier tonight. I was in the bathtub, naked. I thought he was going to kill me. I think he's angry about this case. I hate to admit it, even to myself, but after it was over, after he'd left me alone and I knew I was going to be okay, I was . . . exhilarated. I mean, really pumped up. I'm here at the office tonight because I'm afraid to be at home with him. And I'm here, too, because I'm afraid of what I'll do to him if I see him while I'm this mad. Maybe it's like that for you. With this Harley guy."

"Maybe," Lauren replied, her voice nearly a whisper. What was it that Harley had said to her? *My experience tells me that you know about drunks. And I think you know about good men. Don't you?*

I do, she thought. *I do, indeed.*

"You're content, aren't you, Sam? You like what you do? Your life?"

Alan Gregory posed the question to Purdy just minutes outside of Moab. Alan was driving the hulking gray Land Cruiser south on a lonely stretch of Utah State Highway 191. Purdy sat atypically vigilant on the passenger seat, his eyes peeled for the cutoff to Highway 46, which, if all went according to plan, would return them to Colorado within the hour.

"Huh?" is what he said in response to Alan's question.

"The way you are, I don't see it very often. I think it's the contentedness. The people I see in therapy are almost always . . . not just unhappy, but . . . I don't know. No matter what they come to see me for, it turns out they're unhappy with their job, or their husband, or their friends. Or all of the above. But there's always something. So they end up spending most of their time doing what they don't want to do, working at a job that they hate, screwing somebody they don't really want to be with, generally doing shit they'd rather not be doing.

"I guess what I'm saying is that you don't seem that way. The whole time I've been with you on this trip, I've been perplexed by something about you. And I think that's what it is. You're happy. You like being a cop. You like your wife. You like being with me, learning to ride, helping Lauren out. Everything."

Purdy begrudgingly returned his attention to Alan. He noted the darkness settling inside the car, the dashboard lights beginning to glow. Outside, the pink dusk was in the glory of metamorphosis. He was reluctant to leave it.

"You sound like a goddamn shrink," he muttered, then laughed from deep in his belly. "I do have to admit it's marvelous, though, isn't it?"

"What?" asked Alan, assuming Purdy was again transfixed by the sunset.

"My life. It's marvelous. I like it almost all the time."

Alan glanced over and smiled. "So how do you do it? What's your secret?"

"Is the caller there?" Purdy belted out unexpectedly with an annoying nasal twang. "God, why do I get the feeling you're gonna make me believe I've been magically transported to Donahue or Oprah." He searched his pocket for a stick of gum, unwrapped it, and plopped it onto his tongue. "Want some?"

Alan declined.

Purdy leaned over and checked the odometer. He tried to visualize geographic landmarks in the darkness outside the car. Suddenly his voice filled with pressure and got lower. "Slow down, Alan," he said.

Alan glanced in his mirrors and gently tapped his foot on the brakes.

"This is it. Right about here. Pratt Toomey was killed right about here, right about now, this time of day." Purdy pressed high on his cheekbones with one hand, the web of skin between his thumb and his finger stretched taut across his nose. He pulled down hard toward his chin against the grain of a day's worth of sandstone-colored stubble.

Alan exhaled deeply. He drew the car to a gradual stop on the shoulder.

"You're sure?"

"Pretty sure. Mileage is right. Time of day is right. See that rock face up there?" He pointed to the south. "Remember the pictures we got from Lauren? I bet you that's where he died. Up on top of there."

"Want to look around?"

"Nah. Won't find anything. Especially in the dark. Just want to be here for a minute. Sometimes it helps." He opened the window. Felt the chill in the air, the familiar mountain dryness. Breathed in deeply. Opened the door.

Got out. He walked carefully on the gravel, sand, and dust. He took church steps. Spiritual steps.

"What a gorgeous place this was to die, Alan. Look at the light. I bet something holy happened here once. Who knows, maybe twice."

Alan shut off the engine, walked around the car, and joined his friend in staring at the rock bluff silhouetted against the last light.

"Does that make a difference, Sam? How pretty it is where you die?"

"Everything makes a difference, Alan. The time you die. Where you die. That's the point. Everything makes a difference."

Ten minutes later, Alan turned the big Toyota onto Highway 46, the orange-and-pink glow of the western sky behind them, the black-purple mass of the San Juan Mountains dead ahead.

High in the La Sal National Forest, Utah Highway 46 becomes Colorado Highway 90. The exact point of transition from Utah territory to Colorado territory is not at all clear topographically. The geography doesn't pause with a river or a mountain range to acknowledge the political boundary.

"The more I learn about Utah, the more I feel like I should need to show my passport to get back into Colorado," Alan offered quietly, unsure whether Purdy was asleep in the dark car.

From under the bill of his cap, Purdy said, "I sure as hell don't know what that's supposed to mean."

"Utah. It's like a foreign country, Sam. I guess because of the Mormons and all the morality laws. Lauren and I drove into Canada a couple of months ago, when I was visiting her in New York. Had to go through immigration and customs. On the other side of the border, the Canadian side, it was almost exactly the same as the U.S. side. Here, between Colorado and Utah, the border is wide open, yet the culture couldn't be more different. Did you see any minorities in Moab? Even one?"

Sam scoffed. "How different is that from Boulder? I

mean, really, Alan. What have we got in Boulder, like eleven Asians, six Hispanics, and two blacks?"

"Sam, it's not that bad."

"You know what I mean. Boulder isn't exactly the great melting pot."

"I suppose you're right. I guess that's not it. But there is something foreign about Utah. You know what I'm talking about."

Purdy pulled his hat down lower on his forehead and slumped farther down onto the seat. "It's not that complicated. It's God. It's all about God."

"What do you think, Sam? About God? About the Mormons?"

"I think this whole damn country is God's country. The whole damn world, even. The Mormons are just one of those religions that like to feel particularly precious about it. That's what I think. Enough said. Wake me up if you want me to drive. Does this seat tilt back any farther?"

"Yeah, you got it back farther last night. The latch is on the side, by the door," Alan replied. "Are you religious, Sam? Were you brought up religious?"

Purdy fumbled with the lever on the side of the seat. "Oh, there, I got it. Good. Was I brought up religious? Nah. I was raised Catholic. Buenas noches."

Alan smiled, but he suspected there was more to Sam's preoccupation with cults. "There's something else, isn't there?"

"What? Let me sleep."

"Something about you and religion that's driving you on this trip. Something Lauren knows that I don't."

Purdy didn't look up. He waited half a minute before responding. "It's not about religion for me. It's about fanaticism. I feel good about religion. I go to church regularly, I believe in God. I try to live a Christian life. This isn't about religion. Okay?"

Sam looked across the car, demanding an acknowledgment.

Alan nodded.

"Remember Jonestown, the Kool-Aid? My aunt and uncle—my father's younger brother and his wife—died there."

"Wow. Shit. I'm sorry. I didn't know."

"Fanatical religions—I don't care whether you call them cults, whether you call them evangelicals, whether you call them mainstream—sometimes they hurt real people."

Alan was quiet, hoping Sam would continue on his own.

He did. "Look just about anyplace in the world. Croatia, Ireland, India, Iraq, the Middle East. Look at the abortion battle here in the States, look at Amendment 2 in Colorado, look anywhere on the planet. Most of the conflict in the world is justified on religious grounds. The most noble and the most heinous things done on the face of this earth are done in the name of God. How do you make sense of that? I haven't figured it out yet. For every Mother Teresa there's a David Koresh.

"I get baffled. America thinks it's immune. We aren't. Our time will come. And it won't come from some little sect in Waco, Texas, that has a few bazookas. It'll come from some quote-unquote mainstream religion with high-tech communication and a few hundred thousand obedient believers and some crazy leader who decides that the time is right for a holy war."

Alan didn't know what to say. "You think it will be the Mormons?"

"Hell, I'm no prophet. I've never met a belligerent Mormon. Not one. But I wouldn't be surprised if our trouble comes from one of the millennarian religions. One of the sects, like the Mormons, that believe in the literal truth of the Book of Revelation. Biblically, everything is pointed toward the year 2000, the beginning of the seventh day, the start of the seventh millennium. I think that's when this holy shit's gonna hit the fan. First will come Armageddon. Then the Great New Day. You can count on there being a few bullets fired along the way. You can fucking count on it. Good night."

Alan tried to see Sam's perspective, a view through a lens ground with the ashes of the Reverend Jim Jones.

He floored the car to no avail. Since he had bought the used Land Cruiser from his neighbor, he had discovered that it was chronically underpowered. Nowhere was that more evident than climbing the final leg of the San Miguel River Canyon from Sawpit up into Telluride.

Telluride, Colorado, is tucked into a cul-de-sac canyon in the San Juan Mountains; the road into the narrow pioneer mining town dead-ends at the base of Bridal Veil Falls. No one comes to Telluride on the way to someplace else. These days, people come for the beauty.

In autumn, its gluttony of summer festivals digested, Telluride was sedate. Asleep in the car, Purdy missed all the wonder provided by the dark canyon. He missed the smell of ponderosa and the aroma of woodsmoke. He missed the rhythm of the creeping San Miguel and the echoing bark of a howling dog. He managed to stay asleep in the front seat while Alan checked them into a bed-and-breakfast just a couple of blocks from the center of town. By the time Alan had secured their bikes inside the back of the car, Sam had already moved upstairs and resumed his dreams in a charming little second-floor room.

Robin and Lauren stayed downtown until almost four in the morning, talking about Harley and alcohol and Wiley and hot cider. Lauren had argued vigorously with Robin to try to convince her not to go home. She had offered Robin her sister's bed as a temporary refuge. Lauren thought that Robin's dismissive reply was made too impulsively, but both woman ended up going home alone.

Midmorning the next day, Lauren arrived at the office eager to report on the conversation she'd had with Harley the evening before. Neither she nor Robin even pretended to feel refreshed.

"As I told you, my friend Harley"—Lauren elevated her eyebrows and tried not to blush—"is LDS, and he knows a lot about the Church. He told me that the men Pratt circled on the list from the BYU yearbooks are all Mormon elders. He doesn't know who the woman is. I'll call the alumni association at BYU today, see what they can tell me about her."

"Elders? What do you mean, elders? My paperboy is a Mormon elder." Robin failed to disguise her irritability. Wiley had been asleep on the couch in his study when she got back home. He had already dressed and headed off to work by the time she crawled out of bed and stumbled into the shower behind a carefully locked bathroom door far too few hours later.

"Oh, you know. What do the Mormons call them? Authorities? Yeah. Two of them are authorities. Or apostles? I'm sorry, I'm exhausted from last night and my brain's not working. And one of them is part of the presidency, I think." Lauren tried to make some sense of her recollection of her conversation with Harley at the Side Pocket the night before.

Robin shut her eyes tightly and pulled her hair back over her ears. "Why don't you read me their names."

Lauren unfolded her list. "Leroy Thomas, Bruce Starkle, and Kevin Lee. And a woman, Rachel Misker."

Robin shook her head in dismay at the list. "Bruce Starkle is the one I know. He's a big shot. First Presidency. There are two men in the First Presidency besides the prophet. They're just below the prophet in rank. They're like his cabinet. Those other two men on the list must be run-of-the-mill general authorities. I don't know all of the authorities—there are too many of them. And I don't know the woman.

"Starkle is truly important, though. He was on the BYU Board of Trustees. He's on the news all the time. For someone so powerful in the Church, he's relatively young. He's handsome, eloquent." She smiled to herself. "He's potent, too. I think I remember hearing that he has a dozen kids or something. Although I shouldn't be surprised, I didn't know he was particularly close to Lester Horner. That fact could be crucial for us."

As Lauren reached down to re-examine her list, she was shaking her head. "I'm sorry, but I don't have a context for all of this, Robin. It sounds like these guys are just Church bigwigs, like bishops, but you talk about them like they're as powerful as commissars in the Communist Party or something."

Robin took off her glasses and rubbed the bridge of her nose. "This is the Planet Utah. It's easy to forget it, Lauren. When you look at the mountains it may remind you of Colorado. Don't be fooled. These men run the LDS Church. They provide direction and order for seventy or eighty percent of this state's population. When they suggest how to vote, the population listens. When they tell the legislature what the Church wants, the legislators listen. When they suggest how to think, the faithful listen. If they tell the faithful to stay home with their family on Monday night and make collages of the celestial kingdom or do origami impressions of the angel Moroni, then there's no point having your restaurant open that night—you won't get any LDS business.

"Want to know how it works? Here's how it works. The Church leaders see themselves as persecuted pragmatists. When the U.S. Army was about to start confiscating Church property and when they started arresting Church leaders over polygamy, the prophet then, Wilford Woodruff, issued a manifesto forbidding the practice of polygamy. When the civil rights movement targeted the Mormon Church for not allowing blacks in the priesthood, God miraculously provided a revelation that it was no longer His wish. If the old men who run the Church were to decide that God has changed His mind and that He really wants the faithful to wear Fruit of the Looms and not wear garments anymore, no one would wear garments anymore.

"These old men are behind every bit of the Church's influence, good and bad. The authorities are the force of God in Utah. Government is secondary there, merely an expediency, a practicality. The LDS Church is not always benign."

"You don't sound too fond of the Mormons."

"I'm sure at times I don't, but I can't think of one individual Mormon I dislike. I have plenty of Mormon neighbors. People I work with. Acquaintances. Mostly, in a funny way, I admire them, the way they live their lives, the way they live their values. Living around Mormons in Utah has made me a better person. I've stopped smoking; I drink less. I appreciate the whole idea of family more. LDS I know personally are healthy, respectful, spiritual people, though I personally think they have blinders on about the Church and its doctrine. What I'm so disdainful of is *that* the Mormons run this state and *how* they run this state. Utah is a marvelous place to live. I wish it weren't a theocracy, that's all."

Lauren considered pursuing the Mormon question but didn't. She waited until she had captured Robin's eyes.

"How were things at home? Did you see your husband this morning?"

Robin shook her head and shrugged her shoulders. "He left early. We didn't talk."

"What are you going to do?"

"I don't know. I'm already beginning to convince myself it didn't happen the way I said. Maybe he spilled the cider by accident. I don't know. Listen, I've got depositions on another case this morning. Why don't you go to the conference room and make your calls to Provo? Then you can fill me in this afternoon on what you find out."

"Okay." Lauren felt dismissed. She stood up. "If you want to talk—you know, about Wiley—you'll let me know, right?"

Robin nodded warmly. "Lauren, have you heard from your sister?"

"Yeah," she replied. "Wanted to know what's new with the case. Asked if she can do anything to help. Her gig in Vegas is just a fill-in for a few nights. Who knows, she may prance in here any minute."

"Have her call me."

"Sure. She's at the same number as before, if you want to reach her." Lauren paused one more time before leaving the office. "Please reconsider about staying with me for a while."

Robin didn't respond.

Lauren said, "I mean it."

"Okay, okay, I'll think about it. Get out of here."

The view from the tiny dining room of the inn was to the east. The sharp, juvenile peaks of the Uncompahgre made the steep incline of Black Bear Pass look as forbidding as a path up Everest.

Sam Purdy said, "Yes, ma'am, I think I'd love some of both." Sam was reclining on his chair in the sunlit dining room of the bed-and-breakfast where he and Alan had slept in Telluride. He was responding to an offer of seconds on huevos rancheros and a refill on coffee.

The owners of the inn were a female couple in their late thirties. One, lanky and shy, stayed in the kitchen, while her robust, talkative partner worked the dining room with generosity and wit.

Alan declined more eggs. He asked if he could borrow a local phone book instead.

Sam smiled at him. "My, my. You're getting right to work. That's sure admirable. Except we don't have any names to look up quite yet. What, you gonna check in the yellow pages under 'suspects'?"

Alan had slept well, and he had steeled himself for Purdy. With a smile, he said, "For your information, Sam, I do have names. Or, at least, one name. I talked to Lauren this morning—woke her up, actually. You and I are to see if there's a woman who lives around here named Rachel Misker. If we find her, we call Lauren and get instructions. She doesn't want us to talk with her. She's not even sure she's the one we're looking for."

Sam mimicked Alan's hushed tone. "Why are we whispering all of a sudden?"

Alan leaned forward and lowered his voice as an alternative to whispering. "Sam, maybe Rachel Misker is why this Toomey guy was killed."

"Ah-ha." Purdy leaned over his empty plate and looked left and right before continuing. "So we'd better be *real* careful, right?"

"Sam, why aren't you taking this seriously?"

Purdy sat back on his chair and straightened his napkin in his lap. "I am. But my paranoia isn't metastasizing.

The owner, who had introduced herself as Cilla, delivered the thin phone book to Alan and asked, "Is there anything or anybody I can help you fellas find around here? I know a lot of people."

Alan feared that Sam was about to ask Cilla if she knew Rachel Misker, so he interjected, "No, we're fine. Just looking up an old friend."

Sam shook his head in amusement as Cilla moved on to the only other table that was occupied in the little dining room. "I think Cilla here would turn out to be a safe source for us, Alan. Trust my instincts on this."

"How can you say that, Sam? What makes you so sure?"

"Wouldn't you agree that she and the pretty lady with the ponytail and great eyebrows in the kitchen are an item?"

"Sure." Alan glanced through the open door at the woman with the great eyebrows. Cilla and her partner had been making absolutely no secret of the extent of their affection for each other.

"Well, just how many lesbians do you know who moonlight as secret informers for the Church of Jesus Christ of Latter-day Saints?" Purdy raised his own ample eyebrows. "Got you that time, didn't I?"

Cilla delivered Sam his second breakfast with a smile warm enough to make toast. Purdy ate. Alan plowed through the phone book and didn't find Rachel Misker anywhere, finally concluding that she must be listed under her married name.

A few minutes later Sam said, "So where we gonna

ride today? How different is it riding dirt trails instead of rock ones?"

"What about finding Rachel Misker, Sam?"

"First things first. And the first thing is, I'm on vacation. And unless Ms. Misker is hiding from us—and why should she be, since she doesn't know us from the pope?—we'll find her without even interrupting our holiday." He wiped his mouth with his napkin and smoothed his mustache to the left and then to the right with his tongue. Then he exclaimed, "My God, these women can cook, can't they?"

Alan excused himself to go take a shower.

"She lives in Ouray. Over the hill. Her name is Rachel Baumann now. She's another goddamn attorney."

Purdy was sitting on Alan's bed, talking to him through the closed door of the adjoining bathroom. He had raised his voice enough to ensure that Alan could hear that he was speaking but intentionally didn't speak loudly enough that Alan would understand everything he said.

Alan cracked open the bathroom door. A cloud of steam puffed out near the top of the jamb.

"What?"

"She lives in Ouray. She's married. She's a lawyer."

Alan slammed the door shut and finished shaving. He emerged five minutes later.

"And how do we know this? No, on second thought, don't tell me. I don't want to know."

Purdy made a face intended to demonstrate that he was trying not to gloat. "Sure you do. You'll like this. I used your source." He held up the local phone book. "These people Lauren is looking for all met at BYU, right? A lot of them are lawyers now. I thought she might be, too. Only one lawyer named Rachel in the phone book. Rachel Baumann. I called, pretended I was a prospective client, asked for her credentials. Bingo. Her secretary said she had started out at BYU and finished school in Durango. Did law school later on, in Denver. At DU."

Alan began to get dressed. Purdy stared, perplexed, at Alan's shaved legs. A pair of precise furry rings emerged a few inches above his knees.

"You shave your legs?" Purdy said. His tone implied, *Are you nuts?*

Alan nodded and prayed that this line of inquiry would just go away.

"You do this for Lauren? She likes your legs like that?" Purdy wondered momentarily if his wife would go for it and instantly decided it didn't matter.

"No. It's a bicycling thing. Okay?"

"What? Wind resistance? Like swimmers shaving their heads?"

"No. Road burn. When you fall, you lose less skin and heal quicker if you don't have hair."

"When you fall?" Purdy had taken a hard spill on one of the trails the previous afternoon. "So you think I should shave, too?"

Alan laughed at the mental image but couldn't quite decide if Purdy was being sarcastic. He decided to answer seriously. "Not if you stay off-road, Sam. Then you can stay as hairy as God made you. But if you get serious and start road racing, you need to think about shaving."

Sam shook his head and stared down at Alan's slender calves. "I don't know. I think I'd rather lose a lot of extra skin than have my legs look like aspen trees after the blight."

As quickly as he could, Alan pulled on a pair of jeans. He sat down next to the phone. "I need to call Lauren, tell her we found this woman. You found this woman. I've got a feeling she could use some good news."

Sam said, "Uh-uh. Not yet. I want to do some riding here today. Then we gotta go over to Ouray ourselves and check things out, make sure we're right about Rachel. Anyway, Cilla says there are some great places to ride near Ouray. And she told me which B & B to stay at. Said she'd call ahead and recommend me to the owners. Excuse me—recommend *us* to the owners."

"That's not what Lauren wants us to do, Sam."

Sam snorted. "One thing you learn when you're a cop is that if you listen only to what DAs want you to do, you're hardly ever gonna get anything done. DAs are like football coaches. They like to draw plays on the chalkboard and tell everybody on the team exactly what they're supposed to do to lead the team to victory. But sometimes you have to improvise. When the team wins anyway, then the coach looks good, and they end up as happy as an Iron Ranger on a frozen lake."

Alan knew neither what an Iron Ranger was nor what one would be doing on a frozen lake. "And if the team loses?" he said.

"Ahhh shit. They get over it."

"Fourth floor. Special Collections, please."

The operator said, "Just a moment," in a cheery, singsong voice that made her sound around fifteen years old.

"Special Collections. May I help you?"

"I hope so. Could you please check a listing on a student in an old yearbook for me?"

"I'd be happy to. Do you know the year?"

"She entered in nineteen fifty-nine. Would have graduated with the class of sixty-three, I think."

"Let me pull it. It'll be just a moment."

Lauren Crowder waited impatiently while the librarian went off to retrieve the book. The harsh late-morning glare highlighted a trail of Vanilla Wafer crumbs across the long conference table down the hall from Robin Torr's office. Lauren examined the trail with guilt, as though she were a drunk counting the previous night's empties.

There was a click on the phone line. Lauren thought she was being rescued from being on hold. Muffled noises—possibly voices—followed. Then the librarian said, "I'm very sorry, but those volumes are currently unavailable."

Lauren was immediately suspicious. "I didn't think yearbooks circulated."

"Well, you're so right, they don't. But these are currently unavailable for some reason. I'm terribly sorry. Is there anything else I could help you with?"

"Perhaps if I called later?"

"I don't think that would really help."

"Would someone else have one? The alumni association, maybe?"

"You might just want to check. I don't know what they keep over there. But if you'll stop by with some student identification and your temple recommend, I'll be happy to see what I can do to track one down for you, Miss . . . ?"

"I might do that if I can't find one. Thank you very much."

"You're so welcome."

Lauren's conversation with a man at the BYU alumni association was more terse but no more successful. He didn't have any information on Rachel Misker and couldn't seem to find the association's copy of the pertinent yearbooks. He'd be sure to call if he did. Would she care to leave a name and number?

Lauren said that wouldn't be necessary and hung up, wondering what the hell was going on.

Lauren called Harley for an explanation.

In response to his answer, she said, "What do you mean, you would guess that the BYU yearbook for nineteen sixty-three is no longer considered faith-promoting?"

Harley suppressed a laugh at Lauren's continued ignorance of Mormonism. He adopted a tone as professional as he was capable of mustering. "Certain inquiries, especially ones that might lead to contradictions about the faith, or that, if pursued, may instigate derision amongst non-Mormons, are considered to be not faith-promoting. As you probably know, members of the Church are instructed not to pursue them. What you may not know is that LDS institutions—bookstores and libraries alike—don't make non-faith-promoting materials readily available."

Lauren made no attempt to suppress her incredulity. "Harley, BYU is a major university. And major universities do not ban books. I don't believe that."

"These books don't exactly get banned, Lauren, they merely become unavailable. Don't forget, this is Utah we're talking about. Brigham Young University's own statement of mission allows, quote, 'reasonable' limitations on faculty and student freedom of intellectual exploration and expression if that freedom is likely to interfere with the Mormon Church's spiritual purposes or religious goals."

"*No.* Really? So what does a controversial faculty member do at BYU, publish under a pseudonym?"

"Faculty members uncomfortable with the BYU Honor Code are invited to relocate to a lay institution that permits academic pursuits consistent with more heathen interest. My campus gets a few of the self-banished or tenure-rejected every year."

"Are you one of them?"

"I suppose in a way I am. I never taught at BYU, but the match would not have been a heavenly marriage. The very fact that I am sitting, at this moment, in this messy room I call an office drinking a can of Diet Pepsi would be enough to get me bounced all the way from Provo to Orem." He laughed to himself. "And I can guarantee you that the saints in Orem wouldn't be too happy to see me, either."

Through an exasperated exhale, Lauren said, "The more I know, the more I'm amazed. I've got to run, Harley. Thanks for the continuing sociological tutorial. Will you shoot pool with me tonight?"

"No. But I'd love to watch you play," he said.

"What time works for you?"

"Doesn't matter to me. You know I'll be there. I'm not hard to find."

The same, of course, could not be said for Teresa Crowder.

For the rest of the day, Lauren fretted about her sister's failure to show up in Salt Lake City at the conclusion of her gig in Vegas. Or at least to call again. Lauren pushed away intrusive, anxious memories of her mother's hand-wringing anguish during Teresa's disappearances as a child. She remembered being enlisted to corral her siblings and form posses to go out into the orchards and look for her sister. All day long, she fought the temptation to do it all over again.

Lauren reminded herself that every last time her sister had disappeared she had ended up being all right. Every last time.

Simultaneously, she tried to deny the awareness that Pratt Toomey's family might have said the same thing about him.

Early in the afternoon, worry triumphed over reason, and she called the hotel in Nevada where Teresa had been working. The clerk said that Teresa Crowder had checked out that morning. Did they know where she had gone? They didn't.

A half-dozen phone calls later, Lauren had tracked down the woman who had booked Teresa into one of the casino's lounges. The woman said that she had heard that Teresa had gotten another booking and thought she had left Las Vegas.

"But you don't know where?"

"Sorry. She may have told me, but if she did, I forgot. There are a lot of comedians out there. I don't keep track of them. She doesn't have an agent, does she?"

"No. She's new at this. I mean, at being successful at this. She's been doing her own booking."

"Don't know what to tell you. Your sister's a funny girl. And she's got looks. Her material has some promise. A little more polish, a little more confidence, and, who knows? I'll have her back here for another gig, maybe even before the end of the year. She can count on that."

Lauren thanked her, hung up, and resolved to give up trying to track down her sister. She also resolved to do her best not to worry about Teresa's safety.

But that night, after a funny, flirtatious, diverting time with John Harley at the Side Pocket, she had a long, fretful dream about her father, drunk, about her sister, absent, and about their family dog.

She woke screaming from the dream when the dog's face turned crimson, awash with blood.

In the morning when she woke, she surprised herself by missing Alan. She encouraged the feeling, and before long she ached for him for the first time since she had arrived in Utah. She was glad for the longing, was distracted by it.

Showering, she recalled without wanting to the day she had had her first MRI, lying on the narrow tray, being slid smoothly into the long, dark tube, the hollow rhythmic pounding of the machine, the tinny amplified voice of the technician, the little mirror that helped her see her toes. And, an hour later, the word from her neurologist, the diagnosis: multiple sclerosis. She was as frightened now as she had been then. She had never thought she would be that frightened again. She had been wrong once before. In Aspen. She was wrong again.

In Utah, of all places.

The shower cleared her head. It was time to drop any hope of filing a lawsuit and instead go back to Boulder and get married to Alan Gregory and think about having babies.

A few minutes later, waiting for toast to pop out of her sister's antique Toastmaster, she found herself wondering what John Harley was doing for lunch. Within seconds, she was blinking away tears.

Will Price had thought and prayed about it each day for a week and had concluded that he had accomplished a lot of healing with Lester Horner during the two days they had spent, mostly on their hands and knees, searching for evidence of the ancestors of the enigmatic Anasazi. He had spoken with Horner twice since the justice had returned to Washington, D.C. Lester, he concluded, was now mentally prepared for the new Court term. Will Price felt that his mission had been accomplished.

One mission, anyway. Despite an admirable dedication to the task at hand, the two men had departed the Ute Mountain Tribal Park thinking that once again they had failed to discover anything that would buttress Price's hypotheses about the Lamanites and the cliff-dwelling Anasazi. They had, however, found evidence of a collapsed wall inside the kiva they were working and had begun to uncover some exciting partial petroglyphs. Will Price was a proponent of a controversial theory that significantly stretched existing Mormon hypotheses about the extent to which Lamanite migration had proceeded into the Land Northward from their theorized landing site in Mesoamerica. He considered the new finds from the kiva to be promising. He had carefully photographed the new images so they could be examined by scientists he knew in Provo.

The lack of concrete scientific progress at the dig was almost immaterial to the two men. The path they walked was a long one. They were both patient.

On their last day in the Ute park, a week earlier, as they were packing the car to return to the Farmington airport, Horner had turned to his old friend, and in a voice that begged reminiscence said, "So, how long have we been doing this, Will?"

"I don't know, Lester. What? Twenty-five years? Thirty-five?"

"It's been twenty-seven years. You and I first came to Four Corners twenty-seven years ago. We made that first trip in your dad's rusty old pickup, remember? What color was that thing, anyway?"

Will Price shrugged. "Rust-colored, I guess."

"And now, for the first time in all those years, for some reason I feel like we're finally getting close. I know that there are a lot of people who say we should be digging in Central America or Mexico. Well, I think they're wrong. It's taken us a long time; we've scraped a lot of dirt. But I can feel it now." He shivered involuntarily. "I can."

Price slapped the Supreme Court justice on the back and said, "There's no doubt in my mind but that you might be right, Lester. I've not said anything, but I've received some revelations about this place myself. This is exactly where it is going to happen. Right here. Ute Mountain. Didn't you believe all along that it was going to be Utah? I know I did."

"I did, too."

"You disappointed?"

"No, it's close enough for me. Colorado's fine," offered Lester. "It just means that some cartographer drew the lines a little bit off when the maps were made. When we find what we're after, it will make this place a spiritual part of Zion. Mapmakers make mistakes; the Lord doesn't."

Horner hefted a heavy box of tools into the air and then slid it into the trunk of the car. He paused and looked around at the cliff dwellings high in the canyon. "A thousand Indians—Lamanites, might as well start calling them that—lived in these canyons once, Will. Maybe more. Who knows, right? They were early saints, but their souls were never saved. Well, their wait is almost over. Soon we'll discover the identity of those souls so they can be welcomed into the celestial kingdom."

Lester Horner knew his eyes were teary, but he wasn't sure why. He turned away from Price, into the chill breeze.

Price was moved by his friend's introspection. "Don't doubt yourself, Lester. It's taken me some sweet time to get used to it, but there's no doubt you've been chosen for some special things." He belly-laughed, and the cheerful sound came back bruised as it echoed off the sandstone. "Seriously, who in their right mind would even begin to think that God's wishes could actually be handled by a lawyer?"

Horner smiled and tightened the bungees he was using to wrap the bulky tent.

"Joseph was chosen by Moroni to translate the gold plates. Brigham was chosen by Joseph Smith and by God to lead the saints to Deseret. Apparently you, too, have been chosen. We both know that the president doesn't usually volunteer for the type of scrutiny the Church received during your darn confirmation hearings, Lester. The prophet must have told you that you were called to the Supreme Court, didn't he? The Lord must have chosen you Himself, right?"

Horner nodded, noticed he had missed a tent spike, and reached over for it. He didn't like to think about the Senate hearings. He considered it to have been the most arduous week of his life.

"So the way I look at it, it was the Lord, not the president of the United States, who appointed you to protect the Constitution from the ravages of this society. From homosexuality, from drugs, from women acting like priests. From all the attacks on the family—abortion, pornography, violence. That protection is the work God wants from you. The saints have waited over one hundred years for that shield. You know, Brigham Young wasn't wrong about much, but he thought these mountains would stop the nonbelievers from reaching Utah. Thought that geography would protect the saints. Brigham was wrong about that. President Benson has said that the Church would one day assume leadership in Washington. Well, because of you, that time is now. And it appears that it's up to us. Mostly you, I think, Lester. It's in your hands. They are good hands. Not perfect hands. But they are the hands that the Lord has chosen."

Price checked Lester's reaction.

Horner seemed trapped in a reverie framed by sandstone and sky.

"This, too," Price continued, aware of a need to reel his friend back in, spreading his meaty arms wide to take in the barren majesty of this corner of the Southwest. "You and I are out here living in tents being spiritual fools, looking for proof of the Lamanites. We are like Joseph Smith out here. He had the gold plates and the Urim and the Thummim. He had his wilderness. We have the search for the Lamanites. We have our wilderness. We do, Lester. We persevere to bring the truth. As saints we are often mocked, but constantly we are feared. It is because of our truth. We must always suffer the consequences of that truth gladly."

Horner mused at the beauty around him. "This isn't exactly suffering, Will."

"You know what I mean, Lester."

"Yes, I do. Though if what you and I suspect about my role is correct, I admit to being seriously humbled by what the Lord is asking of me. I know it's only human to doubt one's worthiness, but the enormousness is only starting to become clear to me. You are more righteous than me, Will. You always have been. Why have I been chosen and not you?"

Price shrugged and smiled, and then his deep laugh again filled the canyon. "The Lord, for some good reason He has not yet shared with me, has chosen me to build self-storage lots, Lester. Big ones. With lime-green doors and excellent security. Given my success at it, it's apparently been pretty important to Him that I do it well. I feel good about that, about doing it well. It was an honor to have been called to run the mission in Maryland for a while. But now that's over. I'm happy to be doing the home teaching I'm doing now, but I hope to be called for a mission again soon. Or if God wills it, another bishopric. I've raised a fine family. I am fortunate to be able to tithe the way a rich man tithes. In my spare time I read everything I can to help track down the route of the Lamanites to the Land Northward. It's a good life. It makes me proud."

When Lauren showed up at Lewis, Frank and Zelem the next day, Elsie Smith ushered her directly into Robin Torr's office. Robin didn't bother with a greeting.

"Where's your sister?"

"I don't know."

"You haven't heard from her? You don't know where she is? I thought you expected her back."

"I did expect her back. And, no, she hasn't called in. I don't have any idea where she is."

Robin's eyes were flat and cold. Lauren said, "What's wrong, Robin? You should be getting used to this by now. She'll phone one of us today. What's so urgent that you need to talk to her right away?"

Lauren sat on one of the armchairs across from the desk. She was distracted by an irritating burning on her hand. Her right palm felt as though she had scraped it hard on asphalt. It burned as if from embedded gravel and from fifty little flaps of palm flesh. Absently, she gazed down to examine her wounds and allowed herself the luxury of being surprised at what she saw.

The hand looked fine.

Then it must be someone else's hand; mine is on fire.

Lauren swallowed.

This was multiple sclerosis shooting a round across the bow.

Just a sensory ambush so far. Soon, what? Maybe a frontal assault on one of her vulnerable flanks: her vision, her muscles, her balance. Just an ambush so far, she told herself again, a lone sniper, a flesh wound, just a little pain.

"I said, something's come up," Robin repeated, derision seeping into her tone. "Lauren, are you listening to me? You asked me a question. There's a little something we need to discuss with your sister."

"I'm sorry. What is it, Robin?" She slid the tips of her fingers across her burning palm for evidence of imaginary wounds.

"Read this." Robin handed over a letter on the stark white twenty-five-pound bond that was so ubiquitous in legal communications. An accompanying sheet was on lighter, photocopier bond.

Lauren's spirits sank as she read the stilted politeness of the letter from the lawyer representing Blythe Oaks's estate. The letterhead clearly identified him as a full partner at James and Bartell.

Lauren flipped to the second page and saw the word **"AFFIDAVIT,"** noting the capital letters and bold typeface.

The notarized signature at the bottom of the sheet was that of a young woman Lauren vaguely remembered. She thought she had met her over the Christmas holiday one year on the family apple farm in Washington, a friend Teresa had brought home for Christmas.

Daphne Darrow.

Lauren smiled as she read the name. Daphne had been thin and tall and winsome, with dark, shiny hair and a huge, generous smile. "She has Crowder hair," Jersey Crowder had pronounced from the head of the table, where he had presided over a joyous Christmas dinner at which Daphne had been treated as family. Lauren remembered that particular holiday well, mostly, she thought, because of how magical it had been. It had been especially magical, she knew, because Santa hadn't brought Jersey Crowder any Schlitz that year.

From the accompanying too-polite letter, which actually came close to feigning an apologetic tone at having to bring this "difficult" new information to Robin Torr's attention, Lauren guessed correctly what the affidavit would say.

Daphne's own words were sweet, and despite signs of

obvious coaching at the beginning and the end of the statement by some legal or paralegal type, her brief story managed to convey some true nostalgia and sadness. Her prose was rich with adjectives as she described a brief affair that had ultimately, she felt with apparent regret, ended her friendship with Teresa Crowder.

The opening sentence and the closing sentence of the affidavit both included the word "lesbian" and the phrase "homosexual contact." The three paragraphs in between spoke only of a halting, exploratory love between two young women.

And, yes, sex. Briefly. Awkwardly.

Between two young women.

Lauren read the statement again. She had almost forgotten that Robin Torr was in the room.

When she looked up and saw Robin, Lauren felt embarrassed that her sister's secrets were so starkly stated in black and white. She said, "I remember her. Daphne. She was a sweet kid. She came home from school one holiday break with Teresa." Lauren's voice was wistful at the memory. "It was a great Christmas."

"Especially for your sister, apparently. Not too bad for Daphne, either."

When Lauren spoke again, her eyes were burning almost as much as her hand. "What the hell do you mean by that?"

"I mean, we have ourselves a new problem we don't need."

"I know exactly how damaging this is, Robin. But what I need to know is, what the hell did you mean by your comment?"

"Damn it, Lauren, she should have told me this." She flicked a pencil in the direction of the affidavit.

"What? That she was a kid once? That she didn't always play according to the rules? That she wondered once if she might like girls more than boys? Jesus, Robin, I'm hoping what I'm hearing isn't true."

Robin stared at Lauren for two or three seconds, then past her, out the windows, at the Wasatch. She noticed the white-tipped peaks. Couldn't remember when it had snowed. *How could I miss a goddamn snowstorm?* She tried to still her breathing.

"I didn't mean to sound judgmental. I'm sorry."

"Are you?"

"What, sorry? Yes, I am. Very much so. What I said wasn't . . . right. I'm sorry."

"No, judgmental. Are you judgmental? About lesbians? I need to know."

Robin was silent. She flashed on Wiley, with his mug of cider. Her eyes were clear, sharp, penetrating.

Lauren pressed. "This case isn't about lesbian harassment, Robin. It's about harassment. Period. End of sentence. That Teresa had sex with another woman before Blythe Oaks harassed her is not the point in this case, any more than it was important whether Anita Hill was or was not a virgin when Clarence Thomas asked her about Long Dong Silver."

Lauren sat back, short of breath. She thought she felt the sole of her foot starting to burn. She fought an urge to kick off her shoe and look.

When Robin spoke, her voice was focused, her words cryptic, plated with anger. "I don't like it when you're so righteous. I don't like it at all."

Lauren opened her mouth to speak. Robin cut her off.

"No, it's my turn." She took a deep breath and swallowed. She put both her hands on the edge of her desk, her long, thin fingers curling up over the lip of the wood. "You tell me that if the facts were a little different, if your sister were an out-of-the-closet lesbian, and that if we were sitting in Phoenix, Arizona, and not Salt Lake City, Utah, that the lawyer in you would have been so quick to throw your money and your time at me to support a lawsuit? I'm sorry, I don't think so.

"So don't patronize me with your condescension. And don't condemn me for my legal strategy. *Our* legal strategy. You had your sister call me because we have a fighting chance to win this lawsuit *because* we're in Utah. *Because* Utah is not only a bastion of western frontier conservatism but also the home of the Mormon Church, and it just so happens that we have as many homophobes per capita as just about any place on the face of the earth. And you agreed to press this *because* we just might be able to prove that Blythe Oaks was part of a hated, despised minority. And you've known all along that we were planning to exploit that very ugly fact to help Teresa win her case."

Lauren's jaw was set. Her eyes were hard on Robin.

Robin continued. "Yeah, that's right, we've been planning all along to play dirty. So don't get righteous with me, damn it. This letter"—she glanced down at the papers on her desktop—"hurts our chances simply because it undermines the only leverage we can successfully exploit, given the prevailing prejudice in this state. And that leverage, as you damn well know, is that we were going to make sure that the defendant would be despised more than the plaintiff. And given that our plaintiff is an unmarried gentile woman in Utah who makes her living as a stand-up comic, we both knew that wasn't going to be an easy sell.

"Our defendant was going to end up being despised not because she had sexually harassed someone—which is a seasonal sport here—but because we were going to allow innuendo to paint her with the brush of homosexual hate. Every move we've made has had one intent. We've been gathering information that will help us label Blythe Oaks as a lesbian. In *Utah.*"

Robin uncurled her fingers from the edge of the desk and pointed out the window. "Look at the sign outside of town, Lauren. It says, 'Welcome to Salem.'

"Well, welcome to Salem. Make up your mind. You want to drown the witch, or not?"

Over the course of the rest of the morning, Lauren and Robin negotiated a rationalization about the case that would permit them to press forward. That is, if Teresa ever called with her concurrence. The conciliation process between the two lawyers was cumbersome, because the rationalization needed to be one that they could both stomach. Accomplishing gymnastic moral accommodations was not exactly virgin territory for either of them, but given the tension and fear developing about this case, the decision was not reached gracefully.

Lauren needed a summation. "So the bottom line is, absent finding a smoking gun, like a witness who was in the next stall at the Mayflower, we need to find evidence of prior harassment committed by Blythe."

Robin nodded. "And, I think we agree, given her orientation, any prior harassment would most likely have happened with another woman, right?"

Reluctantly, Lauren said, "Right."

"And"—Robin paused, waiting for Lauren's gaze to find her own—"we also need to do some damage control about the fact that the defense somehow tracked down Daphne Darrow. And we damn well need to find your sister and make sure that there aren't any more Daphne Darrows out there waiting to be tracked down."

Lauren scratched at her burning palm. "If there are, Robin, then this case is a stillbirth. We may be skillful enough to finesse one Daphne, we'll never get away with two."

"Yeah, I know," said Robin. "Let's just pray that Teresa got her period of sexual exploration over with quickly." Robin spoke in a way that permitted Lauren to laugh in response.

Robin moved quickly to take advantage of the change in mood. "You know, there is one other thing that would really help us out."

"What?" Lauren asked.

"What would really help us out is if your sister would find room in her heart to fall in love with a Mormon—preferably a Mormon male—convert, and then get married in Temple Square. That would help us out a lot. I'm speaking purely from a litigation point of view, of course."

Lauren laughed at the image. "You know what's more likely with Teresa? She'll hit the big time as a comic, go on *The Tonight Show*, and spend her four minutes of national attention telling Mormon jokes."

"Please don't even think it. That's my nightmare." Robin rolled her eyes. "One of my nightmares, anyway. That airspace is pretty congested these days."

Elsie Smith knocked on Robin's door and poked her head into the room. "Mr. and Mrs. Nafer are here, Mrs. Torr. And your husband called again. Hello, Miss Crowder." She closed the door silently as she retreated.

"You need to go. So which leg of this monster do you want me to tug on? Should I see if I can find out what Pratt was after, or should I go look around for Blythe Oaks's previous victims?"

Robin feared that Lauren's heart wouldn't be totally invested in finding proof of previous harassment, so she offered her the option of finding out what Toomey had been sniffing out.

Lauren jumped at it. She also decided it was time to begin preparing Robin for the reality of Sam and Alan's assistance. "I've been thinking about it," she said, "and I may be able to enlist some out-of-town help in finding out what happened to Pratt. Some friends from Colorado. That should make things safer for us, at least at first. But the only truly safe thing is quitting. We both know that. And I look at you now, and I don't think it's too likely. Fortunately or unfortunately, Robin Torr, I think I may have finally met my match in the stubbornness department."

Robin said, "I prefer to think of myself as tenacious, thank you."

After a quick morning ride with Sam alongside the San Miguel River near Telluride, Alan packed the car and strapped the bikes onto the roof rack. When Purdy finally emerged from a prolonged visit to the kitchen and good-byes to Cilla and Teri, Alan pointed to Sam's bike chain and told him he had a problem.

"Jammed derailleur," he said.

"Can you fix it?"

"Sure. After we find Rachel Baumann and confirm that she was indeed born Rachel Misker."

Purdy was suspicious that his bike's derailleur problem had been caused by Alan's own brand of petty sabotage, and he was briefly tempted to march into the town of Telluride carrying the bike on his shoulder until he found a bicycle mechanic who would put the chain back on for him.

After a glance at his watch and some calculations, he relented to Alan's demand. He realized that by the time they got settled in Ouray it was going to be well after noon and he wouldn't have yet had lunch. Finding an attorney named Rachel in a town the size of Ouray, he quickly decided, shouldn't delay his midday meal by more than ten minutes.

Lauren walked down the hallway to the conference room that she had co-opted as an office for the duration of the investigation. She started to phone the bed-and-breakfast where Alan said he and Sam Purdy would be staying in Telluride but stopped her finger midpoke. Some of the lights on the panel of the phone in front of her were lit, some were dark, and one was blinking. She shook her head at her own paranoia as she placed the receiver gently back in its cradle. She smiled as she walked back past Elsie Smith's desk and told her that she was going for a walk.

Lauren called the B & B from a pay phone in an alcove just past the bank of elevators in the lobby. Cilla answered after a half-dozen rings and told Lauren that "Sam and Alan" had checked out and were moving over the hill to Ouray. When Lauren asked if Cilla knew why they were heading to Ouray, Cilla said, "To ride, I guess. They really seem to be into mountain biking." Cilla offered the name and number of the inn in Ouray where she had sent them. Lauren jotted down the information on a scrap of paper from her purse.

As she hung up, she muttered, "Come on, Alan, screw the bicycles, you've got work to do." She assumed that her fiancé was the one who was causing Sam Purdy to be distracted by a search for the one perfect trail in southwestern Colorado. She hadn't even considered Purdy to be the culprit; she had never known Sam to do anything but work.

Although only a few miles of the Uncompahgre separate the stunning town of Telluride from the breathtaking town of Ouray, the trip takes about an hour unless it is being made by a bird.

The fifty-mile highway trip from Telluride to Ouray first descends the sharp red canyons carved by the San Miguel River, then goes across and down the splendid Dallas Divide before it traverses the steep sides of the many mountains of the Sneffels Range that tumble down to the banks of the Uncompahgre River. The Uncompahgre is fed by dozens of streams and creeks as it carries snow-melt down the San Juans. At one high, scenic point, the river passes through an impossibly narrow carved canyon into the tiny valley that holds Ouray, the little town that many people consider to be the most exquisite gem in the most perfect setting in Colorado's resplendent crown of mountain jewels.

"I thought when we were in Telluride that we were in heaven. But Ouray must be where the angels get to go on vacation." Purdy leaned forward to look up and out the windshield at the harsh glacial cliffs that towered above Ouray on the west. Their stratified faces were bathed in late-morning early-autumn sunshine, the horizontal striations tinged with purple and gray, the blue sky intensified by the altitude—and, Purdy thought, by the proximity to God.

Alan smiled at Sam but said nothing in reply. He was entranced as he watched a cascade of water shoot through a rock face on the east wall of the canyon, plummeting in a chill mist to the valley below.

He fought memories of his only previous trip to Ouray, a late-spring visit in the company of his wife—now ex-wife. He shook off the thought; he wanted to experience this place for the first time again.

"It's all so steep. Where do we ride?"

"Don't know, Sam. Old mining roads would be my guess. Not to worry. I brought some trail books and maps. First we find Rachel, though, then we ride. Right?"

Purdy replied, "Not exactly. First Rachel. Then lunch. Then you fix the derailleur that you broke. *Then* we ride." Purdy looked out the passenger window at the scenery. Alan couldn't see his face.

"Sam—"

"Save it."

The sign was painted on the glass across the bottom pane of a double-hung window on the second story of a century-old stone building on Seventh Avenue, near Fourth Street.

"R. Baumann, Attorney at Law," it read.

Alan parked the Land Cruiser across the gravel street. He got out of the car and touched his toes a few times. His hamstrings felt like bungees.

Purdy joined him on the cracked sidewalk.

Alan said, "Well?"

"Let's go say 'Hey.' "

"Lauren would prefer—"

"District attorneys would prefer it if you would call 'em before you wipe your ass. Let's just lay our eyes on this lady so we know she's the one. We don't have to tell her why we're here."

"You going to tell her you're a cop?"

Purdy didn't answer; he just hopped over a big rock and started to cross the street.

"What are you going to tell her, Sam?"

Purdy shrugged his shoulders and belatedly looked both ways.

They climbed the stairs to the second-floor landing of the old building and spotted a polished wood door with a glass panel painted with lettering identical to that on the window. The outer office in the suite was set up as an 1890s parlor. At one end, a secretary-receptionist sat at a small desk, her computer neatly screened in an antique cherry armoire against the adjacent wall.

The secretary composed her round face into a pleasant "May help you?" configuration.

Sam Purdy said "Hi" in a cheerful tone.

The receptionist, whose nameplate read "Mrs. Donnelly," said, "May I help you gentlemen with something?"

Purdy was dressed in weary blue jeans and old Adidas and wore his Colorado Rockies cap. Alan's jeans were newer than Sam's, and his sweatshirt was nicer, but the flip-flops on his feet screamed *"Tourist!"*

"Hello. Hello. I'm Sam Grady. This is my brother, Alan." Sam walked over to the reception desk and held out his hand for Mrs. Donnelly. Alan, befuddled, followed him across the room and did the same. Her hand was dry and icy. She smelled of floral bath soap.

"We're from Denver," said Purdy.

"How nice. Is there something I can do for you?" Mrs. Donnelly asked.

"We wanted to see Ms. Baumann. We're looking for an attorney. For our business."

"I'm afraid you will have to wait until Monday, gentlemen. Mrs. Baumann is out for the rest of the day. Would you like to come back, say, ten o'clock Monday morning? With an appointment?"

Purdy didn't bother to check with Alan about his plans. "That will be fine, ma'am, thank you," he said.

"And your name again?" She had a pencil poised over an appointment calendar.

"I'm Sam Grady. This is my brother—"

"Yes, Alan. And this is about?"

"Business. Setting up a business."

"Then we'll see you Monday, Mr. Grady. We'll see you on Monday."

Sam and Alan were exhausted when Monday morning finally rolled around. The weekend had provided the only uninterrupted recreation of their trip, and they had overindulged, riding the steep trails above the Uncompahgre for eight hours both Saturday and Sunday. Alan and Lauren had played phone tag over the course of the weekend but had never connected.

Because Purdy didn't make it out of bed Monday until nine-thirty, they were fifteen minutes late for their ten o'clock appointment with Rachel Baumann. Mrs. Donnelly greeted them as they walked into the waiting room. Rachel Baumann stood next to her secretary's desk.

She was thin and stately. Her thick hair, once blond, now steel, fell almost to her shoulders. The years couldn't disguise her history as a beautiful woman. She wore a simple dress in a floral print. It hung on her as well as if it had been tailored for a queen.

Sam Purdy held out his hand in the waiting room and said, "Azaleas."

Rachel looked confused.

"Your dress. Azaleas. Very pretty. My wife's a florist."

She looked down at her own dress and examined the print. She said, "Thank you." She looked at Alan. He felt as though he were onstage. He didn't know what to do with his hands.

"Won't you come back to my office, gentlemen?"

Sam turned briefly toward Alan and said, "You know, I'm not sure that will be necessary. We actually just wanted to meet you, just need a minute of your time, right now. We're thinking about doing some business up here and wanted to meet a local lawyer, see if we could handle all the legal stuff right here in Ouray. You know, locally."

She waited patiently for Purdy to go on. When he didn't, she asked, "What kind of business are you in, Mr. Grady?"

"Bicycles," Sam said without skipping a beat. "Sales, rentals, repairs. We even fabricate custom frames and wheels."

Alan Gregory, who had been enjoying Purdy's impromptu fantasy, suddenly found himself looking at his friend with incredulity unwillingly plastered across his face.

Sam continued, "We have a successful shop in Denver. Think we can repeat it up here. Actually, we're sure we can. Absolutely. We think this part of the San Juans can be the next hot mountan-biking spot. Get some of the overflow from Moab."

Baumann looked briefly at her unpainted fingernails and perfectly trimmed cuticles, then gazed into Sam Purdy's eyes. "And I assume you have plans to carry you through the winter? A sideline of some kind?"

Purdy felt like kicking himself for not anticipating the question. His smooth delivery faltered. Finally, he said, "Sure, in the winter we'll rent cross-country skis. Do tours. Things like that. Maybe snowmobiles. I like snowmobiles."

"Oh. Things like *that,*" Rachel said. "This isn't Denver, you know, Mr. Grady. It's pretty quiet up here in February, when most of the tourists in these parts are spending their money skiing over in Telluride."

Purdy just nodded. He was trying hard to find his place again.

"And I'm sure you know there are already a couple of bicycle stores in town that are quite established."

"Sure, sure. We're never scared by competition. We can outservice and outprice anybody. So, you do commercial work? Leases, incorporations, et cetera, et cetera?"

"Of course. At least, the kind of commercial work one

might expect to run into in Ouray County. I handle some mine claims, but mostly I have a general practice. I'm just an old country lawyer, gentlemen."

"Then we can call you when we need some help setting up shop? This trip is just for scouting."

"Scouting, I see. Of course you may call again."

Mrs. Donnelly reached into her desk drawer and handed her boss's card across her desktop to each of the visitors.

Rachel Baumann nodded and said, "It's been very nice to meet you." She looked at Alan Gregory quizzically. "Both of you."

As the two men exited the building, Baumann turned to her secretary and said, "That was odd, Arna." She excused herself, walked down a short hallway into her private office, closed the heavy door behind her, and, hands limp at her sides, tried hard not to cry.

Seconds later, Baumann was surprised and perplexed when she looked out her window. She watched the men climb into a big four-wheel-drive car. But the car didn't have the license plates she expected it to have. It was adorned instead with familiar green Colorado plates.

Rachel had been figuring, for sure, that the two men were from Utah.

"Let's get back to the B & B and hope they'll serve us a late breakfast. Then we can ride some more before it gets too late. I need to think about what happened in there."

Purdy couldn't get enough mountain biking.

But the experience in Rachel Baumann's office had precipitated a rapid change in Alan's appetite, from robust to anemic. He said, "That woman was suspicious, Sam. You shook her up somehow with that lame story. I think she knew we weren't in the bike business. She wasn't fooled. Snowmobiles? Shit."

"Yeah, she was suspicious, all right. Contained it well, though. But it wasn't my lame story she was leery of. It was more the *idea* of us, you know? I think she's been expecting somebody to show up. But she wasn't sure we were who she was waiting for. And she wasn't sure we weren't."

"I'd like to pretend I followed that, Sam, but, I didn't."

"That lady in there, she knows two things. She knows we weren't who we said we were. And she knows who she's afraid we really were."

"And who's that? Who is she afraid of?"

"See, we don't know that, do we? That's our disadvantage. We don't know who she's afraid we are. But she's obviously off-balance, too, because she doesn't know who we *are.* Maybe Lauren knows something new by now. I sure as hell hope so."

Alan reached down and started the engine. "I don't know exactly what happened in there, but it doesn't feel good. Maybe we should just go back and tell her who we are, what we're doing. Put her mind at ease about us. Tell her she might be in danger."

Purdy couldn't disguise his disdain. "Civilians are such wusses. Alan, that woman is well aware she's in danger. And you know what? I don't like this new development, either. I'm not having anywhere near as much fun on this trip now as I was fifteen minutes ago. But we don't know the consequences of anything we're doing, so we need to be extra careful about what we tell whom. Agreed? You go ahead and call Lauren if you want. When you do, tell her if she wants me to read any more lines in this play of hers, it's time for her to open the goddamn curtain."

Alan was silent for a couple of blocks. Finally, he turned his head and gazed across the front seat and said, "Sam?"

"Yeah?"

"Did I hear you right in there? You said, 'fabricate custom frames'?"

"That's right, ace, that's what I said."

"You're quite a bullshitter."

"I hang around with pros. I've had some great tutorials."

Lauren was well rested after a weekend of long novels and long naps. A call from Teresa on Sunday night had tempered her anxiety about her sister's safety. And a call from Alan Gregory minutes before she left her sister's house Monday morning had provided the first encouragement she had felt in days.

She drove Teresa's car downtown. After dropping her things in the conference room, she poked her head into Robin's office. Robin was stuffing her briefcase full of files she needed for a late-morning court appearance.

Lauren said, "I found Teresa. Or she found me. She's on a cruise ship."

"She's on a cruise ship?" Robin asked, her tone dubious.

"Well, not exactly. Not yet. She leaves tomorrow. She's on her way down to San Diego right now. She apologized for being out of touch. She got offered a job doing short cruises in Mexico for a couple of weeks. Apparently somebody who saw her show in Vegas called her to fill in when another comedian got sick."

"Where in Mexico?"

"Pacific coast. Cabo San Lucas, Mazatlán, Puerto Vallarta, maybe to Manzanillo. How far do you think you could go in four days?"

"You give me four days and I promise you that I could get lost so far into the Amazon that nobody would find me."

"Having escapist fantasies, Robin?"

"I'm afraid they've become routine at this point. By

any chance, did you ask your sister to *call* me? Perhaps even convince her that it might be in her best interest to consult with her attorney about this case occasionally?"

"I told her to call you. She said she would. I actually hoped you would have already talked with her by now." Lauren was tempted to apologize for her sister's awkward unreliability, but didn't.

Robin Torr looked exasperated as she shook her head twice in each direction.

Lauren said sheepishly, "I guess she didn't call."

"Good guess. Did you ask her about Daphne?"

"I didn't ask her. But I told her about the affidavit."

"What did she say?"

"She got a little huffy."

Robin muttered, "Apparently runs in the family."

Lauren ignored the dig. "From the tone of her response, I got the impression that Daphne's story is basically true and that the—um, affair? liaison? whatever—was a one-time thing for Teresa."

"So there are no more Daphnes in the woodwork?"

Lauren shook her head. What she said to herself was *God, I hope not.*

"You have a number for your sister where I can reach her?"

"No."

Robin sighed. "Did you by any chance ask her what her feelings were about continuing this dubious crusade? In her absence, and in her stead, I might add."

"Not directly. I told her I thought all of us were in some danger. She said she understood that, then she said she would consider dropping it if you and I felt too threatened. I told her that we felt plenty threatened and that she needed to think carefully about what she wanted to do."

"And she said?"

"She said she would."

"When? Between routines? On the promenade deck in the mornings? How the hell am I supposed to run this case without access to my client?"

Lauren looked down at her burning hand, then back up at Robin. "I guess we'll just run it the same way the defense is running their case without access to a defendant."

Robin removed her glasses and rubbed her eyes.

"You said you had something else. If it's good, tell me now. If it's going to upset me, wait till after I get back from court."

Lauren chose to be silent.

Robin placed her glasses carefully back on her nose, using the ear pieces to try to corral her hair. "Oh, God. I can't wait. Tell me now."

"It's good and bad, actually. The good part is that I think I found out what Pratt was after on his trip."

"Yeah? That's great. So far I like it."

"And the bad part is that what I said last week about maybe enlisting some help from Colorado wasn't exactly true. The truth is that I found out about Pratt by involving some other people without asking you whether or not it was okay."

The glasses came off again. Robin Torr sat all the way back on her leather desk chair. "You did what?"

Lauren looked at the credenza behind Robin and said, "Those flowers sure are pretty."

"The flowers are Wiley's way of saying he doesn't want me to be mad at him. You gonna send me some now, too?"

"Oh, go ahead and be mad, Robin. What I did was I asked some people from Boulder, some friends, to check on a few things in Moab. Discreetly. I did it because I was afraid that anybody we sent from Utah would be followed, like Pratt was. My friends found out some useful things in Moab that they don't think the police know. They followed Pratt's trail and ended up in Ouray. In Colorado. They found Rachel Misker. She's on that list we put together; she's part of Lester Horner's old BYU crowd. It looks like maybe Pratt was on his way to talk with her when he was killed."

"Ouray's in the mountains, right?"

"Yeah, near Telluride."

"Have your friends talked with her? Do we know where she fits in our puzzle?"

"They didn't interview her, but they met with her this morning. They introduced themselves to her as potential clients. She's an attorney. Their impression is that she's scared of something. Real scared. They're waiting for instructions from us—something, unfortunately, neither of them is particularly good at."

"Waiting?"

"No. Taking instructions."

"Who are they?"

"One's a detective from Boulder. A policeman. His name is Sam Purdy. He's good. We've worked together quite a bit. Right now he's officially on vacation; he's doing this thing in Ouray as a favor to me. The other half of this little team of mine is Alan Gregory. My very own."

"Why did you do this without asking me?"

"I figured you would say no."

"You figured right." She paused and looked out the window. "This doesn't do a whole lot for the level of trust between us, does it?"

"I suppose not, Robin. But it may do a hell of a lot for Teresa's case."

"I don't play that way, Lauren."

"Well, this isn't a game anymore, Robin. As far as I can tell, the other side has started to use live ammo."

"So you called out the cavalry? On your own authority?"

Lauren laughed. "Sam Purdy may be the cavalry, Robin. Alan is more like Dennis the Menace. He's a magnet for trouble. Whatever Alan manages to attract in the way of mayhem, I wanted Sam around to protect him."

"Well. Although I'm happy for the new information, I'm angry you didn't trust me enough to allow me to be part of this decision."

"I'm sorry. I truly am. I did what I thought was best."

Robin Torr looked over her shoulder at the dozen yellow long stems. "For the record, I'm not fond of roses. Wiley's never gotten it right. I have to wonder how much of an apology he's actually making when he sends me a big bouquet of flowers that he knows I don't particularly like. And you know what else? I'm beginning to realize I'm a little envious of that boyfriend of yours. Wiley wouldn't do something insane for me like

Alan is doing for you, even if I got down on my knees and begged him. Your guy may be truly short on smarts, but it sounds to me like he sure loves you."

Lauren smiled, shrugged, nodded.

Robin sculpted a mischievous smile from her thin lips. "So, now that he's finished doing his job in Ouray, are you going to invite Alan to Salt Lake and take him to the Side Pocket to meet Harley? Maybe play some eight ball?"

Lauren winced, then blushed. She didn't smile. She said, "These days it's nine ball. And why don't we just make it a fivesome? You come along and bring Wiley. I'm sure he and Alan and Harley will get along famously."

Robin drummed her fingers on the desktop.

"We're quite a pair, aren't we? I mean, we are *soooo* together. Have our lives in such perfect order."

"Yeah. That's us. We're role models for our generation. We are absolutely fit to be the moral judges of the cosmos."

By midafternoon Robin Torr was completing the last of a dozen phone calls to people who she thought, perhaps, might have been in a position to, maybe, hear if Blythe Oaks had ever before been accused of any sexual impropriety. The time spent on the phone had been dispiriting. She had been hung up on more times than she had been spoken to politely, and she had received no information of any value to the case. She feared she had burned more than a few bridges. For nothing.

She was packing her briefcase to make an early exit from the office when Elsie Smith buzzed her with an incoming call.

"Who is it, Elsie?"

"She says her name is Mary Brown."

"What does she want?"

"She wouldn't say."

Irritated, Robin fingered the button blinking on her phone and said, "Robin Torr."

"Hello, I'm, um, calling to offer you some information for your case."

Robin sat forward, reflexively grabbed a pencil, and dropped it into her electric sharpener. The machine whirred.

She stilled her voice. "And what case might that be?"

"You know. The comedian one."

Yes. "With whom am I speaking?"

"You can call me Mary. Mary Brown."

"But that's not your name?" Robin regretted the question the moment she asked it. She squeezed her eyes tightly, wishing she could retrieve the words.

Silence from Mary Brown. Robin thought she'd blown it. She rushed on, hopefully, lightly, "What would you like to tell me?"

"I've heard you're trying to find evidence about Blythe Oaks. About her relationships with women. You're calling people. I know some things from a long time ago. I think you need to know them. It's not at all what you think." She paused.

Robin's heart leapt, then sank. From the woman's tone, Robin sensed that she was waiting to be disbelieved.

Robin gave her time to resume on her own, then said, "I'm eager and grateful for any information you can offer me." Torr wasn't yet sure of the woman's motivation for calling. Was she interested in helping or in diverting Teresa Crowder's efforts against Oaks?

"Blythe believed—" The woman started, then stopped.

Robin analyzed the voice. Middle-aged. Blythe's age. Confident. Educated. "Yes?" *Please.*

"Blythe always had special friends. Special friendships with girls—with women, I mean."

"I'm not sure I understand." *Go on, please. Just keep talking.*

"We girls relied on each other in those days, in ways that might not be easily understood. Especially by outsiders."

Another pause. Robin guessed that her caller was waiting for some affirmation that she comprehended what she was talking about. But she didn't understand.

"The way we were with each other was important for us. It gave us, well, sustenance. And affection. It was our only source of . . . I don't know what. We were away from home. We needed each other."

Robin Torr waited, counting silently to three, before she responded. "Those days?"

"When we were girls. At school. Before we married. Don't get me wrong—we all married. But the times were chaste times. We were chaste girls. We stuck together. In every way. We still do."

"You were at BYU with Blythe?"

"I'd rather not say."

Robin wondered if she was talking with Rachel Baumann. A break, finally. Finally. *Don't screw this up, Robin.* She scratched notes with her yellow pencil, trying to catch up with the conversation thus far.

"So Blythe had special friendships. What made them special?"

The woman's voice fell into the soft cushion of reminiscence. "We were so caring then, so close. And warm. We pampered each other. We loved each other. Blythe used to say we were romantic friends, not just girlfriends."

Robin wanted to know if they were sexual friends, but she knew she couldn't ask yet. She was trying to reel this woman in slowly, gently. She pondered her next move, wishing she could plan this conversation as though it were a deposition, the questions penned out in advance, the answers anticipated.

Before she spoke again, the woman said, "A kiss didn't mean anything then. Doesn't. But it does, of course. You know what I'm talking about, don't you? It was another way of caressing each other, of caring. It was part of showing how special we were to each other. Of avoiding the dangers that the devil planted with . . . boys."

Robin thought: *There are kisses and there are kisses. Friendly pecks, even on the lips, don't usually occur in bathroom stalls.* Without thinking it through, Robin asked, "Where did the boys fit in?"

"The boys came later, after their missions. But before we married, we couldn't be familiar with boys. Decent girls didn't. Decent girls *don't.*" Some condescension infiltrated her voice. "It would have been immoral. Christian men and women unite to form Christian families. Not before. Never. We didn't dance with Satan."

"But you girls had each other?"

"Yes." The tone Robin Torr heard softened again. "We had each other. It was very special. A treasure. Truly, a treasure."

"I see," Robin said, though she didn't. She was at a loss as to what else she might say.

"And we still do have each other. Some of us are as close as we ever were. And I'm relieved that you seem to understand. I didn't expect you to. Whatever might have happened to Blythe in Washington is absolutely not what the papers are saying it was. What happened was nothing degrading or sinful at all."

Robin heard background noises in the receiver pressed against her ear.

"You are just hurting people, decent people, by pursuing this. Stop your calls. Please let her rest in peace. I need to go now."

"Please. May I call you? If I have more questions? If I need to know more?"

"I don't think that would be wise."

"Will you call me again? Please. Let's say, in a week. As you can imagine, I need to speak with my client about this. I may have new questions."

The woman said, "I won't promise," and hung up.

Robin slowly replaced the receiver in its cradle. She was mildly surprised to discover she'd been squeezing it in her hand. When she looked up she saw Elsie Smith standing in the doorway to her office. Torr hadn't heard the door open.

"Yes."

"Anything else before I go, Mrs. Torr?"

"No, Elsie."

"Will Mrs. Brown be a new client?"

"No, Elsie, she won't. Go on home. I'll be done here in a minute. I'll lock up."

That's odd, Robin thought, as her secretary closed the door behind her. Elsie is never curious about clients.

Robin resharpened a pencil that didn't need it and

returned to her legal pad to expound on the quick notes she had made during the phone conversation with Mary Brown. The door to her office opened again.

Wiley Torr stood in the doorway this time.

The Mary Brown notes sat conspicuously in the middle of the desk blotter. Robin looked down at them furtively, as though they were letters from a lover she wished to hide from her husband. Wiley's blue eyes followed Robin's to the pad.

She ripped the sheets along their perforation and slid them into the filing tray on the credenza behind her desk. She tried to act nonchalantly.

"Want to get some dinner, Robin? We need to talk."

"I wish you had called."

"I had a meeting on the fourth floor. Just finished. Hoped you might be happy to see me."

"I'm, uh, not quite done here."

"Really? I saw Elsie at the elevator. She said you were finished for the day."

"I just gave her that impression so she wouldn't feel bad about going home."

Wiley shifted his weight from his left foot to his right and adjusted his grip on his briefcase. His nervous energy was spilling over despite his attempts to control it. Lately, Robin had been giving him the impression that his agitation was something she barely tolerated.

"So that means no? About dinner?"

Robin hesitated. *What could it hurt?*

Be cautious. "I need a little time to finish up. I'll meet you somewhere in, say, half an hour, forty-five minutes."

Wiley smiled as though he had just been awarded a prize in a raffle. He suggested a trendy restaurant that would cost twice what he was usually willing to pay.

Robin said, "That's fine, Wiley." She glanced at her watch. "Six o'clock?"

Wiley Torr waited impatiently, aware of the passage of each minute, until their waiter was almost ready to deliver the entrees. Satisfied with his restraint, he finally began pressing his wife for an update on her strategy regarding Teresa Crowder's case.

Robin, on the other hand, passed much of the same interlude growing annoyed at Wiley, who had been mindlessly scraping his salad fork from side to side next to his plate. The dinner had been a bad idea. How could she think Wiley would be any different now than he had been a few days before? She consoled herself and passively expressed her irritation by not offering to share her appetizer. And by reminding herself of the wince on Wiley's face when she had ordered it. The shrimp fritters were the most expensive appetizer on the menu. She knew; she had checked.

"Wiley," she said in response to his query about her client, "please stop sliding your fork around for a second and listen to me."

He looked at his left hand, which held the offending fork, as though it were a renegade part of his body. He dropped both hands to his lap, configured a self-conscious smile, and looked at his wife. "In case you have forgotten, our firms are representing opposing sides in this matter. I don't want to talk about the Crowder case again until it's over. Let me be clear. I *will not* talk with you about the Crowder case again until it's over. And that includes the time it might take to exhaust any appeals. Got it?" Robin raised her wineglass to her lips and considered the merits of ordering a full bottle and really pissing her husband off.

"Appeals?" Wiley blurted, his voice as out of control as his hand had been seconds before. Other diners quieted their conversations in the expansive dining room. Heads turned toward the booth the Torrs occupied.

"You'll actually file this thing and carry it to trial? And after you get slaughtered in court, an appeal? You can't do that. Think of your client. Think of the expense for your firm. Think of the poor Oaks family. Think about me. What you're doing is cruel. This can't go on, Robin. Darn! Give it up!" He sat back and straightened his tie, as though that would punctuate a completion of his return to decorum.

The outburst neither surprised nor upset Robin. She felt as though she were watching it on film. "Are you done making a fool of yourself yet, Wiley? If you're not, I'm walking out of here right now. Don't push me tonight. I'm not in the mood."

He glared at her, and his face flushed in exasperation. Almost under his breath, he said, "I'm sure you'll reconsider when your hormones subside."

The waiter approached with their entrees. He slid an artfully presented platter in front of each of them. When he asked if there would be anything else, Robin smiled pleasantly and asked him to bring a certain bottle of vintage Burgundy.

The waiter eagerly returned with the bottle, opened it ceremoniously, and filled her glass. Wiley covered his glass with his hand and said nothing. Robin hesitated briefly, permitting the waiter to retreat from their table, then raised her glass, took one sip of what turned out to be a truly fine wine, and said, "To you, Wiley. A real jerk."

Then Robin stood, retrieved her coat and purse from next to her on the upholstered bench, and headed toward the front door of the restaurant. Two steps from the table, she turned back toward her husband and said over her shoulder, "Don't have a coronary about the tab, honey. Give the bill to James and Bartell. God knows, this was a business dinner if I've ever been to one."

Robin drove straight from the restaurant to Teresa Crowder's bungalow, which was lit up, inside and out, like Temple Square at Christmas.

Lauren yanked open the front door before Robin was halfway down the cracked cement walk.

"Oh, Robin, thank God you're here. I've left messages for you all over town."

Robin, sensing the urgency, broke into a run the last few steps. "What's wrong? Is it Teresa? Is she okay?"

"No—yes—I don't know. Come here." She grabbed Robin's gloved hand and pulled her down the hallway to the little house's main bedroom. Teresa's bedroom. Lauren entered the brightly lit room first and then turned to watch the expression on her friend's face.

Robin Torr jumped back involuntarily at what she saw. She bumped against the open door. It crashed into the wall.

Teresa's brass bed sat beside a window against the long wall that faced the door. The sheetcase was turned down, as though a maid had been in to prepare the room. The rest of the room was Teresa's version of neat. Some clean laundry had been folded, waiting to be put away, in a tall pile on top of a small desk strewn with papers. A pair of cotton sweats that Teresa used as pajamas on cold nights was thrown over the back of a chair. The door to the small closet was open. Two pairs of shoes spilled into the opening.

Robin's gloved hands covered her mouth as she turned her attention back to the bed.

A kitchen knife, a big one, with an eight- or ten-inch blade and a wooden handle, stood impaled, erect and mean, in the center of the sheets, a foot below the pillows.

Through her gloved fingers Robin managed to say, "That's it, just the knife? No note? Nothing?"

"It's from the kitchen. They stuck it right where Teresa's heart would be, Robin. They want to kill her. They want to kill my little sister."

"Have you called the police?"

Lauren shook her head. "I didn't know if I should."

Torr looked at her, puzzled. "Why the hell not?"

"Are you sure that they're not part of this? Part of everything, Pratt's death?"

"The police aren't corrupt here, Lauren. They may be too deferential at times where the Church is concerned. But they sure as hell need to know about this."

A loud knock on the front door caused both women to jump.

Lauren ran to respond. Robin followed right after.

A man dressed in corduroys, a flannel shirt, old moccasins, and a green down jacket stood at the door.

"Harley, thanks for coming." Lauren turned back toward the living room and addressed Robin. "I called Harley when I couldn't reach you. I was scared. I didn't know what else to do."

John Harley took two long steps across the room and extended his hand. "Hello, I'm John Harley. People call me Harley. I'm a friend of Lauren's."

"Yes, I know, she's mentioned you. Robin Torr. Nice to meet you."

"Robin is Teresa's attorney, Harley. Come on, let me show you what they did. This way."

Harley followed Lauren down the narrow hall. Robin trailed after them.

Harley didn't stop in the doorway. He strode directly over to the bed and stuffed his hands in the pockets of his coat. He leaned over and looked at the knife. He stared at it for half a minute and said, "Darn it. That's something, isn't it?"

When nobody responded, Harley asked, "How did they get in?"

Lauren answered, "I don't know. There are no broken windows or anything. But, then, this place isn't exactly Fort Knox. I don't even know when this happened. I haven't been in Teresa's bedroom in a couple of days. At least I don't think so."

Robin Torr interjected, "I'm going to go call the police. Lauren. Where is there another phone? I don't want to use the one by the bed. In case"—she paused—"he touched it."

Lauren shivered at the image of the person—the man—actually in the house, wandering around, touching things. Fouling things. "There's one in the kitchen. Back through the living room. It's on the wall next to the refrigerator."

Robin headed for the kitchen. Lauren edged over to Harley and gratefully accepted a hug and an arm around her shoulder.

"This is out of my league. But I can tell you that I'm absolutely terrified for you. You can't stay here. It looks to me like somebody is seriously threatening you."

"Me?" The thought that she, not her sister, might be the addressee of this terrorism was a novel one for Lauren.

"It's Teresa's lawsuit, Harley, not mine. I'm just a volunteer."

"It's always been her lawsuit. That hasn't kept other people from dying so far, has it?"

"This is my sister's bedroom. I'm staying in the guest room across the hall."

"And you want to assume this guy knew that? Exactly where each of you sleeps?"

She buried her face in Harley's chest and said, "Don't, Harley, please."

Robin Torr walked back into the room. She felt awkward stumbling in on their embrace.

"The police are on their way," she said. "We probably shouldn't wait in this room. We might screw something up. Let's go back out to the living room, okay?" *At the very least, get you two out of the bedroom.*

Lauren and Harley sat chastely at opposite ends of the sofa. Robin took the room's only chair. The phone rang immediately, startling all of them. They stared at each other and listened to it ring a second time.

"We should answer it. Maybe it's my sister."

Reluctantly, Robin accepted Lauren's suggestion. "I'll get it," she said, and walked into the kitchen. Seconds later she returned, some playfulness in her eyes. She said, "Lauren, it's for you." As Lauren walked past her, Robin raised her eyebrows and whispered, "It's Alan. From Colorado. It looks like all hands are on deck, now."

"He wants me to fly to Telluride tomorrow and meet him. Sam Purdy—the cop I told you about—needed to get back to Boulder early for some reason. He took Alan's car so he could return his rented bike. I guess it's about time I met Rachel Misker, anyway. But I won't go unless I know that Teresa is safe."

Robin Torr said, "And as is par for the course, we don't even know where the hell your sister is. How on earth are we going to ensure her safety?"

Harley had grown uncharacteristically quiet. He was examining his cuticles.

Robin continued, "Well, at least we know where she's supposed to be tomorrow, right? She should be in San Diego getting on that cruise ship. We do know which cruise ship, don't we?"

Lauren didn't respond.

Harley, too, seemed lost in space.

"We know which cruise ship, Lauren, don't we?"

"Yeah. Yes, we do. I do."

"Well, if you're going to Telluride, I guess that means I'm going off to San Diego to find my client."

"Would you, Robin? That would make me feel a whole lot better. Thanks."

A loud conversation between two police officers intruded from outside. A rap on the door followed instantly.

Harley said, "The cops are here."

Close to midnight, the police gone, Lauren and Harley resumed their seats in the living room.

Robin joined them a minute later. "I got a seat to San Diego first thing tomorrow morning. It looks like I'm going on a cruise. My first." She did a little dance.

Lauren smiled gratefully at her friend. "Not exactly a vacation, though, is it? Can't we just get the cops to watch her? I mean, the Salt Lake police think this knife is indication of a serious threat."

"And which cops do we try to enlist? California? San Diego? Mexico? The U.S. Coast Guard?"

Lauren felt exhausted. She shrugged her shoulders at Robin's question.

With an edge in his voice that Lauren had never heard before, Harley said, "What makes you two think you're immune from whatever is happening here? Although I find it fascinating, the reality is that the two of you are behaving as though Teresa is the only possible victim of this madness."

The attorneys both looked at Harley. Each of them used a gaze that they employed with reluctant witnesses.

"She's the obvious choice, isn't she?"

"No, she isn't. I don't think so, anyway."

Robin was intrigued. "Why do you say that, Harley?"

"With what I've heard here tonight, Lauren, it sounds like your sister is willing to fight this battle as long as she doesn't have to go too close to the front lines. If either of you weren't putting in the energy to continue her fight, I think she would drop it. And I think whatever adversary you're fighting wouldn't have too hard a time figuring that out. If I was against you—if I was the one who wanted you to cut this stuff out—I wouldn't go after Teresa. I would go after the one of you who is most likely to press to continue this thing."

Robin said, "That's you, Lauren."

Harley nodded. "That's right."

Lauren looked back and forth between the two of them as though she were watching a tennis match.

"Lauren," Robin said, "if this nut kills you, Teresa won't press this. She isn't strong enough to do that. She'll tell me to drop the investigation. I'll have no choice without a client. You know that's true. Harley's got a valid point. If Teresa got hurt, you would push this until the day you died, and you know it."

Lauren didn't want to hear it. "But what about the press? The media? These assholes can't just start killing us and avoid scrutiny. What about all the Mormon-bashing press the Church is always complaining about? They would feast on this."

Robin persisted. "Really? Have you read very much about Pratt's death lately? I haven't. Is Blythe Oaks's murder still filling the front pages? The press has a short memory. The Church absorbed ten times this much publicity about the Salamander thing in the late eighties without even a blip in their image. I don't think we can count on the free press as being a significant deterrent where the Church is concerned. The LDS leadership has been stonewalling the national press since before Richard Nixon had even heard of Watergate."

Harley nodded in agreement. "You're the most likely target, Lauren. If they're smart, anyway. And this guy is smart. Sure, it's prudent to protect your sister. But I think you're in the most danger here, not her."

"I'm surprised at you, Harley. You think the Church is behind all this, too, don't you? Why? This is your church we're trashing here."

Harley fidgeted. "Let's just say tonight's events leave me with some new concerns. I've also got to do some serious contemplating, and I've got to read a few things. Then I'll know better exactly what I think." Harley was growing unnaturally nervous. "Can I interest anybody in some breakfast at Bill & Nada's?"

Despite her fatigue, Lauren was tempted.

But Robin answered first. "Not me, thanks," she said.

Lauren declined, too.

Harley made them repeat the promise they had made to the cops not to stay in Teresa's house that night. After accepting Lauren's gratitude for coming over, he made his exit to Bill & Nada's, alone. Given what he had just seen in Teresa's bedroom, what he really wanted, desperately, was a drink.

Robin waited for Harley to leave before telling Lauren about the phone call from Mary Brown. They discussed the ramifications for a few minutes before the futility created by Mary Brown's pseudonym caused the conversation to degenerate into silence.

Lauren finally cracked the quiet. "If you didn't get any of the frantic messages I left earlier, Robin, why were you coming over here tonight?"

Robin Torr started to laugh—gently at first, but soon she was laughing so hard, she had to bend over to catch her breath in order to speak.

"I came over here tonight because I didn't think it would be safe to go home to Wiley. I was going to ask you if I could sleep here. I think that would have left me to sleep in Teresa's bed."

Lauren didn't join in the laughter.

Robin stopped, too. In seconds, her eyes started to tear. "You know, for some reason I can't precisely pinpoint, I feel like a dolphin that's being flushed into a drift net. I can see the danger coming, but I'm afraid I can't escape it."

Lauren stepped over to her friend and embraced her. "You got a favorite hotel in town? Want to share a room?"

They shared not only a hotel room but also a taxi to Salt Lake City's airport the next morning.

Before leaving the Hilton, Robin had called her office from the lobby and told Elsie that she would be out of town attending to family matters for a few days. She said she couldn't give Elsie a number but would call in for messages. On the way to the airport they directed the cab driver to stop at Robin and Wiley Torr's town house. Lauren questioned the judiciousness of stopping by so early in the day. Robin assured her that Wiley would already have gone to work.

He either had gone to work or had never home come from the restaurant the night before.

Robin packed a bag as quickly as she could and left Wiley a note saying that she needed some time to think and would be in touch with him within a week.

Checking in at the airport, Robin changed her reservation to San Diego so that she would have to switch planes in Phoenix to get to California.

Lauren chose a flight to Telluride that would involve a two-hour stopover in Denver and two different airlines.

Each of them made up fictitious names for their reservations.

Lauren felt overtly paranoid.

Although she jokingly complained about remorse at not being able to get any frequent-flyer credit, Robin labeled the fake names and indirect flights to their destinations "prudent."

As she saw her friend off to Phoenix, Lauren argued, "All paranoids consider their actions prudent. We're no different."

Sitting alone, waiting for her flight to Denver, Lauren was troubled by the mood that had descended over John Harley the night before. Unable to make sense of it, she finally wrote it off as a reasonable response to the bizarre, difficult circumstances.

She was looking forward to being back in Colorado. And to seeing Alan. And she was glad for that.

Freezing rain and faulty de-icing equipment in Chicago caused the plane that was to carry Robin Torr from Phoenix to California to arrive an hour and fifteen minutes behind schedule in Arizona. Torr's connecting flight subsequently arrived two hours late in San Diego. After a brief but maniacal taxi ride from the airport to the port, Robin discovered that she had missed the sailing of Teresa Crowder's cruise ship by about twenty minutes.

Lauren Crowder's journey to Telluride was less eventful. Although the sheer scale of Denver's mammoth new airport made the task of changing concourses and finding her gate slightly overwhelming to her, the connecting flight to Telluride was on time, and the plane's descent into the mountain airport was turbulence-free.

Alan Gregory spotted Lauren while she stood on the tarmac, fumbling in her carry-on trying to find her sunglasses. He was two steps from the door to the terminal when she walked in and saw his open arms. They embraced. They stared. They kissed. At the exact same moment, both said, "It's so good to see you." He grabbed her bag and slung it over his shoulder and led her to the rental car he had hired after Sam Purdy left town with the Land Cruiser.

On the long ride around the mountain from Telluride to Ouray, relief seeped into Lauren's spirit, offering some freedom from the constant tension that had been plaguing her in Utah. Within minutes of seeing Alan, she was animated and affectionate, even playful. She watched herself, mistrustful. She asked about friends in Boulder. Whether Alan had heard any news or gossip from the DA's office. Why Sam had had to go back to Boulder so suddenly.

"He had to testify at a hearing this morning. Something he hadn't anticipated."

With a little prompting from Alan, Lauren began a detail-laden exposition of the new chapters of her sister's story. Intermittently, she also lapsed into lengthy periods of poignant silence, her fingers stretched on his knee or twirling the hair that hung over his collar, the whole time awestruck at the beauty of the San Juans, which she was seeing for the first time.

A rule that had developed early in their relationship proscribed Alan from asking Lauren about the state of her multiple sclerosis immediately upon seeing her or speaking with her on the phone. Even if a limp was visible in her walk, or if she never took one hand from a coat pocket, or if fatigue seemed to be holding her hostage, he was to refrain from overt query or concern for some variable amount of time that she had preset in her head. Sometimes five minutes was sufficient, other times not. Alan hated the guessing game.

Just past the turn north toward Ridgway he finally asked, in as matter-of-fact a tone as he could muster, "How's your health?"

"I'm all right. Fine."

"You know what I mean."

"I know what you mean. I'm all right." She smiled, trying to be convincing.

He didn't turn toward her but said in a low, gentle tone, "Which, if my rusty translation skills are functioning okay, means in English, 'I've got some symptoms but they're pretty invisible, and I'm managing them, and I don't want to honor them with any discussion.' "

"Not bad. You been practicing on somebody else while I've been away?"

Her tone was light. He forced a smile in relief.

"Can I be permitted just a couple of"—he took his

right hand from the wheel and crushed his index finger and thumb together tightly—"tiny, tiny clarifications?"

"Depends."

He was surprised at the latitude she offered. He didn't hesitate. "Your vision is okay?"

"Yes. It's stable." Translation: not the same as good, but not awful.

"Are you falling down much?"

"Not too bad." Translation: my balance isn't any better, but I don't fall down very often.

"One more?"

"You're pressing your luck."

"Anything new? Any new exacerbations?"

Lauren was quiet.

"You'll tell me when you're ready?"

"Yes." She was looking away from him, out the window, at the endless miles of split-rail fence that bordered Ralph Lauren's ranch on the Dallas Divide.

Minutes later, on her own, she resumed her narrative about events in Salt Lake City.

When she got to the point in her story where she began talking about the previous night, where she described the knife impaled in her sister's mattress—"It was obscene, that's all, just obscene"—she abruptly stopped and looked out the side window. She started to cry, quietly. Alan took one of his hands from the steering wheel and touched her leg, fearful of stealing his eyes from the curvy road for even a moment. She seemed oblivious to his touch. She was rocking gently, her arms wrapped below her breasts, hugging herself.

At the first opportunity, he pulled the car to a stop on a small clearing off a dusty shoulder, the front of the car facing the Uncompahgre range. Swollen white clouds hung like ornaments above the jagged peaks. He reached across the front seat to hold her. With his touch, her sobs grew audible. She began shaking and leaned into him, her head buried in the crook of his neck. He could feel her sharp fingernails pressing into his skin through the thick yarn of his sweater.

"You must be terrified," he said a while later, after her crying had progressed from the stage of dark weeping to the stage where her primary interest was successful completion of a frantic search for a tissue.

She wiped her nose and stole a glance at him, her antennae sensitive to his judgment. None identified, she nodded a reply to his question, then blew her nose. She turned the rear-view mirror toward herself and used a fresh tissue to wipe away a torrent of mascara that had begun a trail down her right cheek.

She knew that he had assumed the tears were tears of fear for her sister and herself. She didn't tell him she was crying partly about the confusion she felt seeing him. Partly about the attraction to John Harley she couldn't explain. Partly about the odd repulsion she felt to the stability Alan offered.

She faced him and almost said, *I'm really confused.* Instead, she said, "I'm really frightened for Teresa, Alan."

Alan nodded. "Me too. Are the police watching her? Is somebody with her?"

"She's on a damn cruise ship, if you can believe it. Her lawyer, the woman I've told you about, Robin Torr, left this morning to find her, to make sure she's safe."

"She's on a cruise? Really?"

"Yes, she's on a ship, but, no, she's not vacationing. She's working. She got a gig. She's been working every week now for a while. Anyway, she's on one of those three- or four-day cruises they do off Mexico."

"Good for her, I guess."

"I would be happier for her if I knew that she was safe."

Alan watched a couple of bicyclists pause on the clearing where they were parked. The riders were winded and exhilarated, their faces pink and triumphant.

Alan reached out and began to rub Lauren's neck, pressing hard on the taut muscles across her shoulders, tracing her shoulder blades. She dropped her head, stretched her neck, murmured, and occasionally flinched at his touch. He rubbed and pressed until the murmurs outnumbered the moans, and then, with a few fingers below her chin, he gently raised her head, leaned in, and found her lips with his tongue. She offered hers in response. He moved his fingers into her soft hair and smelled her.

She slid her hands below his sweater and tugged his shirttail from his jeans. She wanted to feel flesh. He was so warm. Her fingers were cool. He shivered. She probed. He fiddled with her buttons and hoped she wasn't wearing a bra.

They made love in the car. The act felt as awkward as it did illicit.

For Lauren, the sex was liberating. She was so relieved, simply, that she still wanted him.

Alan struggled to respond to a question about Rachel Baumann. "She's proper. That's the best word I can use to describe her. She's composed and intelligent and formal. Proper."

"Like prissy?" Lauren asked.

"No, not at all, she's like . . . like a female version of Gregory Peck in *To Kill a Mockingbird.*"

"And you guys told her what?"

"Not me. I didn't tell her anything. Sam Purdy told her that we were thinking of opening up a bike shop here and might need some legal help."

Lauren shook her head in dismay at the image. "And you don't think she bought it?"

"I doubt it. Don't get me wrong; Sam was good. He has true talent as an actor. But she was suspicious, I thought, even before we opened our mouths."

"You said that when we talked on the phone. But what exactly do you mean? What kind of suspicious was she?"

"Given what you've told me, I think she's been expecting that somebody she either doesn't know or doesn't want to see is going to come to talk with her about something she doesn't want very much to talk about. Sam and I went back and forth about it after we left her office. He agrees with me. The lady's suspicious. Bordering on scared. But she's composed, not about to panic. I think she's waiting for something to happen up here that she wants nothing to do with."

Lauren sighed. "Which is where I come in, I guess."

"It looks like it's your role to play if you choose it. Can you tell me what it is you think she knows? What might be frightening her?"

"I guess I can tell you what we know. It isn't much. The problem is that we don't know exactly what she knows. We're guessing. We think she knows something incriminating about Blythe Oaks—either a history of harassment or evidence of her being a lesbian. But we're not sure. We're working on the assumption that Pratt Toomey was on his way up here to talk with her when somebody ambushed him. But we're making barely educated guesses about exactly what he was following up on."

Alan and Lauren were walking down Third Street in Ouray. The mountain light was brash and the air dry, the temperature cold enough to caution about the coming winter yet warm enough for just sweaters. She interrupted the progress of his aimless stroll by sliding her hand from his loose grip and touching him on the shoulder. As they turned to face each other, the sun, falling closer each day to its winter posture in the southern sky, shone on her black hair and into both their eyes. He pushed his sunglasses back up on his nose and brushed his sandy hair from his forehead with the back of his hand.

Lauren looked into his blue eyes and felt warm. "I haven't thanked you properly—you and Sam—for all you've done to help me and Teresa out. It was great, what you found out in Moab. And then coming up here. Without you guys, I wouldn't even know about Rachel Misker."

"Baumann."

"Baumann. I mean it, Alan. Don't joke. Given how dangerous this has gotten, I feel foolish for dragging the two of you into it. But you did great. Better than I had any right to hope. Thank you." She perched up on her tiptoes and pecked him lightly on his dry lips.

"I'm sure he'll tell you, so I might as well. Sam did almost all of it. I was Pancho; he was the Cisco Kid. I felt more like his valet than I did his partner."

Lauren smiled. "He's a pro, honey. Anyway, he

wouldn't even have been here if you hadn't come. And I'm sure you're underestimating your contribution."

They resumed their walk. He broke the silence. "You going to talk to her today? Rachel?"

"I think so. Yes. No reason to put it off."

"What are you going to tell her?"

"That's a tough one. You guys used the bicycle-store bit that I was planning on using, so that's out." She squeezed Alan's hand. He smiled. "So I think I'm going to tell her the truth."

"And what, just hope she'll spill her guts and rat on a fellow Mormon?"

"I've got some things I can ask her about. Hopefully, get her talking. We know her background. Some of it, anyway. When she was young, she was at BYU with a group of kids that included Blythe Oaks and Lester Horner and a bunch of other people, including a few guys who are now major players in the LDS Church."

"LDS? That's the Mormons?"

"Yeah, that's the Mormons, the Latter-day Saints. God, a couple of weeks in Salt Lake and I'm talking like a Utahan. It's scary. If I turn to you suddenly and ask you if you want some ice cream, or if I have an overwhelming need to know how the Jazz did, take me to see somebody, okay?" She exhaled, then continued. "Anyway, like at least half of this BYU group, Rachel ended up going to law school. But she never moved back to Utah, which makes her unusual among her peers. The other thing that makes me curious and suspicious about this college group is the fact that nobody in Provo at BYU will tell us anything about them. They seem to have misplaced everything related to attendance there in those years."

"That's odd."

"I thought so, too. It *would* be odd in Colorado—very odd. But it's apparently quite commonplace for documents to evaporate at LDS institutions in Utah. Nobody I talked to in Salt Lake City was very surprised that all these things turned out to be gone." Lauren thought for a moment about trying to explain to Alan the Mormon concept of faith-promoting and non-faith-promoting literature, but decided to save it for another time.

"And we have some information—which, unfortunately, comes from an anonymous phone call and therefore may be pretty unreliable—that leads us to believe that this group of friends included a clique of girls who were closer to each other than Mormon propriety might tolerate."

Alan looked askance at Lauren. "You think a group of them were lesbians?"

Hearing the question asked out loud jolted Lauren out of her assurance. "You know, the truth is, I don't think that. One of them, maybe even two of them, might have been lesbian, or maybe just believed they were." She thought about Teresa and Daphne. "My guess is—I mean, if any of this is true—that they were probably just experimenting, like kids do. But the social environment may have been even more bizarre in Provo in the sixties than it was everywhere else. The pressure on these Mormon kids is incredible. The Church pressure on teenagers to abstain from sex is pretty overwhelming."

"So your speculation leaves you where with Rachel? You're going to waltz into her law office and ask her, lawyer to lawyer, if her old buddy Blythe was a lesbian? Whether Blythe ever hit on her during the old schoolgirl days? Doesn't sound too promising a line of inquiry. If I were you, I wouldn't totally rule out the bicycle-store bit." He pointed down a side street. "Her office is just a couple of blocks down that way."

"Show me."

"You're not going to call first?"

"No. I think I want to surprise her. Take advantage of whatever suspicion or fear you and Sam saw in her face."

They walked to the east past an array of century-old wood buildings. Alan said, "I don't envy you this, honey. It sounds like what you're trying to do is to dig up dirt to discredit the woman who harassed your sister. I can understand why it would help, but it can't feel very good. In a perfect world, whether or not this woman was a lesbian should be absolutely irrelevant to what she did in Washington, D.C."

Lauren walked half a block, counting sidewalk cracks,

before responding. "You're right, of course. It doesn't feel good. But the truth is, for us to suggest that she would sexually harass another woman presupposes that she would be interested in sexual contact with one. I don't want to convict her of being lesbian. Clarence Thomas's crime wasn't that he was heterosexual. It was that he harassed a subordinate female using sexual coercion. But Anita Hill's charges would have fallen on deaf ears if Thomas had announced he'd always been gay. The rules aren't any different for Blythe Oaks. This isn't a perfect world we're fighting in—far from it. It's Utah."

Alan responded. "Don't misunderstand me. I'm not arguing you shouldn't pursue this, but what actually happened a few years ago is that when his confirmation was completed, nobody looked down on Clarence Thomas for being heterosexual. The same won't be true if Rachel Baumann confirms what you already suspect. Blythe Oaks's memory will be gored because she was a lesbian long before she gets crucified because she was guilty of harassing your sister. I can see how that will help Teresa win her case. I can't see how it will help you sleep at night."

Lauren had spotted the stenciled lettering on the second-story window of the gray stone building before Alan pointed it out.

"It's that one. The second floor," he said, giving her hand a final squeeze.

Lauren nodded. "Give me some time with her. I have no idea how long this will take." She looked at her watch. "Why don't we plan to meet for coffee. Same place we had lunch. Say, three o'clock?"

"You don't want me to come up with you?"

"I don't want to have to explain you and Sam and the bicycle business. Believe me, it was hard enough explaining the two of you to Teresa's lawyer."

"Well, good luck up there. I'll wait around a few minutes. At least let you make sure she's in."

"Thanks. I may need the luck." She reached up and kissed him, sliding her hands behind his neck, pressing hard. "And you'll get extra credit for tracking down a place to see an early movie. I think I'll be ready for some escape when this is all over."

She began walking toward the entrance to the building. To her back, he asked, "If I find an early movie, what form will the extra credit take?"

Lauren stopped on the second stone step, turned back to him with a mischievous smile, and replied, "A form illegal in the state of Utah." She bounced up to the door.

Arna Donnelly greeted Lauren with a pleasant smile. Lauren introduced herself and asked if she could speak briefly with Mrs. Baumann about a personal matter.

"I'm so sorry, Miss—is it Miss?—Crowder, but Mrs. Baumann is with a client right now. Would you like to make an appointment and come back another time?"

"Would you mind terribly if I waited? What I have won't take long, I promise."

"Well, I don't like to encourage people to wait without an appointment, but if you would like, when Mrs. Baumann is free, I'll be happy to ask her if she has just a moment to have a word with you. How's that?"

"That sounds great."

"May I get you some tea or coffee? Or a soft drink? I have diet."

Lauren was flipping through a neat row of magazines that sat on a polished table beside a Victorian loveseat. She had three choices: *Smithsonian, Self* or *Field & Stream.* Nothing topical or newsy. She smiled at Mrs. Donnelly. "No, nothing for me, thanks. I just had lunch."

She settled in for a long read about Indian artifact robbing in the Southwest.

About fifteen minutes later, a short, muscular man with hair the color of unpeeled carrots exited through an adjoining door into the waiting room. Lauren listened as Mrs. Donnelly chatted with him about whether or not he was ripening the green tomatoes from his garden in his basement again this year, and whether he was having any luck. Hers, apparently, were turning to mush for a reason she hadn't been able to discover. He assured her his tomatoes were fine and offered to stop by and see if he could be of any help. She declined. "Too late this year, I'm afraid, Andrew." He said a cordial good-bye to her and went on his way.

Mrs. Donnelly scribbled something on a piece of paper, rose from her desk, and walked through the door that Andrew had entered moments before. Lauren supposed she was on her way to inform Mrs. Baumann about her afternoon interloper.

A minute later, with Mrs. Donnelly back at her desk, Mrs. Baumann stood in the same doorway and said, "Ms. Crowder, won't you please come in? Though I'm afraid I can give you only a few minutes."

Lauren entered Mrs. Baumann's office. The stenciled pane—R. Baumann, Attorney at Law—she had seen from the street was on the bottom of one of the double-hung windows that faced the stunning southern end of the tiny valley. The big office was brightly lit, the sunlight filtered only by thin cotton tab curtains the color of wheat awaiting the thresher. Big overstuffed furniture—two chairs upholstered in a rich plaid, and a deep sofa of subdued greens and grays—almost covered a large Persian rug at one end of the room. Rachel Baumann guided Lauren to one of the chairs. She took the other, carefully smoothing her skirt as she sat. A primitive table of miter-cut knotty pine and quarter-sawn oak separated the two women. A spray of freesia spilled from a brass urn in the center of the table.

"Your office is gorgeous. I'm surprised, I expected, um—"

"Cowboy Victorian?" interjected Rachel Baumann with a tiny, satisfied smile.

"Yes."

"Mrs. Donnelly has been with me for years. That's her office out there. I let her do what she wants with it. It seems only fair. This office is mine. I like to feel like I'm working at home."

"Well, you must have a beautiful home."

"Thank you." Rachel tightened her lips into a narrow line.

Lauren thought she noticed a new set to Rachel's jaw.

"I apologize for having to rush you. But I have very little time. I have an appointment away from the office at two-thirty. What can I do for you, Ms. Crowder? Briefly, please." Baumann's face was kind and warm, but her manner was assertive and assured.

Lauren read the lines of the face for suspicion or fear. She saw none. She already liked this woman.

"I'm an attorney, Mrs. Baumann. I'm currently on leave from my position as a deputy district attorney in Boulder County. On the Front Range."

"I know where Boulder is, dear."

"Sorry. The reason I'm here is that I'm currently helping my sister, who lives in Salt Lake City"—Lauren paused and examined Mrs. Baumann's expression for any sign of distress at the mention of Utah but again saw nothing—"who is contemplating a lawsuit against an old classmate and onetime friend of yours at BYU."

"Blythe Truste."

Lauren wondered if there was a new timbre in Baumann's voice. She wasn't sure. "Yes. Blythe Truste. Blythe Oaks. I'm sure you've heard. I mean, about her tragic death."

"The whole—for want of a better word—affair has been terribly disconcerting to me. I need to warn you, Ms. Crowder, that although I'm sure you are sincerely interested in helping your sister, and I'm sure you have no reason to doubt the veracity of her accusations, my sympathies, which are influenced by history and allegiance, and not by reports in tawdry publications, rest firmly with the Oaks family. They seem to be the most certain victims here, so far."

Lauren had actually expected a stronger first volley from Rachel Baumann. Her confidence bolstered by the tepid defense, she pressed on. "I know this must be awkward for you. It is for me. But may I ask you just a few more questions?"

"I suppose you may. You have certainly come a long way for the privilege."

"You were at BYU together?"

"Yes, for a while."

"Your group of friends from college has become quite prominent. An amazing record of achievement, actually, for an entire graduating class, let alone a small group of close friends."

"There were some remarkable minds among us. That's true. Some more pedestrian ones as well, I assure you. But BYU is a Church school, and much of the advancement of my old friends has taken place in the Church."

Lauren found Baumann's disclaimer odd, as if advancement within the Church were somehow less valid or less valuable than other achievements.

"Certainly not Lester Horner," Lauren said.

"He is definitely an exception."

Lauren detected a tightening in Rachel's expression, a twitch in the corner of her mouth. "You knew Lester Horner?"

"Of course. He was remarkable even then, Ms. Crowder. We all suspected he was destined for great things." The calm in Rachel Baumann's countenance had returned.

Lauren advanced without pause. "We have statements that the women, the girls, in this BYU group considered themselves special friends—'romantic friends' is the term that's been used. Could you shed any light on that?"

"I could deny it, I suppose. It was a very long time ago. But you obviously have talked with someone from those days already. 'Romantic friends' was Blythe's term—well, Blythe's and Audrey's, anyway. A few of the other girls adopted it. I wasn't one of the ones that did. But, yes, although I haven't thought of it in years, I certainly heard it."

Audrey? "Did these romantic friendships included sexual activity?" Lauren expected offense to flash onto Rachel's smooth countenance. It didn't.

"I wouldn't know. I certainly never saw anything. But, then, we're not talking about hugs and holding hands, are we?"

"No."

"Sorry. Keep in mind that the morality constraints on students at BYU are severe. To my mind proper, but severe. And they were perhaps even more severe in those days. What you are suggesting would be out of the ordinary, to say the least."

For the first time, Rachel Baumann displayed some overt discomfort. She stared at her hands, then reached across the table and picked a dry petal from a freesia bud. The bud was the color of custard, the petal the color of dirt. Lauren held her breath and waited.

Rachel looked up at her. "Ms. Crowder, I don't know who in that old group you have been talking with, but I've had no contact with any of those women for years. I don't know how or why you've found me. I was an outsider in those days at school. I was a hanger-on, not part of Blythe's precious club. They may have considered each other to be some kind of special friends. They never considered me one, I can assure you. There was a time early on when I would have done anything for admission to that clique. By my sophomore year, I had grown uninterested in them. And they were never interested in me."

Resentment? Is this resentment?

"And Audrey is . . . ?" Lauren tried to make the question sound less than important to her than it was.

But Rachel recognized immediately that she had inadvertently supplied some new fuel for her visitor's stalling investigatory engine. "Oh, I don't remember what might have happened to Audrey. I can't even remember her last name. As I implied, it's not as though I've exactly been invited to reunions with those girls."

"By any chance, do you have a BYU yearbook from those days?"

"Again, sorry, but no. I'm not sentimental about those years. I'm a practical woman. It's not the sort of thing I would want to keep around." She looked discreetly at her watch, then intently at her visitor. "The past is always buried in a restless grave, Ms. Crowder. Always."

Lauren moved forward on her chair, trying to be sensitive to the time. She pointed to a pair of photographs in a hinged hammered-silver frame on the table. "Your family?"

Rachel smiled. "My daughter, Anita. My husband, Walter. He died, um, a long time ago."

"I'm sorry."

Rachel merely nodded.

"Your daughter is very attractive. She looks like you."

"Thank you. That's kind of you to say."

"Does she live with you?" Rachel Baumann was reluctant to answer, Lauren thought.

After a hesitation and a slight wavering in her commanding presence, she said, "No, she lives in Denver. On the Front Range." She smiled.

Lauren returned her smile.

"Anita teaches third grade at a private school. I'm very proud of her. She honors me every day just by being who she is."

"What a wonderful thing to say, Mrs. Baumann."

"She's a wonderful person, Ms. Crowder. I'm sure you would like her."

"I'm sure I would. Well, thank you so much for your time. You've been very gracious."

"Mountain hospitality. But I'm afraid I haven't been of much assistance."

"You never can tell with these things. You must know how it goes."

"Yes I do. Lawyering and fishing. Same sport. Different hooks, different bait. I decided a long time ago that fishing is more fun."

Lauren stood and turned toward the door, then stopped. She turned back toward Rachel, whose face was only eighteen inches from her own. "Are you still a member of the Church, Mrs. Baumann?"

Rachel smiled, almost laughed. "My, I haven't been asked that in a long time. The answer, I suppose, is that I'm a Jack Mormon. Which means no. And which means yes. Good day, Ms. Crowder."

Rachel stood erect by the closed door until she heard Mrs. Donnelly's ever-polite good-bye to Lauren Crowder and until she heard the door to the outer office thud close. She permitted her shoulders to sag a centimeter and felt her eyelids flutter shut.

Out loud, to the mountains, she said, "I can't believe that's all they wanted. They don't know. *They don't know.*"

For the first time since Lester Horner's appointment to the Supreme Court, she felt free.

The bounce in her step that had been generated by discovery—an old name, a new lead: *Audrey!*—deserted Lauren's walk two blocks from Rachel's office, and fatigue started to grip her with a tenacity that she knew from experience wouldn't be loosened by a jolt of caffeine. A short way from the restaurant where she was to meet Alan she succumbed to the exhaustion and weakness and lowered herself onto a splintered bench in front of a small market. She rested, trying to still her panic by getting lost in the view up toward Box Canyon Falls. The effort failed. The skin of her right leg was tingling, and weakness was robbing the muscles of their tone.

Until she boarded the plane for Utah to help her sister pursue her lawsuit, Lauren had been in New York, at the Albert Einstein College of Medicine, participating in medication trials for a new drug under development to treat MS. For six months she had endured the injections into her thighs. And for those six months she had been free of any new exacerbations of her illness and had been troubled only minimally by her old, familiar symptoms.

Now, after—what?—only a couple of weeks on her own, away from New York, her hand was on fire, her leg felt as heavy as a wet log, and she feared that soon she wouldn't be able to walk. Lauren felt tears spring up in her eyes. She blinked them away. *Not now.*

Not now. No. At least I can control that.

Minutes later she stood, and everything was worse.

The leg that had so easily followed her brain's instructions five minutes before was now an absolutely reluctant soldier. She said march; it dragged. She said straighten; it hung limply.

She slunk back onto the bench, looked at her watch, and waited. It was a quarter past three. Alan would come looking for her soon. Her tears, she knew, wouldn't wait for him.

Back at the B & B, Alan supported Lauren up the stairs to their second-floor room. He helped her settle onto the bed and then pulled off her shoes. She insisted that he get her luggage from the car. Dutifully, he went down to retrieve it. When he returned to the room with her black shoulder bag, she was lying on her side, curled away from the door, her breathing already in retreat into the shallow rhythm of sleep.

All along, he had assumed that she would sleep away a segment of that afternoon. It was part of their leisure routine together—part of the daily accommodation she made to multiple sclerosis. In all the days he had ever spent with her, he could remember only a few times when she hadn't rested during the day. He had planned to use the time she was in bed to hike southwest out of Ouray and explore Box Canyon Falls and maybe check out some of the nearby hot springs.

From anywhere in the room he could smell her fear, even as she slept. "Sometimes," she had said once after recovering from a spell of temporary blindness in her left eye, "I think I can actually feel the myelin dissolve in my brain. It's hot; it's like dripping boiling water onto sugar. The myelin burns at first, then flows away and leaves my nerves bare underneath. It feels raw, red. As it cools, it takes a piece of my freedom with it."

Alan pulled a book he had been reading from the floor next to the bed, kicked off his shoes, and angled himself onto a floral chintz chair in front of the room's solitary window. He watched her chest heave gently, as shadows inched across the bed until the darkness of the late afternoon began to merge with the darkness of her hair. Discrete, narrow shadows cast by the vertical posts from the frame of the stately bed etched her in long, dark prison stripes. He read a sentence from his book. Watched her. Read the same sentence. Watched her some more. Within ten minutes, the book was back on the floor, and he was on the bed beside her, asleep.

Awake, he could do nothing.

In his dreams, he could rescue her from her jail. And feel triumphant.

A gentle tapping sound stirred both Alan and Lauren as their eyes opened to a dark room. Disoriented, Alan reached for the phone, then stopped himself. The room didn't have one. He then propped himself up on his elbows and tried to shake away his sleep before leaning over Lauren, who still lay curled on her side. She blinked. He pulled her hair back from her face and kissed her cheek.

"Hi," he said in a low voice. She didn't answer.

Tap, tap, tap. A quiet voice said, "Excuse me. Mr. Gregory? Mr. Gregory?"

A louder, deeper, critical voice said, "Helena, he's a *doctor.*"

"Shhhhh!"

Alan jumped up and made his way to the door. Opening it, he noticed that he hadn't locked it when he had come up from the car.

The innkeeper, Helena Cocetti, stood at the door. Alan raised a hand to shade his eyes from the relatively bright light in the hallway.

Helena surprised him by looking fetching. Her brown hair, pulled into a tight bun each morning at breakfast, was swept back in a loose ponytail, which framed her narrow face in an attractive way. Sometime during the day she had traded her trademark pleated skirt and cotton blouse for faded jeans and a new flannel shirt of rich browns and blues. All in all, Alan quickly decided, a nice transformation. Her husband, Palmer, stood a few steps behind her, his hands in his pockets. He, too, had traded his morning clothes for denim and flannel.

"We've been horseback riding," Helena whispered, at once respectful of the sleep lines etched in Alan's face and apologetic for her casual garb. "I'm so sorry to have to wake you. I hope I did the right thing." She rubbed her hands on the hips of her jeans. "I didn't even take five minutes to change. And I bet I smell like Jane." She sniffed the air.

Alan didn't quite have his wits about him. "Did you have a nice ride?"

"Lovely. Just lovely. Palmer and I love autumn rides the best."

"Maybe spring," piped in Palmer.

"Maybe spring," agreed Helena, "but it's so muddy."

"There is that," Palmer said.

"Yes?" Alan interjected, hoping to discover the purpose of their visit.

"Oh. As I said, we've been riding. Most all day, since we served you breakfast. We've had the machine on, though."

"We stopped in town for groceries, too," offered Palmer in clarification. "Needed some fresh fruit for tomorrow."

The answering machine? Alan's face was full of concern for Lauren and full of longing for the warm nap he had barely left.

Helena leaned forward. "You got some calls from your friend Sam. Quite a few, actually. Three, Palmer?"

"At least three."

She paused and crinkled her forehead. "Sam isn't always as pleasant as he was when he was visiting here with us, is he?" Helena was still whispering.

"No, he's not," Alan agreed, quickly ascertaining that Helena wasn't being sarcastic. What did Sam want so urgently? God, I hope he didn't wreck my car. Or, worse, my bike.

"And your lady friend got a message, too." Helena nodded in the direction of the bed. She couldn't actually see it from where she stood, but she was an experienced innkeeper; she could sense that the bed was occupied.

"Helena, Palmer, thanks, let me throw some water on my face and I'll be down to take a look at the messages in a minute or two."

Palmer said, "That'll be just fine, Doctor. But you don't have to *read* 'em. We'll play 'em right back for you. They're still there on the machine."

Helena turned toward her husband, nodded eagerly, returned her gaze to Alan, and said, "Of course we will, Palmer. That's a fine idea." She leaned back in toward Alan. "You can hear it for yourself if you would like, but take it from me, our Sam has not had a very nice day."

He crawled back into the dark bed and snuggled Lauren from behind.

"You haven't moved."

"I haven't tried."

"You going to park here till morning?"

"No. Gotta pee."

He kissed the back of her neck. "You'll probably have to move, then."

"I'm not being silly. There's logic here, Alan. If I don't try to move, I don't have to find out what parts don't work."

"The leg?"

"That's an important part. Certainly one of the ones I'm worried about."

"We've got messages downstairs. Sam has apparently been calling me all day. And you got a message from somebody. Do you want me to pick yours up?"

She felt a jolt. "Teresa?" Well, she thought ironically, at least my adrenals still work. "Please. Go get the message. Let me know as soon as you know. Go. Go." He got up.

"Do you want some help getting to the bathroom?"

"No. I'll manage somehow. But, Alan?"

"Yeah?"

She crinkled her nose and looked around the small room. "We do have our own bathroom, don't we?" Concern about her sister had erased the thickness of sleep from her voice.

"Yeah. That door there. I'll be right downstairs. And I'll be back up as soon as I can."

Purdy had been calling the B & B to talk with Alan since shortly after ten o'clock in the morning. He had called four times, not three, and his patience had diminished drastically with each subsequent call. The last call had been at lunchtime.

Just before the end of the final message, Helena said to Alan, "This is when he starts to curse," shook her head, and walked out of the room.

With his credit card in hand, Alan used the parlor phone to try to track Purdy down at the Public Safety Building in Boulder. Madeleine, the person in his office whom Sam relied on for "investigatory support"—"Don't ever call her a secretary; she can be lethal"—couldn't find him, thought he might have gone home or off-duty. Alan tried his home number. No answer there.

The message that had been left for Lauren was from Robin Torr. Robin sounded almost as irritated as Purdy at being forced to communicate with the answering machine, but she, unlike Sam, never sacrificed her equanimity. She had arrived too late in San Diego to catch up with Teresa before the cruise ship sailed. She had tried to reach her ship-to-shore—"or shore-to-ship, or whatever it's called"—but the operator on board the ship couldn't find a listing for Teresa in the crew directory, so Robin never spoke with her. She was going to fly down to Cabo San Lucas and meet the ship there and try again. She didn't know where she could be reached, so she suggested that Lauren call somebody named John Harley with any messages. If for any reason she couldn't track Lauren down in Colorado, Robin would communicate through Harley, too.

Lauren was sitting on the edge of the bed brushing her hair when Alan returned. Her light makeup had been refreshed and she had pulled a sweater on over her shirt. She looked up at him eagerly when he pushed open the door.

"No news on Teresa."

She exhaled. "Who was it, then? Robin?"

"Yes, it was Robin. She called from San Diego." He relayed the gist of Robin's message.

Quietly, to herself, as she resumed brushing her hair, Lauren said, "I hope Teresa made it onto that cruise."

Alan sat beside her. He placed an arm across her back, hooking his fingers at her waist, and said, "You look beautiful. I'm sorry that everyone needs to be so scared."

"Thanks. I feel better being here with you. What did Sam want?"

Alan shrugged. "Who knows? He called four times this morning. Never really said what it was about. Just wanted to talk with me, then with us. He's not happy. I called Boulder, but I couldn't find him. I left messages all over the place. Helena and Palmer said that they would be here all evening, and promised to find out what he wants if he calls." He touched her hair and waited impatiently for her to turn to him. "How did it go?" He tilted his head toward the bathroom door.

She smiled. "My bladder still works. That's something."

"Lauren."

She widened her gray eyes in mild consternation. "Look, I made it there and back, didn't I?" He stared. She stared back. "The leg's really heavy, but I can move it—sort of."

He hugged her and felt her wince.

"Did I hurt you?"

"No. I've, um, got some pain in my hand. It's okay. Listen, I think I need a cane. Will you please walk into town and get me one?"

"Of course."

"I have one in Boulder that I got at a mountaineering store. I don't think you've ever seen me use it. It's like an adjustable walking stick type of thing. It works pretty well. I bet you can find one up here."

He nodded. "I'm sure I can." He stood to leave, patted his hip for his wallet, then began to search for where in the room he may have misplaced it. He saw it on the bureau, grabbed it, slithered into a jacket, gave Lauren a kiss, and headed out. He stopped by the door and said,

"I almost forgot. Robin Torr said that since she doesn't know where she's going to be, you should communicate with her through someone named John Harley. If she can't find you, she'll leave a message there as well. I hope you know who that is." He smiled at her and left her alone.

The hairbrush had stopped midstroke. Out loud, Lauren said, "I hope I know who that is, too."

Alan heard voices as he approached the second-floor room with Lauren's new walking stick in his hand. He paused, perplexed, then opened the door. Lauren had moved from the edge of the bed to the chintz chair. Sam Purdy was stretched out on the bed, four pillows shoved between his back and the pot-metal headboard.

Alan laughed at the sight of him. "Comfortable, Sam? Welcome back." As nonchalantly as possible, he stuck the walking stick, its tag still on it, into a corner by the door.

Lauren's face was alive and determined. "Sam brought us some news. Some troubling news."

Purdy seemed to be attempting to look modest. It struck Alan as similar to a viper trying to look cuddly.

"You tell him, Sam."

Purdy reached over his shoulder and fluffed one of the pillows. Alan moved across the room and sat on the arm of the chair, next to Lauren. She mouthed, "Thanks," tilting her head at the corner of the room.

Purdy started. "You know how strange we felt after we talked to Rachel Baumann? Shit, was that just yesterday? You know, that she seemed so suspicious, even worried? Well, I stayed uncomfortable about it on the absolutely interminable drive back to Boulder in your stupid car. I swear I could have pedaled up to the tunnel faster than that thing can climb up a mountain. Anyway, I went back over everything we had—what I know about the lawsuit, the murder of the defendant in D.C. (Virginia, actually), the private investigator getting killed outside of Moab—and I just felt funny about it all.

"I had that stuff about Toomey's murder from Lauren,

the stuff she had faxed to me. I knew what she told us later about the dog-print coincidence, but I didn't know anything else about the murder back east. So I gave them a call—the Virginia cops. Said I had a throat slashing in a mountain park outside of Boulder, wondered if I could see some of their stuff, see if we might have us a serial on our hands, kill a couple of birds with one stone, yada yada. They were pretty nice about it, and they faxed me a bunch of paperwork right away this morning.

"Well, I'm, like, *working.* You know, for the city. So I don't get a chance to look at this stuff right away. When I do, I read it, it's pretty much the same story that Lauren has already given me from news reports and what the lawyers have heard. Lady sitting alone in a remote part of a park, no sign of struggle, throat slashed with a sharp knife from somebody standing above her, bleeds to death. No robbery, no sexual assault. Nothing new.

"Except that in addition to dog prints, it turns out the cops in Virginia have got dog *hair.*"

Lauren looked up at Alan as if to say, *This is important, pay attention.*

"The crime-scene people in Virginia found two dog prints in the blood by the body. We already knew that. Initially, they wrote it off as prints from a stray, a loose dog that compromised the scene before they arrived. Well, these reports say they also found some dog hairs in the fabric of this lady's sleeve—the sweater sleeve on her left arm. You know, the cuff. Not many—a couple, three hairs. Not like she had grabbed the dog, like she was defending herself. So they decide, reasonably, that she had petted *some* dog at *some* time with her left hand while she was wearing that sweater. The bottom of her sleeve was facing down when her body was discovered, so they conclude that there's no way the hairs come from a stray that came by after she's dead. And dead people usually don't pet dogs. All in all, the hairs just become a typical investigatory artifact. We get them all the time. Just a loose end, right?

"Well, maybe, I say. Because we know that the state cops in Utah say they found dog prints in the dirt and blood around Pratt Toomey's body, too. I just wish there was some way to find out if the Utah police found any hair—"

"To match with the hair from Virginia?"

"Right. But—"

"Tell him about the blood, Sam. And about the cut in Pratt's jacket."

"Yeah, okay. I've seen some dead bodies in my time, more than I would like. And it may surprise you, but most people don't die too messy. Even if they're shot or stabbed or beat up or whatever, most people only bleed a certain amount before they die. Sometimes you get a bleeder, but not usually. But both these deaths—Oaks and Toomey—were bloody. The neck slashing, absolutely, that's a bloody way to go. But Toomey is more interesting because he was a gunshot of the chest, which isn't always a bloody death. Can be, but isn't always. Pratt was shot in the center of the back, through the heart, exit wound through the center chest. And he bled plenty. Could have been incidental, not intentional, but the damn shot almost drained him. And according to Lauren's lawyer friend, the analysis of the crime scene by the Utah forensic investigators is that the murderer then lifted his body and cut his nylon shell with a sharp something, probably a knife, so that the blood wouldn't pool close to his body. So that it would flow out, away."

"After? His shell was cut *after* he was shot?"

"That's what they think."

"Why? Why would somebody do that?"

"Well, they apparently don't know, and I certainly don't have any idea. But it's interesting. The blood's important, somehow. It may well be linked to the dog. Maybe the dog likes the blood. I don't know."

"Lauren? Do you know?" Alan asked. She shook her head.

"Have you called the Utah police, Sam?"

Purdy shook his head. "Not a good idea. I'm sure they have the same stuff I have from Virginia. And I'm in kind of a vulnerable position here, since I really shouldn't have these reports at all. Before I flew back up here, I called the guy I had talked with in Virginia and told him thanks for his help, but I had been wrong, my crime scene was much more chaotic than theirs, the neck cut on my victim came from a left-hander, and there were signs of sexual assault."

Alan turned his attention from Sam to Lauren, who in his judgment wasn't acting sufficiently frightened. "What do you think, sweets?"

"I think this means it's possible that we're right about everything. I can't wait to tell Robin."

"Anybody want to know what I think?" Alan asked.

Sam smiled at Lauren and shrugged, making sure that Alan knew he was humoring him. "Sure, Watson, what do you think?"

"I think," Alan said, "that it means that you and your sister and Robin are in incredible danger. Somebody absolutely doesn't want this lawsuit of yours to proceed. The fear that Sam and I saw in Rachel Baumann's face must be part of all of it, too."

Sam sat forward on the bed and waited until Lauren looked at him. He narrowed his eyes and lowered his thick voice. "That's really why I came up here, Lauren. I didn't come up here just to tell you that maybe you were right. I came up here to try to convince you to back off until the cops in Virginia and Utah and the people at the FBI figure out what the hell is going on. You three—you, your sister, and your lawyer friend—are in serious jeopardy. And Rachel Baumann, too. She knows something that somebody doesn't want you to find out. I'm afraid that they're going to kill either you or her or both of you to keep that from happening."

Both men knew Lauren well enough to be able to assess how receptive she would be to their advice, especially given the paternalistic tone. She might heed it in the end, but she would reject it, or at least scoff at it, in the beginning.

Instead, she merely ignored it. "I spoke with her today, Sam, at length. She didn't seem that frightened to me. I don't know exactly what you guys saw the other day. Maybe it was that you're men and there were two of you and you weren't lying as well as you thought you were, but she just wasn't that frightened today. And she doesn't know that much. I—"

Purdy pulled himself up from the bed and interrupted.

"I'm not convinced. And I do want to hear all about your interview with Rachel Baumann. But I want to hear all about it over dinner. I'm starving. First, I need to go downstairs and make some apologies to Helena and beg her to forgive me for being so rude on the phone today. Otherwise, I'm afraid that she won't give me one of those omelettes of hers in the morning. Lauren, you gotta try one. Swiss chard and, I think, Asiago. Then, the three of us are gonna go out and find some supper."

Lauren said, "If we're going out to eat, will you two excuse me for a minute?" The two men looked at each other. "You know, like leave," she explained.

They stood and left the room.

At the bottom of the stairs, Alan confronted Sam. "Why did you really come back up here, Sam? You didn't get in an airplane just to argue with Lauren about the danger she's in. I'm sure that you know as well as I do that arguing with her in person is no more effective than arguing with her on the phone."

"I know that. I'm here because I'm feeling creepy about Rachel Baumann. I can't leave this thing so unfinished."

"What are you going to do?"

"Don't know. I'll listen to Lauren's story about her visit with Rachel today. Then I'll decide what to do. But something. I came up here to do something."

Alan went back upstairs and found Lauren exiting the bathroom.

"He's right about the danger you're in. You need to listen to him."

"It's not as bad as he says. He's exaggerating." She stood and hopped toward the corner of the room. "Thanks for getting the walking stick. And, Alan?" She softened her tone. "If Sam asks, please let's just tell him that I twisted my leg today. Okay?"

"Whatever you want."

She kissed him. "That's what I want."

Helena and Parker Cocetti argued politely for a few minutes before reaching a consensus about sending their trio of guests down Main Street to a restaurant called the Outlaw. At the inn, Purdy perused a tattered copy of the menu offered to him by Palmer, saw plenty of red meat listed, and declared the choice perfect.

Open only during the tourist season, the Outlaw was preparing for its winter shutdown. A few tables near the bar were occupied by locals saying their good-byes to the tavern until the spring thaw, but the restaurant was mostly quiet and welcoming and western and warm.

Sam and Alan ate. Lauren, who wasn't hungry, picked at a salad and then asked the bartender where she could find a pool table. He directed her to the Silver Eagle Saloon, across Main Street.

She hobbled across the street and made her way to a battered coin-operated Brunswick in the back of the bar. Given that she was playing with a house cue and on one leg, she was relatively pleased with her game. Two elderly men twirled around on their barstools to watch her play, cradling whiskeys in their laps. Before long they started making side bets on the length of her runs.

After Sam and Alan finished dinner they crossed the street to the Silver Eagle and carried chairs over to the pool table. Never once interrupting her game, Lauren filled them in on her visit with Rachel Baumann.

Sam listened intently, distracted only by the quality of her play. When she was through he said, "So that's all you got this afternoon? Just this name—Audrey—and Rachel's protests that she wasn't in the in-group and shouldn't be expected to know anything about Blythe Oaks or Lester Horner?"

"I guess that's it," Lauren said, feeling chastised. Purdy's synopsis made the meeting feel more inconsequential than it had been. "But I also think I know who Audrey is. Pratt had mentioned her once. I checked class records and some other documents I have, and it seems that she is now Audrey Payne, married to a church big shot. And, what's most important, Sam, is that I got confirmation from Rachel that a zillion years ago these girls had special relationships that even they themselves labeled as romantic."

Sam sat back on his chair, wiped the grain of his red mustache left and right with his fingers, and drained the dregs of the beer on the table in front of him. "That may be good news for your sister and her lawsuit, but I don't see how it adds up to a motive for murder. An old story of a bunch of nineteen-year-old girls checking out each other's bodies is not exactly the stuff that tends to motivate a rash of murders."

"It could be, Sam," Lauren asserted, "if it establishes a foundation for convincing a jury that Blythe Oaks was lesbian. Because that would stain Oaks's family and add credibility to Teresa's accusations, which would stain Justice Horner for having hired her. And if Horner is stained, it obviously would stain the LDS Church. Motive everywhere."

In a soft voice, Sam argued gently, "Put on your prosecutor's cap for a second, Lauren. Would you kill Pratt Toomey to keep him from hearing what Rachel Baumann told you this afternoon? I sure wouldn't take that risk. Especially since, by your own research, and her own admission, there are, what—a half-dozen other girls? more?—who know the same information. Maybe the other kids from BYU know even more information, since Rachel professes to have been such a blessed outsider. Is this murderer going to systematically start killing off the entire coed half of the class of 'sixty-three in order to keep some post-adolescent lesbian petting hidden?"

Lauren lined up a shot and fought to maintain her calm. She tried not to think about her leg and her myelin. "What are you saying, Sam? That I spent the afternoon talking to the wrong person? That Pratt wasn't really coming up here to talk to Rachel at all?"

"Sure, that's one possibility. It's possible that Pratt was coming up here to talk with somebody else. Alan and I tracked down Rachel Baumann without breaking a sweat. That sure doesn't mean we tracked down the right person. Perhaps it even argues that we didn't." He paused. "But it's also possible that we did find the right person and that she lied to you through her teeth. Or—"

The bartender, an emaciated man with a baseball cap on a head that looked as if it had been rendered bald by chemotherapy, and with suspenders holding up his oversized Levi's, interrupted the developing tension by asking if anybody wanted another round. Sam said yes. No one else bit.

Alan's eyes were on Lauren. He read impatience and frustration in her face and tried to gauge whether Sam was sufficiently sensitive to the impact of what he was saying to her.

"Or what, Sam?"

"Lauren, please don't take offense at what I'm telling you. I think I'm here to help, okay? I lied to my boss to come up this mountain today. I flew in an airplane the size of a condor into an airport the size of a commemorative stamp to get here. I've already been away from my family much longer than I like. Regardless of your fantasies, I would not go to these lengths just to annoy you. You know from experience that tact is not my long suit, but I'm not doing all this just to get a chance to critique your work this afternoon. My intent"—he took a long draw on his fresh beer—"my intent is to try, for want of a better phrase, to keep you alive. But if I'm not being helpful, just let me know. I'll be gone as soon I get that omelette in my gut tomorrow morning." He smiled. "You could call out the local militia, and you still couldn't get me out of town before that."

She pursed her lips and thought about Pratt and about Teresa. She massaged the burning in her hand. "I'm sorry, Sam. I'm under a lot of pressure. What's your other hypothesis? Please."

"My other hypothesis is, I think, an obvious one. That maybe we've been right all along, that talking with Rachel Baumann was indeed the purpose of Toomey's last trip. But a problem none of us has solved is that we're only guessing what he planned to talk with her about. You and your attorney friend think he wanted to discuss this little romantic girls' club from thirty years ago. But we don't really know that, do we? And Rachel's ease in dealing with you today is"—he lowered his voice here for emphasis—"absolutely inconsistent with what Alan and I saw in her office a couple of days ago. If she was lying to you today, I think you would have smelled it. You're too close to all this, no doubt about it, but I know your bullshit threshold, Lauren. You would have smelled it if she was lying. That lady may have some sociopathic blood in her veins, but it runs thin. She can't lie like a pro. You would have caught it.

"So I think what's happening is that maybe, just maybe, we don't know the right questions. And that what you saw today on Rachel Baumann's face wasn't the absence of fear; it was the presence of relief. If Alan and I read her right the other day and she sees the three of us as the second coming of the big bad wolf, maybe she realized today that although we've found our way to the woods, we don't have a clue where Grandmother's house really is."

"I don't like what you're suggesting, Sam, mostly because it makes me feel lost. Back almost to square one. But it makes some sense. I'd like to discount whatever fear you and Alan saw in Rachel's face. It would make my job easier. But I shouldn't." She sank the four ball off the far cushion.

Purdy raised his eyebrows and stared at the pool table. "How the hell do you do that? Shit."

"Practice. You were saying?"

"An hour ago, whatever, back at Helena and Palmer's, I told you why I came back up here. It still holds. I absolutely think you should can this thing until the cops sort it out. We—you, me, and Alan—don't know enough to even begin to protect you and your sister from whoever's killing these people."

"I'm not good at giving up. You both know that." She traded glances first with Alan, then with Sam. "And I won't give up, even temporarily, until my sister's safe. Sam, we don't even know where she is." Her eyes filled with tears.

Alan explained to Sam about Teresa's unexpected gig and the cruise ship and the late airplane and Robin Torr's trip to Mexico to find her to ascertain that she was safe.

"But when she's safe, when you know that she's safe," Sam said after processing the details of the story, "you'll take a break from all this?"

Lauren widened her eyes. "Yeah. I'll think seriously about it. How's that?"

"It's about all the cooperation I ever hope for from a prosecutor. Let's pray we get some good news from your lawyer friend in the very near future."

When he finished his beer, Purdy thanked Lauren, who insisted on paying for the drinks, and excused himself to take a walk around town. While Lauren had made an excursion to the ladies' room, he had told Alan that he was planning the stroll and made him promise to take Lauren straight back to the B & B when she was done playing pool.

Purdy exited the Silver Eagle and headed down Main Street for a block before circling around to the east past Rachel Baumann's office. The building was, as he expected, dark.

He kept walking.

The night air in the Uncompahgre was cold, and he was under-dressed in a sweatshirt and down vest. Insulating clouds jostled the peaks above the valley but couldn't quite surmount the sharp ridges to settle over the town like a blanket and hold in the day's heat.

Around the corner, not far from where Baumann practiced law, Purdy mounted the steps of the building that held the Ouray Police Department.

Purdy smiled to himself at the calm he found inside and the contrast in atmosphere with the Boulder Public Safety Building. A solitary uniformed officer sat at a worn but elegant oak desk in the front of a small room. Purdy approached calmly and asked for the duty officer.

"You're looking at him. What can I do for you? Officer Miklowski." Miklowski didn't offer his hand.

"May I sit?"

"Suit yourself."

"Officer Miklowski, I'm Sam Purdy of the Boulder Police Department, and I'm here unofficially." Purdy waited for the officer to react to his introduction. He didn't. Purdy checked out the man's name tag. "May I call you Bill? Please call me Sam."

"Can I see some ID, sir? Badge would be nice."

Purdy reached into his vest pocket and flipped his badge wallet open on the desk in front of him. Miklowski viewed it carefully, glanced up at Purdy, then back to the shield.

"You're not on the job right now, correct, Detective?"

"It's Sam. But that's correct I'm on vacation."

"But you didn't exactly drop in here tonight just to pay your respects to a fellow officer?"

"That's correct, too, Bill." Purdy felt awkward, had hoped for more camaraderie. "I'm kind of worried about something I'm afraid might be happening here in town. Thought you guys might like to know about it."

About five minutes later, after Purdy had outlined the general nature of his concerns about Rachel Baumann's welfare—"Rachel? Really?"—and detailed the two distant deaths that had fomented his concerns, Bill Miklowski interrupted him for only the second time and said that he thought he should run this one by the chief.

Sam and Bill spent about ten minutes getting better acquainted. Purdy was trying to explain in as non-self-incriminating a manner as possible what his involvement was in this interstate mess when the chief arrived, apparently through a back entrance, and buzzed Officer Miklowski's phone extension.

"Let the recorder answer the phone for a while, Bill. Call Marian and tell her you're going to be away from the desk. Offer our guest something to drink and bring me a Coke. Then both of you come on back."

From his chair opposite Chief Long's desk, Sam Purdy thought things were going well.

The police chief of Ouray was a slender man who didn't stand when Miklowski ushered Purdy into his office. Chief Long's posture was admirable. Even this late in the evening he sat as straight, Sam surmised, as if he had a stick up his ass. Purdy was offering himself side bets on how tall the guy was. Five seven, five nine max. By the terms of his silent wager, if he was correct, Purdy won the right to stop someplace for dessert on his way back to the inn.

Miklowski, for some reason Purdy couldn't discern, felt a compelling need to recount Purdy's story himself, despite the fact that the originator of the tale was sitting four feet away from him. Chief Long, for some reason Purdy couldn't discern, listened as attentively as if his officer were a primary source of impeccable credentials. Purdy half listened, having long ago developed an immunity to personal irritation over police department inefficiency. He found himself impressed at Miklowski's quick grasp of the general thrust of his story. A couple of small errors cropped up, but in the interest of good will, Sam chose not to correct him.

"Your officer has it pretty straight, Chief." Sam turned to his left. "I'm impressed, Bill."

Brian Long brushed his full but obviously newly barbered hair back on the sides of his head with both hands. He said, "I don't know why you don't think that maybe you and your buddy didn't spook Rachel with your little charade the other day, and that's why she was frightened."

Sam sat forward and put his elbows on his knees. "I considered that, Chief—at least until I got back to Boulder and learned about this dog thing that Bill just described so well. I then came to the conclusion that it was no longer prudent to assume that those two murders were random acts of violence. In fact, I have come to believe that everyone with anything to do with this case has something to worry about in relation to their continued existence on this planet. And I think Rachel knows it, too, and that's why she was afraid. She thought my friend and I were the bad guys. But I sure don't know her well enough to know if she would share that fear with the local authorities. So I thought I would do it myself. Clue you in."

Staring at something inconsequential on his desk, Brian Long said under his breath, "And we're certainly grateful for that." He finally looked up, one hand wrapped around his can of Coke. He spoke evenly. "What is it you would like, exactly, Detective Purdy? You want me to put a patrol car outside Rachel's house and hope she doesn't notice? Or you want me to do your dirty work for you and go tell her the danger she just might be in to try to scare her into divulging some information I'm not sure you and your 'friends' have any right to know? Is that it? You looking for some free help getting some dirt on a very fine lady who plays her cards as carefully as anybody I've ever met?"

Purdy took his elbows from his knees and began to rub his eyes with his thick fingers. *This,* he thought, *is no longer going as well as I'd hoped.* Before he was finished massaging his tired eyes, he began his reply. "Personally? I don't give a shit what you do, *Chief.* Me? I have this bias about my work. I like to know what's going on in my town. I like to know if any of the local citizens are in any unusual danger. I like to keep at least a part of my attention on any strangers in town, on new faces. Like that.

"So, no, I'm not looking for you to offer a free assist on this case I keep being called off the bench to help on. I personally don't give a fuck if you tell Rachel that she needs protection 'cause she's on the hit list of a drunken driver who just escaped from County with a grudge against her for not getting him off.

"I like my friends. I'm helping them out. I liked Rachel when I met her. It would be nice if she were alive for a while. That's why I'm here. And I think perhaps I've worn out my welcome. Good evening, gentlemen."

He twisted around, searching for his vest, found it on the floor behind his chair, stooped down to get it, and stood to leave.

"Sit back down and cool your jets, Detective."

"Excuse me?" Purdy asked, not bothering to turn around.

Without even the slightest change in tone, Long acknowledged Purdy's protest. "Sit back down and cool your jets, Detective. Please."

"Be happy to, Chief."

Brian Long said, "You're from Boulder. You get yourselves a few tourists. You city guys got any new and special ways for determining the difference between a stranger and a tourist? I always find that particular discrimination poses a bit of a dilemma around here."

Purdy smiled at Miklowski as he answered. "It's high-tech stuff. We ourselves only recently learned it after getting funding on an LEAA grant. Some of the brass even spent time at the FBI Academy. Basically, in this case, stranger versus tourist identification would involve increased suspicion of anybody traveling, probably alone, with a long-haired dog in the golden-to-red color range, who is probably driving his own car, that car most likely being adorned by Utah plates."

Brian Long had a smirk on his face. "And if I'm following this new technique correctly, then if somebody fitting that profile seemed to be hanging around Rachel's home or office, we should probably be more than mildly concerned."

"Gosh," Purdy exclaimed. "And to think it took us a hundred and sixty-five thousand dollars to figure out stuff like that."

Brian Long called Rachel Baumann's home to try to set up a meeting that Purdy said he would be happy to attend. But nobody answered the phone at Rachel's house.

"I guess she's out," Purdy said as Chief Long replaced the receiver in its cradle.

"Not likely," Miklowski offered.

Long nodded, agreeing with his officer. "More likely not answering. Rachel doesn't go out too often. Not since Walter died, anyway. Certainly not since Anita moved away. She stays home, mostly. If she doesn't feel like talking, she doesn't answer her phone."

"When did Walter die?"

"When was that, Bill? Sometime before I got the job."

"I was a kid, maybe ten or eleven, when Walter got killed. So, what's that? Fifteen, sixteen years ago."

"Walter was killed?"

Both men nodded.

"Could be relevant," Purdy said, succumbing to the laconism apparently endemic to the law-enforcement community in Ouray.

"Don't see how," said Bill.

"Me neither," said Brian Long, after a contemplative pause.

"Well, then," concluded Purdy.

They walked ten minutes to Rachel's house.

The stroll carried them six blocks closer to the steep, striated faces of the western canyon walls, across the trickling flow of the Uncompahgre in autumn, to a quiet dirt lane above Oak Creek. Even only this far away from town, the change in light made a million stars seem to leap from the sky. The high walls of the San Juans loomed above the neighborhood like dark, vertical clouds.

The locals were prepared for the season and the short trek out of town. They wore hats and gloves, and their coats came equipped with sleeves. In contrast, Sam Purdy was nearly frozen when they arrived at Rachel's house, a sprawling log cabin of indeterminate age on a woody promontory that enjoyed an expansive view of the valley. Purdy was encouraged by the quantity and vibrancy of interior and exterior lights adorning the house, discouraged by its visual isolation from the neighbors.

Why couldn't Rachel live in town? Like across the street from the damn police station.

The path to the front door was a mix of packed dirt, railroad ties, and stones that meandered through a grove of small aspen. The entrance itself was partly obscured by a pair of large ponderosas flanking a narrow porch.

Brian Long led the procession to the planked deck outside the door. He pounded heavily and yelled, "Rachel, it's Brian Long, you home?" Purdy watched a light come on in a distant structure through the trees.

No one came to the door. Miklowski looked bored.

Long knocked and yelled again.

Nothing.

Purdy suggested they take a quick look around. Long said nothing but seemed to concur. Miklowski carried the only flashlight, so the other two men followed him as he leapt a low railing on the porch and scrambled up a steep grade toward a big bay window.

Miklowski shined his light inside, then dropped its beam when it was apparent that the interior lighting was rendering his torch redundant.

He whistled through his gaped teeth and said, "Shit, would you look at that."

Lauren had phoned John Harley as soon as she got back to the B & B after dinner. When he didn't answer at his apartment, she tried Salt Lake City directory assistance and asked for the number of the Side Pocket. Across the room, to Alan, she explained, "I've been playing pool there." He was puzzled by her explanation.

Odelle answered at the Side Pocket. No, she hadn't seen Harley. It was a little early for him, though, wasn't it? Any message? Okay, I'll tell him you called.

Lauren forced a smile at Alan, who was reclining sideways on a small sofa in Helena and Palmer's parlor, reading last week's *Newsweek.* "It's where I met him. The guy who Robin's leaving messages with. At the Side Pocket."

Alan waited for her to elucidate on her own. When she didn't, he said, without looking over at her, "He's just a friend, right?"

As naturally as she could manage, she said, "That's right. Just a friend. He's taught me a lot about the Church. He's a Mormon. Maybe a Jack Mormon."

Although Alan wouldn't have known a Jack Mormon from an Easter Catholic, he nodded and returned to his magazine. Given the day, the new symptoms, her fears about her sister, and the conundrum about Rachel Baumann, he decided to forgo exploring the opening Lauren had created.

He followed Lauren and her heavy leg and her new cane up the stairs to their room. No harm would come from giving her the benefit of the doubt.

Robin Torr's flight to Cabo San Lucas was scheduled to depart at 9:10 the next morning. She booked a room in a hotel near the airport and spent the evening shopping for some clothes more suitable for the tropics than those she had grabbed in her rush out of Utah.

Robin never crossed paths with Teresa Crowder, who was staying on a different floor at the same hotel. Teresa's flight out of San Diego was scheduled to leave an hour earlier than Robin Torr's.

Although Teresa had been disappointed at how things had turned out with the cruise ship, she was proud of the fact that she had acceded to Lauren's wishes and called her bungalow in Salt Lake City and left a message on the answering machine for her sister telling her where she would be instead.

It was, after all, the responsible thing to do.

"Whattya make of that, Chief?" Miklowski asked as he again raised his ineffective flashlight and swept it in a wide arc from one side of the spacious room to the other. The main room of Rachel Baumann's house was deep, traversing the entire width of the structure. Matching bay windows anchored each end. A dividing walkway framed by low cabinetry was all that separated a livingroom area at the front of the house from a smaller, dining-room area at the rear. The rooms were brightened by the exposed polished wood of the log walls and by a high beamed ceiling, and warmed by huge acrylic landscapes and stunning antique tapestries.

Purdy thought, *All this place needs is some furniture and rugs to go straight into* Architectural Digest.

"Where's her piano?" asked Long. "Where's all her furniture?"

"Is Rachel moving out?" wondered Miklowski. "She sell this place? I never heard anything."

"Where the hell is she?" asked Purdy, no longer feeling the night chill at all.

The three policemen accomplished little as they circled Rachel Baumann's home, peeking through every accessible window. The perplexing absence of furniture and rugs that they had discovered in her main rooms was not repeated in any other part of the house.

Purdy and Long argued briefly over the meaning of the absence of disarray, over how neatly the furniture and rugs seemed to have been removed from the living room and dining room. Purdy kept to himself a troublesome image of Rachel's body rolled up in a nice big Persian carpet. Miklowski noted the absence of packing boxes. Chief Long noted the absence of any rumors in town about Rachel moving.

Purdy mentioned the absence of a body, either standing at the door welcoming them in for cookies or crumpled in a pool of blood anywhere in the house.

"I thought she never went out," he said.

"Not never. Rarely."

"It's almost ten-thirty, Chief," Miklowski said. "That is a little late for Rachel to be out."

"So where is she?" Purdy demanded.

The chief tugged on the end of his gloves and then stared up at Purdy. "Sam, is everybody in Boulder exactly where they are supposed to be every night at ten-thirty?"

Purdy was growing cold again. He shoved his hands farther into the shallow pockets of his vest. "Who might know where she is? Who are her friends?"

"I betcha Arna Donnelly would know, Chief," suggested Miklowski.

"Then let's go call Arna Donnelly," Purdy snapped. He remembered Mrs. Donnelly's name from the plaque on the reception desk in Baumann's office.

Chief Long wasn't convinced. "Arna will be in bed. It's almost ten-thirty. I don't want to worry her."

Purdy responded, "Well, *shit.* It's *only* ten-thirty. Arna will have plenty of chance to still get a good night's sleep after she answers a couple of questions. We have a suspicious situation here, Chief Long."

"So you seem to think." Long thought about it for fifteen seconds before he said, "Okay, I'll call Arna."

They walked back into town and used the phone at the Coachlight Restaurant to make the call. Arna had been up waiting for *The Tonight Show* to start.

In reply to Chief Long's question, she said, "Rachel had her floors refinished this week, Brian. You know, her wood floors? I think they're pine. The wide boards, those are pine, aren't they? Yes, I think they are. I imagine the fumes were just too bad for Rachel to stay in the house. Ever had your floor refinished, Brian? You and Beth have carpet, don't you? Well, we did, just a couple of years ago. But our boards are the skinny ones. Oak. Don't matter, I imagine. Ooooeeee, it stinks. We stayed next door with the Lightharts."

"Where would Rachel go if she wasn't going to sleep at home, Arna? Any idea? She mention anything to you?"

"Well, if tomorrow wasn't a work day, I'd expect that she would have gone over the hill to see Anita. But since we're open tomorrow and she's got some appointments, I bet Rachel would just go down and visit with Donna at the Wiesbaden and take a room there."

Of course, he thought. "I should've thought of that myself, Arna. I'm real sorry to bother you so late at night. You will forgive me?"

"Oh, Brian," she scolded.

Chief Long hung up the phone and turned to Purdy. He said, "I feel kind of stupid. She's getting her floors refinished. Rachel's best friend here in town is a woman named Donna Tarkett. She used to be Dr. Brown's nurse before he retired. Anyway, when Doc Brown retired, Donna bought a small lodge here in town with Rachel's help. It's called the Wiesbaden. I bet Rachel's there. If she's not, Donna will know where she is."

The Wiesbaden Hot Springs Spa and Lodging was a few blocks away at the east side of town. Purdy, his toes still numb, suggested a phone call to ascertain that Rachel was indeed staying at her friend's lodge. Chief Long didn't see any reason to wake Donna Tarkett with a phone call and felt that walking by and making sure that Rachel's car was in the Wiesbaden lot would take care of all their questions just fine.

"Can we drive? Please?" asked Sam Purdy, meekly.

"It's only a few blocks, Sam. No real need for that."

"I give up. I can't feel my toes. I'm frozen."

Chief Long turned to Miklowski. "In deference to our flatland guest, we'll all head back to the station. Bill, you can go back on your shift. I'll drive our visitor all the way over to the Wiesbaden."

Purdy ignored the sarcasm and cranked the heat up on the Ouray Police Department's white Jeep Cherokee as soon as Brian Long started the engine. Purdy's fingers and toes were so numb he couldn't even tell if the air blowing out of the vents was warm or not.

Within a minute they arrived at the lodge. The Wiesbaden consisted of an L-shaped motel building and a larger guest house surrounding some natural hot springs fed by Ouray's abundant geothermal resources. A few exterior lights indicated to Purdy that the lodge hadn't closed for the winter, but the absence of interior lighting in more than a couple of rooms suggested that business wasn't exactly booming, either.

Only three cars lined the street in front of the lodge. "That's Donna Tarkett's truck," Brian Long said as they passed a full-size Dodge with the Wiesbaden logo painted on the side, "and this one belongs to a tourist," he continued as he made the Jeep crawl past a Buick with Arizona plates. "And this one here is Rachel's old Wagoneer."

The wood-paneled Wagoneer was indeed old. It was, in addition, battered, rust-patched, and filthy. Mostly, though, it was distinctive.

"You're sure it's hers?" Purdy asked, assuming that Long was.

"Absolutely. Only one other one this old in town. And the other one's pretty. Rachel's got an immaculate house and an immaculate office, but her car is for shit."

Purdy made Long drive around the block surrounding the grounds of the lodge and the adjacent streets to check for vehicles with Utah plates. They didn't find any. He turned to face Chief Long. "You don't want to wake her, right?"

"These other two murders, they both took place in remote locations?"

Purdy considered the question, then nodded.

"Well, Rachel's in a public place right now. I'd be more worried if she were at home, up on the hill by herself. But there are other people around here. Donna's pretty alert. There's regular traffic passing by. Bill will be on patrol tonight. I'll remind him to keep an eye out for strangers with dogs and cars with Utah plates. She'll be fine, Sam."

A gnawing in Purdy's gut screamed that waiting was foolish. But his leverage with Chief Long was almost nonexistent, so he didn't argue. "We'll talk to her in the morning, right?"

"First thing, Sam. Promise." Purdy missed the condescension in Brian Long's voice because his toes had defrosted to a stage where he could tell that the air blowing on his running shoes was warm. He was liking that.

"Take you back to Palmer and Helena's place, Detective?"

"That would be great."

A block from the Wiesbaden, Purdy said, "Brian?"

"Mmm-hmmm?"

"Anyplace in town I could stop for something sweet this late at night?"

Without even a second's delay, Long said, "Nope."

"Damn, I was afraid of that," Purdy muttered into the dark car.

Purdy was joined for an early breakfast the next morning by Alan and Lauren. Sam had already decided that the fact that he had visited the police department the night before would probably precipitate an argument from Lauren, so he had no plans to mention it to her.

Alan asked him how his walk had been.

"Great. A little cold."

"Where'd you go?"

"All over. Walked around town some. Saw some hot springs. Even crossed the river and went a little ways into the hills."

Lauren, who was eagerly accepting Helena's offer of breakfast, said, "That's admirable, Sam. You usually a night walker?"

"I don't need much sleep."

Alan offered, loud enough so Helena would be sure to hear, "No, what Sam needs is much breakfast."

Purdy smiled at his hostess and said, "Amen." He had already stopped by the kitchen and discussed the possibility of an omelette with her.

"Palmer likes to call them frittatas, Sam," she'd whispered.

"Well, if he'll cook me a couple, I'll call them anything Palmer would like," Purdy had said.

To Sam, it appeared that Lauren and Alan were being overly polite with each other, and he was curious what had transpired the night before. He asked a couple of questions, which Lauren answered, and learned only that they hadn't heard anything about her sister's whereabouts from the intermediary in Salt Lake City.

The first of the two promised frittatas arrived in front of Purdy just as Officer Bill Miklowski burst into the sun-washed dining room of the inn.

Helena was startled by how bedraggled he looked. He was breathing hard, his eyes were jumpy, and his heavy beard was well into the stage where anyone could tell it had been a long time since he had shaved. "Well, Bill, hello. Are you all right?"

Immediately, Purdy guessed what was coming and was out of his chair, ready to rush Miklowski to another, more private room, when the policeman blurted out words that would soon echo in every corner of the quiet little town of Ouray.

"Rachel's dead, Sam. The chief wants you. You gotta come with me. Now. Come on, hurry." His voice was pressured and frightened. His face was pasty, his lips pale.

Purdy grimaced, mouthed the word "Fuck!" and turned to Miklowski. "I need to grab my coat. The time for hurrying is a little past, I'm afraid, Bill." He turned to Lauren and Alan. "You two stay here, and stay together. If you see anybody you don't know who's paying attention to this place, call Chief Long immediately. Alan, you got that?"

Somberly, he said, "Yes, Sam."

Purdy turned to Helena. Helena stood hugging herself, a solitary tear tracing a path down her left cheek. "Helena, you and Palmer going to be home?" She nodded. "Does Palmer have a gun, a rifle, anything?" She nodded. "Get Palmer, tell him to get the gun, and everybody stay together, okay?"

She nodded.

Purdy walked upstairs deliberately and descended a minute later with his coat and his gloves.

"Let's go, Bill," he said, and walked out the door.

Lauren felt her breathing grow so shallow, she wondered if her lungs had literally filled with fear.

With the arrival of Officer Miklowski's car at the Wiesbaden, all three patrol vehicles from the Ouray Police Department were on the scene. Cars from the county sheriff were just arriving from their offices, a block away. The officers were overwhelmed in number by a concerned, tearful gathering of local residents, who knew too few facts and were already busy spreading too many rumors.

Purdy raised the collar of his leather jacket and hunched his shoulders high as he meandered through a line of locals, politely saying, "Excuse me, please." Officer Miklowski, looking lost, trailed in his wake.

Purdy read the scene quickly. The glass-enclosed lobby of the main lodge was quiet, a solitary uniformed sentry guarding the door that faced to the south. None of the motel-room doors was either open or guarded. A small crowd, however, had gathered on Sixth Avenue, adjacent to a stone path that led to a tall cedar fence that ran in a rough semicircle out toward the back of the property, against a steep slope. Purdy followed the sidewalk toward the gathering.

Long's control of the scene pleased Purdy. The townspeople weren't trampling evidence; instead, the group was well contained behind a deep perimeter that had been established by Long. Purdy stopped his approach on the periphery of the scene, looking for clues as to what had happened, waiting for Long to invite him inside the crime-scene perimeter.

In the brief car ride through Ouray's sleepy streets, Miklowski had told Purdy three times that Rachel was dead. Each time he repeated his message, it was as though it were the first. "She's dead. You were right. She's dead." Although his mood was agitated, his tone was flat. Purdy had tried a few questions that Miklowski had answered with "Don't know." The only question that he had been able to answer was "How did she die?" It had been answered with "She drowned. Rachel drowned."

Purdy had been silent the last couple of blocks to the Wiesbaden.

Brian Long finally stepped through the gate in the cedar fence and spotted Purdy. Long's face was somber; his eyes were heavy with responsibility and regret. He took Sam Purdy by the arm and tugged him across the stone path to create some space between them and the restless group on the sidewalk.

"This is awful, Sam," he said.

"I'm terribly sorry, Brian."

"Eight years I've been here. This is my first murder. And I could've stopped it." He looked to Purdy for forgiveness for his lack of diligence.

Purdy tried to do the best he could to provide a cushion for Long's guilt. "You don't know that, Brian. Last night we may have been in the murder-prevention business, or we may have just been kidding ourselves and really only been in the murder-postponement business. I'm afraid that you've got yourself a dedicated killer on your hands."

"You're homicide, aren't you?"

"Boulder's not a big enough department to have detectives just do homicide. But, yeah, I do homicide sometimes."

"Give me a hand here?"

"You seem to know what you're doing, Brian." Purdy tilted his head toward the crime scene.

"Maybe I do. I did a long time ago, Sam. I was a division chief in Fort Collins before I came up here. But I'm rusty and I don't want to screw this up. Help me?"

Purdy turned his body to face the gate. He wanted to shift Long's focus. "What have you got?"

Long took a deep breath. "Donna Tarkett, Rachel's best friend, found her this morning at seven-thirty, face-down in the tub." He saw Purdy look once more at the closed gate. "There's a private hot tub in there that Donna rents by the hour. She calls it the Lorelei. It's got a little stone waterfall that flows into the tub from one of the hot springs."

Involuntarily, Purdy began to imagine what a body would look like after bobbing around all night in a hot tub. "Miklowski said she drowned," he said.

Brian Long shook his head once. "Bill's a good small-town cop, Sam. Knows basically what to overlook. Knows what to press. But he doesn't know shit about homicide. Rachel's in the water, I guess he figures she drowned."

"So what do you think it is?" Purdy edged closer to the gate. He wanted to see the scene. And despite his fears about the condition it would be in, he wanted to see the body.

Brian Long slid dark aviator glasses onto his nose and hooked the rims behind his ears. "Rachel looks like she's been boiled, Sam. The water from the hot springs is one hundred six to one hundred ten degrees this time of year. That's real hot. And I think she's been in there all night. If I had to bet, I'll bet she didn't drown. Or if she did drown, I'll bet somebody drowned her. It's unbelievable what she looks like. It's like a horror movie. You ever seen a body after a night in hot water?"

Purdy shivered. He had only dealt with one floater in his career, in Duluth, in the late fall, in water that was much closer to freezing than to steaming. He didn't really want to know what Rachel Baumann looked like after bobbing around for ten hours in water that was damn near scalding. The image in his head was of swollen, lobster-red skin. Something told him the reality would not even be that pleasant.

"Is she still in the water?"

"No. Donna jumped in and tried to pull her out first thing. She got her halfway out, then . . ." His voice trailed off.

"Then what? Brian, what?"

"Then . . . when she pulled on Rachel's hand to pull her the rest of the way out of the tub, the skin on Rachel's hand slid right off. Just like a glove. But with the fingernails still attached."

Purdy grimaced at the image. "Oh, shit. Poor Donna."

"Yeah."

"Can I take a look?"

Brian Long said, "Please," and waited for Purdy to precede him to the gate.

"Who assists on this stuff for you guys? County? State?"

"Both. County's here already. Mobile crime lab is on its way. We're still trying to find the coroner. CBI will do lab and forensics for us if we need it. We'll need it. The coroner here's an M.D., and he's good, but if I know him, once he sees Rachel's body he'll get a forensic pathologist from Montrose to do the post."

Purdy picked a spot a couple of feet up from the handle and pushed on the gate with his gloved fingertips.

Rachel Baumann's body had been moved the rest of the way out of the hot tub. The corpse was completely draped with a white motel sheet. To Purdy, the sheet seemed to be covering a body at least twice the size of the woman he had met a couple of days before. A big towel, still folded, sat unused on an old Adirondack chair. The hot tub, which Purdy had expected to be made of redwood, was actually of molded fiberglass. A gentle flow of steaming water bubbled melodically down adjacent rocks, spilling into the tub. The setting was serene and beautiful. The irony could not have been more complete.

"Can you turn that thing off?"

"We're trying. It's a natural spring. There's a chute up the hill to divert the water to the street so Donna can do maintenance. Her handyman isn't around, and nobody can find the key to the lock on the access door."

Purdy said evenly, "The access door isn't evidence. This is. Pry it open. Or blow the damn lock off if you need to. God only knows what the hell's washing away down here."

Like dog hairs, he thought.

Long set his solid jaw and pursed his lips. He left, Purdy hoped, to give somebody an order. Purdy lowered himself to a crouch on the cedar decking. He raised the sheet. Immediately he dropped the shroud back onto the body and stood. He said, "Oh, my God," and warded off an impulse to flee the pool enclosure.

Rachel's corpse had been lain flat on its back on the worn wood deck. The body Purdy examined the second time he raised the sheet had bulged to become the size of a two-hundred-pound person's. Alive, Rachel had weighed in the vicinity of one thirty-five. The face on the bloated corpse was rippled from changes greatly accelerated by the moist heat of the hot spring. The color of the skin was chalky white. The individual features of the face—the lips, the tongue, the nose—were swollen to grotesque proportions that made it impossible for Purdy to be certain that he was even looking at Rachel Baumann's remains. Purdy guessed that the onset of decomposition might be more pronounced in the face because hot water had entered Rachel's throat and sinuses through her mouth and nose. Rachel's once-clear eyes had receded to invisibility behind the tumescent folds of ribbed cheek and forehead flesh. Purdy wondered about rigor. What about lividity? He could have guessed what the heat had done to accelerate those processes but didn't bother.

If he stayed on this case, he knew that soon he would

be an unwilling expert on the acute postmortem consequences of extreme sustained high body temperature.

Without touching the body, Purdy visually examined the swimsuit-clad corpse for evidence of trauma. He couldn't identify any. The bloating of the torso had been restrained by the tight fabric of the swimsuit. But Rachel's hands and feet were swollen and ribbed deeply, like a washerwoman's. Quietly, as he respread the sheet, he said to Rachel, "God, I hope they have a good ME around here. Somebody's gonna have their hands full trying to figure out what happened to you."

Brian Long said, "You talking to me?"

Purdy looked over at the gate, away from the corpse. "Brian, how do you even know it's Rachel? I can't recognize her."

Long shook his head, the whole time looking away from the body. "I can't, either. Donna recognizes her swimsuit. And she says that Rachel was the last one with the key to the Lorelei. You see what the water did to her skin? I'm not even sure we can retrieve prints off of those fingers. We might have to confirm identity with dental records. I'm just working under the assumption it's Rachel."

"Don't worry. The techs will get prints." He looked back down at the sheet. "The body is awful, Brian. Is Donna doing all right?"

"Donna's a basket case, Sam. An absolute wreck."

"Rachel have any family?"

"A daughter in Denver. Anita. Sweet, sweet kid. It's gonna kill her. This is just gonna kill her."

PART THREE

SINNERS AND SAINTS

Better dead clean, than alive unclean.
MORMON MAXIM OF THE 1940S

The child of a Mormon family undergoes what must be one of the most powerful indoctrinations of any society, so that in adult life, that child is incapable of admitting publicly, and sometimes not even to himself, that he does not believe in some or even in all of the basic teachings of the church. To do so is to drain himself of one hundred and forty years of Mormon blood.
RODELLO HUNTER,
A DAUGHTER OF ZION

Palmer Cocetti rocked gently in the front room of the inn with his deer rifle across his lap. His eyes were focused on the street. Alan prayed to himself that a minivan full of innocent Mormons from Utah didn't choose that day to drive up to Helena and Palmer's door looking for accommodations.

Lauren had been on the phone since minutes after Purdy left, frantically and unsuccessfully trying to reach Robin Torr, John Harley, or her sister.

The domestic office of the cruise line provided no help in determining that Teresa was or wasn't actually on their ship on the Mexican coast. After a half-dozen calls to airport hotels near Lindbergh Field in San Diego, she finally succeeded in tracking down the one where Robin Torr had spent the night. Lauren was told that Ms. Torr had checked out about twenty minutes before.

Lauren begged to have Torr paged. She waited while the clerk checked with a manager, who finally relented. *Please, Robin. Be there.*

"I'm very sorry, but she's not answering the page."

A secretary in his department said that John Harley was in class already. She would be happy to give him a message.

With her cane for support, Lauren walked from the parlor to the front room and announced to Alan that she wanted to go to the scene of the murder.

"Sam wants us to stay here, Lauren."

She fought despair. She leaned the cane against a chair and slid her arms around his neck and welcomed his reflexive embrace. "As though I'm safer here by myself than I would be out there surrounded by every cop in the county. I doubt it. Sam's just being controlling. I know him pretty well. It's in his nature."

"What about the phone? What if Teresa or Robin calls? Or your friend from Salt Lake?"

Lauren examined Alan's face for evidence of accusation. She couldn't tell. She turned away from him. "Palmer, will you take messages for me?"

He hefted his rifle somberly. "Anything to help, Miss. I used to be Military Police. We got us a situation. That's what we used to say. I'll do my part."

The mobile crime-scene truck arrived in Ouray, and its investigators immediately began to process the scene. The coroner showed up minutes later.

The coroner was a dour-looking man with a large shiny forehead and an ill-fitting suitcoat with six-inch-wide lapels. After hearing a shortened version of the facts from Chief Long and taking a cursory look at Rachel Baumann's swollen remains, he recognized that he was out of his league. He excused himself and retreated to the lodge office to make some phone calls to try to track down the forensic pathologist in Montrose to do an autopsy. Whatever the coroner lacked in specialized skill as a medical examiner, he apparently made up for in modesty and prudence.

"Do you think that water looks pink?" Purdy gestured to the spa water, which was finally undisturbed now that the mineral spring feeding it had been diverted. Brian Long had been watching the crime-scene techs go about their jobs—sketching, measuring, photographing, videotaping, scouring for trace evidence. He glanced over at the water distractedly.

"Not especially. I think it's just the tint of the tub. See the red streaks there in the plastic?"

Purdy shook his head. "Nah. I think it's pink. I think Rachel may have been bleeding." He approached one of the forensic technicians. "Do me a favor? Grab some water samples from that tub. Test for blood."

The investigator reached into a molded plastic case and extracted two vials. "Got them already."

"Did you skim the surface for trace materials?"

"Done. Swabbed the sides at the water line, too. In a few minutes we'll drain the water and check the filter and the trap."

Purdy shook his head a little, pleased at the professionalism and competence of this rural crew, dismayed at his own urban chauvinism. He asked whether they were done photographing and videotaping the scene.

"This part we are. We haven't done her room yet or the path in between."

Purdy went in search of the coroner. He chose an alternative from the usual path that led from the Lorelei to the lodge office. He tapped the coroner on the shoulder as the man spoke on the phone. The coroner covered the mouthpiece with his palm, and Purdy asked the man to come with him so that he and Chief Long could turn the corpse to examine the back of the body for wounds.

He reluctantly assented, said a quick good-bye into the mouthpiece, and hung up the phone.

The coroner and Purdy found Chief Long at the gate to the enclosure, and together they proceeded inside. The coroner warned the two policeman not to tug on Rachel's limbs when turning her. "I'm afraid they might come right off in your hands," he said. Gently, the three men rolled Rachel Baumann's body onto its left side. Purdy suspected they would discover wounds. He also knew that if wounds were there, it was going to be difficult to find them in the engorged, rippled flesh.

"Here," said the coroner, pointing to a spot below the right shoulder blade. "There's a hole or something right here. See? I wouldn't be surprised if there's a wound in there somewhere."

"Knife?" asked Chief Long.

"Who the hell knows," replied the coroner, reluctant to probe the decaying flesh, even with gloved fingers.

"I'm not sure, either," said Purdy, who had lowered his face to within a foot of the wound. "I think maybe it's a round hole."

The coroner was trying hard to be useful. He was

palpating Rachel's head through her damp hair. "Brian, I got something else. Rachel's got a depression on her head. She was hit pretty hard. I'd say from above and behind. Good-size skull depression. Yeah, definitely. Lacerated skin, too. Given the location, so high up on her skull, I'd guess this isn't from a fall. We'll know better after thc autopsy."

He pulled his hand away from Rachel's head. His examination gloves were covered with her hair.

Lauren was just settling into the passenger seat of Alan's rental car when Helena burst outside waving her arms.

"Your call! Your call! The man from Utah."

John Harley was on the line, finally. Lauren hurried back inside as quickly as her cane and her heavy leg would permit.

"Harley. Thank you. Have you heard from Robin Torr? Any news about Teresa?"

"No. Why would she call me?"

Lauren explained about the system that she and Robin had arranged to use to stay in touch. "I hope you don't mind. It was kind of impromptu."

"I don't mind. Are you with your man friend?"

"Yes, Harley, I am." Alan Gregory was sitting across the parlor, listening, Lauren assumed, to every word.

"Harley, there's been another murder. The woman I came to Colorado to talk with. She was killed last night. The rumor in town is that she was drowned. I was just—Alan and I were just heading over there to see what happened."

John Harley's end of the conversation was silent for a moment. Then he said, "Drowned? That doesn't fit. Have the police check carefully for blood. See if she bled before she died. The time of death—after she bled—is very important. Then call me back. I'll stay in my office until I hear from you."

"Harley, what do you mean, doesn't fit? Why should they look for blood? Tell me what you're thinking."

"No. Go find out what you can. Call me back as soon as possible."

Back in the car a few minutes later, Alan said, "Your friend hasn't heard anything?"

Lauren shook her head. "No. But he seems to think it's important whether Rachel actually drowned or died after something caused her to bleed. He wants me to check with Sam and call him back." She looked out the window at three women huddled together outside a small market. She was reminded of the small town near the apple farm where she grew up.

Alan said, "I don't get it."

"I don't, either," Lauren said. "Alan, he reminds me of my dad. This guy in Salt Lake City. It's pretty confusing to me."

Alan swallowed and permitted some mental connections to develop. "Your friend drinks?"

"He's sober now, for a while."

"You trying to rescue him?"

"I don't know. Maybe."

"You attracted to him?"

Her pause was a second too long. "To him? I don't know. To something, I guess." She finally turned to him in the car just as he was pulling to a stop outside the Wiesbaden. "I love you, Alan."

Alan felt his stomach flip. He tried to smile at her but failed.

Lauren held Alan's hand as she walked. Her right hand gripped the cane. A sheriff's deputy refused to let them past the parking area in front of the Wiesbaden. Alan called out to Purdy when he noticed him emerging from the cedar gate that seemed to be the center of everyone's attention. Sam shoved his hands into his pockets and strode over. He was acting as though he were in charge of the world and was growing irritated at the help.

He walked straight to Alan Gregory. Lauren felt ignored and annoyed. "I thought I told you to—"

"Lauren talked to her friend, Sam. We may know something new."

Purdy looked at Lauren, who said, "I need to sit first." Her leg felt like lumber.

Purdy walked over to some patio furniture by the large hot-springs pool in front of the main lodge and told the four people seated at a table there to "beat it." He never asked Alan and Lauren to follow; he just expected them to.

"What's so damn important?" There was no attempt to keep the skepticism from his voice.

"Harley, my friend in Salt Lake, is acting as an intermediary between Robin Torr and me. He called a few minutes ago, said he hadn't heard anything from Robin. Then I told Harley that Rachel was dead—that she had drowned—and the first thing out of his mouth was something like 'That doesn't fit.' He immediately asked me to ask you if there was any sign that she bled before she died and to call him right away with the answer. That's why we're here." The last sentence was a lie she was grateful to be able to tell. She would have come anyway.

Purdy's interest was piqued. He furrowed his brow and played dumb. "Why is blood so important? Dead's dead."

"Harley wouldn't tell me. Just said that it was. That he'd tell me more when I called him back."

"You know his number?"

"Yes."

"Let's go call him, then. Follow me."

Sam led them into the office and commandeered a phone. Lauren pulled out her credit card and punched in Harley's number, said a brief hello, and told Harley she was going to give the telephone to a detective from Boulder named Sam Purdy.

Sam was in an impolite frame of mind and didn't bother with any pleasantries. "What's with your interest in the blood, Mr. Harley?"

Harley was amused by the detective's authoritarian tone. In some respects it reminded him of his most recent interview with his bishop. Unfortunately, impertinence had come easily to him then, too.

"Is there any blood spilled where she was murdered? Like on the ground?" Harley asked.

Purdy didn't answer.

"There is, isn't there? I knew it. I knew there would be blood. I knew she didn't drown."

Purdy was silent while he strategized.

"Assume you're right, Mr. Harley. What's the significance? And how would you know?" Purdy was skeptical but curious. Most murder scenes were at least a little bloody. He wondered what Lauren's friend was getting at by predicting bloodletting.

"How much do you know about the LDS Church, Sam?" Harley never asked Purdy what he wished to be called.

Sam decided on ignorance as being the strategy of choice. "About as much as I know about professional soccer."

"Have you ever heard of blood atonement?"

"Doesn't ring any bells. Is that some Mormon ritual or something?"

"Hardly. But some of the most fervent faithful believe, based on some old but rather specific preaching by Brigham Young, that certain sins are so vile that the sinner can only be forgiven for them once his own blood is spilled and mixed with the earth. It's absolutely the only way the sinner can be reunited for eternity with his family in heaven."

"What kinds of sins are we talking about?"

"Murder, for one. But most often, the historical penalty of blood atonement was sanctioned against those who defiled the Church or belittled the prophet or his teachings."

"And what makes you think that this blood-atonement thing is particularly pertinent today, Mr. Harley?"

Harley loved the sardonic tone of the question and immediately felt that Purdy and he would get along famously if they ever had a chance to meet. "Everybody calls me Harley, okay? I take it Lauren told you about the knife? In her sister's bed? Right where her heart would be? Well, I saw it. And it got me thinking about the other two murders. The woman in D.C.—her throat was cut, right? And that investigator in Moab? Lauren said that somebody went to some significant trouble to make sure this guy's blood spilled out of his waterproof jacket after he was shot. Those two deaths, the spilling-of-blood part specifically, are consistent with the practice of blood atonement. Consistent, anyway, if you make the assumption that the victims were guilty of sins against the prophet. And if you make the assumption that the murders were committed by a member of the Church."

"Please excuse my ignorance. Who is the prophet?"

"The prophet is the current president of the Church. The prophet, seer, and revelator of all Mormondom. It's always an old man. The Church is a male gerontocracy."

"Okay. Let me see if I got all this. So, if we determine that the victims were all in a position, in someone's eyes, to bring ridicule on either the Church or the prophet, then some radical Mormon might take on for himself the title of enforcer and spill their blood as dictated a hundred years ago by Brigham Young."

"So far, so good."

"And if this latest death were to involve the spilling of blood onto the earth, and if we assume that Rachel Baumann was a danger to the Church, it would fit the pattern you're describing as well?"

"That's right. You get an A."

"How literal is all this, Harley? I mean, does the blood actually have to spill into the dirt? Would flowing into water suffice? Like down a sewer line?"

"I'm no specialist on these things. Brigham Young said ground. I know that, because I recently looked it up. But, then again, he said it at a time when there weren't a whole lot of sewer lines to be concerned with.

"In the early days of the Church, these enforcers of the faith were called Danites, or sometimes Brigham's Avenging Angels. Historians, both LDS and gentile, think that in the beginning they reported directly to Joseph Smith, and later to Brigham Young. Those two were the founding fathers of the Church. These days, though, the Church denies the existence of Danites, and if they're around, we're not talking mainstream Church members anymore; we're probably talking zealots."

"Zealots?"

"Fundamentalist Mormons who still believe in the Principle—polygamy. Other LDS sometimes call them polygs."

"Like those polygamists who got into that thing with the FBI? What are their names? It's like the car. The LeBarons, that's it. Zealots like them?"

"Yeah. Most of the fringe Mormons that the press likes to sensationalize would be considered zealots by mainstream Mormons. The LeBarons, Bruce Longo, Paul Singer. Yeah, I would guess all of them would have endorsed blood atonement. Heck, some of them even practiced it. But—may I indulge in some irony here, Sam?"

"Be my guest, Harley. When I'm investigating a murder I always have a few spare moments to indulge in a little irony."

Harley loved that response. "Well, the irony is that

the only condoned practice of blood atonement these days is committed by the State of Utah itself."

"What?"

"Remember Gary Gilmore? He was a murderer executed by the State of Utah a few years back. Norman Mailer wrote a book about him. His capital punishment was not by lethal injection. Not by the electric chair. Not by hanging. Not by the gas chamber. Gary Gilmore was killed, by his choice, by firing squad. His blood was spilled upon the ground."

"And he had that option because of the state's Mormon heritage?"

"Yeah. That's Utah's heritage."

Purdy took a deep breath and exhaled slowly. "So if all your suppositions are true, Harley, the murderer we're discussing might be a fringe Mormon who's protecting the prophet from heretical Church members."

"Or from outsiders eager to damage the credibility of the Church through ridicule. By outsiders I mean gentiles, or maybe even Jack Mormons."

"Okay, you got me again. What's a Jack Mormon?"

"Someone who was born or converted into the Church but who has strayed. Doesn't tithe, doesn't attend services, drinks a bit—or even a bit more than that—wakes up to a cup of coffee, is full of doubts. A jackrabbit isn't really a hare. To a devout member of the LDS Church, a Jack Mormon isn't really a Mormon. So your murderer could be a zealot, a Jack Mormon, or a gentile with a grudge."

Purdy scratched his ear under the phone. "That doesn't narrow down my suspect pool very much, Harley. I take it you may be one of these Jack Mormons?"

"I may be on my way. My bishop and I discuss it quite frequently."

"So if you're still so ambivalent about the Mormon Church, why are you telling me all this?"

"There are no state secrets here, Sam. You could learn all this stuff in an hour in the library. A secular library, anyway."

"What you're suggesting smacks of the practices of the ayatollah, not of a major American church, Harley."

"Well. I'm already having enough doubts about the faith that it's probably best that I leave the judgment to others. Like I said, if it's true, we're talking radical LDS, not mainstream LDS. But there's another possibility to consider. This murderer could be somebody who wants people to *believe* that he's acting like a Danite, so that the Church would suffer even more ridicule."

"There's a nice comforting thought, Harley: an imposter fanatic. Great." Purdy searched his usually reliable memory for a dangling fragment. "But there's some precedent there, too, isn't there? Like the bombing guy in Salt Lake City, what was his name?"

"Mark Hofmann. Yeah, Hofmann's the guy you're thinking of. He forged historical Church documents that would have undermined the foundations of Church doctrine if made public, and then he tricked the Church into buying the documents so they would never see the light of day."

"I'm getting the impression that, as a general rule, the Church isn't terribly fond of criticism."

"The Church has been known to be a little sensitive at times, yes."

Lauren rested on a settee across the lobby while Purdy talked with Harley. Alan sat next to her, sensed her struggling with her symptoms, and offered whatever support he could.

Purdy hung up without asking Lauren whether she wanted to speak again with Harley. He pulled an oak ladder-back chair to the settee and straddled it, facing Lauren and Alan.

"He may have something. I don't want to talk about it right now; too many people around. It'll take me just a few minutes to finish up here and check out with Chief Long. Stay right where you are. I'll find you."

He stood and left the building.

Lauren said, "Isn't he charming?"

As was his preference for any conversation of consequence, Purdy ended up sharing Harley's theory about blood atonement over an ample meal. This one, because of the early-morning sacrifice of his frittatas, encompassed both breakfast and lunch, in both size and makeup.

The last thing that Brian Long had told him before Purdy had corralled Alan and Lauren and left the Wiesbaden was that there didn't seem to be any other wounds on the body.

Alan and Lauren nursed iced teas while they watched Sam eat. At first he offered them his theory between bites. To both his friends, the exposition of the hypothesis seemed like the second most important thing he was doing. Alan suggested that he finish eating; then they could talk.

When Sam finally pushed his plate away, he said, "Rachel's in the hot tub. He watched her go in from the hill above the tub. He climbs the fence and gets in behind her somehow. She's got the jets on in the tub, maybe, and she doesn't hear a thing. He hits her on the head hard enough to crack her skull open. She collapses into the tub. But maybe he doesn't hit her in a way that makes her bleed. He's afraid she's going to drown without spilling blood, so he stabs her with whatever he's got with him. Maybe he hadn't really planned on it—on stabbing her. I don't know. He watches her start to bleed. He's accomplished what he wants. Even more than he wants. Because since Rachel's body is bobbing around in hot running water, trace evidence likely goes down the drain. And God knows what the fact that the body was poached all night is going to do to the autopsy.

"Anyway, our murderer splits. And he's got an eight- to ten-hour head start before anybody even finds her. He could've been having breakfast in Salt Lake City just as I was sitting down to Palmer's frittata this morning."

"Any evidence of the dog?" The question was Lauren's.

"Didn't see any paw prints. They're still looking, mostly up the hill, assuming that was his entrance. Of course, it'll take the lab a while to analyze for trace evidence, like dog hair."

"Any witnesses?"

"They haven't come up with any yet."

"Anybody see any cars with Utah plates close by?"

"There's only a couple in town that anybody recalls. The police chief is going to interview those people himself. Our guy's gone, though. Long gone. Getaways are his specialty, remember?"

Alan asked, "But you're sure it's the same guy?"

"Yeah."

Alan didn't see the logic. "But why? I mean, other than the obvious link to Teresa's case. The weapons and cause of death have been different each time, haven't they?"

"The weapons are different. But a lot about the MO is the same. Isolated, rural killings providing great escape access. Focus on blood and bleeding. Smart, well-planned crimes. Guy is not at all interested in being caught. This is not a killer with an impulse. This is a killer with a mission. He doesn't enjoy it, isn't getting off on it. No revelry. He's gotta get it done and get away."

Lauren leaned forward. "Sam, who is going to get the feds in on this? We both know this isn't a small-town murder."

"And what, the big-city cops in D.C. and Salt Lake City have done so well with *their* murder investigations? The local chief isn't an idiot. He knows he's got a complicated crime. He's got a call into the bureau's Denver office. He's waiting to hear back from them. He's at a bit of a disadvantage, though, because he only has hearsay evidence that Rachel was even part of the same set of circumstances that may or may not have something to do with the other two deaths. My own opinion is that the bureau's interest is going to be lukewarm until your lawyer friend provides some confirmation that they can actually hold in their hands that Rachel was really part of this mess—and I mean that in an interstate sense—or until the CBI lab finds evidence that a dog was around for the third time. My word on this ain't worth shit, Lauren. And your word, unfortunately, ain't worth much more than mine."

Purdy looked at his watch and decided it really wasn't too early for dessert. He motioned the waitress over and asked how the cherry pie was.

Alan waited until the waitress had responded and departed. "How much danger is Lauren in, Sam?"

Lauren shot a warning glance at Alan.

Purdy spent a moment trying to clean his teeth with his tongue. "Depends," he said, as the waitress returned and slid an oversized plate in front of him. Thc wedge of pie seeped plump sour cherries.

"On?" To Alan's surprise, Lauren forced the question. He grabbed her hand and held it loosely.

"Our underlying assumption—" Purdy cut and shoveled in an initial mouthful of pie. "You sure you don't want some of this? What's wrong with you people? Our assumption is that these people are dying because they know something, or, in Pratt Toomey's case, because he was on the verge of knowing something. So if our assumptions are correct—and I'm beginning to believe they are—how much danger Lauren or her sister or her attorney friend are in is directly related to how much they know. Which at this point, I think, fortunately or unfortunately, is not very much."

"Or to how close we are to discovering something," Lauren pointed out.

Purdy nodded almost imperceptibly.

"The reality, ladies and gentlemen," Alan said, pausing until both of his friends were looking at him, "is that the danger is related to how much somebody *thinks* these women know. How much they actually know doesn't mean shit."

By the end of the afternoon Lauren had completed a nap precipitated at least in part by a grueling interrogation conducted by Chief Brian Long. Long had wanted to know why she was in town to see Rachel Baumann and what Rachel had told her. While she was answering the chief's questions, and later, while she slept, Alan and Sam rented bikes and pounded up a steep dirt road near the Bachelor Mine. When they met in the late afternoon in Helena and Palmer's parlor, all three of them agreed that there was not much to be gained by remaining in Ouray.

Sam booked a seat on the last flight of the day from Telluride to Denver. Lauren was adamant about staying available until she heard from Robin Torr. Although Alan was due back at work in Boulder the next day, he decided to catch the early flight out the next morning, hoping he could use the extra time to talk Lauren into coming home with him.

They checked out of the B & B after saying good-bye to Helena and Palmer. Alan and Lauren drove Sam over the Dallas Divide and up the canyons above the San Miguel to Telluride's airport. Before boarding his plane, Sam admonished Lauren, "Find your little sister and get your butts to Boulder, where I can keep an eye on you."

Alan drove slowly from the airport into the town of Telluride. During the quiet, blustery days of fall the old mining town managed to be quaint without even an echo of cuteness. He rolled the car to a crackling stop on loose gravel in front of a modest Victorian inn near the

Oak Street chair lift. A minute later he introduced Lauren to Cilla and Teri and their fine little B & B. The women raised Lauren's reluctant, deflated spirit with the exuberance of their welcome. They asked after Sam. Cilla offered her guests a thin brown bottle of sweet white wine on a silver tray that looked as if it had once been somebody's wedding present. Teri appeared moments later with a platter of quesadillas and pico de gallo.

After the wine was gone and had been replaced by another bottle, and that was gone, Alan asked his hostesses for a room with a bath. Cilla left to prepare it.

Telluride's corner of the San Juans was small and cozy, the air was thin, and bad news tended to travel the canyons with the speed of a spooked buck. Given Lauren's fears and the tenuousness of her mood, Alan was grateful that neither Cilla nor Teri had asked about the day's events in Ouray.

When Lauren and Alan finally went upstairs, they discovered that the bathroom was candlelit, the tub was full and steaming and bubbly, and a huge spray of fresh flowers adorned the top of the commode. Of one mind, they undressed each other in the dim light and sank slowly into the water. She watched the water and seemed to find despair. He watched her, her flesh, and tried not to think about Rachel Baumann's last bath at the Wiesbaden. He held her from behind with both arms, supporting her, and traced the sides of her face with his fingertips. She pressed her back tightly to his chest, and within a few quiet moments she began to cry gently and privately, until the water lost its fire.

Her fear, too.

She held his arms with her own, across her abdomen, as though she would never let him go.

The single candle, on the sink across the room, flickered and then extinguished itself, and a pale glow from the moon tumbled through the lace curtains. With the toes of her good foot she twisted the hot-water tap until a torrent of steam and water began spilling into the tub. She took one of his hands and placed it between her legs, and took the other and placed it on her breast, and she turned her head and kissed him.

The bedroom had a cove ceiling and a burgundy velvet chaise and a four-poster pine bed and a dwindling fire and a southern view of treetops and vaulting mountain faces covered with the black-green of ponderosa. And when Lauren rocked the four-poster and met his thrust and pulled him as far into her as she could and came at the exact stroke of nine o'clock, her good leg locked around Alan's ass, they discovered that somewhere in the inn there was a cuckoo clock.

The bird began chirping seconds into Lauren's climax. By the third cuckoo she was crying, and by the fifth, laughing. And by the time the bird stopped clucking and retreated to its den, she was absolutely spent.

She wiped her eyes and inhaled deeply to try to find some oxygen, then asked in a quiet, breathy voice, "I couldn't even tell. Did you come?"

He rolled off her onto his side, lay his head on her chest, and touched her gently on the soft skin beneath her ear.

Lauren bolted straight up in bed shortly after the distant cuckoo clock announced 2:00 A.M. She leaped to the floor, where she promptly crumpled into a ball onto a threadbare kilim with a loud thud and a muffled "Damn."

Alan barely stirred as Lauren fumbled around in the dark for something to cover herself. She found her jeans and slithered into them, tugging them awkwardly over her hips while still seated on the floor. The next clothing she found was his sweatshirt, and she pulled it over her head and flipped her hair out from under the collar. She smelled him.

Where is that stupid cane?

The sky was clear and freckled with stars, and the moon hung lazily, a little fuller than a crescent. There was not enough celestial light, however, for Lauren to see her cane. She finally spotted it leaning against the wall between the closet and the bathroom door. She struggled over toward it, raised herself on her good leg, and, as quietly as she could, let herself out into the stillness of the second-floor hallway.

She remembered a phone on a side table downstairs in the big room with the fireplace where they had chatted with Cilla and Teri. The combination of the stairs and the cane presented a challenge in the dark, but she adjusted with silent determination and patience she didn't feel.

"Harley, please be home," she whispered into the receiver as she punched the long chain of numbers.

Three rings, four. A voice gorged with sleep. "Yeah? Jules? What's wrong? Are the girls okay?"

"Harley, it's not Jules. It's me, Lauren."

"Lauren, hi." The phone call was beginning to win the battle for his attention. Barely.

"I should've called earlier. I'm at a new number. I'm sorry. Have you heard from Robin, Harley?"

"Yeah. Gimme a second. I did." He dropped the receiver to the sheets. It promptly bounced to the carpeted floor next to his bed. Harley was oblivious. He looked around the room and felt thick, smooth muck in his head and welcomed the sensation of waking up drunk. The experience was similar to awakening beside an old lover with whom he had never really wanted to break up.

He stumbled across the room and lifted a bottle of cheap vodka off the top of the TV, raising it to his dry lips just to be sure it was empty. In the bathroom, he peeled off his corduroys, stepped clumsily out of them, freed his penis from his garments, and peed loudly. Neither hand guided the flow of urine; both were propped flat on the wall behind the toilet in an absolutely essential effort to help ensure a continued vertical orientation while he relieved himself.

When he walked back into the bedroom he was wearing only gray socks, his garments, and an old cotton turtleneck. He tripped over the phone on the floor by the bed, stubbed the big toe of his left foot, screeched "Ouch," and remembered. Sort of.

"Yeah?" he said after picking up the receiver.

"Are you feeling all right, Harley?"

"Sure, who's this?"

"Lauren. Lauren Crowder. Harley, are you awake?"

"Yeah. Your friend called, Lauren. Said she couldn't find you. Said she didn't find your sister. Said to tell you she wasn't on the boat. I guess she couldn't find anybody. 'Cept me." Harley found that pretty funny.

"What do you mean she wasn't on the boat? Harley! What do you mean?"

"She—wasn't—on—the—boat."

Lauren was frantic. Her intent to keep the volume of her voice under control was forgotten. "Where is she, Harley? Where's my sister?"

He shrugged his shoulders. He was trying to remember whether he had any more vodka in the kitchen.

"Harley! Answer me." Lauren wondered if Harley might be drunk. She tried to dismiss it but involuntarily pictured a vintage can of Schlitz. "Harley, wake up!"

"Okay."

"Where's Teresa?"

"She doesn't know. She's coming back here. The lawyer."

"When?"

In a lilting, childlike voice, Harley said, "Soon?" He couldn't actually remember. But the goal of his memory was fluid. Maybe the kitchen? He wanted to check the kitchen. Maybe he left a bottle in there. He hung up the phone.

Alan sat on the stairs, listening to Lauren's end of the conversation, feeling like an eavesdropper. He was trying to weigh the relative merits of retreating to their bedroom and awaiting her return or joining her downstairs during the remainder of her conversation with her friend.

Since she was wearing his sweatshirt, he'd left the bedroom barechested and was soon chilled. The cold helped him reach a decision; he walked down the rest of the stairs when he heard her place the receiver back in its cradle.

She sat sideways on the sofa, her good leg drawn up to her chest, her dead leg beached on the cushions. She rocked and stared.

Alan perched on the couch next to her and hugged her gently. "What is it?"

"Teresa wasn't on the ship, Alan. Robin couldn't find her anywhere."

"Maybe she's back in Salt Lake wondering where the hell you are."

"No. I left a note at the house, just in case she got home before I reached her. I told her not to sleep at the house under any circumstances. Told her where I would be. I listed all the numbers you had left for me up here."

"Well, who knows, maybe Teresa is developing a responsible streak in her old age, and she left you a message at the house, too."

Lauren pounded the back of the sofa with her hand. "God! Why didn't I think of that? Maybe she left me a message on her machine. Or at Robin's office."

Alan was relieved at the animation Lauren displayed. "Can you retrieve messages remotely from her machine? Do you know the code?"

"No. It's an old machine, with one of those beeping things to pick up messages. She keeps it with her." She looked up at him. "Alan, I've got to get back to Salt Lake."

Alan rubbed her back and nodded, resigned.

In a minute of mutual silence, her tense muscles did not even pretend to slacken under his touch. His voice as devoid of confrontation as he could make it, he asked, "How's your friend? Harley?"

For what to her felt like the tenth time that day, Lauren cried.

They parted in the underground train station at Denver's new airport the next morning before Lauren caught her connection to Salt Lake City.

She had awakened him early with a kiss on the back of his neck that was more tongue than lips. She'd swung an arm across his chest. He'd shivered once and moaned, and in seconds his breathing had changed.

Slowly, with her fingers and her mouth and her long, silky hair, she made sure this time that he came.

Over coffee and flaky rolls, Lauren had insisted that Alan go back to Boulder. She did it in the voice he knew precluded argument. She promised to stay in a hotel with Robin Torr until everything with the case started to settle out. She promised to call him that night.

"Every night," he insisted.

"Every night," she said, meaning it, grateful for his concern.

Lauren's connection into Salt Lake beat Robin Torr's connection from L.A. to Utah by only an hour. If she had known, she would have waited.

Instead, she took a cab across town to her sister's bungalow, paid the driver, accepted her small suitcase, and stood at the foot of the path that led to the front door. The combination of her ambivalence and her fear was causing her to feel that her shoes were merged with the cracked cement.

The house was locked. She knocked on the door. The wishful logic in her head stipulated that any self-respecting intruder would voluntarily retreat out the back door at the sound of an insistent knock. She waited ten or fifteen seconds to give him time to leave. Then, one hand on the key, the other on a can of pepper gas from her purse, she let herself into the living room and smelled the stale air.

What she smelled, she decided, *was* stale air. I've only been gone a couple of days, she reminded herself, too short a time for decomposition to begin, anyway. The thought didn't reassure her. She dropped her shoulder bag and her purse and hobbled with her cane across the room.

The air in the kitchen was much more redolent than stale. The room seemed to be in the same state in which she had left it. A coffee mug and a spoon sat upright in the sink. A water glass and a single plate had long since dried in the dish rack. Lauren knew Teresa had not been home. Housekeeping was not one of Teresa's strengths. Teresa could not be home more than an hour without a spoon crusted with yogurt or a knife slathered with peanut butter making its way to the kitchen counter.

Lauren took a deep breath and opened the cupboard beneath the sink. Her nostrils were blasted with the sour stink of fermenting trash. She slammed the door shut and glanced to her left; the knife drawer was closed. Gingerly, she slid it open. The knives, save the big French knife that the police had confiscated, were all in their usual places.

The note she had left for Teresa sat on the small metal kitchen table. The single sheet of pink paper was oriented so that the script angled away from someone standing next to the table. *Is that the way I left it?*

She couldn't remember. She tried to assure herself it didn't matter.

She pulled her coat tightly around her neck with one hand, grabbed the cane firmly with the other, and made her way to the end of the narrow hallway that led to the back of the house. She listened. The refrigerator seemed to be purring more loudly than usual. The furnace igniter clicked in the basement and a muffled *whooosh* from the gas burners tainted the hollow silence, sifting up through the tarnished brass grate in the floor in front of her.

Teresa's bedroom door was closed.

Had she left it that way? *Come on, Lauren, think. Think.*

She couldn't remember.

The blower fan from the furnace kicked on. To her, that day, the air seemed to blow with the volume of a gale.

With her index finger on the button of the pepper gas, she threw the bedroom door open all the way. Fast, hard.

The bedroom was devoid of corpses. Or any evidence of recent blood atonement. The mattress was gone—the police had taken that—but except for that glaring omission, the room looked undisturbed.

The message light on the answering machine on the painted trunk by the bed was blinking, "3 . . . 3 . . . 3."

Her lips turned up in a hopeful smile, Lauren sat on the box spring and pushed the playback button.

The first message, the earliest call on the tape, was from Teresa. Lauren's spirit soared at the sound of her sister's voice. "Hello, Lauren, it's me. The stupid cruise line screwed me. The person I was replacing had a miraculous recovery. How the hell does someone get better in twenty-four hours from an ovarian cyst? I think maybe I'd better change gynecologists. I got bumped only an hour before boarding and I'd already spent eighty bucks for a new swimsuit. It's a great suit, even makes me look like I have boobs. Can you believe it? I pouted and cried and the booking person for the line took pity on me and found me a few days' work in New Mexico. So I'm off to Taos. Have joke, will travel. Pretty neat that I called, huh? You tell Robin Torr for me, okay? Bye. I'll be in touch when I know where I'll be staying. I hope there's good news on the case."

The next message consisted of a long pause and a hangup.

Then there was a call from their mother. Her voice sounded older to Lauren, who felt a stab of guilt for not having called recently. "Either of you girls there? I got that stupid machine. Jersey, you got a message or should I just tell them we called? What? I can't hear you. Yes, I got the machine. Okay." Louder, "Teresa, Lauren, it's your mother. Give us a call when you get a chance."

The last message on the recorder, the most recent call, was from a guy Teresa had been dating on and off. He wanted to know if she wanted to go gambling in Wendover.

Lauren glared at the machine, replayed the message once, and punched the reset button.

She muttered, "New Mexico? You're in New Mexico, Teresa? Shit."

Lauren called Robin Torr's law firm and got Elsie Smith on the line. Elsie told Lauren that she hadn't heard from either Robin or Teresa.

Lauren began thinking clearly enough to realize that the puzzle in front of her wasn't that severe. The number of comedy venues in Taos, New Mexico, was probably pretty finite. It shouldn't be too hard to find Teresa.

She picked up the Salt Lake City phone book and checked the listing for the number of One Hand Laughing. She dialed, and a few seconds later was talking with Harold O'Shay, who answered his own phone by saying, "O'Shay, tell me something funny."

Lauren introduced herself.

"You're her sister? Well, well. Your sister's one hot little comic. Let me tell you. I knew she had it. I did. I mean, I gave her the minutes 'cause I knew she had the material. I mean, I'm getting calls about her all the time now. All the time. Even from the East. People in Baltimore can't even find Salt Lake City on a map, and they calling me 'bout your sister."

"That's very nice of you, Mr. O'Shay. I'm proud of what Teresa is doing, too. I've, um, been out of town, and—you haven't heard from her, have you?"

"No, no. But I been thinking. I can headline her if she stays this hot. I'd love to be the first club to headline her. Shoot, I *will* be the first club to headline her. Maybe December. Is she booked in December? She got an agent yet? She needs an agent."

"I'll be sure to tell her that, Mr. O'Shay. I'm sure she'll be terribly excited. The reason I'm calling today, though, is that she left me a message that she got some work in New Mexico, in Taos. She didn't tell me what club or where she would be staying. I really need to talk with her, and I'm hoping you might be able to tell me the names of the clubs that operate down there."

Harold O'Shay knew about a comedy club in Albuquerque, and he thought there was a hotel in Santa Fe that hired national acts into its lounge during the tourist season. But that was the totality of what O'Shay knew about comedy in New Mexico. Nothing in Taos.

Lauren called the club in Albuquerque and the hotel in Santa Fe but still wasn't successful at tracking down the name of any place in Taos that hired stand-up comedians.

Baffled as to what to do next, Lauren returned down the hallway to the kitchen to wrap the offensive garbage and get it outside to a trash can in the alley. She found a twist tie and held her breath as she secured the plastic bag. After grabbing her cane and the bag, she began walking deliberately into the yard.

Lauren was most of the way down a narrow cement path that led to a solitary gate from the tiny fenced yard into the adjacent alley when she glanced down and dropped the bag of trash. She dropped the cane, too, and covered her mouth with both hands. Her gray eyes widened and she stopped breathing. Yanking her head left, then right, she scrutinized the yard, even looked up into the trees, then back at the house, up to the roof.

Seeing nothing, she turned and ran. Or tried to run. Her leg failed her, and she collapsed to the ground. Like a blind woman, she groped for the fallen cane, her eyes of little help because they were locked involuntarily onto the small, brown mound of dog shit that rested three feet from her nose.

She stared at the turd as though it were a grenade with the pin pulled.

When Robin Torr's taxi arrived at Teresa's house, she found Lauren sitting on the front stoop with her overnight bag beside her. Surprised, Robin paid her driver and called up to Lauren, "You lock yourself out?"

Not quite loudly enough for Robin to hear, Lauren said, "Thank God you're here." She didn't stand; didn't trust her leg. Robin was halfway down the walk. Lauren said, with some urgency, "We can't stay here, Robin. Do you know where Teresa is?"

Robin lugged her suitcase off the sidewalk and shook her head. "Just not on that ship. You got my message?"

Lauren nodded and chewed on her upper lip.

She turned her head to the house, then back at Robin. She pointed in the general direction of the backyard. "He's been back. The guy with the knife. With his dog. He's gonna kill us. He's gonna kill Teresa. He knows where she is. He read my note. He knew I went to Ouray. He followed me and killed Rachel. I led him to her, Robin. I led him right to her, and he killed her."

Robin was at the bottom of the three cement steps.

"Rachel Baumann is dead?"

"Murdered. Yesterday. Right after I talked to her." Lauren was gazing away from Robin, down the block, transfixed watching two small girls play in a pile of newly raked leaves. She and Teresa used to do that.

"After you talked with her? So you found out what Rachel knows?" *Then you're going to be next.* Fear for Lauren rocketed through Robin.

"Rachel didn't know anything. She either fooled me during the interview or she doesn't know anything. Didn't. She died simply for talking with me, that's all. That's all she did. She just talked to me. She was so nice." Lauren yanked her attention away from the reverie of the little girls and the leaves and locked her eyes onto Robin Torr's. With horror in her tone, she said, "He *boiled* her, Robin."

Robin moved up the concrete steps and settled close to her friend. "We need to find your sister. And then we need to stop this madness. Once and for all."

Robin accompanied Lauren back inside so she could grab a suitcase and some fresh clothing. On the way down the hall Lauren tugged Robin into Teresa's bedroom and replayed her sister's taped message about the canceled cruise-ship engagement and the replacement gig in New Mexico.

"So that's why I couldn't find her. Do you have any idea where she might be staying in Taos?"

Lauren briefly recounted her conversation with Harold O'Shay at One Hand Laughing and her subsequent calls to Santa Fe and Albuquerque. She hadn't yet called the cruise line to see if the person who had found Teresa the booking in Taos knew where she was staying.

Robin gestured toward the answering machine and said, "We should take that tape with us."

Lauren wasn't thinking clearly. She said, "Why? We know what's on it."

"Yes, but we don't want anyone else to know what's on it, do we? If somebody keeps coming into this house, we don't want them to be able to find out where your sister is just by playing her answering machine."

Lauren remembered the blinking red beacon: "3 . . . 3 . . . 3." How many calls had there been? "I hadn't thought of that. Why not just erase it?"

"What if she calls back and leaves a new message that tells exactly where she is? We have to turn the machine off. We can't afford to have her leave directions to where she's gone, can we?"

"Then how is she going to reach us? I have to leave her a way to reach me."

"If she can't get through here, she'll call my office."

Lauren didn't like the plan. "Do you trust Elsie?"

"I can handle Elsie."

"Robin?"

"Yeah."

"What if whoever was here has already heard the message and is on his way to New Mexico?"

When the cab that Lauren had ordered finally arrived, the women told the driver they wanted to go to the downtown Marriott.

Robin got around to asking Lauren about the cane.

"I'm having a little trouble with my MS. It'll pass." She forced herself to mount a smile.

"Have you had this symptom before, or is this an exacerbation?"

Lauren was puzzled at the intelligence of the question. She was accustomed to confronting ignorance about her disease. "How do you know to ask that?"

"My aunt, remember?"

"Yes, now I do. I'd forgotten." The cab was heading straight down South Temple to downtown. Lauren knew that if the taxi continued on to the north, they would soon cross the street that led to the Side Pocket. She was tempted to talk with Robin about Harley and the middle-of-the-night phone call. And about Alan and how nice he had been in Colorado. "It's a new symptom, I guess. I've had weakness before. Never this bad, though. It'll pass," she repeated, forcing another weak grin.

"You don't want to talk about it?"

Lauren tightened her jaw and willed her tears to dry. "No, I don't. I need to ignore it right now. There's so much else. I just don't have any time to be sick." Her voice trailed off.

Outside, the air in Salt Lake City was cool. High clouds feathered the western sky. A slight breeze blew off the distant lake.

Checking in at the big hotel was banal. In their tenth-floor room, Robin said, "You can stay here, you know, Lauren, and rest. I can take care of things at the office myself."

"Teresa might call. If she does, I want to be there. And I want to look at the case file again. Maybe we keep missing something."

"All right. We'll get a cab."

Lauren knew the office was only five or six blocks away and that the taxi was an accommodation on Robin's part, but she didn't argue about it. She was exhausted.

At the law office, Lauren left messages with three different people at the cruise line who she hoped might know where her sister had gone in New Mexico. Over the next couple of hours, between phone calls and other interruptions, she and Robin caught each other up with the events of their recent travels.

Lauren went into elaborate detail about her meeting with Rachel Baumann.

"And I think I know who Audrey is. There was an Audrey Hayes in Blythe's class at BYU, and a woman named Audrey Payne spoke at her memorial service in Provo. There's a chance, I guess, that it's one and the same person."

"You said Payne?"

"Yeah."

"Did you cross-check that name with the rest of the class, looking for a husband?"

"Yes. Husband might be Neal Payne."

"Shit. He's a general authority. If she was part of this romantic girls' club at BYU, that gives the Paynes a motive in this mess, too."

"Why don't we call her? I'll speak to her. You listen on an extension, see if you recognize her voice. See if she's your Mary Brown. If she is, if we ever need one again, we have us a witness."

Robin argued the ethics of what they were doing while spending most of five minutes tracking down a home phone number for the Paynes. Lauren dialed. She pretended she was raising funds for the Nature Conservancy and had a pleasant two-minute conversation with Audrey Payne. She hung up.

Robin said, "She's the one. Too late to do us any damn good. But she's the one."

Lauren had been reluctant to divulge Harley's theory about blood atonement to Robin. But she'd now come to believe it. As Lauren described the apparent credibility that Sam Purdy gave the hypothesis, Robin Torr felt her general uneasiness balloon into something more palpable. Although Robin retained some skepticism about the lengths to which the LDS Church would go to quiet its enemies, she had no such illusions about a small fraction of the Church's most ardent believers. She had lived through a turbulent decade in Salt Lake City.

She had seen the Church mount a successful campaign against the Equal Rights Amendment. She had seen the Church leadership make fools of themselves buying up "historic" LDS documents from the counterfeiter Mark Hofmann for the sole purpose of hiding them from the faithful. And she had seen half a dozen instances of fundamentalist Church members killing each other, and killing others, over the words of nineteenth-century preachers and prophets.

If some modern-day freelance Danite was behind all this, Robin Torr wanted nothing to do with it. She made her position clear to Lauren, who needed surprisingly little convincing. Although Lauren wasn't eager to quit the investigation, she was growing more and more fearful her sister would be its next victim.

They agreed that when they found Teresa, they would lock themselves in a room with her until she agreed to drop the harassment action. In addition, they knew they needed to get quick word to the opposing attorneys about the change of heart. Robin pointed out that, ethically, she couldn't notify the defendant's counsel of their intent to drop the investigation without Teresa's explicit directive.

Lauren suggested a middle ground.

Robin Torr called the attorney at James and Bartell who was counsel for the Oaks family and stated that, given some "new information" she had recently uncovered, she thought there was a strong likelihood that the investigation would soon be stopped. Torr explained that her client was traveling but that she expected to be able to reach her shortly and anticipated a rapid determination to cease all action against Blythe Oaks and the Women's Symposium.

The lawyer at James and Bartell was polite and did Robin the courtesy of not overtly relishing the surrender over the phone. Robin assumed, however, that the partners at James and Bartell would be cheering and high-fiving each other within minutes after her adversary got off the line, and that moments later phones would be ringing in the executive offices of the LDS World Headquarters to pass along the good news.

"I hate it when the bullies win," Robin said to Lauren after hanging up the phone.

In an attempt at comfort, Lauren said, "We probably could have won if we were willing to kill anybody who got in our way, too."

Elsie Smith buzzed. "It's Mr. Torr, Mrs. Torr."

"Speaking of bullies."

"You want me to go?"

"No. It's not necessary. I'm sure Sterling immediately called Wiley and told him the good news. He'll be nice to me now. Watch." She punched the button that was blinking on her phone.

She was right. Wiley was pleasant; he even came perilously close to apologizing for being difficult lately. Then he asked if she would be home for dinner. She said no, not until they had a chance to talk, and she wouldn't be free to do that until this case wrapped up, hopefully in the next couple of days.

Wiley didn't bother to feign surprise about the termination of the case, but he did have trouble masking his irritation that Robin wasn't coming right home.

"Don't push me, Wiley. This case is still consuming my attention. I'll be done as soon as I can, and then I can focus on us."

He began to argue.

"Wiley, stop. You're not helping things." She listened. "If you need something and you can't find me, just leave a message with Elsie. I'll check in."

He said he loved her. She thought it sounded ironic.

She said, "Bye."

Lauren watched as Robin laid the phone back in its cradle. "See, Robin, the bullies don't always win, do they? You hungry? I haven't eaten, and I'm not thinking straight, and we still need to figure out some way to find my sister."

Will Price phoned the Supreme Court to tell Lester Horner the news.

Lester Horner's secretary told him that the justice was in a meeting with his clerks and couldn't be disturbed. Will dictated a carefully worded message to his friend. It was intentionally cryptic, and he had the secretary read it back to be certain she had transcribed it correctly. The message was "Heard back from BYU. It looks like we finally found what we've been after. I'm going down this weekend to confirm. Can you get away?"

After his meeting with his clerks had concluded, Horner read the message from Will Price. Immediately, he knew what Will was alluding to. Price and Horner had made a careful photographic record of some petroglyphs that they had begun to uncover at the dig site they were working in the Ute Mountain Tribal Park. As was his habit, Price had taken the proofs to BYU so they could be examined by some of his anthropologist and archaeologist friends. Something important must have shown up. Will Price was a cautious man. He didn't jump at shadows.

Horner slapped the top of his desk. *We've found evidence of the Lamanites!*

He sat back in the big chair at his desk and blessed the day. A phone message two hours earlier had been from an old friend at James and Bartell in Salt Lake City. Easily as cryptic as Will Price's, the message had suggested that the Oaks matter "should be favorably resolved by week's end."

Given his position of prominence within the Church, Lester Horner knew that his involvement in any discovery about the Lamanites would add a measure of credibility to what would certainly be contentious findings. If he permitted himself the luxury, he could fantasize that the discoveries would be dramatic enough that they might bring secular attention as well. But in his heart he knew better than to believe that gentiles would view Mormon archaeology with anything but disdain.

Regardless, Horner felt he had to get back to the Rockies to be with Will Price for this momentous weekend. He would fly out Friday night, then back into D.C. Sunday night on the red-eye. He hoped it would be enough time. It had to be.

Horner called his secretary and asked her to make the travel arrangements and to confirm details on hooking up with Will Price.

He realized, suddenly, that he was happy.

In the LDS hierarchy, stake presidents are higher in rank than bishops. Bishops preside over wards, the basic congregational unit. Wards are combined into stakes, where presidents preside. Neither bishops nor stake presidents are actually clergy in the traditional, ecumenical sense of the word. All males who are members in good standing of the LDS Church are Aaronic priests. Aaronic priests hold the keys to baptize and the keys to other powers, including the power to heal and to receive revelations from God. Higher priests, holders of the Melchizedek priesthood, have greater powers still. Bishops hold more keys than Melchizedek priests, stake presidents more than bishops. The progression continues until it reaches the prophet.

John Harley hadn't been to his stake house in a few months. Maybe six, he thought, but he couldn't actually remember. To his surprise, he had been summoned there this morning by an early phone call from the stake president himself.

Although Harley knew who his stake president was, he had never before had occasion to meet with him individually.

He was tempted to call Jules to see if she knew what this was all about. He wondered why this interview wasn't going to be with Bishop Fortin, from his ward, the same cretin credit-union manager with whom Harley had already endured a dozen interviews. He considered the possibility that he was about to be excommunicated. Or was this merely another intrusive attempt to determine if he was worthy enough to have his temple recommend returned?

He couldn't imagine that they were considering letting him back into the temple. Just two weeks before he had admitted to Bishop Fortin that he was still drinking "hot drinks," that he still craved alcohol, and that he still doubted that he was righteous enough to be the priesthood holder in his household. And, no, he wasn't praying as much as he should. And, no, he apparently wasn't very receptive to the Lord currently, because revelations were passing him by.

The stake president was a prominent real estate agent who sold homes almost exclusively in the No-Pill Hill section of the Upper Avenues of Salt Lake City. The man's face was plastered across busstop benches all over the city. He was a husky man in his late forties whose wide head wasn't marred by a single gray hair. Incredibly large pores lined the sides of his nose. He introduced himself to Harley as "President Randall Johnson" and asked him to have a seat in a small, windowless room decorated with two different framed romantic images of Jesus, one above each of two chairs.

Harley sat, as instructed. The president departed and didn't come back for almost ten minutes.

"We have grave matters to discuss, Brother Harley," President Johnson intoned upon his return. Harley thought the stake president's manner would be more appropriate to a discussion of the insufficiency of a proposed counteroffer in a real estate negotiation than to some supposed spiritual inadequacy.

Harley waited. The residue of alcohol from the previous night had left enough of a deficit in his attention that he considered silence to be his best strategy.

President Johnson looked at Harley with a stern, paternal glare. "I'm speaking with you today at the specific request of the First Quorum of the Seventy, Brother Harley."

Harley had trouble believing that the general authorities knew him from the angel Moroni. But by invoking the power of the upper tier of the church leadership, the stake president had simultaneously captured Harley's attention and frightened him a little bit as well. Although his bishop might be a bit of a buffoon, Harley knew this stake president was a powerful spiritual leader on his way up the Mormon leadership ladder. And Harley was well aware that any member of the First Quorum of the Seventy possessed the ability to make him miserable in this world and a second-class citizen in the next.

The interview immediately tumbled from the dramatic precipice of President Johnson's introduction to a familiar banality that reminded Harley of a visit from his assigned home teacher, or of the more recent insult of his invited interviews with Bishop Fortin.

It began with a request that Harley renew his testimony to the veracity of the Book of Mormon, that Harley restate his belief that Joseph Smith was a true prophet of God and that the Church of Jesus Christ of Latter-day Saints is the one and only true and living church on the face of the earth.

Harley testified that he believed that all these were true.

Harley was then asked if he would sustain the authority of Bishop Fortin. Yes. Of President Johnson? Yes. And so on up the hierarchy, until Harley sustained his belief in the authority of the prophet.

Then, "Are you tithing, Brother Harley?" As though they didn't know.

"Are you following the Word of Wisdom, Brother Harley?"

"Do you contribute to the well-being of your ward?"

"Do you regularly have family home evenings?"

"Do you engage in adulterous practices, Brother Harley?"

"Are you honoring your marital vows?"

"Are you wearing your garments?"

"Are you keeping your tokens and honoring the secrets of the temple?"

Harley's answers were honest and forthright and, although they were not everything the president wished to hear, there was nothing in the questions that indicated to Harley why he had been requested to attend this meeting.

Soon the pace picked up.

"Are you honoring the teachings of the general authorities?"

"Are you reading only faith-promoting materials?"

"Are you contributing to any disrespect of the Church?"

To the last question Harley answered, "No," after a slight pause. The hesitance had been generated by the novelty of the query. He'd never been asked that one before.

His favorites from previous interviews with Bishop Fortin had been "Have you murdered anyone since our last interview?" and "Do you and your wife engage in oral copulation?" Harley's reply to Bishop Fortin—"I didn't think you guys asked that one anymore"—had caused the bishop to move immediately on to the next question in his spiritual deposition.

President Johnson's subsequent question covered virgin territory, too.

"Brother Harley, when you socialize with nonmembers, especially those who might be antagonistic to the Church, do you always represent the Church in a manner that will generate the maximum respect and honor for the prophet and for Jesus Christ the Lord?"

A sudden awareness hit Harley like a punch in the kidney. *They know about Lauren. How the hell did they find out about Lauren? Somebody probably saw us together at Bill & Nada's. Or maybe the Side Pocket. That doesn't make any sense, though. How many LDS are there who hang out at the Side Pocket and Bill & Nada's?*

Harley remembered: Pratt Toomey had seen Lauren and him together at Bill & Nada's. Maybe Pratt thought that Harley was helping Lauren mount the case against Blythe Oaks and informed Bishop Fortin of his suspicion. Brother Pratt Toomey would have done that in a Deseret second.

Harley said, "Yes, President Johnson, I do."

President Johnson removed his glasses and held them in one hand at the side of his head. "Do you wish to think more about that answer, Brother Harley?"

"No, President Johnson, I'm comfortable with my answer. And with my conduct."

Randall Johnson frowned before placing the glasses

back in front of his eyes. He maintained his grip on them, however, and never placed the earpieces back on his head. "But you are currently socializing at an establishment that is certainly not consistent with the proper values of the Church or of Jesus Christ the Lord."

That one wasn't a question, so Harley fought a sense of obligation to provide an answer. He failed.

"I play pool, President Johnson."

"In a bar."

"That's where the pool tables are."

"Are you being impertinent, Brother Harley? What we are discussing here is your salvation, your ultimate place in the celestial kingdom. I hope and pray that you will not leave this interview satisfied to be facing an eternity in the terrestrial kingdom."

Harley realized that he had just been addressed as though he were on a downhill slide to Jack Mormondom. Mormons who died clutching temple recommends attained the highest level of the three planes of heaven, the celestial kingdom. Mormons who had strayed but who had already enjoyed the blessings and endowments of church ritual were relegated to the terrestrial kingdom. Unsaved gentiles spent eternity in the lowest plane of heaven, the telestial kingdom. Once elevated to the celestial plane after death, the holiest of the male faithful could hope to progress to become gods themselves and attain the power to reign over other planets as God rules over this one from a planet circling the star Kolob.

Harley didn't respond right away. His mouth felt pasty. He desperately wanted a drink. He thought of Jules and her unquestioned faith and her love for him. He remembered why he endured these inquisitions.

Jules and the girls. His family. Harley knew that the irony of the intense Mormon focus on family values was that, when spiritual push came to spiritual shove, the values would always be judged to be more important than the family. And Harley knew that any prayer he had of being able to return home to his wife and children required that he appease the bureaucratic real estate agent/religious leader sitting across him.

Harley swallowed hard and framed his reply carefully. "I remain eager, President Johnson, to once again demonstrate to Bishop Fortin and to you and to the members of the First Quorum that I am worthy to live the gospel of the Lord, to hold a temple recommend, and to ascend to the celestial kingdom. I also remain eager"—he paused and blinked twice, hoping to keep his head clear enough to continue—"to regain my rightful priesthood position in my home, to strive always for perfection, and, once again, to demonstrate spiritual leadership for my wife and daughters on this earth. I am grateful to the Church and to the Relief Society and to Bishop Fortin and to you for all your patience with me and all your assistance to my family during this difficult period when I have been spiritually adrift and under the influence of the devil."

President Johnson replaced the glasses on his head and sat back on his chair. He eyed Harley skeptically.

"On behalf of the general authorities, Brother Harley, I would like to accept your testimony as sincere and honest. But a matter still clouds the issue of the genuineness of your, um, faith. The authorities have asked me to have you prepare a letter detailing all aspects of your relationship to a woman named . . ." President Johnson looked down at the palm of his left hand. Harley couldn't tell if he had a tiny piece of paper there or if he had written something directly onto his skin. "Lauren Crowder."

Harley opened his eyes wide. "A letter?" His head ached with the effort. "What kind of letter?"

"You know Miss Crowder, then, Brother Harley?"

"Yes." Level voice, Harley, level voice.

"Then you know she isn't a member?"

Harley nodded.

"And that she is paying a large sum of money to bring legal action against a revered *dead* member of our Church alleging that the member practiced homosexuality?" President Johnson spoke the last word with abject disgust, as though he had been required to curse in the presence of his grandmother.

Harley searched his memory. Did Lauren ever tell him that she was paying her sister's legal fees? No, she hadn't. So he didn't know that. Relieved, he affected a perplexed face and responded, "No, President Johnson,

I didn't know that she was paying to bring legal action against a member of the Church."

President Johnson huffed at Harley's answer. He stood and took a step toward the door. He said, "In writing. By the end of the week. *All* aspects of your relationship with this woman, Brother Harley. Good-bye."

After lunch, Lauren napped in the hotel room for almost two hours. When she woke, she bathed in tepid water in the cramped confines of the shallow tub, not trusting her leg to behave in the shower.

Wrapped in a hotel robe, she sat on the bed and gazed down at Temple Square. She phoned John Harley at the university.

"Harley, it's Lauren."

Harley heard echoes in her voice. He didn't know exactly what they meant. He looked up to be certain his office door was closed. "Hi, you're back in town," he said. The echoes? Oh, no. He thought he knew. Did we talk last night? Yup. We talked last night. He knew.

Lauren thought Harley's voice sounded flat, cautious. "You free for dinner, Harley? I mean, a normal dinner, early. Not a Bill & Nada's dinner. I'm too tired for that today."

"I don't think that's possible tonight, Lauren. Um, where are you now?"

"I'm at—"

"No, no, don't tell me. What I meant was, are you at your sister's house?"

She puzzled at his interruption. "No, I'm at—"

"Good, good. Are you at your lawyer friend's office?"

She was growing annoyed. "No, Harley, I'm . . . ." and then before he could interrupt her again, as though a flash had gone off in her face, she got it. "I'm, ah, I'm at a pay phone."

"Well," he said, exhaling, and then adding some artificial levity to his voice, "that's good. Because I'm not."

She was certain what was going on now. Harley was warning her that he thought that the phone lines were being bugged. By whom? What had he learned? She wanted to ask a thousand questions and she knew she couldn't. "If you're not free for dinner, Harley, is there someplace else we can meet, you know, just for a soft drink or something? Maybe someplace we've met before?"

Harley thought about it. It was a good idea, not a great one. Either of them could be followed to a rendezvous. He needed to choose someplace public and noisy, and hope they wouldn't be overheard. "That place where we had drinks outside the bookstore, remember that?"

She did. Harley had taken her on a sociological tour of the downtown ZCMI Mall. ZCMI—the Zion's Cooperative Mercantile Institution—was a department-store chain, partly owned by the LDS Church, that sold brand-name merchandise to the masses and also faith-promoting items to holders of temple recommends. Harley had told Lauren that ZCMI was where he and Jules bought their garments, their sacred underwear. In the same mall was an outlet of Deseret Books, part of a Church-owned bookstore chain that sold only faith-promoting literature. Lauren had been fascinated at the selection of books. Later, nearby, she and Harley had stopped briefly and had drinks at Orange Julius.

"Five o'clock?" she suggested.

The downtown offices would just be letting out. The streets would be busy. "Perfect," he said, not believing it.

As soon as she hung up, the phone rang again.

She lifted the receiver and said, "Hello."

"Lauren, it's Robin. Somebody at the cruise line returned one of your calls. We've got the name of the club Teresa is playing in Taos."

Lauren's paranoia erupted again. "Robin, did you talk with this person yourself?"

The line grew quiet for a few moments. In a heavy voice, Robin replied, "No. Elsie took the message. Shit."

Lauren's spirit felt as heavy as her leg. She thought, it doesn't matter. If the phones are really tapped, it doesn't matter.

Harley stood with his arms folded over his chest while he examined a long wall of books that all appeared to have been written by general authorities of the LDS Church. From a corner of his eye he caught sight of Lauren hobbling up to the Orange Julius stand in the middle of the ZCMI Mall. She wore a long plaid skirt of blues and browns and a pale yellow sweater and, he noted immediately, was leaning heavily on a black walking stick topped with a round purple knob. She perched herself against an unused end of the store counter and began to scan the crowd for Harley.

He had arrived early at Deseret Books, hoping to find a volume or two to give to Lauren so she could read up on blood atonement, at least as a historical entity, but came away from the store empty-handed and feeling slightly foolish.

The fact that a subject was historically Mormon, and even spiritually Mormon, was no indication that it would be judged to be faith-promoting by the general authorities. A few years before, Harley had been sitting next to his wife at a Semiannual General Conference of the LDS Church and had listened in mild horror and major consternation as Boyd Packer, a senior member of the Quorum of the Twelve Apostles, warned the assembled Church members about the dangers of participating in the study of Mormon history, doctrine, and culture. He restated the long-held convictions of other Church elders that critical examination of the origins and beliefs of the Church should be avoided by members because such investigations would be likely to erode faith. "If doctrines and behaviors are measured by the intellect alone," Packer had warned his audience, "we will be misled."

Walking back out of the bookstore, Harley assumed that blood atonement was probably one of the doctrines and behaviors the study of which Elder Packer would consider particularly faith-eroding.

As stealthily as he could, he sneaked up behind Lauren outside Orange Julius and whispered in a husky voice the first line he had ever said to her as he had admired her playing pool in the Side Pocket.

"Only drunks and Englishmen drink them warm, you know."

She turned to him and threw an arm around his neck and embraced him. The walking stick clattered to the floor.

He'd been hoping not to draw any attention to them. Gesturing at the stick, he pulled back from the embrace. "What's with the cane?"

"It's nothing. A little problem with my leg. It'll pass." Even to Lauren, the "It'll pass" was beginning to sound suspiciously like a mantra.

Harley paused, giving her a moment to expound on her own. She didn't. Puzzled, he prodded. "I was going to suggest we walk."

"Not my best thing right now, Harley, I'm afraid. I'm currently much more proficient at sitting." They moved to an empty table ten feet away. A slime of spilled Julius varnished half the table. Harley wondered how the bubbles could crust without popping.

Intermittent white noise generated by the blenders provided some auditory cover. Harley looked at his watch. Lauren noticed Harley's unease. "You're worried, Harley. That's not like you. And that worries me. A lot."

He leaned closer, carefully placing his elbow just outside the tidal flow of the pale citrus muck on the table.

"My stake president—a church leader I absolutely can't ignore—called me in for an interview this morning. The authorities—the general authorities—want to know about you. What I know about you. About us. Whether

I'm helping you. Everything." Indications of alarm began to assemble in Lauren's eyes. He was encouraged and recognized that he wanted her to be afraid with him. "So in case we had any doubt whether you and your sister had captured the attention of the old men in the Church Administration Building, well, now we know you have, big-time. I'm supposed to write a report about you—about us—for somebody on the First Quorum."

"They can make you do that?"

"They can make the consequences intolerable if I don't."

"How?"

"If they excommunicate me, I'll be shunned by members of the Church. I'm lucky I don't own a store or sell insurance. Members would just stop doing business with me. But if I'm excommunicated, Jules won't take me back. No way. And I'd lose the girls for sure. That's their leverage. And they'll use it in a second."

"Wow. They can do that? That sounds like blackmail."

"It's their club, their clubhouse. They know the secret handshakes. If they don't like me, I don't get in anymore."

Lauren wasn't at all surprised to learn that the Church was interested in the lawsuit. She and Robin Torr had been working under that assumption all along. But she was shocked that the Church had managed to link her and Harley, and that they would use his family as pawns to try to force Teresa to stop pursuing the lawsuit. Homosexual harassment by a prominent Church member would certainly be a blemish on the LDS Church, but this response seemed way out of proportion.

Why were the Church leaders treating this wart as though it were a melanoma?

"How? How do they know about us? Isn't this risky? Should you be meeting with me like this?"

"I'm not sure exactly what's going on. Either somebody saw us together, like Pratt did that time at Bill & Nada's, and the authorities are fishing. Or they're listening to us, and they *know*. Today, I'm just hoping that the two of us weren't followed."

Lauren looked around for the followers, realized she

wouldn't even know what she was looking for, and turned back to Harley. "Listening to us how?"

Harley fell back on the chair and scanned the thin crowd in the mall. Meeting here, he thought, was a mistake. How could he identify a Mormon tail in this place? Everybody in here looks like they could be working for the Church. He should have told Lauren to meet him at the Side Pocket. Odelle and Jerry would have known in a second if a stranger had come in after them.

Irritated at himself for his misjudgment, he barked, "How the hell do I know? By tapping my phone? Bugging your sister's house? Microwave listening devices?" He recognized the recoil in Lauren's face as she reacted to his tone. He softened his voice. "LDS Church security is a huge operation, Lauren, and it's mostly headed by ex-FBI and CIA types, real professionals. The LDS presence in U.S. security and intelligence operations is truly significant, way out of proportion to the population. Mormons raise the type of kids that intelligence and police agencies like—polite, patriotic, respectful. And the boys who have been on missions are usually fluent in at least one foreign language, as well. I'm digressing—my point is that if they wanted to listen to us, they wouldn't have any trouble figuring out how to do it. They've got the experts and they've got the money."

"That's illegal," Lauren pointed out, and immediately felt foolish.

"You find your sister?"

"Not exactly, but I think I know where she is."

"She's okay?"

Lauren fought tears. "I hope so, Harley." She had promised herself she wouldn't ask about the phone call, but she did. "Were you drunk last night?"

"Yes," he said without nuance or delay. "Am I supposed to apologize now?"

She tightened her jaw and raised her eyebrows, then looked away from him.

"Why?" she said. She waited, then continued, her voice taking on a supple, unfamiliar form. "Oh, don't answer that, Harley. That's stupid. I know why. No, I don't. It doesn't matter why. Oh, shit, I hate it that you drink, Harley. I hate it."

He shook his head. "I don't think so, Lauren. I don't think you hate it. I think you get some perverted need met by watching me battle with it. For some reason I don't understand, you don't seem to feel safe unless you can face danger and then watch it slip away. The routine seems to bore you. You were crazy to go into the Side Pocket that first night with your cute little pool cue and your cute little ass and act like nothing was out of the ordinary, the whole time you're surrounded by grunting low-lifes and drunk Tongans. But you thrive on surviving it. You struck me then and you strike me now as someone who would feel better having a tiger on a leash than you would being in a room without a tiger. I don't pretend to get it. But I think it's true."

She thought of Alan. To her, she knew, he'd become a room without a tiger.

She turned her gaze toward the Deseret Bookstore. She recalled the John Harley she had met at the Side Pocket, so impertinent and impish and seductive and *fun*. She mused about the transformation that had occurred. Harley now looked frightened and acted defeated. The culprit, she concluded, was his church. She felt sadness for him, and she shivered at the irony. She said, "Your tiger's not leashed now, is it, Harley?"

"Not mine. Uh-uh. Not yours, either." He tilted his head toward the bookshop. "Not theirs. Nope. There are fangs and claws everywhere."

"Well, maybe there's some hope. We're planning on dropping our investigation as soon as we find Teresa. I'm sure the Church knows of our intentions by now. Robin Torr told the plaintiff's law firm this afternoon to be sure the Church finds out immediately. So they can call off their dogs. And maybe they'll leave you and your family alone."

Harley ran his fingers through the hair on the side of his head. "Well, if all of us have just one lucky day, then maybe dropping your investigation will bring an end to this mess."

"That's my hope, too, Harley. But I still need to find my sister. Robin Torr is on the phone right now trying to track her down. I'm going to try to leave tonight to be with her. If I can't get out tonight, then I'll go first thing tomorrow."

"Where is she?"

She knew she paused long enough to hear her heart beat once. She said, "New Mexico. Taos."

He'd noticed the pause, too. "I hope she's okay." He looked down, then back up. "Believe me when I say this. I won't betray you, Lauren." He made sure she was looking right at him. "My family will come first in every decision I make. But I won't betray you."

She reached out and touched the top of his hand. With warm eyes she said to him, "I know. I hope you're able to lasso your tiger again, Harley."

"I don't have much hope for me today." He grinned at her in the devilish way she had found irresistible from the first day she had met him. "My problem all along has been that I enjoy it too much when my tiger's on the loose."

The vagaries of airline scheduling prohibited Lauren from getting a flight into Albuquerque that night, and the first flight out of Salt Lake City the next morning was booked solid. There were no non-stops into Santa Fe from Utah at all. Her choices were either to fly standby and hope to get lucky, to try to get a connection into Albuquerque or Santa Fe through Denver or Phoenix, or to take an early commuter flight into Durango, Colorado, or Farmington, New Mexico, and drive across northern New Mexico to Taos. Despite the extra driving time, Lauren calculated that the Farmington choice should get her into Taos at least ninety minutes earlier than any of the other options.

She made reservations for Farmington and told Robin the plan. Robin was reading the room-service menu in their hotel room.

Late that afternoon, Robin had tracked down the owner of the small club in Taos where Teresa was scheduled to perform. The owner had confirmed the booking but didn't know where Teresa was staying. Her first performance wasn't until the next evening, Friday.

Robin looked up from the menu and asked, "Can you drive? With your leg so weak, I mean."

"I think I can drive. I can't support much weight, but I can move my foot enough to control the pedals. I've driven with my left foot before, anyway."

"Well, I don't like the idea of you driving that far across New Mexico by yourself. I'm coming with you."

Lauren protested meekly. She said, "You don't have to do that, Robin." But she was relieved. She didn't want to go to New Mexico alone. She had already thought of calling Alan in Colorado and seeing if he would meet her in Farmington.

"Your leg's not getting any better. Without wanting to be crass, hon, the truth is that you could be half paralyzed and half blind before you're halfway across New Mexico. So I'm coming. I'm worried about my client, anyway. Please call the airline back and get me a seat." Torr stood, crossed her arms, and started to tug her sweater over her head. "I can't tell you how badly I need a bath." As she closed the bathroom door behind her she began to hum a happy tune that Lauren recognized but couldn't quite place.

Lauren tried to consider a world where people were happy and hummed happy tunes. For a moment she thought she did. She tried to make the image last. She couldn't.

She used the private time while Robin was in the bathroom to phone Alan in Boulder. He was eager to know how she was and how her leg was and was eager for news about Teresa. He spoke in hushed tones about his longing for her. He told her he loved her long before the conversation was over. Then he told her again.

She knew he meant it.

Sam Purdy had called Alan with news from the police chief in Ouray. The FBI was interested in Rachel Baumann's murder—not committed, but interested. The Colorado Bureau of Investigation hadn't completed its analysis of the material from the crime scene. But something in the preliminary findings had jostled the FBI's interest. Chief Long didn't volunteer what the preliminary findings were.

She told Alan about Robin Torr's phone call of surrender to the opposing attorney that afternoon.

Alan's voice grew soft, full of hollow places where she could hide if she chose. "I know how disappointed you must be at backing down, but I'm very relieved that it's over."

"To be honest, I'm relieved, too, Alan. I'm used to seeing my adversaries across a room. But since I got to Utah, I feel like I've been boxing with ghosts. I just hope this decision hasn't come too late for Teresa. I'll deal with my anger at being intimidated once I know that she's safe."

"You're sure you don't want me to come with you? I think I can get to Farmington from Denver pretty easily."

Small, intimate sounds emanated from behind the closed bathroom door. Faint overtones of an argument invaded from the room next door. Alan's quiet breathing sang in her ear.

"No, it's okay, but thanks. Robin's coming with me. She'll drive. We'll just find Teresa and bring her home. Nobody has any reason to fear any of us now that the case is over."

"And then?"

"Then I'll come home. And I'll marry you and do wicked things to your body. But not necessarily in that order."

The bathroom door opened and Robin entered in a cloud of steam. Her hair was wet and shiny. A towel was wrapped around her torso. She sang in a whisper and smiled warmly at Lauren. Robin fumbled for something in an overnight bag and then nestled against the headboard of the other bed and began to push back her cuticles with a wooden stick.

Lauren was sprawled on the bed. She told Alan she loved him and would call from Taos. She hung up.

A minute later, without looking up, Robin asked Lauren if she could guess why she was feeling so happy.

Lauren shook her head.

"One, because this Morrison looks like the real thing for the Jazz, and two, because I know I can live just fine without Wiley. When we get back from our little road trip, I'll talk with him, see if things can change in our marriage the way I need them to. If they can't, I'll move on. I'm smiling at the freedom I feel. I want a baby."

Lauren thought about her ex-husband, Jacob. "Can Wiley change?"

Robin gripped a cuticle scissors in her hand and clipped at the edge of her thumbnail. "I doubt he wants to. But if he does, I'll listen to what he has in mind. I don't need to decide any of that right now."

Lauren looked at her own shabby nails but felt too tired to repair them. "It's ironic, Robin. You're feeling free, and I'm worried that I'm about to give my freedom up—to Alan. I love him—I do—and yet I agonize about being married to him. Maybe to anybody. It didn't work the first time." She sighed and looked over at the next bed.

Robin twisted open a tiny bottle of red nail polish before looking up. "But you love him?"

Lauren nodded. "Yeah, but that's nothing new for me. What's odd is that I feel loved by him, too. And that's very different from last time. I loved Jake. Jake loved Jake. My being loved was never part of our marital equation."

"Do you need Alan?"

She considered it. "No, not in any way that worries me." She pondered her useless leg, and thought, *Unless I get sick.*

"Then you're free, too."

Not of MS. Not of men like Harley, of tigers without leashes, thought Lauren. *I'm not free of those things.*

Robin was having trouble staying modest in her wrapped towel.

"There's another robe in the closet, Robin. I'll get it for you." Despite Robin's protest, Lauren hopped over to the closet on her good leg and then hopped back over to Robin's bed with the robe. Robin stood, turned her back to Lauren, and permitted the towel to drop to the carpet. Large, pale freckles trailed from her thin shoulders down her back. Lauren helped slide the bulky terry cloth over Robin's arms so she wouldn't ruin her newly painted nails, then tied the belt.

Robin said, "Thanks." She slid her arms under

Lauren's and reached up and embraced her, her hands spread on the wide bones of Lauren's shoulder blades. "Teresa will be okay. We'll be okay. You watch."

Lauren returned the embrace, then fell back on her own bed, exhausted but momentarily not feeling so scared. She held the remote control aloft and said, "You want to watch the news?"

Robin fumbled in her purse and held up two small rectangular pieces of stiff paper adorned with the logo and colors of the Utah Jazz. "No, not really. You up for a basketball game? You'll get to see Karl Malone *and* Shaquille O'Neal. An amazing opportunity. Preseason, I know, and he may not get many minutes, but still, it's Shaquille O'Neal."

"Who?" asked Lauren.

The regional airport at Farmington, New Mexico, was a time warp away from Salt Lake City. Salt Lake tried hard not to be a high desert; Farmington didn't bother. It was one of those wondrous southwestern places that didn't have to stretch to remind visitors whose land this used to be.

The faces that greeted Lauren and Robin as they made their way down the shaky stairs from the plane and across the narrow tarmac were mostly red and brown. The people were stocky, their faces round, their noses wide. Their hair was Crowder hair, the color of the night.

The compact Hertz counter wasn't far from the gate. A young man with a worn Stetson and a cocked hip was finishing up a seemingly unsuccessful flirtation with the solitary female clerk behind the counter. The man stepped aside and waited as though his day had no duties while Robin and Lauren exchanged their driver's licenses and credit cards for a set of car keys. When they departed he resumed his seduction, as though they had never been there. The clerk seemed to welcome the return of his advances.

The rental car, a new Toyota, was parked in a lot across the street from the brown stucco terminal.

Both women were dressed in blue jeans and sweaters. Robin wore old aerobics shoes that were mostly pink. She had bought them during a period of exaggerated guilt over her lack of exercise. She had worn them to three step-aerobics classes.

Lauren wore cowboy boots that had been polished and repolished to a deep black-brown, with a pattern of fanciful stitching of lazy interlocking hearts running up the sides. The boots had been a gift from her ex-husband, Jacob, on some ancient Valentine's Day. Lauren remembered receiving the gift with glee. Each boot had concealed a vase holding an abundant bouquet of gerbera daisies.

Jake had been one of her tigers.

Robin stalled her walk to match the meager progress Lauren made with her cane. They carried jackets and shoulder bags and made jokes about Thelma and Louise.

It was Robin who noticed the big burgundy Ford Bronco parked in front of the terminal. She had been folding and unfolding the accordion creases of a road map and then glancing around at the terrain, trying to get oriented to the east, toward Taos. She noticed the big Bronco because of the Utah plates.

And because the man climbing into the passenger seat bore a striking resemblance to Supreme Court Justice Lester Horner.

She poked Lauren, who was fumbling for the buckle to her shoulder harness. "Lauren! Look, over there. That big car." She pointed toward the Bronco. "Isn't that Lester Horner? On the passenger side?"

The big 4 × 4 was in the shadows, and the glare of the light off the windshield interfered with Lauren's getting a clear look at the man inside.

"Maybe." She peered intently. "I can't tell. Why would he be here? The Supreme Court just started its new term, didn't it?"

"I know the damn Court's in session. But I also know Lester Horner. That was him, I'm sure of it."

"Could you see who he's with?"

"Some guy, about his age. I didn't pay much attention. I was just too shocked at seeing that it *was* Lester Horner."

Lauren shrugged her shoulders, weary of new pieces showing up to complicate this puzzle. Robin looked away from the car and back at Lauren. They each raised their eyebrows.

Robin defended her appraisal. "That's weird. I swear that's Horner."

Lauren said, "It doesn't make any sense. Why would he be here?"

The truck pulled away from the curb of the loading zone. Both women watched, speechless, as the frisky head of a terribly happy dog plunged out the open window of the passenger door. As the truck turned left onto the access road that led down from the mesa toward Farmington, it crawled past the Toyota at a measured pace. The dog seemed to look right at them, his golden-red snout pointing into an imaginary wind.

Lauren felt an agony she had not even imagined possible. She felt it surge through her blood with tremendous velocity, as though sharp crystals were ripping at her veins.

She blurted, "Teresa."

Robin Torr said, "Damn."

Robin punched the accelerator before sliding the gearshift lever out of park. The engine howled and then slowly quieted. She waited, then pulled the stick toward her and eased the car out of the lot.

"You see him?" she asked.

"Yeah, about a block up on the right. Thank God he's big." Talking struck Lauren as mundane. She was mildly surprised that she was able to do it at all but appreciated the feeling of normalcy the act provided.

"Is this the way to Taos? Are we heading east?"

Lauren looked up for the sun but saw nothing but thin interlocking sheets of high gray clouds. She alternately scrambled to find a section of the Hertz map that might correspond to their location and scanned the roadside for highway markers. "I can't tell where we are. I'm not oriented yet."

Robin murmured, "Tell me about it."

The access road to the airport veered down a mesa toward Farmington. Not far from the terminal the big Ford slowed and turned right, and then quickly right again. A highway marker near the intersection indicated that the road was New Mexico Highway 64.

Robin barked, "Where does it go? Where does that road go? Is this the way to Taos?"

Lauren puzzled at the highway marker, then at the map. After Robin had copied the Bronco's turn onto Highway 64, Lauren blurted out, "No. I don't think so, anyway. This road does go east and west, but I think we're going west, away from Taos. If we stay on it, we'll be heading right toward Four Corners."

Four Corners? In addition to New Mexico, that means Arizona, Colorado, and Utah. Arizona or *Colorado* or *Utah. But Teresa is in New Mexico. In Taos. Safe.*

Teresa is safe.

"You're sure? There's no way to get to Taos on this road?"

She examined the map. Definitively, she said, "No, it's absolutely the wrong direction."

The pressure in Robin's tone subsided. "Well, then maybe these guys aren't after your sister. Maybe it's just a coincidence that they're here at all."

"And it's a coincidence that they have a dog?"

"There are lots of dogs, Lauren."

The windows of the Bronco up ahead were darkly tinted. Lauren pressed her hypothesis. "Robin, what if they already have her in that car?"

Robin checked the location of the Ford, then peered across the front seat at Lauren. She forced a softness into her voice. "Jesus, Lauren. That's a justice of the U.S. Supreme Court up there, not a kidnapper. Not a murderer. Anyway, who would bring along a hostage and then park curbside at an airport?"

"Somebody who's real certain that their hostage isn't going to cause any trouble."

Teresa is safe.

Lauren laid out her case. "So why is Horner here? Why is he in Farmington? Why today, with my sister only a few hours away? Why with that dog?"

"Do you really think your sister's in the back of that car, Lauren? Do you want me to ram it or something?" Robin's forced calm was deserting her.

Before Lauren could answer, the Bronco's brake lights flashed on, the right-turn signal started flashing, and the truck began an abrupt turn into a wide gap in a chain-link construction fence.

"Keep going, Robin. There's a gas station across the street. Go in there. I'm going to find out whose car that is." With a pen from her purse, Lauren jotted the license plate number of the Bronco onto the soft pad of skin at the base of her thumb.

She grabbed her cane and her coin purse and hobbled to a pay phone. She punched in what seemed like a thousand numbers and thought she'd faint with relief when Sam Purdy answered his phone.

"Sam, it's Lauren."

Purdy heard the desperation in her tone. He said, "What's wrong?"

"Maybe nothing. I'm not sure. Can you run a Utah vehicle check for me ASAP?"

Sam wanted to quiz her. His instincts told him to say instead, "Okay, give me what you've got."

"Late-model Ford four-wheel drive. A big one. Burgundy and tan."

"What? An Explorer?"

"No, bigger."

"Bronco?"

"Whatever. I don't know." She read him the license plate number.

"I'll call you right back."

"I'm at a pay phone. The number has been vandalized to oblivion. I don't know what it is. I'll just wait here on the line."

Calmly, he said, "This could take a while."

"It's really urgent, Sam. I'll wait. No! Before you go, listen. I think somebody needs to know what's going on here. Robin Torr and I are in Farmington, New Mexico, heading, um, west on Highway 64. We're driving a red Hertz Toyota something or other with New Mexico tags, number . . ." She squinted and read the license plate number to Purdy. "We're following that Ford I told you about, and they've just pulled into a construction site outside of Farmington. The construction project is apparently for a self-storage lot they're building here. Wait a second, the sign is already up. The place is called 'Your Garage—Self Storage.' It's huge. Cinder-block, bright ugly green, you can't miss it. On 64, real close to Farmington."

Purdy recognized a couple of gaps in Lauren's story that were large enough to drive an earthmover through. "Why are you in New Mexico?"

"We finally tracked down Teresa. She got a weekend

gig in Taos. We're here to talk her into withdrawing her complaint and coming home."

"But you're in Farmington, not Taos."

"It's a long story. We couldn't get a flight into Albuquerque. When we were getting ready to leave the airport in Farmington to drive to Taos, we saw Lester Horner climbing into the big Ford I just told you about, and we followed it here."

"Justice Lester Horner?"

"Yeah."

Sam generally considered Lauren to be cautious, even as prosecutors go. He wondered about her judgment in this affair. "So you followed him? Why? I don't get it."

Lauren recognized the omission she had made in her narrative.

"Because of the dog, Sam. The guy who picked Horner up at the Farmington airport had a big red dog with him."

Sam paused and felt an adrenaline surge. "Shit."

"That assessment doesn't begin to cover it, Sam."

"What are you gonna do, Lauren? I mean, besides wait for me to get a make on that Ford? What are your plans?"

"I guess we'll stick with them and hope they're just going fishing or something. Mostly I'm hoping that they don't turn around and head for Taos."

"What else can I do from this end?"

She looked across the highway and answered, "Not much I can think of. We certainly don't have anything to take to the New Mexico police that would make them eager to detain a justice of the United States Supreme Court, do we? Wait! I know what you can do. You can help me find Teresa in Taos. I haven't talked with her yet. But I have the number of the club where she's working." She dug in her change purse and dictated the phone number to Purdy. "See if you can find out if she's checked in with them, where in town she's staying, and make sure she's safe. I'll call you back in a while. I think that's a better idea than staying on the line while you wait for the check on the Ford to come through."

Sam said, "I can do even better than that. How about I phone down to the Taos police and tell them we got an anonymous threat against your sister, ask them to keep an eye on her while we verify it up here?"

"That would be great. I'll call you soon to get the results of that vehicle check. Bye, Sam. And thanks."

Purdy said, "Don't do anything stupid, Lauren." But she had already hung up. He knew it didn't make any difference at all that she hadn't heard his warning.

She hobbled back to the car.

"I haven't seen a thing. They're still in back someplace. Did you find out whose car it is?"

"My friend in Boulder, Sam Purdy, the detective, is checking for me. I'll call him back in a little while to see what he's found out. He's going to try to find Teresa in Taos, too. Make sure she's all right."

Robin touched Lauren's shoulder. "I'm sorry if I'm on edge. I know you must want some support for what we're doing, but this seems crazy to me. Lester Horner is a justice of the United States Supreme Court. What we're doing is this: We're following a Supreme Court justice around northern New Mexico, basically because he's traveling with a dog."

Lauren didn't respond. Horner being here, now, in Farmington, New Mexico, had to be important. It had to. Though how would Horner or his friend know where to find Teresa? *Maybe,* she thought, *the booking in Taos was a ruse to lure Teresa here. Or maybe the nightclub is owned by a Mormon. No, not likely.*

Lauren flashed on the image of the red dog and then on the turd in her sister's backyard. She had discovered that Teresa was in Taos by listening to the answering machine in the house. What if the guy with the dog had done the same thing? What if he had broken in and played the tape and reset the machine? It was possible. She tried to recall the number of calls that had been flashing on the machine's readout and the number that were on the tape. Did they match? And Lauren's note to Teresa had been in plain view on the kitchen table, with her itinerary in Ouray and Telluride spelled out in great detail.

Did I lead these murderers to Rachel Baumann? Did Teresa leave directions to herself? Lauren felt a deep chill and turned away from Robin Torr.

"What are we going to do, Lauren? Just sit here and wait?"

Before Lauren answered, she recognized the change in status between the two of them. With sudden deference, Robin was assigning her the power of "boss." Lauren said, "I guess. We'll sit here and wait to see what they do next."

"You know, I thought we came to New Mexico to put an end to this craziness, not to take it to an absurd new level. Why don't we just go to Taos and get your sister and go home?"

Lauren turned across the front seat and touched her friend on the side of her chin. "We've been kidding ourselves, Robin. We can plan this any of ten ways that we would like. But the truth is that we don't have any control. Nonc, not really. And we haven't had any in a long time. We should have stopped this after Pratt was killed. Who knows? Maybe it was already too late, even then.

"I'll call Sam Purdy back in a little while. See if he's found Teresa in Taos and whether she's okay. If she is, we'll go there and get her. In the meantime, I need to play out this hunch. I don't want to lose track of that guy and his dog until my sister is sitting safely right next to me."

"And Lester Horner? I need to remind you that you're keeping track of him, too." Robin's tone had grown hopelessly sardonic.

Lauren hardly noticed. She said, "Yeah. And Lester Horner, too."

To Lester Horner, the supplies that Will Price had set aside for their short drive back to the Ute Mountain Tribal Park seemed double what he had ever packed for their previous visits to the reservation.

Horner enjoyed the break from traveling and walked the perimeter of the huge construction project. Will Price corraled a couple of laborers to help him move the boxes and crates from a completed storage unit to his Bronco.

On the short ride from the airport to Price's newest self-storage facility, Horner had pressed his old friend for details of the nature of their discovery. Price had been effusive. A few of the tiny petroglyphs that they had begun uncovering on their last couple of digs contained some symbols that Price thought were consistent with images described in the Book of Mormon. Will had brought some high-resolution photographic and video equipment and lights to record the dig site and to chronicle their efforts as they checked a section of the dwelling they were excavating for some further petroglyphs. The anthropologists and archaeologists at BYU had made some recommendations on where to dig next based on the sketches that Price had completed of the site thus far.

Horner was excited. He couldn't wait to get back to Lion Canyon and the tribal lands and get the brushes and tools back in his hands. He couldn't wait to see the enhanced photographs that Will had brought back from BYU. Looking down the road, he couldn't wait to announce their discovery to the Church. The president would be thrilled.

The president of the LDS Church, anyway. The other president—of the U.S.—what he thought about one of the Supreme Court justices digging in God's dirt in southwestern Colorado didn't much matter to Horner.

In uncharacteristic style, Horner permitted his revelry to turn to fantasy. In an open-minded world, this discovery, he imagined, would have every Mormon-basher and every Utah-basher eating their words, and every scavenging journalist would forget about the Mark Hofmanns and the Ervil LeBarons and the Bruce Longos and the Paul Singers and would be writing treatises about the rightful restoration of the true Church of Jesus Christ.

In an open-minded world, people would begin talking about the biblical prediction of the restitution of all things and the necessity of preparing for the coming millennium. And the conversion of millions to the Church of Jesus Christ of Latter-day Saints would complete the transfer of religious power on this earth away from Tehran and Jerusalem and the Vatican right to Temple Square in Salt Lake City, Utah, where it belonged.

Will Price would get a deserved seat on the First Quorum of the Seventy, maybe someday even on the Twelve. If God wishes, mused Horner, I will return there as well—wherever I belong, wherever I am called by the Lord or by the prophet.

The images reverberating in Lester Horner's mind seemed to float from the clouds as if on the wings of angels. Horner would not have been surprised to see the angel Moroni himself alight on a mesa and speak to him.

He had never felt closer to the Lord and more blessed with God's grace than he did that day as he stood on the periphery of Your Garage, staring north toward Ute country through the galvanized diamonds of a portable cyclone construction fence. He stuffed his hands far into the pockets of his down vest. If he raised them up, he felt, he could float away.

Horner was experiencing a peace and a fullness that he had always thought would elude him until he entered the celestial kingdom.

Price's booming voice intruded into Horner's reverie and blanketed the high plateau. "All set over here, Lester. You ready to hit the road and make some history?"

Horner nodded to the clouds and to God and jogged eagerly over to join his friend in the bulging Bronco.

A single phone call from Boulder to Utah revealed that the Ford Bronco was registered to a development company, Your Garage, Inc., of Orem, Utah.

Purdy assessed the information to be slightly less than revelatory, since the vehicle had last been seen pulling into a construction site where the world's latest Your Garage was being built. But, then, Purdy didn't know that Your Garage was entirely owned by Will Price and his brothers. And Purdy didn't know that Will Price was currently driving the truck. In fact, Purdy didn't know Will Price from Brigham Young.

A dead end is what it felt like, so Sam scrambled to

find Teresa Crowder in Taos before Lauren called back. He wanted to be able to tell her something useful. He phoned the club owners, who told him that Teresa had called late the previous evening from a motel where she was saying in old Taos, but that they hadn't actually seen her. She was due to show up for her first set by eight o'clock or so. She had asked if she could run through part of her act on stage prior to opening, so they figured she would be in sometime that afternoon for her rehearsal.

That's all Sam Purdy had been able to discover when Lauren phoned him back from the same pay phone in Farmington about twenty minutes after her first call.

"I was just about to call the motel. Call me back in five minutes. I should know something."

"Okay, Sam. Five minutes."

Robin stopped by the filthy phone kiosk just as Lauren was hanging up. She told Lauren she was on her way to the bathroom and asked her if she wanted a can of pop or a snack. Lauren declined, unaware that she had any appetite or any needs unrelated to her sister.

Lauren's leg was beginning to feel like less of a weight as she trundled back to the car. She tried a step without the stick. Maybe this exacerbation is remitting, she hoped, and I can ditch the cane. I could use some good news.

She stopped in her tracks and stared directly across the street. As she watched in dismay, the burgundy Bronco bobbed slowly over a deeply rutted unpaved section of the storage-yard lot, squeezing between parallel sets of scaffolding that fronted opposing lines of garish green garage doors.

Lauren observed the tedious progression of the truck's big chrome grill and felt crippled by fate. She pirouetted on her good leg, praying to see Robin Torr's return from the ladies' room. She didn't. She thought, *I hope she only had to pee. I hope it's so filthy in there, she can't bear the thought of staying one second too long.*

She turned back to the construction site.

The Bronco pulled to a stop at the entrance to the highway. Two silhouettes could be clearly discerned through the windshield. A dog's head protruded out the passenger-side window. No blinker flashed.

Left or right? Taos or Four Corners?

Please, not Taos. Not Taos.

The truck waited for a long break in the traffic and then pulled out to the right. To the west.

Four Corners. Where the hell are they going?

Lauren whipped around. Robin!

As the truck accelerated, she tried to run and get Robin, but her leg wasn't ready for that kind of action and she tumbled instantly to the dirty asphalt. She scraped her hands and tore her jeans and, lying on her side, watched the Bronco disappear in the distance.

Robin arrived seconds later and lifted her up and dusted her off. She saw blood through the hole in Lauren's jeans.

"They left. That way. To the west." Lauren was breathing the way a miser spends money. Her eyes said *Please.*

Robin helped Lauren into the car and, against her better judgment, tore off into traffic after the big burgundy Ford Bronco.

Purdy waited fifteen minutes for his return call from Lauren. He had spent ten of the minutes chewing out a Boulder patrolman who had dropped the ball on canvassing a block on University Hill where a rape had taken place. Patience wasn't Sam Purdy's long suit. To fill some time, he called Alan Gregory and alerted him of the new developments, promising to stay in touch.

Purdy's calls to Taos had been fruitful but disconcerting. Teresa Crowder had come into the motel office in Taos shortly after seven o'clock that morning inquiring about a good place for breakfast. The manager had sent her to Domingo's, a little Mexican bakery about a block away. They hadn't seen her since. Her rented car was still in the lot, right in front of her motel room.

A soft-spoken woman whose excellent English was presented with a thick Oaxacan accent answered the phone at Domingo's. Her name was Rosa. She remembered the girl. Coffee, two churros. She had been joined by a man. No coffee. Chocolate milk, two churros. They had talked for a while. They had left together. Was the young woman distressed?

Didn't seem to be.

Did she remember a car? Did she notice what kind of car the man was driving?

Sorry, no.

Anything? A description?

"There was the dog," she had said.

A thin stream of blood snaked down the soft skin of Lauren's calf and soaked the sock inside her cowboy boot. She didn't really notice. Her attention was focused on the road ahead; she shifted her eyes left and right to check down every intersecting street for signs of the burgundy Bronco. Robin scanned her mirrors for cops while she restrained herself from pressing the car from going any faster than sixty-five.

Without even looking, Lauren picked gravel from beneath loose flaps of skin on her palm. She had no sensation of her fingernails digging into the wounds.

Dejectedly, after a half-mile, she said, "I don't see them, Robin."

"You know we're following them away from Taos, hon?" Robin's pulse was quieting. She was battling the undertow caused by the wake of Lauren's adrenaline surge while simultaneously pushing to keep some objectivity in their planning.

"I know. But if we know where they are, where they're going, then Teresa will be safe. Sam Purdy is going to find her in Taos. He'll look after her."

"You're sure, you're absolutely sure, that it's these two guys we should be after?"

"Yes."

"What are we going to do if we catch them?"

"I don't have a clue, Robin. Not a damn clue."

"This is Detective Sam Purdy of the Boulder Police Department. Just find him, please. Patch me through. I'll wait. Hurry, it's a police emergency."

Less than a minute later, Chief Brian Long of the Ouray Police Department came on the line. The connection was questionable and both voices crackled.

"Sam, nice to hear from you. What's up?"

"We may have a break, Brian. I know you know stuff that I don't know. That's fine. But you need to tell me if any of what I've got here is important. Okay?"

"Tell me what you have."

"We have a middle-aged white male—sorry, I don't have a better description than that—traveling with a medium-size long-haired brown-red dog, possibly a setter or a retriever, driving a burgundy-and-tan 'ninety-one Ford Bronco with Utah plates, last seen in northern New Mexico in the company of one of the principals in this Utah sexual-harassment lawsuit that you heard so much about a few days ago."

A long pause was filled with static and a prolonged, fractured hum.

"Well, whattya know? That is interesting. It may be—let me repeat, may be—somebody I've already talked to, Sam. Can't say for sure. After the murder, we canvassed the whole valley for sightings of unfamiliar dogs and cars with Utah plates. Came up with a few of each. This guy had both. His dog is a retriever, a red one. The guy's in his early to mid-fifties—is that still considered middle-aged? His name is—wait a second, let me think—um, William Price, I think. Lives in Lehi, a small town in Utah. But he wasn't driving a Bronco; he was in a Cadillac. Like I said, we talked to him. He checked out. No priors. Owns his own business. Long family ties in Utah. His alibi was fair to good. Other than that he had a dog and was from Utah, there was nothing particularly suspicious about him. I'm sure I can find him if I need him."

Purdy was encouraged by the thoroughness of the work that had already been done in Ouray. "I've run a check on that Bronco already, Brian. It's registered to a self-storage company that's located in Orem, Utah. Is that anywhere close to Lehi? You know your way around Utah? You got a map where you are?"

"Yeah, hold on a second." Long leaned across the front seat and pulled a compact road atlas from the glove box of his department Cherokee.

Purdy's anxiety leapt into an even higher gear the second Long said, "Whattya know? Orem's right next door to Lehi, Sam. Right next door."

Sam told Long that he was feeling suspicious about all the coincidences and that he was going to go to New Mexico to find Lauren. He promised to stay in touch. He clicked off the call and then phoned the motel and the comedy club in Taos and left instructions with their owners to call Detective Lucy Tanner at the Boulder Police Department the second Teresa Crowder showed up. He phoned Lucy Tanner about his plans and told her he'd check in with her the second he got to New Mexico.

Sam again called Alan Gregory, who was waiting by the phone. When Sam said he was heading to New Mexico, Alan said he would be ready to go in five minutes. On his way out of town, Sam picked Alan up at his house in east Boulder. They took turns cursing the immense distance to Denver's new airport. The airport's tent roof was intended to evoke the jutting peaks of the Rockies but loomed instead like an amusement park in the distant plains, so far away from the metropolitan area that it seemed fanciful to associate it with Denver, let alone the distant mountains.

Purdy drove them right to the top-level departure curb, flashed his badge at one of the Denver cops working airport security, placed a hand on his shoulder, spoke into his ear for half a minute, and then gave him the keys to the car. He pushed Alan through the glass doors into the terminal. They descended a long escalator to the main floor. Sam cut into line, flashed his badge at a ticket agent, checked his small bag, and got tickets. The two men ran downstairs, where they boarded an underground train to a distant concourse. They jogged straight to the remote commuter gate and boarded their flight to Farmington, New Mexico, with a good two or three minutes to spare.

"Slow down, Robin! There he is. Don't hit him! Jesus."

"Sorry. I was checking my mirror for cops."

"We've got him again now. Don't get too close."

Steep hogbacks and high mesas dominated the barren plateau of the Navajo reservation. At Shiprock, the Ford turned off New Mexico Highway 64 and headed almost due north up U.S. Highway 666. Robin Torr was trying to keep the Toyota a half-mile back on the sparsely traveled road. She had moved in closer to her prey as they approached Shiprock and then copied the truck's turn to the north onto Highway 666. She fell back again while the minicaravan moved toward the Colorado border.

"Where the hell are they going?" Lauren mused, barely audibly, to herself.

"What the hell are *we* doing?" Robin responded.

Lauren looked over at her, and they both started laughing. When Robin pulled her attention back to the road she realized she had swerved halfway across the center stripe. An oncoming cattle truck began blaring an air horn at her. She pulled abruptly back into her own lane. The wake of the passing truck shook the little car.

The sign on the right side of the road said, "Welcome to Colorado."

"And what do you suggest I tell the New Mexico police? That is, if we're still talking fucking New Mexico at all."

Clear-air turbulence above the Palmer Divide jolted the narrow commuter plane. Sam Purdy paused. He gripped the arms of his seat, peeked outside, and wondered how the plane's wings were managing to stay on.

"Farmington is right next to Four Corners, you know. In less than an hour these people could all go from New Mexico to Arizona or Utah or Colorado—and back again. So let's say we get lucky and we even discover what state they're in. We call the state cops and we tell them that there's this guy who has been questioned—and, basically, cleared—in a Colorado murder and who is driving around in their state in his own car, while visiting his own legal business. And, by the way, *Trooper,* his traveling companion happens to be a justice of the United States Supreme Court.

"And I'm gonna suggest that the police do what? Pull them over? Search their car? For what? On what grounds? Sorry, Alan, we ain't got shit that'll interest the police in New Mexico or any other state, especially with Lester Horner riding shotgun in that car. If they were in Boulder, even I wouldn't dare to stop them based on what we have."

Alan wasn't surprised by either Purdy's answer or his sarcasm. But he had been hoping for some police magic, for Sam to do one of those special things that cops can do that ordinary citizens don't know anything about.

Turbulence yanked the plane in an abrupt astral direction and shushed the cabin.

Purdy checked the wings again.

Alan said, "Do you think this guy has already kidnapped Teresa?"

Purdy looked out the window at the Front Range of the Rockies. He thought he could see the Air Force Academy chapel. "The truth?" He turned back to Alan, who was crammed into a knee-crushing seat across the aisle.

Alan nodded.

"I think what you think. I think Lauren's sister is already dead. Although everything we've got is circumstantial, it sounds to me like William Price is our guy. And if you take a close look at his record, up until now he hasn't shown any particular inclination to age his victims before he kills them."

In a somber, disbelieving voice, Alan said, "This is going to devastate Lauren, Sam."

"I know. I hope we're wrong, but if we're not, we'd better be there with her when she finds out."

By noon the sun glowed high in the southern sky, cutting sandstone-colored ribbons through the breaking clouds above the southwest corner of Colorado. Robin Torr shifted her sun visor from the windshield to the side window and squinted through her sunglasses to locate the dot on the horizon that she hoped was the big burgundy Bronco. Lauren sat mute beside her, entranced by her fears and by the stunning buttes and imposing rock towers of the southernmost edge of the Ute Mountain Tribal Park.

Soon they approached a road that headed west to the town of Towaoc, a place neither of them knew existed, and, not knowing what else to do, Robin followed Price and Horner's car as it headed up the slope of Sleeping Ute Mountain. The truck stopped in front of a nondescript building that housed the Cultural Research and Education Center of the Ute Mountain Tribal Park.

"Act like you're looking for something. Don't let them see your face." Each of the women twisted away and bowed her head, allowing her long hair to shroud her face. They listened to a door slam in the Bronco. Seconds later, another. Then voices, they couldn't tell whose.

Lauren chanced a glance out the window. The men were disappearing into the building. The dog was tied to a post near the door. She released her seat belt and said, "I want to see inside that truck. I'm going for a walk."

"Bullshit, Lauren. If they see you, they'll never forget you with that stupid cane. I'll go take a look." She struggled into her jacket. "Shit," she muttered. "I can't believe I'm doing this."

"All you're doing is going for a walk."

She shot a caustic look at Lauren. "Yeah, right, Pollyanna."

The air was cold, and the dry winds pierced her jeans. Robin hurried to close her jacket. She stuffed her hair into the neck of her jacket, pulled the collar high around her ears, and wished she had packed a hat.

The Bronco was dusty and creaked quietly. The breeze gusted and whistled as it snaked through a solitary piñon. Robin looked over at the dog. In response to her glance, it wagged its tail, clearing an arc in the red dust.

The Bronco's windows were darkly tinted and filmed with grit, but even from five feet away Robin could see that the vehicle was packed full of something. She saw square shadows and flat planes through each of the windows as she walked past. On the back bumper she recognized the simple emblem of the Ute Mountain Tribal Park on a decal that read "Friends of the Park."

She knew that she would have to walk directly in front of the car in order to see through the windshield into the front seat. That meant she had to pass within a few feet of the dog. Has this happy dog, she wondered, watched people die?

She stooped and held out the back of her hand for the dog's perusal, then began to pet the animal while she strained to see inside the building. She couldn't tell where the men had gone. She pulled the dog's collar around and read the tag. "Hi, my name is Satchel. I belong to W Price." Below the names of the dog and its owner were a phone number and an address in Lehi, Utah.

She shivered and reflexively glanced back at the door. As she stood, the dog stood with her.

Robin turned to the truck. The tint on the windshield was much lighter than the tint on the rest of the glass. From her vantage point it appeared that almost half the cargo area behind the front seats was filled with a single large black trunk. The rest of what she could see seemed to consist of camping supplies and unmarked boxes. She exhaled. Not much to go on.

Lauren had cracked open a window of the car. She heard the door of the building creak before she saw the shadowy light change behind Robin. She gasped, and immediately covered her mouth with her hand. The two men were approaching Robin.

Instinctively, Robin lowered herself back down to the dog and rubbed a spot on her neck below her collar. Satchel strained her head around to try to locate her master without having to give up the kind touch of this stranger.

Robin's heart drummed. *What do I do? Do I turn? Do I pretend they're not there? What would I do if this happened outside the grocery store in Salt Lake City?*

Robin turned her head but didn't actually look up. She smiled. "Is this your dog? She's real sweet."

"Yeah. She's a good dog." The man's voice was like muted thunder; it bellowed deep and twanged her bones. He stooped right beside Robin and unclipped the lead from Satchel's collar. His jean-covered hips and hers touched momentarily. Robin fought panic. She stood to remove herself from proximity to him and said "Bye," more to Satchel than to the men, and without making eye contact she retreated through the door into the tribal education center.

Lauren took her hand from the horn of the Toyota and exhaled loudly. She thought, *We're going to lose them now. Damn.*

The Bronco rumbled to life. It backed up, then took off down the same road on which it had arrived.

Despairing at the departure of the Bronco, Lauren grabbed her stick and joined Robin Torr inside the building. She found Robin in the middle of a conversation with a weathered man who she assumed was a Ute. He was telling Robin that years ago, in the early sixties, the men who had just left had befriended his brother at BYU. With his brother's blessing the men had been coming to the park for years, digging at a few minor sites in Lion Canyon near the cliff dwellings. They were two of only a handful of people who had permits for long-term research on the tribal lands.

Lauren piped in that she would love to see an actual dig, and began negotiating to arrange a special tour in the park with a Ute Indian guide. The man explained that visitors were not allowed in the park without a guide and that special tours were usually reserved for a minimum of five people. Lauren pulled out her wallet and told him she would be happy to pay for five special tours. He gladly took her money, told the women where they could buy some food and water in Towaoc, and instructed them to meet their guide at the Ute Mountain Tribal Park Visitors Center in a converted gas station on Highway 666 in about an hour.

"Please don't argue with me. I'm going to get us a car and I have to call Boulder and see whether Lucy has heard from New Mexico since we got on board this aerial roller coaster. Maybe Lauren has called. Or maybe her sister has shown up in Taos. The guy behind me on the plane told me that the best restaurant in all of Farmington is this little Mexican place at the airport, Señor Whats-its. Your job is to go get us some food—a lot of it—while I go do what I have to do."

"Sam, I'm not hungry."

"Alan," Purdy said evenly, his eyebrows arched, "I don't give a fuck. Later on, when you are hungry, it may just not be convenient for us to stop at McDonald's. Just do it." He looked across the small terminal. "That's it over there. Señor Pepe's. Remember, I want a lot of food. At least a couple of meals' worth. The guy said to try the crab enchiladas. And I like tamales and I like green chile."

"Crab enchiladas? In the middle of the desert?"

"The restaurant's in an airport. Maybe they fly the fucking crabs in first-class." Purdy shook his head as though he were talking with an idiot and made his way to the nearest bank of pay phones.

Alan caught up with Sam fifteen minutes later at the Hertz counter. The bag Alan carried away from the restaurant was bigger than his carry-on from the plane.

Purdy saw him coming. "This is Trudy. She remembers them from this morning. Lauren's still got that cane. What did she do to her leg, anyway?"

Alan dodged the question. He grinned at Trudy. Trudy seemed pleased. "Do you remember anything else?"

Purdy answered for her. "No, she doesn't."

Annoyed, Alan faced him. "What did you find out from Boulder? Anything?"

"They're not in New Mexico. They're back in Colorado. They followed these two guys to the Ute Mountain Ute Indian reservation. They called my office from there. The guys they're following apparently have a longstanding permit to do archaeological research on the cliff dwellings, or near the cliff dwellings, or whatever, on the reservation."

"You mean Mesa Verde?"

"That's what I asked. No. Lauren told Lucy—Detective Tanner—it was the Ute Mountain Park. It's on tribal land, not federal land. Lucy got the impression Lauren was quoting from something she was reading."

Trudy looked up from her keyboard with a trained smile. "Did you know we're quite close to the Ute Mountain Park? Would you gentlemen like a brochure? And a map?" She looked down and pecked a few more times at her keyboard. "And would a Ford Tempo be okay today? I have a nice red one."

Alan said, "Please, not a Tempo. I hate Tempos." He'd momentarily forgotten that Purdy's police-issued vehicle was a Tempo.

"We'll take the Tempo," Purdy said to Trudy, eyeing Alan critically. "I like Tempos."

Alan wondered why Purdy had bothered to ask him along on this trip, but he kept the question to himself. Instead, he said, "Any word from Taos, Sam?"

Purdy shook his head gravely.

In apparent consonance with his character and in deference to a worn set of shock absorbers on his pickup, the Ute guide drove with admirable patience as he led Robin and Lauren past the dramatic vault of Chimney Rock and into the spacious canyon of the Mancos River.

The sun had already begun to drop to the west by the time the Ute guide pulled his Chevy pickup to the side of the two-lane dirt-and-gravel road that bisected the tribal park. This section of the canyon of the Mancos River was wide and flat. The mesa tops to the north and south were carved like fanciful castles.

The Ute Mountain Tribal Park attracts relatively few visitors. A million tourists a year may visit Mesa Verde National Park, while only a few thousand find the more remote Ute Mountain Park. But the same ancient people who inhabited and inexplicably deserted Mesa Verde also developed their enduring culture and built spectacular cliff dwellings in the land of the modern Ute Mountain Utes. The Ute Mountain Tribal Park is less accessible, more primitive, and less studied than its northern neighbor. It is no less majestic.

In late autumn there are days when the Ute Mountain Tribal Park draws no tourists at all. The dirt-and-gravel road that snakes off Highway 666 to the ruins is quiet, the potsherds and dust undisturbed, the Anasazi petroglyphs and Ute pictographs unexamined, and the cliff dwellings and ruins as lonesome as during the centuries before their rediscovery.

"It's so desolate," Robin said.

"But pretty spectacular," added Lauren. She was awed by the desert canyon that was surrounded by rock-rimmed buttes and sprawling mesas and spectacular stone towers that seemed to have been carved from mountains of red sand. The mesa tops and the floors of the canyons that hugged the listless Mancos River were the only areas that supported vegetation. The sky above was the soft blue of a baby's eyes.

Before climbing in his truck to lead the women into the park, the young Ute had told them they were going to stop and see some ruins in the Mancos River Canyon prior to heading to the archaeological dig site, farther east in Lion Canyon. Lauren had protested. She argued that they wanted to go directly to the dig. The Ute told her simply that his boss had told him to give the men time to get their camp set up without being disturbed.

That was that.

If it wasn't too dark when they left the archaeological site, then perhaps they would stop on the way back up the canyon and see some of the petroglyphs and pictographs at the site of the torched hogan of the Ute chief Jack House—"but probably not." The Ute guide said that he wanted to be on the dirt road out of the park by dark.

As the truck in front of them proceeded farther into the park, Lauren turned to Robin and said, "Why are they here, Robin? I mean, really, why are they here?"

"I don't know. They're amateur archaeologists. It's not an uncommon pastime among Mormons. There are a lot of LDS who scour around old Indian sites hoping to find evidence of the Lamanites and the Nephites." She touched the brake pedal to try to escape a cloud of dust thrown up by the pickup. "I think the real question continues to be: Why are *we* here, Lauren?"

Lauren knew the answer to that. "Because as long as we know where they are, they can't hurt my sister."

In a kind voice, Robin said, "Their reason for being here, I think, is more compelling." She fiddled unsuccessfully with the radio. A station from Cortez drifted in and out, something country-and-western. "At least it's pretty here. You know, I think at first, when we left Farmington, I was kind of disappointed about not going to Taos. I was looking forward to seeing Taos for some reason. I don't know why, I just really was. I've never been to New Mexico before. After we found your sister, I was secretly hoping I could talk you guys into going to Santa Fe before we went back to Utah. But, you know, fate isn't always unkind. I've always wanted to see these Anasazi ruins, too. I never really thought I would. Wiley's restrictions on travel are pretty severe. He doesn't do luxury and he doesn't do primitive. This is primitive. He would want a tram and a Ramada Inn." She rubbed the back of her neck, sore and stiff from the waxing and waning exhilaration of the day.

Lauren longed to talk with Alan. He would understand her need to save Teresa. He would hold her. He would let her go again.

She had insisted that Robin twice describe the black trunk in the back of the Bronco. Each time she dug for new details. Robin wasn't cynical enough to share Lauren's fear about its contents. Lauren didn't press the matter—couldn't. Maybe with Alan. She needed room for her fear. But she couldn't stop thinking about it. She thought, over and over, *The case is big enough to hold Teresa. They have her.*

She's dead. She's not dead.

He loves me. He loves me not.

As a child, she had always tried to count the petals of the daisies before she plucked them, one by one, and let them fall to the grass. She had always needed to know how it would come out in the end. Now was no different.

In front of her, the Chevy stopped abruptly in a sliver of stark light. The young Ute got out of the truck and walked toward the Toyota.

Robin Torr and the Ute, who had introduced himself as Ransom Gray, made a compelling pair as they began walking a worn path toward the ruins at Train Rock. Robin stretched naturally to match the guide's easy stride down the trail that sloped gently from the road toward the Mancos. Lauren had declined to accompany them. She remained suspicious of her leg and felt anchored to the car by her fatigue.

"Please make it quick, Robin. I want to catch up with that Ford as soon as possible. Okay?" she had pleaded as her friend left the car. Robin had nodded before jogging over to Ransom.

From her roost in the front seat, Lauren watched them descend the trail and minutes later climb to the base of a stunning rock formation across the canyon. She could see their destination above their heads—a set of ruins perched on top of a series of rocks across the river. The rock formation bore the vague shape of a locomotive and freight cars.

About thirty minutes later, Ransom walked Robin back to the Toyota, then climbed into his Chevy and drove east down the wide dirt road that traversed the huge park. Lauren had fallen asleep while Ransom and Robin were gone. One side of her face was red and creased.

She asked, "How was it up there?"

Robin said, "The ruins are spectacular. And there are artifacts—potsherds—everywhere, all over the ground. I'm definitely coming back when we have more time.

Ransom said that if I'm willing to rappel he'll show me some ruins almost nobody gets to see." She paused and turned her head toward Lauren. "Rappel means ropes, doesn't it?"

Lauren nodded.

Robin squinted at something on the road ahead and pursed her lips. "Oh, well, why not, huh?" Some levity entered her voice. "What was fun is that he wanted advice about his girlfriend. He's a nice kid. He lives in Cortez, north of here, on that highway we were on. His girlfriend's an Anglo named Cindy. He sees me as an expert on Anglo girls. It's all kind of cute."

As they drove east, the dirt road began a gradual climb out of the canyon floor and up the side of a mesa that rimmed Johnson Canyon and Lion Canyon. The shadows of the scrub and sagebrush that reached out to the east were noticeably longer than before. The vehicles traversed a series of switchbacks before they reached the top of the mesa southeast of the river. The mesa top was thick with dense forests of juniper and piñon. The sweet smells of evergreen saturated the dry air. An eastern breeze rustled the trees.

After driving a few more minutes, Ransom pulled his truck to the edge of a promontory and stopped. The entire southwestern landscape seemed to be visible. Sleeping Ute Mountain dominated the bright western sky, the sharp, steep mountains of the La Plata hovered above Mesa Verde to the north, and the carved volcanic ruins near Shiprock, New Mexico, framed the south.

Ransom watched the faces of his guests for a few minutes, then drove to the juncture of Lion and Johnson canyons. He leaned his head out the window, gestured into the adjacent abyss, and called out, "Lion Canyon."

The women pulled themselves from the car and made their way to the edge of the cliff. Ransom followed. Robin and Lauren gaped down at the steep stone walls, at the stunning ruins Ransom called Eagle's Nest and Lion House. The colors—the bleached blond rock of the cliff dwellings, the red sandstone, the gray-greens of the piñons and junipers, the browns of the soil—were muted and in transition, fighting to find the right blend of day hues and night hues to meld into a balance for dusk. But

Lauren hardly noticed the beauty. In a small clearing she had spotted the last direct rays of the day dancing off the burgundy top of a big 4 × 4.

She was transfixed.

"Gotcha," she said under her breath.

She searched the surrounding ground with her eyes. The narrows at the entrance to Lion Canyon were dense with sagebrush and grasses. A solitary cottonwood that had already shed its leaves stood sentinel at one end. But she didn't see Lester Horner. She didn't see the damn red dog. She didn't see Will Price. And, despite scrutinizing a wide perimeter around the truck, she couldn't see the big black case.

Robin stood at her left shoulder and faced the canyon. She, too, saw the Ford. She said into the wind, her words blown back in her face, "Aren't you scared? Even a little bit?"

Lauren turned to her friend and hugged her with her free arm. Their untied hair gusted out and wove together. She said, "Robin, I'm so terrified that I'm afraid I'm going to pee on myself."

Robin's shoulders slackened. "You seem so determined. I was afraid you weren't scared."

"It's my DA face. And my MS face, I guess. You know, in my work I deal with some real creeps. I tell myself before I go into an interrogation room with some asshole who has just brutalized some kid or raped some woman, I tell myself he's just scum. But sometimes, when I actually let myself feel how monstrous he really is, I want to run for my life—just run. And sometimes, instead, I have this impulse to go berserk and scratch out his eyes with my fingernails, and I want to watch him die. Those feelings—those crazy feelings—I think they're because I know I'm already too late to save his last victim. But this time it's different.

"I'm so scared this time because I don't know whether my little sister is his latest victim or is about to become his next one. I don't know whether she's been kidnapped and stuffed into that trunk, or murdered and stuffed into that trunk, or if she's sitting on the plaza in Taos right now sipping a margarita. I'm just afraid I'm too late. There's a big part of me that doesn't want to see what's in that black case. I don't want to go down and talk with those men. I want to run. But I have to make sure they don't have Teresa with them. Believe me, I'm praying that I'm wrong about everything."

Robin took Lauren's hand. "If you're right, we're confronting one, maybe two murderers. If you're wrong, we're merely going to have to admit to tracking a U.S. Supreme Court justice across two states because we thought he was a madman. But for whatever it's worth, I'm with you—all the way. This one's your call. I'll go ask Ransom to lead us down there. At least we'll have us a witness."

On the drive west from Farmington onto Navajo lands, then through Shiprock, and finally north into Colorado, Purdy ate all of his lunch and, with his friend's consent, most of Alan's as well.

Alan's anxiety was accelerating while Sam's was diminishing. Sam was on the hunt, in his element. Alan fought despair over Teresa's fate and gut-ache fear for Lauren.

"This tribal policeman is going to meet us outside the reservation and take us in to find them, right, Sam?"

"Yeah. That's what Lucy told me she arranged from Boulder."

"What did she tell them to get them to agree to help?"

"I don't know for sure. But she said Brian Long—the police chief from Ouray—helped her out. Lucy's pretty imaginative. She might have even tried telling them the truth. But knowing her, I doubt it. So please let me do the talking. I can promise you, from personal experience with your act, I'm a much more convincing liar than you are."

"And what do we do with these people when we catch up with them?"

"Depends. When we get to the visitors center, I'll call Boulder and see if Lauren's sister has shown up in Taos. If she hasn't, then our first job is to find her. Or her body. If we find either one, we have us a delicate situation, given the presence of Justice Horner. But I don't think that'll happen. I think her body's someplace in or around Taos. So I think what we do is we get Lauren and her lawyer friend from Utah, and we make sure that they're safe. We give this guy from Lehi assurance that we're on him like white on rice until we know for sure he's not holding Teresa. And we hope we can find something to link him to all these murders."

"Lauren's and Teresa's safety comes first, Sam."

"Absolutely."

The Ute Mountain Ute tribal policeman wasn't waiting alone at the visitors center across the road from the unmarked entrance to the tribal park. He was with Chief Brian Long of the Ouray Police Department.

Long leapt from the passenger seat of the tribal-police car and ran to the rental car as soon as he recognized Purdy's face through the windshield.

Long said, "It's him. It's Price, Sam."

"What? Whattya got?"

Alan's heart sank at the news. He wanted them to be on a wild-goose chase. He didn't want Lauren to be on the tail of a murderer. Long introduced the tribal policeman, who had ambled up to join the rendezvous. Alan and Sam got out of their car.

Long started to explain: "The murder scene at the Wiesbaden showed no traces of dog hair—none in the water in the hot springs, none in her room. And there were no fresh dog prints close to the enclosure where Rachel was killed. Nothing developed in any of the forensics to link Rachel's killing with the other two murders.

"But remember, I told you that we did track down a few people in town who were traveling with dogs? One of whom, this William Price, also was driving a car with Utah tags. Well, while I was interviewing all these people last week, I played with their dogs and kind of accidentally managed to pull hairs from each of them. At that point, I was still hoping we would find dog hairs in the water from the tub and maybe we could get a match.

I even got casts of paw prints that one of the dogs left in the flower beds outside the house where it was staying. That wasn't Price's dog, though—I just got hair from his dog. Anyway, although I didn't expect anything to come of it, mostly because the evidence was gathered slightly, well, unconventionally, I sent all this stuff to the FBI to see if they could get a match between these hairs I pilfered and the hairs they took off the sleeve of that woman who had her throat slashed in Virginia. A couple of hours ago I heard back. The hairs match. It turns out that a dog of the same breed and color as William Price's dog was in that park in Virginia when that woman had her throat slit. And we know that Price's dog was in Ouray when Rachel was killed. So the way I'm looking at it, William Price is my prime suspect for both murders. It can't be confirmed until the FBI gets final DNA confirmation of the dog-hair match. But it's him, I know it's him. Lucy, that detective in your office, told me you were on your way here, so I got a friend of mine to fly me down to Cortez in his plane." He kicked his boot in the dust.

"What about the FBI? Don't they want in on this?" asked Sam.

"I called them in Denver. They want the final DNA analysis, and they're arguing about whether this should be handled out of the Farmington field office. I don't much feel like waiting for them to sort out their turf battles. Especially not with your DA friend chasing Price. By the way, when I talked to Detective Tanner in Boulder, she said to tell you the other sister hasn't shown up. You wanna wait for the feds?"

Purdy said, "Like hell."

Alan had a hard time keeping his mouth shut.

Purdy headlined the obvious. "Brian, you know there's a Supreme Court justice in there, apparently a friend of William Price?" Purdy tilted his head toward the tribal park.

Brian Long shrugged. "I just hope he's not involved. I've never arrested even a regular judge before." He turned his head away from the group. "But I don't think the procedure's any different, is it?"

Purdy directed his attention to the Ute Mountain cop. "How far in are we going? How long will it take us?"

The Ute rubbed his left eye and tugged a Colorado Rockies baseball cap down on his brow. "Thirty, maybe thirty-two miles. Good gravel roads. A little wash-boarded. Take us maybe forty-five, fifty minutes."

"How much light do we have left?"

The Indian faced the western sky and scrutinized the position of the sun behind Sleeping Ute Mountain. "Maybe a little more than that, maybe a little less," he said.

"This is your land, your jurisdiction. You okay with what we're doing?"

"Because of the justice, you mean?"

"Yeah." Purdy was stone-faced.

The Ute spit into the dust. "Don't bother me none. Won't be the first time justice has been arrested around here."

Will Price and Lester Horner had set up their camp in the usual spot, a parched clearing a few dozen yards from the entrance to Lion Canyon.

As was their custom, Price had driven the Bronco all the way to the southern-facing cliffs and unloaded the supplies—which this time included the black trunk—that he would later lug up a ladder to the dig. He had then driven the truck back to the spot where Horner would pull out what he needed to set up camp. The campsite was flanked to the east and south by a few scraggly junipers, which served to blunt the force of the sharp breezes that they knew from experience could knife down the stony canyon. The camp was only fifty yards from the partly excavated kiva that Horner and Price had been working, on and off, for almost six years. In the spring, during the runoff, flash floods could make the crossing to the kiva tricky. Now, in the fall, the canyon floor was dry.

Dozens of ancient kivas—some excavated, most not—dotted the canyons and cliff dwellings of the Ute Mountain Tribal Park. As far as Anasazi kivas went, the one to where Will Price lugged their supplies was small and unspectacular. Only eleven feet in diameter, it sat on a rock shelf twenty-five feet above the floor of Lion Canyon. It had been built and abandoned long before the other, larger kivas in Lion Canyon. Experts in Provo had told Price and Horner that the kiva's location, so close to the canyon's entrance and only twenty-five feet above the arroyo, probably rendered it too vulnerable to both enemies and flash floods. Unlike the newer, more spectacular cliff dwellings built above it nearer the canyon rim, the kiva wasn't in a protected rock alcove. The archaeologists hypothesized that the ancient ones abandoned this kiva when they constructed the sheltered dwellings farther into the canyon at Eagle's Nest and Tree House.

The age of the site and the fact that it had never before been completely excavated accounted for the scientific and spiritual interest of Price and Horner. The older Indian sites, they theorized, were more likely to show evidence of the migration of the followers of Lehi—the ancestors of the Lamanites and the Nephites—to the New World hundreds of years before the birth of Christ, as chronicled in the Book of Mormon.

The rich panorama of petroglyphs that had been discovered over the years in Mesa Verde and on Ute Mountain Ute land had drawn Will Price's interest like a magnet. He'd long maintained to his friend that the most likely source of evidence of the substantiation of the migration of the lost tribes of Israel to the New World would come from symbols pecked laboriously into rock.

"Our role is to close the distance between faith and fact, Lester. We'll do that on our hands and knees so that others with less faith can do it with their eyes."

Now they believed that they had it.

On their most recent expedition, the one shortly after Blythe Oaks's death, the men had begun to uncover and photograph a segment of collapsed wall that had once formed the southernmost curve of a kiva, a small, round ceremonial room dug below ground level. On a narrow band of rock behind a crumbled section of a banquette were fragments of small petroglyphs. The designs pecked into the rock were in various states of disintegration, ranging from negligible to severe, but the images hadn't been vandalized. Price's consultants at BYU had sharpened his photographs with computer enhancement and had begun to reconstruct the pictures that had been notched into the rock wall over a thousand years before. Encouraging him, they had told him where to dig next.

When the men settled down into the kiva, each braced

against a pilaster of stone and brick, Will Price showed Lester Horner the sketch from BYU. Then they got down to the tedious work of excavation.

Satchel lifted her head and cocked an ear. Will Price noticed and listened himself. At first he heard nothing but the wind. Then a distant vehicle. Some tourists leaving the park. He worked slowly, waiting for darkness. He needed the darkness.

He was philosophical while he worked. "These kivas, this is where they kept their legends, Lester. This is where they told the old stories, the special stories. And this is where our story will be told." The men were on the banquette that rimmed the kiva a few feet above the floor, Horner sitting cross-legged, alternately using his fingertips and a soft brush on the edges of the collapsed wall; Price was on his knees, working with brushes at the border of an image pecked into rock. A pair of battery-operated lanterns intensified the dim light in the depths of the cutout room.

Horner struggled to keep his excitement from causing him to be careless with his tools. Although the justice considered himself a scholar of the Book of Mormon, he had never done the detailed research necessary to be an expert on what modern archaeologists would need to find to verify the ancient record. His understanding of what the Book of Mormon predicted about artifacts left by the Lamanites and the Nephites was perfunctory, even elementary. But his friend Will was a lifelong scholar of Mormon archaeology and had, over the years, developed a clear sense of what the petroglyphs would look like to reflect the story of the followers of the prophet Lehi as they left Jerusalem and traversed the wilderness of the Arabian Peninsula before sailing to the New World in 600 B.C. The geographic area that included Colorado and Utah was far north of what the Book of Mormon referred to as "Desolation" or "the Land Northward." Price and Horner were looking for evidence of northern migration by the Lamanites sometime after they annihilated the Nephites in battle around the fourth century A.D.

"At the end of the weekend, we'll get those big lights up here and we'll get us a video record and a photo record, and we'll have a meeting with the authorities and show some movies in the Church Administration Building. How's that sound, Lester?"

"Like a ticket to heaven," said Horner, smiling.

Satchel ran to the rim of the kiva and barked.

That's when Ransom Gray's quiet voice skipped eerily off the kiva's stepped stone walls. "Anybody up there? I'm a Ute guide. And you got visitors."

Will Price said, "Darn it to heck," and sounded like he meant it.

A primitive but sturdy wooden pole ladder over twenty feet long separated Ransom, Lauren, and Robin from the elevated kiva.

"I can't get up that," Lauren said, pounding her cane into the dirt at the foot of the ladder, frustration spilling out of her.

"I'll help. You'll get up," said Ransom evenly. He handed Lauren's cane to Robin Torr and stood behind Lauren as she placed her good leg on the thick wood of the first rung. "I'll support you from below each time as you move your good leg up a rung. Then you pull yourself up with your arms and your strong leg. Got it?"

Lauren tried. It worked. "Okay."

"Howdy." Price's voice was booming but pleasant as he greeted the three visitors who appeared above him on the rim of the round room. Satchel approached the women eagerly but sniffed close to Ransom only after he held out his hand for inspection.

Ransom said, "Hello. These women wanted to see a dig. We won't disturb you long." He sounded apologetic.

The lanterns washed the three newcomers with light from their feet to their knees. Their upper bodies were silhouetted against a sky that was retreating from day to night. Price adjusted one of the lanterns, and the halogen light sprayed across their faces. Immediately, he recognized one of the women from the brief encounter on the porch outside tribal headquarters. She was the one who had been playing with Satchel. He didn't like the fact that she was here. Had she followed him? He thought he had seen the Ute kid in the park before; he really was a guide. The woman with the cane he didn't know, though she did look vaguely familiar.

"It's a surprise seeing you again, Miss." Will Price directed himself to Robin, his words and his tone almost insisting on an explanation. Lester Horner, eager not to have his anonymity disturbed, and hoping that these visitors would get bored and leave, kept his back turned and continued to brush at the rocks with his tools.

"We heard that you were archaeologists. The man at tribal headquarters said we could visit your dig, see how it works. It's a great opportunity for us. Thanks." *Twenty minutes on a stair machine and I can't get my heart beating like this,* Robin reflected in disgust at her incipient panic. The dirt from the rungs of the ladder was turning to a dusty red paste on her sweaty palms. "We're not bothering you, are we?"

"Well, we are quite busy. Maybe just a few minutes won't hurt." He shifted his gaze from one woman to the other. He locked his hard brown eyes on Lauren, wondering, *Do I know you? Why are you staring at me?*

Lauren stood on the rim of the kiva. The command in her voice surprised everyone, including herself. She recognized the tone she was employing even before she knew exactly what she as going to say. She was at the podium now, speaking in her opening-argument voice. She said, "I, for one, didn't come all the way here to see you two gentlemen playing archaeologist."

Even Lester Horner turned and faced the visitors when he heard that.

"Hello, Mr. Justice," she said, acknowledging him, before rotating her gaze back to his companion. "It's Mr. Price, isn't it? Hello to you, too, Mr. Price."

The sound of his name being spoken caused Price to tense even further. How does this woman know my name? Did the Utes give that out, too? Who is she? What on earth do they want with us?

"And who are you, Miss?" Price was glad his voice

was more robust than everyone else's. With its thick fabric and full body, his voice could manage to package an astonishing amount of rebuke without sounding the least bit snide.

"I'm a deputy district attorney." She paused and let the words settle. Price's face stiffened, she thought. Horner looked befuddled and glanced momentarily at his friend. "My name is Lauren Crowder, and I'm looking for my sister. Her name is Teresa. Teresa Crowder."

Horner dropped the tool he was holding.

Trouble, Will Price reflected. *It's time to institute Plan B.*

Lester Horner stood before he spoke. His knees cracked loudly. He brushed dirt and sand off his clothing with his grimy hands, then let his arms hang at his side.

"What the heck's going on here, Will?"

Price surveyed Lauren's three-legged silhouette above him. He absolutely did not want her speaking alone with Lester Horner. As quietly as his voice could manage, he whispered to Horner, "There may actually be something I need to discuss with this woman, Lester. It may be a little sticky—about Blythe. You know, the accusations against her. All in all, it's probably better that you not be part of it, given your position. I hope you can understand what I mean. Trust me on this."

Horner felt confusion and anger. He was grateful that his friend was willing to shield him, furious that he had somehow managed to get him into a position where it was necessary.

The justice addressed Lauren, noting for the first time the resemblance between her and Teresa. "Ms. Crowder, although I have no idea why you are here, given that I may be a witness in the legal action your sister is contemplating, I don't feel it's proper for me to engage in any discussions with you that may involve her or her contact with Blythe Oaks. I will need to excuse myself."

Robin took a step forward. "My name is Robin Torr, Mr. Justice. I'm Teresa Crowder's attorney. The action you've just mentioned has not been filed. As soon as I have a chance to consult with my client, I'm certain the whole thing will be dropped. You have my assurance of that. There isn't a conflict."

"In my mind, Miss, your admission means that the investigation is still active, and I judge it only proper to excuse myself from this conversation. I suggest you consider the propriety of your presence here as well, based on the current state of affairs rather than on your ability to predict the future."

Torr thought, *Great. I'm being lectured on the ethics of my behavior by a Supreme Court justice, and I'm supposed to ignore him?* She opened her mouth to reply.

But Price interrupted and directed a question at Lauren. "May we discuss your concerns alone, Miss Crowder? Just you and I? I think that's the most efficient way that, uh, we can come to an understanding. Because I won't speak in front of your attorney friend, either." Price had two agendas: He needed to know what Lauren knew, and he needed to split up the group.

Price turned to the Ute guide and said, "Ransom, why don't you take your other guest on a visit to the big lodge above us. Give the lady and me fifteen minutes or so?"

Ransom Gray was eager to leave the tension in this kiva behind. "Robin, you want to go up and see a cliff house? It's close."

Robin looked at Lauren, who noted the skepticism in her friend's eyes. "It's okay, Robin. Too many people know we're here. Just don't go far. I'd actually love to have a private chat with Mr. Price. And I'm certainly not in any shape to hike somewhere else to do it."

"I'll wait for you in camp, Will," Horner said with some derision in his voice. He began to climb up from the bottom level of the kiva.

Lauren didn't want anybody going back down into the canyon alone.

"I don't think so, Mr. Justice. I think until Mr. Price and I talk about where my sister is, we all need to keep some distance between ourselves and those cars down there." If Teresa is down there, she thought, I sure as hell don't want you hightailing it out of this park with her. I'm tired of chasing you jerks across this desert.

Horner was startled at Lauren's words. *Where her sis-*

ter is? What on earth is she talking about? "Well, where exactly *do* you want me to go, Miss? I'm certainly not going to go on a hike with the lawyer of the woman who has accused my dear friend of dreadful things. She may be planning to use me as a witness, for heaven's sake." *Will, what have you done to get yourself involved with this case? How do you even know Teresa Crowder? What could you know about the accusations against Blythe?*

Will Price completed a quick read of the situation and saw an opportunity developing. Modifications to his plan took shape in his mind as he spoke. "Lester, why don't you go on up to the broken tower." In explanation to the two women on the rim of the kiva, he said, "It's a decrepit ruin right above us." He faced Horner again. "Take some tools with you. It's the other place we needed to do some work this weekend, anyway."

The broken tower above the kiva could be reached only by a nearby ladder. Horner gazed at the ladder and nodded reluctantly.

The kiva was filling with gray-brown light and cold shadows. The dwindling daylight remained sharper on the path that led from the kiva to the large cliff dwelling high up on the canyon wall. Ransom took Robin's hand and they climbed to the trailhead above the kiva.

"Call if you need anything, Lauren. We'll be close by," Robin said, her tone reflecting her reluctance to accept the plan. To herself, she muttered, "I don't like this." She kept reminding herself that Lester Horner was a justice of the United States Supreme Court.

Ransom led her up the trail.

Lester Horner began to pack some tools. Lauren couldn't tell whether he was merely being methodical or whether his dawdling was some sort of delaying tactic. Will Price seemed unconcerned as the minutes passed.

Finally, Horner appeared to be finished. He lifted a small pack and grabbed one of the lights.

Price stood. "You know, I hate to admit it, but my old bladder is not going to make it through our discussion, Miss Crowder. Lester, do you mind staying with my things for two minutes while I relieve myself?" He didn't wait for a reply; he knew Horner wouldn't leave the dig unprotected. To Satchel, he said, "Stay." Price then hurdled himself adroitly up from the banquette to the top of a pilaster and exited the kiva onto the trail where Ransom and Robin had gone.

Horner wanted to ask Lauren why she thought Will Price would have any idea where her sister was. He knew that asking would not be particularly prudent, though, because he didn't know in what position her answer would leave him. So he didn't ask. He lowered himself to the dirt floor of the kiva to sit and wait. Lauren sat on the upper rim of shaped rock, her cane across her lap.

Above them, out of their sight, Price darted up the trail. In a minute he reached the base of the long pole ladder that led up the steep canyon face to the next rock shelf. Ransom and Robin were already up the ladder, exploring the big cliff dwelling above them.

With every bit of strength he had in his thick arms, Price yanked on the rungs and frame of the heavy pole ladder. He was just able to pull the base out far enough so that the top rung slid down the rock face to a position that was unreachable from the shelf above.

Immediately, Price bolted back down the trail. He slowed to a walk as he reached the open rim of the kiva.

"Go on, Lester. We'll try to be brief," he called down to his annoyed-looking friend.

Lauren noted that Price's breathing had changed. She wrote it off to anxiety. *This asshole should be worried.*

Lester Horner climbed out of the kiva with surprising agility, walked down a short path, and then pulled himself up a nearby wooden ladder to the ruins of the small tower.

From the upper rim of the kiva, Lauren and Price watched Horner clear the top rung and then disappear into the ruin.

Lauren turned to Price, eager to press him about the black trunk and about Teresa, and then gaped open-mouthed as he darted past her down the short path to the nearby ladder that Horner had just ascended. In a single smooth motion, Price yanked it from position.

At the same instant, above her, she heard Lester Horner scream, "Oh, no. Oh, no. No! Will, Will! What have you done?" Horner's head emerged over the lip of the stone ledge, and he screamed, "The ladder! Will! No. *NO!* Miss Crowder, run, run!"

Another scream echoed in the canyon. Robin shouted, "Lauren? What's wrong? Are you okay? Damn it! We're on our way! Hold on." Then, seconds later, Robin screamed again, "They moved the ladder, Lauren. Shit! We can't get down."

Teresa!

Will Price walked back to the kiva and sat so close to Lauren that she could smell his sour breath as he said, "Not likely you're going to run, is it?" He flung her cane out of the kiva into the canyon and said, "Now, let's have that talk. You had some questions?" He noticed Satchel laying forlornly where he had put her on stay, her snout nestled between her front paws.

He released her. "Okay. Good girl."

Satchel waddled, tail wagging, right over to Lauren, who had wrapped her arms around her upper body to try to contain her panic. She tried to think.

From above them, a shrill male voice filled the canyon. "Miss Crowder, she's alive. Your sister, she's alive!"

Teresa.

In a resonant voice so deep that it shook her bones, Will Price said, "For now, anyway. You know, you really shouldn't have come here. It would have all been okay if you had just left us alone."

"How much farther? Can you tell anything from that map?"

Purdy had a photocopied map of the Ute Mountain Tribal Park sitting on his lap. He leaned across the front seat and checked the odometer. He raised the map closer to his face.

"I'd say we're halfway in, maybe a little more. The Ute cop thinks we'll find everybody at this dig that Price and Horner are working."

Alan glanced at the dashboard clock, then, for confirmation, at his watch. "That's going to take at least another twenty or twenty-five minutes at this pace." The dusty pickup was still fifty yards ahead. "Can't that guy speed up? There's not much light left."

Purdy, too, surveyed the dust cloud being raised behind the truck in front of them. With a wisp of irony in his voice, he said, "My guess is that he *is* hurrying."

"What do you think the chances are that the FBI will show up? Like with a helicopter?"

Purdy smiled to himself. "It's possible. Shit, anything is possible with the FBI. But the problem is that the FBI always seems to show up with too much of something. Too many people. Too many guns. Too many experts. Most consistently, though, they show up after too much time. So don't hold your breath waiting for the cavalry."

He fumbled behind him and pulled his automatic pistol from its holster. "We're all right. We got us a good posse—three good cops in case things get rough, and one marvelous shrink in case anybody gets real upset and needs to talk."

Sam Purdy was too preoccupied with the functioning of his weapon to notice the dirty look flung his way by Alan Gregory.

"Do you have any idea how stubborn your sister is? My, my . . ." Price's tremulous voice trailed off.

Lauren thought she heard echoes of admiration in his words. He rubbed at the hard gray stubble on his left cheek with his fingertips. She could hear the crackle.

She ran her tongue slowly over her scummy teeth.

"What do you want, Mr. Price? I'm not stubborn. Give me back my sister and you can have whatever you want. The lawsuit's dead. It's history. What else do you want? Name it. My sister will say she made up everything." She fought an impulse to impale her fingernails into his eyes and scream "Bastard" until her lungs burned.

"It's not what I want that's important. You need to understand that. It's what the Lord wants. And in the Lord's name, I need to know what you've learned so far."

What had Harley called them? Danites? Yeah. God's Avenging Angels. "You mean what we've discovered to help with the lawsuit? We haven't had too much success, I'm afraid—"

"No, not the lawsuit. Not that." He flitted his large fingers in a dismissive gesture. "Not anymore. What's important is what you leaned from Rachel Misker. In Ouray. I know you talked to her. I wish you hadn't done that. But you did. Your sister said she didn't even know you'd had a chat with Rachel. I had a little trouble believing that. But it's irrelevant now. Though I do need to know what Rachel told you before—"

"Before you killed her." Lauren immediately wondered if she had interrupted him before he could finish the sentence the way he had intended: *before I kill you.* Is that what he was going to say?

"Before she died," Price said.

"What do I get for telling you about my conversation with Rachel Baumann?"

"I'm afraid you're in no position to bargain, Miss Crowder." Price's voice was cordial, matter-of-fact. His posture was slackened. He looked tired—maybe relieved, she thought.

"If that's the case, Mr. Price, if you're going to kill me anyway, then I guess I prefer to die with what I know."

He shook his head slowly. "How valiant. I'm impressed. But I can't really permit that. I'm sorry. I think I'll have to go get your sister. Maybe her presence will motivate you to be more forthcoming. Excuse me."

She had to stop him. "Ransom and Robin are going to get help, Mr. Price."

"You're right. Eventually, they will get out of that ruin. There's a trail up over the top of the canyon. It's a tough climb up to the mesa and a long way back down this canyon, though. Even if the Ute kid knows his way around in the dark, they won't get back here for an hour or so. No matter how this goes, I'll be done in an hour. You have my word on that. And my word is gold."

"Stop, then. Okay. What do you want to know?"

"Tell me about your chat with Rachel. Why did you want to talk with her?"

Lauren took a deep breath. She explained about the BYU yearbooks and the interviews that Pratt Toomey had done with some of Blythe Oaks's old classmates and how Rachel's name had come up. "When Pratt was murdered on the way to see her, we figured she might have known something important. That's why I went to Ouray. To see what she knew."

She looked down at her hands. "You killed Pratt, didn't you?' Her tone carried a drop of accusation, a wave of confusion. *Why?*

Price already knew all that Lauren was telling him. He had heard this much of the story from Pratt before he shot him.

"And what did Rachel tell you?"

"Not much. I was surprised by how little she knew. All she told me about was this romantic girls' club that Blythe Oaks was at the center of during her first couple of years in Provo. We thought she could tell us about some overt lesbian behavior by Blythe, something that would give us leverage with my sister's case. But she said she didn't know about any. Just this 'romantic friends' thing that a number of the girls were part of. She tried to explain the culture at BYU in the sixties. I didn't really get it."

Will Price shook his head. *Of course you didn't get it. That's the whole point.* Lauren's story confirmed Rachel's version of what the two had talked about. Almost exactly. Price was smiling slightly, his gaze drowning in the darkness of the bottom of the kiva. Rachel had assured him twice that all the secrets were safe. She had been relaxed, celebratory even, telling her little story. She thought she was going to live. The circle couldn't be open, though. It had to be closed. He had to do his part for God.

Rachel knew that. *She* knew.

Lauren shrank from Price's silent reverie. She pondered all that she didn't know. She didn't know what shape her sister was in, why she wasn't calling out. Is she drugged? Gagged? Dying? She didn't know why it had grown so quiet above her. Where were Horner and Robin and Ransom? She didn't know if Lester Horner could escape from that tower and get some help.

She didn't know what to make of Will Price's calm.

She did know that she was sitting, crippled, without her cane, on a twenty-five-foot-high ledge, next to a man who had probably already murdered at least two people over some piece of information that she had come close to discovering. But had never discovered.

"Why?" she asked, her question more perplexed than prosecutorial. "Why did you kill Pratt and Rachel?" Blythe, too, for all she knew. "Why did you bring my sister here?" Why the hell didn't you just kill her in Taos?

Price considered answering, then ignored her. He was pondering his next move, relieved that the knowledge had never escaped its exile in Ouray. At the beginning, he had hoped to spare Horner. The Lord knew he had tried. Now that wasn't possible. Too many dominoes had toppled. The risk to the Church was too great. The alternative would be awful. Intolerable to the Seventies, to the prophet.

He said, "I brought your sister here as a pawn. I was going to frame her for a murder. That's all. I thought the Lord wanted me to go on with my life. Now that can't happen. Now that you've showed up I can't use her at all. I'm afraid it's time for me to finish my job, Miss Crowder. Please stay here. Believe me, being courageous won't do you any good."

"No," Lauren said defiantly. She tried to stand. To stop him. She took a single step toward the ladder, toward her sister, stumbled, and fell.

Price walked past her without looking back.

She crawled after him. She screamed, "Noooooo! Teresa, run! Oh God, oh God."

She heard the loud crunching of rubber on gravel before she noticed the tops of a stand of juniper brighten on the opposing mesa top. A jiggling beam of light was coming up the dirt road leading to the promontory where Ransom had stopped his truck and pointed out the view of Lion Canyon.

Will Price, too, heard the crisp sound of the approaching vehicles penetrate the canyon. He had pushed the ladder back into position and was halfway up the ten rungs to the ruins of the old tower. He turned and spotted the headlights. He guessed the worst, calculated how much time he had to finish his job, decided it would be just enough, and reached up for the next rung.

Lauren screamed, "Help! Help!" and waved her arms. She despaired that no one would see her against the dark background of the shadowed cliff. If the vehicle's windows were closed and some music was playing inside, the occupants might not even hear her. She let herself hope it was Sam Purdy in the car.

High in the canyon, Robin cried out, "Look! Someone's here. Help us! Help!"

Lauren waited desperately to hear her sister's voice.

Nothing.

She told herself to breathe. She needed a beacon to

draw the attention of whoever was in the vehicles across the canyon. Could it be Sam? Or maybe someone he had sent to help?

She scrambled over the edge of the rock ledge back into the kiva to retrieve the other lantern.

Price cleared the top rung of the ladder and hoisted himself into the debris of the tower.

It was empty.

He shook his head, looked around at the mess, and hissed, "Darn!"

Lester Horner thought that if life were a rope, Teresa Crowder was holding on to the last few inches. And they were frayed.

The Anasazi tower where he had found her bound and gagged, and apparently drugged, filled the highest and most exposed end of a rock shelf that ran parallel to the one that held the small kiva below. The bulk of the man-made portion of the wall of the two-story tower had collapsed centuries ago, and the roughly round ruin that remained was now little more than a repository of ancient stonemasonry. A natural twenty-foot-long alcove slashed out horizontally into the rock at the back of the shelf.

The long alcove had been walled in by the Anazasi as a granary, a storage area for food. It extended out past the edge of the rock ledge that once supported the back of the tower. The last eight feet of the alcove were exposed, hanging out over the depths of Lion Canyon. At its widest, the gash in the wall was five feet deep. At its highest, it extended four feet.

Almost immediately upon discovering Teresa Crowder, Lester Horner had freed her and dragged her up the incline of crumbled rocks into the opening of the alcove. To make room for himself between her and the entrance to the tower, he had edged her, half awake, down the slash in the sandstone face. Slowly, carefully, he had extended her horizontally into the exposed end of the granary, out over the arroyo. Praying first that she wasn't already dying and then that she would stay immobile, he grabbed an assortment of fist-sized rocks to use as weapons and parked himself as a sentry in front of her, waiting for Will Price's inevitable return.

Teresa grew vaguely aware of being alive. She felt an instant of dread that was textured with memories. Each shallow breath filled her with the scent of green apples and wet black soil. Her open eyes were washed with the pink and orange of the desert sky, and her parched throat was pebbled with grains of sand and the dust of dry clay. With each gulp of cool night air the apprehension in her heart grew more fertile.

Through her diminishing mental fog and the developing ink of night she watched the jagged progress of the pickup truck silhouetted across the canyon.

Instantly, she knew. *It's coming down the lane. Run. Now.*

She squeezed her eyes shut tightly, then opened them again. She squinted and tried to count the cases in the back.

Run. Now.

She pushed out from her perch and saw the sky. *I'm in a tree.* She relaxed, constrained from fleeing farther by space and jeopardy. If she moved, she was certain she would fall. If she remained still—up here, in the dark—he wouldn't find her. She was safe. Up here, in the orchard, she was safe.

Quiet, now, Teresa. Wait.

Sometime during the day she had urinated on herself. It confused her. *Why'd you pee on yourself?* The denim of her black jeans was wet and sticky. The uric acid and the damp cold chafed her thighs and buttocks. Now the discomfort focused her, helped her fight the malaise encouraged by the chemicals roaming her brain. Her wrists hurt badly from being bound together behind her, and her shoulders ached from having been stuffed in the trunk. *Why'd you pee on yourself girl?*

Teresa had no memory of the trunk. Clearly, though, she remembered the pickup. Down the lane. And the orchard. And the Schlitz.

If her thinking had been lucid enough to make the distinction, she would have wondered whether the shivers that traveled in rolling bursts up and down her body were from the desert cold or from her anguish.

Suddenly, in an instant of awareness as clear as fresh water, she recognized the man with her as Lester Horner.

This isn't the orchard. Is it?

Will Price hopped deftly from the top rung of the ladder into the ruins of the tower and soon spotted Horner crouching ten feet above him at the peak of a steep fifteen-foot incline of loose rock and rubble.

The man's deep voice carried a ton of frustration. "Come on. Where is she, Lester?"

"Will, what have you done?" Horner despaired at the answer he might receive.

"What have I done? I've been protecting the Church from its enemies, that's all. I'm doing the Lord's work. Joseph's work. Brigham's work."

"Why this woman? What did you want with her?"

"She's nothing, Lester. But she wanted to expose Blythe's sins, and that, that was something I couldn't allow. They would have used Blythe's abominations to ruin you and destroy your calling. You know that. I asked Blythe to leave Washington. As a priest. For your sake. She laughed at me. She *laughed* at me, Lester. Then I tried to scare her into leaving Washington. But she wouldn't budge. I had to stop her from defiling your position on the Court with her abominations against the Lord."

Horner gripped a rock and squeezed it until the flesh on his hand hurt. "Blythe? You killed Blythe, Will?" His voice carried the hollow tones of his incredulity. "Why, Will? Why?"

Price was weary. He didn't really have the stamina for this role anymore. He felt grateful that Horner apparently had not even heard about Rachel Misker's death. At least they wouldn't have to discuss that.

"Necessary, Lester. She was a homosexual. She

danced with Satan. I needed to protect you from that ever becoming public. I needed to protect the Church from that becoming public. I warned you about her, Lester. And I warned her."

"You're nuts, Will."

Price looked at his feet, then back at Horner. "Nuts? Not me. But it's ironic. That's what they said about Joseph Smith, too, isn't it?"

Horner scoffed, his tone flush with ridicule. "So now you're elevating yourself to the same plane as the prophet?"

"You didn't have any trouble seeing yourself on that path, did you? But this is no time to argue about the nature of our respective journeys to the celestial kingdom, Lester. Not anymore. Come on down, please. It's all over for us. Satan's tornado has cut too wide a swath."

"Leave her alone, Will. Don't sin anymore."

Price's robust tone became clipped and hostile. "Her? This isn't about her. Don't you get it? She was just a tool of the enemies of the Church. And today I was going to turn the tables. She was going to be my tool. That's all. All along, I thought I could protect the Church by protecting you. But—though it breaks my heart—now I know I need to protect the Church from you and your sins as well." He kicked the sun-bleached dust at his feet. His voice grew sharp, as though his words were stitched together with razor wire. "So *don't!* Don't preach to me about sinning, Lester. The sins that threaten our Church are yours. Your sins have threatened the preparations for the coming of the Lord. Not mine. Come down here. Now. I'm a tired man. Please don't make me come up there."

"My sins?" Horner was genuinely puzzled.

Price shook his head in exasperation and began to climb the incline of rubble toward Lester Horner.

Horner hurled a rock and missed his friend's head by inches. A second struck Price a glancing blow to his upper back. He grunted and raised a forearm to protect his face.

"My sins, Will?" Horner stood and raised another

stone high above his head. "My sins?" He flung the stone.

The lemon-sized chunk pounded Price's shoulder and tore his flesh. *Five more feet,* he told himself. *That's all I need.*

He looked up from under his raised arm and admonished his friend. "Lester, you killed a soul. The spirit is coming back to haunt you. Now your soul must be redeemed for eternity."

It's that simple.

Price lunged up at Lester Horner. Just before he reached him, his body shook with the crushing power of another sharp crack, this one to his face. Once, when he was eleven or twelve, he had caught a hardball flush in his upper cheek. The pain hadn't come for a few seconds. This was like that. This time the pain didn't start until he had his hands wrapped around Horner's leg.

Price dragged the justice back down the incline with him, his grip firm, gravity doing most of the work. Then the pain came. Blood rushed out of his torn eye.

Teresa began to scream.

Lauren waved the lantern in the direction of the approaching vehicles for half a minute. Finally she heard a long bleating reply from a car horn. When the commotion started above her, afraid the rescuers would arrive too late, she scooted over to the base of the ladder and pulled herself to standing.

She visualized Ransom behind her, imagined his strong arms supporting her weight. She tensed the muscles in her own arms to hold herself tight to the ladder as she hopped one-footed—too slowly—from rung to rung.

Two more. Near the top. Just two more rungs.

She wasn't sure exactly what happened next. Maybe the perceptions she had were simultaneous.

From the corner of her eye, to her left, she saw a flailing shadow darken a segment of the gray-brown sky. A winged bird, a cameo of death, it was there, then it was gone. Ricocheting, mocking—everywhere around her, everywhere at once—she heard a horrified

"Noooooooooo." Half plea, half protest, the mournful sound trailed off into the distant desert, bouncing softly off rock walls, entering ancient dwellings and holy places to be still, and coming back again and again until the refrain was only a whisper.

She was certain the wail she heard was her sister's.

A dull thud punctuated the sequence.

Footsteps thundered behind her and she heard a frantic call—Alan's. "We're coming, Lauren! Hang on."

A spark of exhilaration ignited in Lauren's gut. Then, in an instant, the relief melted as if consumed by fire. They were just getting out of their car. *They're too far away. They're too late . . .*

With a surge of power she had never before felt, she pulled herself over the top of the ladder into the ruins of the tower. Her muscles sizzled. She raised herself and stood gazing into the bloody face of a monster.

Will Price reached out for her.

She fell to her right to elude him.

He stared down at her momentarily and then seemed to lose interest. He stepped away from her, stopping at the edge of the old tower. Blood poured generously from his eye socket and glistened black on his face as he raised his head and spread his arms to the desert sky. He inhaled deeply and leaned forward, as though he expected a current to lift him, as though he expected to fly.

He didn't fly. An instant later his heavy body crashed with a sharp crack and a dull thud on the rocks of Lion Canyon.

Lauren shook her head in confusion and rage and felt tears migrating through the filth on her face. The salt stung her lips.

Although the approaching rescuers made their share of noise, the only sounds Lauren heard as she huddled in the rocks and dust of the tower were old ranch sounds and desert sounds and sounds she was certain were voices of the ancients, scolding her for her failure to protect her sister.

The wind hummed and paused, whistled and stilled through the canyon and the piñon and the junipers.

Her lover called her name. Again. In the distance,

still, but closer. Like a morning dream, on the cusp of awareness.

Too late.

The night seemed to be catching its breath. A voice, low and halting, said, "Lauren, is that you? Is he asleep?"

Lauren looked up into the shadows of the wall that loomed behind her. The wall seemed to be talking, and she saw faces in the rocks. Feeling only slightly crazy, she said, "Yes, it's me. Everyone's asleep. But I'm too late to help. Again."

Teresa replied, "Not for me, you're not."

"Teresa?"

"I'm on a tiny ledge above you. I don't know what's going on. But I can't get down without some help."

Lauren, fighting disbelief, laughed in relief at their predicament. "Well, that makes two of us. Are you okay?"

"I think so. But I have a feeling I'm going to be late for my set."

What remained of the day's light was all to the west. The dark sky on the horizon was stained with splintered streaks of raspberry.

As the colors dissipated to black, the sounds of the desert wind and the night insects reigned, interrupted only by the percussion of heavy feet and the frantic calls to Lauren from Alan and Sam below her in the arroyo and from Robin above her on the mesa rim.

"We're okay," she yelled in response. "Teresa's here. She's okay. She's okay."

Lauren inhaled to call out again, but her voice was drowned by the rhythmic pounding of helicopter blades cutting swaths through the parched air. The machine littered the solemn landscape with its profane roar and its probing searchlights.

As the chopper hovered to the west, Sam and Alan pulled themselves clear of the top of the ladder and into the ruins of the tower. Below them, Brian Long and the

Ute tribal policeman gingerly approached the two bodies on the canyon floor.

The helicopter descended a few hundred feet and hung just above the mesa rim, its irreverent profile winged with the last of the raspberry light. An amplified, booming voice yelled, "FBI!" The searchlight flitted and swooped over the cliffs and the arroyo and finally focused its beam on the ruins of the tower. With the aid of the illumination, Alan and Sam edged Teresa from her perch and carried her to Lauren.

The sisters embraced.

Sam turned to Alan, leaned his face close to his friend's ear, and yelled, "We may have been too late to be of much help, but at least we didn't bring a helicopter along to use as a fucking flashlight."

Teresa was airlifted to Farmington, where a couple of local physicians recommended a night of observation in the hospital. The rest of the group drove on the dirt road out of Lion Canyon back to tribal headquarters in Towaoc. By the time they arrived on the slopes of Sleeping Ute Mountain, the Ute policeman seemed to have learned everything he wanted to know about the events that had taken place on Ute Mountain Ute land. The FBI agents from both Farmington and Denver, however, insisted on knowing a lot more. They interviewed everyone until exhaustion prevailed.

The group was finally dismissed around midnight. They drove south to Shiprock and then across to Farmington to find Teresa, get some sleep, and arrange to fly Satchel back to Will Price's family in Utah.

Sometime after ten o'clock the next morning, with Lauren and Alan and Teresa in one rented car, Sam and Robin in the other, they caravaned to Taos. They had agreed over breakfast that they would celebrate everyone's well-being by taking in Teresa's show that night.

It took almost twenty-four hours for everyone to accept that Teresa was truly out of danger. Finally, when the national press and the tabloids pieced together the rudiments of the story and tracked Teresa to northern New Mexico, Robin and Sam were able to convince Lauren that, given the spotlight provided by the media, Teresa was as safe as she was going to be for a while.

The next day, the group parted company reluctantly. Robin returned to Utah, and Sam and Alan and Lauren flew home to Colorado.

Alan was aware that Lauren was continuing to brood long after Teresa's safety was assured. He wrote it off to the residue of the trauma in Lion Canyon. Although he found it difficult, he tried to give her some latitude to find her equilibrium. He also promised to try to honor her unusual request to find a couple of good seats for some upcoming Denver Nuggets games.

Lauren appreciated his concern. But it didn't change anything.

She knew that this thing wasn't over.

The streets east of Washington Park were carpeted with the drying ornaments of elm and ash and willow. The morning air in Denver was still and sharp. A few trees—some birch, some aspen, a lonely oak or two—clung to their fading leaves. But the colors that dominated Denver's landscape in late autumn were the blues of the sky and the greens of the spruces and pines.

In-line skaters and bicyclists rocketed on paved trails in the nearby city park. Sweatshirted couples migrated toward well-deserved Sunday-morning indolence with fat newspapers under their arms, seeking respite at nearby cafes.

Lauren had trouble finding a place to park in the block of South Gaylord Street where Anita Baumann shared a brick bungalow with a friend. She finally had to walk back a couple of blocks to Anita's little house. *It's almost exactly like Teresa's place in Salt Lake,* she thought.

Her walking stick was not as necessary to her now as it had been a week before. She carried it for security. Her neurologist in Boulder had stoked her full of enough IV Solu-Medrol to slow the progression of her symptoms and to fill her brain with high-octane mud.

The drive into Denver from her own home in Boulder had taken forty-five minutes. She had passed the time listening to *Weekend Edition* on NPR and had mused at the lack of acumen displayed by the media as they recounted one more time the oft-repeated speculations surrounding the bizarre murder of Supreme Court Justice Lester Horner by his lifelong friend William Price and of Price's subsequent suicide. The reports universally played up Teresa's instigatory role in bringing accusations of harassment against Blythe Oaks. Teresa was being transformed daily in the media from victim to vamp to victor and back again.

The attention also transformed her into one of the hottest young comedians in America. Now Teresa Crowder had an agent, and she was scheduled to do Letterman on Friday night.

Will Price had become the latest in a series of crazed Mormons to be lionized and chastised by the national press. His zealousness and fanaticism in protecting the LDS Church from the consequences of Teresa Crowder's accusations against Blythe Oaks temporarily renewed national interest in the obscure religion from Salt Lake City. But the very fact of his fanaticism guaranteed that no real critical public examination of the fastest-growing Christian religion in the world would actually take place.

The authorities in Salt Lake City rode out the controversy with characteristic quiet. With the prayed-for showcase of the 2002 Winter Olympic Games on the horizon, and with the stupendous effort that continually went into choreographing and packaging the LDS Church for public consumption, they knew that they could not risk embroiling the Church in the daily polemics of the Horner affair. Recent history in controlling the fallout from Ervil LeBaron, Mark Hofmann, Paul Singer, Evan Mecham, and Bruce Longo told the Church leadership that their safest position was to let this fiasco pass on its own.

Robin Torr had been contacted by three true-crime writers and more people who called themselves movie producers than she had ever thought existed. She had moved into an apartment and was trying to decide what to do about her marriage.

Lauren had returned to Boulder, and she and Alan had talked about going somewhere and eloping over Thanksgiving.

John Harley's apartment phone had been disconnected. Lauren had left messages for him at the Side

Pocket and at Bill & Nada's and at the university. She had heard nothing back. If she didn't reach him soon, she knew she would fly to Salt Lake City to make sure he was all right.

Lauren hadn't told anyone—not Robin, not Alan, not Sam Purdy—about the purpose of her Sunday morning visit to Denver.

Anita Baumann opened the door to her small blond-brick house wearing a sleek, all-white outfit that was as loose on the upper half of her body as it was tight on the lower half. Her blond hair was short and unstyled. She was blessed with her mother's clear eyes and thin-lipped, warm smile.

And, Lauren thought, she has her mother's grace.

"Hi. I'm Lauren Crowder. Thanks for agreeing to meet with me."

"Hello. Come in."

Anita's roommate, a beautiful Asian woman who barely looked old enough to be living independently, grabbed a pile of newspapers from the living-room sofa and, after smiling a shy greeting, retired to another part of the house.

Lauren sat on a beige chenille sofa that had seen better days. She said, "I'm so sorry about your mother. I met her only once, but she seemed like a wonderful woman."

The mention of her mother brought immediate tears to Anita's eyes. She lowered them and said, "Thank you. Can I get you something? Some tea?"

Lauren ran her tongue over her dry teeth. "If it's not too much trouble, please. That would be nice." She wondered how puffy her face looked from the steroids.

Anita returned with two cups and saucers and fine china dishes for milk and sugar. "They were Mom's," she said poignantly.

Anita's skin was moist and rich and seemed immune to wrinkles, but her eyes conveyed the magnitude of the grief and hurt she had suffered in the last fortnight. She handed Lauren a cup and said, "About your coming.

There's something I don't understand. Why haven't you just gone and talked to the papers? Like everyone else."

Lauren raised her cup and drank, grateful for the lubrication in her mouth. "I really don't know if I know anything, Anita. I'm only guessing at what I told you on the phone. All that I'm reasonably certain of is that your mother died to protect something. It's the piece that everybody, so far, seems willing to write off without bothering to explain. As I told you already, I don't think your mother lied to me. I do think that maybe I didn't know enough to ask her the right questions. But I don't think she lied. Your mother didn't strike me as the type of woman who would lie to protect the thirty-year-old adolescent sexual experimentation of a bunch of girls she hadn't talked with in years."

For a moment, neither woman spoke.

Lauren continued. "At the end, a week ago, on the Ute reservation, Will Price had a chance to kill me. He had a chance to kill my sister. He didn't kill us. Which says to me that although it may have started that way, in the end this rampage he was on didn't have anything to do with my sister's accusations against Blythe Oaks.

"Price also had a chance to kill Lester Horner. In fact, I think he kidnapped my sister to frame *her* for killing Justice Horner. But Price did end up killing Justice Horner. Then he killed himself. And, of course, before any of it, he killed your mother."

Anita's gaze didn't quite meet Lauren's.

"It's convenient to blame this whole mess on my sister's being assaulted in a bathroom in Washington, D.C. But it really doesn't make much sense. Not enough sense, anyway. Your mother shouldn't have had to die for that. Even if she knew something inflammatory about Blythe Oaks's past. Blythe Oaks being a lesbian would just not be a big enough scandal. The Church could have just blamed it on Satan and excommunicated Blythe Oaks and hung her out to dry. The Church would have weathered that. God knows they've weathered worse."

Lauren examined her hostess's face, hoping to ascertain how well her argument was being received. But she couldn't tell.

"As you've probably already read, my sister said that

as they fought in the kiva, she thought Will Price said to Lester Horner that he had sinned. He said something like 'It's because you killed a child' or 'because you killed a soul.' "

Anita raised the index finger of her left hand and touched herself on the tip of her nose as her palm covered her mouth. She gently closed her eyes. She said, "And you think he was talking about old times?"

Lauren nodded, relieved. It sounded almost like an admission. "That's what I'm wondering about. Yes."

"What do you want me to say? If I tell you you're right, what are you going to do? Are you going to go talk to *The New York Times?* You want to go on *Nightline* and tell Ted Koppel that Justice Horner was a hyprocrite? Or are you just interested in announcing to the world that my mother was a horrible person?" Anita burst into contained sobs. She turned straight on the sofa, away from Lauren.

Lauren resisted a temptation to touch her. "Your mother was one of the most gentle, proper women I have ever had the pleasure of meeting. I just want to know what was so important that she had to die. Why Pratt Toomey had to die. Why my sister almost had to die. The answer can only come from understanding why your mother and Horner and Price did have to die."

"And you think I know?"

"I got the impression from the people in Ouray that you and your mother were very close."

Anita didn't respond.

"Anita, I think I already know."

"Take your best shot, then." Defiance and helplessness mingled in her eyes. Her voice remained level.

Lauren took a deep breath before she began. "Your mother left BYU abruptly when she was twenty. She didn't finish her sophomore year. She didn't marry some guy right after he came back from his mission like most of the young women did. What does that tell me? Not much. Maybe that she was more of an independent thinker than her peers. I know she moved to Ouray for a while, and as far as I can tell, she left the Church. Your grandparents don't live in Ouray. None of your family does. When she married your father, your mother didn't marry in the temple. I think something of an epiphany occurred for your mother thirty years ago. I don't know what. But I'm afraid you do."

Lauren watched Anita Baumann juggle her emotions and her conflicts.

"You know, as reluctant as you are to have me visit you today, that's how troubled your mother was by me and my friends showing up in Ouray a couple of weeks ago. Your mother has been keeping an old secret for a terribly long time, waiting to be discovered, fearing she would be discovered. That secret, I think, eventually killed her. And I think she left it to you. *I fear* that she left it to you. I don't want it to kill you, too."

Anita's eyes flashed. "What? I'm supposed to sacrifice my mother's reputation—and my father's memory—just to buy a little piece of mind for myself? That's not who I am, Ms. Crowder. That's not how they raised me."

"I suspect that's true. After only a few minutes with you, I think I already know that much about you. But you also need to know something about me." Lauren paused, waiting until Anita faced her. "I don't want to write a book about this. I don't want to give interviews to *Time* and *Newsweek.* Whatever you tell me won't ever get public because of me.

"Today, despite everything, I still have doubts that the Mormon Church killed your mother. Whether or not somebody in Salt Lake City ordered Will Price to kill her is something we'll probably never know. But I am sure that an authoritarian culture did kill your mother. And I believe that there are more fanatics out there like Will Price who are capable of doing great harm to someone to protect their beliefs.

"Lester Horner is a Mormon martyr right now. The Church can live with that. Nicely, I'm afraid. They would have much preferred to have an LDS Supreme Court justice, but they'll settle for having a wonderful martyr. Because the alternative is unthinkable to them. The alternative is that the real truth might come out.

"If I'm putting this together right, the truth has something to do with your mother and Lester Horner. Cheating on an exam? Ridiculing the prophet? Breaking the Honor Code? An illicit romance? I don't know. But I think that when she left BYU and went to Ouray, she did it for a reason. And that reason had something to do with Lester Horner.

"I think that Will Price's efforts to stop my sister's lawsuit were at first simply an attempt to protect Horner from being stained by Blythe Oaks's current or past homosexual behavior. Later, when we stumbled on your mother's existence, the risks skyrocketed in somebody's eyes—certainly Price's. Horner was in danger of something scandalous about his own past being discovered. I think that that something involved your mother, and Will Price knew about it. And I think eventually he killed everybody else who knew about it in order to keep it a secret."

Anita Baumann adopted the same stoic face that Lauren remembered seeing the day she visited Anita's mother.

"Anita, I think that Will Price killed your mother and then killed Lester Horner to keep something secret. I have nothing but guesses about what it might be. But Price killed to protect the Church from the consequences of the disclosure of *something*. Right now, that something is still a secret. But I'm afraid—hell, I'm terrified—that other fanatics might be capable of killing to protect that secret, too."

Anita turned her gaze away from Lauren, out the front window of the house. She was silent for almost a minute. Then she asked, "Lauren, do you believe in God?"

Without thinking, Lauren stammered, "I believe . . . in believing in God."

Anita Baumann stared at her with flat eyes and then left the room. Lauren couldn't tell if she was planning on coming back.

She was gone only a minute or two.

"I have some things to show you.

"First, though, you have to tell me something. If you don't want to make this public, then why are you here? I've been assuming that the whole point of your coming to see me was to find ammunition to bash the Mormons or to bash the conservatives in Utah. Mother would have hated all of that. *Hated* it. So what is it that you want?"

Lauren's response was composed, her voice soft. "If I'm right about my version of what happened, I want to take a statement from you"—she tilted her head toward the portfolio Anita was holding—"along with whatever documents you have, and send everything to a couple of prominent attorneys I know, in sealed envelopes, with instructions for them to open the envelopes only if you die of any cause in the next few years or of any suspicious causes later. I will also send a copy of your statement, along with the letter to the lawyers, to the members of the First Presidency of the LDS Church in Utah."

Lauren twisted a paper napkin between her fingers. Her eyes teared.

"My determination to help my sister fight her own demons may have caused your mother to be reunited with hers. I can't stand the thought that those demons might engulf you, too."

Anita handed Lauren an old, battered document folder and told her to read. She took both of their cups and went to the kitchen to make fresh tea.

Rachel Misker Baumann was a born lawyer. She had kept everything.

Pages from a journal documented her horror as the days passed and her menstrual period didn't come. She told no one at first. At first, she just prayed. Finally, she told Lester Horner, who, disbelieving and ashen-faced, sent her away and told her that he, too, would pray about it. He was sure, *sure,* it was the work of evil spirits. He would seek a revelation from the Lord.

News of the revelation came to Rachel two days later in the form of a note from Lester Horner. In the note was the name and address of a nurse in Ouray, Colorado, who would "take care of the problem." Horner gave Rachel detailed written instructions on how to find Ouray, on how to find the nurse, and on what to say to her friends, and he gave her a check for one hundred dollars.

After two wrenching days, Rachel Misker felt as if her soul had been torn and shredded. She was in love with Lester Horner, wanted to do what he thought was right, felt he was the man, the priest, she would be obeying all through this life, all the way until he pulled her through the veil into the celestial kingdom, where they would share eternity together.

But she also knew in every Mormon bone in her body that abortion was a sin worse than murder.

Worse than murder.

Murdered people can be elevated to the celestial kingdom; unborn souls cannot.

She decided to ask Horner's best friend, Will Price, for a blessing, for guidance.

Price was cold and stern with her and told her only that she had obviously been doing the devil's work. She needed to have faith in God's revelations, and she needed to obey the priesthood holder. Price chastised her ruthlessly for cavorting with Satan and luring Horner into sin. After five minutes, he dismissed her.

On her own, in the course of a marathon of prayer that filled a week's worth of sleepless nights, Rachel Misker concluded that this dictate from Lester Horner wasn't about God's will. And that despite Will Price's rebuke, she wasn't doing the devil's work.

The revelation from Lester Horner was about protecting Lester Horner. His reputation. His future career. But Rachel felt powerless. She could bring Horner down with her. *Maybe.* But the bottom line was that, unmarried and Mormon and pregnant in Provo, Utah, in 1961, *she* was going down.

She left BYU and went to Ouray.

She never cashed Horner's check.

And she never had the abortion.

Anita stood, her focus locked on some imaginary spot above Lauren's head. She inhaled deeply and began to speak in the tired, sad voice of a woman who has felt great pain. "I found these papers in my mom's things. I read them the very day that William Price killed him. Killed my father. Price killed them both. He murdered my mother and he murdered my father. He killed them both in the name of God."

She sat stiffly and began to cry.

Lauren approached Anita and pulled her head to her abdomen. She said, "I'm so sorry," and she, too, began to cry.

It frightened her to know that in Utah, this whole tragedy might somehow make perfect sense.

AUTHOR'S NOTE

I relied upon a wide range of source material in preparing this book. These references included *America's Saints: The Rise of Mormon Power,* by Robert Gottlieb and Peter Wiley; *What Do Mormons Believe?,* by Rex E. Lee; *In Mormon Circles: Gentiles, Jack Mormons, and Latter-day Saints,* by James Coates; *The American Religion: The Emergence of the Post-Christian Nation,* by Harold Bloom; *This Is the Place: Brigham Young and the New Zion,* by Ernest H. Taves; *Mormon Country,* by Wallace Stegner; *Roughing It,* by Mark Twain; *Utah: A History,* by Charles S. Peterson; *A Gathering of Saints: A True Story of Murder, Money, and Deceit,* by Robert Lindsey; *Secret Ceremonies: A Mormon Woman's Intimate Diary of Marriage and Beyond,* by Deborah Laake; *Odd Girls and Twilight Lovers: A History of Lesbian Life in Twentieth-Century America,* by Lillian Faderman; *Brigham Young University: A School of Destiny,* by Ernest L. Wilkinson and W. Cleon Skousen; *The Mormon Murders: A True Story of Greed, Forgery, Deceit and Death,* by Steven Naifeh and Gregory White Smith; *Ute Mountain Tribal Park: The Other Mesa Verde,* by Jean Akens; *Exploring the Lands of the Book of Mormon,* by Joseph L. Allen, Ph.D.; *Family Home Evening Resource Book,* published by the Church of Jesus Christ of Latter-day Saints; and the Book of Mormon, translated by Joseph Smith.

Although the wonders of the Ute Mountain Tribal Park are described as accurately as possible, the kiva and "broken tower" in Part Three are entirely fictitious sites.

ACKNOWLEDGMENTS

For their inspiration, my deepest gratitude goes to Beverly Purrington and to the memory of Patty VanBenthuysen.

With this book, I had a lot of help in a lot of ways. My heartfelt thanks to Richard White, Harry MacLean, Mark Graham, Marc Vick, John Graham, Mary Malatesta, Tom Faure, Jeffrey and Patricia Limerick, Elyse Morgan, Enid Schantz, Robin Purdy, Paul E. Johnson, Norm Avery, Rob and Virginia Bayless, Ann Nemeth, Richard Blakely, Jean Naggar, Carolyn Carlson, Matthew Bradley, Michaela Hamilton, and Al Silverman. In addition, I am grateful to a number of people who generously shared their perspectives on various aspects of life in Utah but have chosen to remain anonymous.

I gladly acknowledge a special indebtedness to Dr. Richard Finkel, whose compassion and skill made completion of this project possible; to Alice Price Knight, who offered important direction when I couldn't get my compass to work; and to Rose and Alexander, who provide light during the gray times.

And finally, my enduring thanks to my family, from coast to coast. They believe in me, and there's simply no way to express sufficient gratitude for that.

A warm Friday night in April, the air still and perfumed by lilacs.

Emily had to pee. I fingered her leash as she circled and sniffed the ground for whatever peculiar scent would tell her she had found the right spot.

Peter was on his way out the lane. He slowed his old Volvo and thrust his left arm through the open window in greeting. "Hi, Em," he called.

I returned his wave and watched the wagon's lights trail away. Emily cocked her ears as she squatted in the dust.

She would have preferred that we continue on for a walk, but I was eager to get back inside, where my wife waited for me with chilled pepper vodka, a videocassette, and a cozy spot on the couch.

When it became important that I know, I had to speak with a lot of people before I understood what happened later that night.

The Community Hospital Emergency Department records show that at 2:10 A.M. two men carried Peter through the door of the ER. He was immediately stretched out on a gurney covered with sheets already bloodied by a fourth-grade casualty of a school bus crash near Allenspark. One look at Peter made it clear that there was no time for clean linen. In seconds he was surrounded by exhausted ER staff.

"He's got a faint pulse. Hurry, please! He's lost a lot of blood!" yelled one of the two men who had carted Peter from the Boulder Theatre to the nearby hospital. The man was burly, with thick arms and short legs and unruly hair that was a memorable mix of copper and silver. His face was flushed red from the exertion, and his tiny eyes communicated urgency. The man had been a medic in Vietnam, and he swore that he'd detected a faint carotid pulse when he'd found Peter in the theatre while he arrived to do his after-show clean-up. Experienced in triage, he had decided that there was no time to call an ambulance and had rushed Peter to the hospital in his own car, an old El Camino with a sleek golden cover over the back.

The ex-medic had corraled a university student off the sidewalk adjacent to the alley behind the theatre to ride in the back of the El Camino with Peter. Earlier, the sophomore had been at a party at one of the fraternities on the Hill and gotten so blitzed he'd lost his keys and had to walk home to his apartment on Spruce Street. At the time he was shanghaied he had been taking a brief respite from his hike home in order to vomit in the alley.

In the frantic atmosphere in the ER, the inebriated kid from the university looked bewildered. He shadowed the ex-medic wherever the man moved.

"I don't get a pulse. Anyone getting a pulse?" called a tall gray-haired nurse who had been first to appear at the head of Peter's gurney in the wide hallway outside the treatment rooms.

An ER doc arrived at a trot and scanned Peter slowly from head to toe. "Bag him. Where's the bag? Do we have an open room?" he said in an even, airline-pilot voice.

"In your dreams."

"Get some O-neg. BP?"

No one answered at first, then someone said, "Not yet, I'm trying."

"Call cardiac over here. Get me a line wide open."

"Respirations are zero. Still no pulse. No pressure."

"Stay with the CPR. We're going to need a central line. *Get me a room!*"

Down the hall, someone yelled, "Is cardiac three open yet?"

"When did you have that pulse? How long ago?" The ER doc, a guy in his forties with acne scars, a receding hairline, and a ponytail, looked squarely at the big man with the red face.

The ex-medic barked, "Five minutes, sir! That's all, maybe four. I know this one, sir! He's worth saving." Blood stained the man's clothing and his skin. It was Peter's blood, and it had started to lose its sheen. The pasty film was cracking and separating on the thick red hair of the man's forearms. The ex-medic had been Peter's friend. Now he stood at attention, crying. Wearing painter's coveralls over a sleeveless T-shirt, drenched with Peter's blood, his eyes illuminated as though they were powered by the sun, he was somehow the most dignified person in the ER.

He sobered everyone in his presence.

My dear friend Adrienne, Peter's wife, was the urologist on call for the ER that night. She was just completing a difficult catheterization of a ten-year-old girl who'd had a pelvic fracture from the bus accident. Outside the trauma room she heard the commotion in the hall, knew instinctively there was a code, and concluded that one of the casualties from the school bus had crashed. As soon as she finished inserting the cath, she stripped her gloves and went out to see what was going on.

Adrienne was five feet tall in spike heels. Maybe. From her vantage she had no chance of seeing over the half-dozen people surrounding the gurney, so she squeezed into a tiny space left open near the patient's feet. The pony-tailed emergency medicine doc leaned over the body, counting silently while he performed CPR. A nurse kept time with the breathing bag she pressed firmly over her patient's mouth and nose. With thick wads of gauze another nurse sopped amber blood from countless short linear wounds. Needles were being plunged into his veins—"I'm not getting a flash, nothing. This guy's got no pressure, zero"—plastic bags of fluid were being hung, and leads were being taped with remarkable precision to newly cleaned places on Peter's hairless chest.

"He's going out. Damn. Anybody got a pulse?"

Adrienne couldn't tell who said that. The voice she heard was tired, not urgent. A female voice, she thought. But no one at the table responded to the open question.

From down the corridor someone called, "C-3 is open."

"Stay with the CPR. We're moving into cardiac three. Everybody together, let's go. One, two, now!" The ER doc, the one rhythmically thrusting his weight onto Peter's chest, spoke clearly, expecting his directions to be obeyed.

Cardiac three was in Adrienne's direction. She hopped back to keep from being plowed over by the wheeled table and its multiple attendants.

As the gurney sped by she saw her husband's open eyes looking right at her. Through her. Her heart dropped to her toes.

She said, "Oh, Jonas, your daddy."

You think you know someone.

Peter had been my neighbor for almost ten years. I'd dined with him a hundred times. I'd helped him build fences, dig holes to plant shade trees, clean gutters. For hours I'd watched him shape and smooth wood in his studio. He'd comforted me after my first wife left me, and he soaked up my tears when my dog died. When his baby was born, I was there next to him. He had invited me to hold the cord while he cut it. I did, although I never knew why.

In Peter's company and at his insistence I'd finished many bottles of his good wine that I had no business finishing, and ran a handful of 10K's that I had no business running. I had never beaten him in tennis. Not once. I doubt it had ever crossed his mind to let me win.

Peter liked being the best.

He liked being an anachronism, too.

The music that blarred constantly in his studio always

came from old records. LP's. Creedence Clearwater, Grand Funk, Cream. Early Airplane. Peter relished an opportunity to serve tournedos Rossini or beef Wellington to a dining room full of Boulder cholesterol phobics. He drove a 1976 Volvo station wagon with an AM radio. If he ever owned new clothing I never saw it.

Peter loved the back country and the mountains and yet had married a woman who thought the *city* of Boulder was a wilderness. He camped and hiked alone, usually in the Indian Peaks, and on days when inspiration avoided him in his studio, he could often be found hanging at some gravitationally defiant angle on a rock face in Eldorado Canyon. Peter was a regular practitioner of "free-soloing"—which involves climbing high rock faces without ropes or safety gear. I wouldn't have gone near those same vertical walls without scaffolding.

One night at a dinner of fiery jerked shrimp that Peter had prepared shortly after he and his wife, Adrienne, had gotten pregnant, Adrienne asked him to give it up. Just like that.

"No more free-soloing?" he said without looking up from his meal.

"That's right, Geppetto. No more free-soloing. The guys that do it are, literally, a dying breed. I want you around to change diapers."

He exhaled before asking, "Can I still sport climb?"

Adrienne nodded. Sport climbing meant ropes, and hardware, and, if Adrienne got her way, a helmet. To me, the difference between free-soloing and sport climbing was akin to the difference between swimming with sharks unarmed and swimming with sharks while carrying a pen knife. But no one asked my opinion, and I kept it to myself.

Adrienne nodded again. She said, "Sport climbing's okay."

Peter's eyes smiled, but the corners of his mouth never turned up.

I was only an observer that night, but the interchange had appeared to be a graceful marital contract negotiated without rancor. Over the next year, though, I heard through mutual friends that more than once Peter had been seen on the Diving Board, or another world-class climb in Eldorado, no ropes, no helmet.

A colleague, a clinical psychologist like myself, who had witnessed one of these remarkable solo climbs reasoned that every successful ascent Peter made was really nothing more than a failed suicide attempt.

Peter Arvin wore his blond hair down to his shoulders and shaved once a week, whether his wispy beard needed it or not. His smile was that of a leprechaun, and he was miserly enough with it that you knew it was special when he directed one your way. His eyes were one shade more golden than hazel, and they always seemed sadder and wiser than everyone else's.

Even in metaphysical Boulder, Peter could bring a roomful of locals to awkward silence with his musings on the meaning of some aspect of life that none of us had ever considered thoroughly. He was big on extraterrestrials one year, on phantom governments the next. The rain forest problem had him stumped.

It was always something with Peter, who was as spiritual a man as I had ever known. The nature of his spirituality was personal and idiosyncratic and at times plain weird, but Peter's determined sense was that there was a higher energy at work, a deity at least in-the-making, somewhere in the universe. He talked about his spiritual beliefs constantly, as other people might speak about politics, or sports, or the weather. "If there is actually a God—a single God," he'd told me one spring while we were working manure into his wife's vegetable garden, "I think we're talking about an adolescent. It's got to be a kid God who's trying to take care of this planet. Face it, there's just too many fuck-ups for this to be a full-grown supreme being with four hundred million years of experience. I mean, losing the dinosaurs, for instance; can you imagine a God who's actually paying attention allowing *that* to happen? Sorry, no way.

"This planet is being run like it's something somebody's doing on the side, when what they're really interested in is the celestial equivalent of getting laid or starting a rock and roll band."

He preferred to read biographies to anything but science fiction, which he called, "anticipatory nonfiction." He loved the theatre. From Shakespeare to Broadway road shows to local rep companies. He was always an enthusiastic groupie and eager volunteer, and at times a generous benefactor.

In his studio he was a magician. He fashioned wood as though only he knew the meaning of the grain and the whorls. Acclaim for his pieces was widespread, and he had recently been profiled for his work in the Denver newspapers and in "Colorado Homes and Lifestyles." Peter didn't feign modesty about his carpentry. "The right piece of wood is a piece of wood that's waiting to become a chest, or a bed, or a chair. The wrong piece you have to *make into* a chest or a bed or a chair. I find the wood that is waiting." His work was usually commissioned a year in advance. He never charged enough for any of it.

Becoming a father had seemed to change him in intrinsic ways. Not enough to shake his character, but he was five degrees less frivolous here, ten degrees more responsible there. He was more focused. He smiled more.

I knew all these things about Peter. In retrospect, I didn't know obvious things. I didn't know much about his life before he moved into the house up the hill. I knew little about his family in Wyoming. I didn't know if he had ever been a cub scout or played second base in Little League or puffed into a clarinet in the high school band.

Still, I lived next to him for ten years with the illusion that I knew him well. But then so did Adrienne, his wife.

After he was murdered, we both found out we didn't know shit.